THE
TRAITOR'S
CONTRACT

Also by Paul Mann:

The Libyan Contract
The Beirut Contract

THE TRAITOR'S CONTRACT

Knightsbridge Publishing Company
New York

Published in the United States by
Knightsbridge Publishing Company
255 East 49th Street, Suite 25D
New York, New York 10017

Library of Congress Cataloging-in-Publication Data

Mann, Paul
    The traitor's contract / by Paul Mann.
      p. cm.
    ISBN 1-56129-021-1 : $19.95
    I. Title.
    PS3563.A53623T7   1991
    813'.54—dc20   90-46555
                                                 CIP

Designed by Gary Hespenheide/Hespenheide Design

10 9 8 7 6 5 4 3 2
First Edition

For Jenni, who was worth waiting for

Contents

Turning and turning in the widening gyre
The falcon cannot hear the falconer;
Things fall apart; the centre cannot hold;
Mere anarchy is loosed upon the world,
The blood-dimmed tide is loosed, and everywhere
The ceremony of inocence is drowned . . .

"The Second Coming,"
W. B. Yeats

1 The Hot Lunch

Corinne looked her best the day she died. The lobby guard told her so as she stepped into the elevator that carried her to the forty-fifth floor of the STC Building. So did Henry, the friendly black security guard on her floor.

"Good mornin', Miss Castillo," Henry said as Corinne got out of the elevator. "Lookin' good today, Miss Castillo . . . if you don't mind my sayin' so."

Corinne didn't. Her cheeks flushed a little redder and she smiled her good-morning smile. Henry was the elder of the two guards who manned the security desk on her floor. Corinne liked Henry, but she wasn't too sure about the younger of the two men who wore the blue-and-gray uniform of STC's in-house security squad. Pete was a young Hispanic with a mustache and limpid, sleepy eyes. Even though he had never said or done anything to offend Corinne, there was something about him she couldn't warm to. Something sly about those eyes, she had decided. She said good morning back to Henry and nodded coolly to Pete.

She could feel their eyes roaming up and down her body as she walked past the security desk and clacked on expensive high heels down the smoky-blue marble corridor to the vice president's office. She knew what they were thinking. The blush flared in her cheeks all over again. Corinne had chosen the figure-hugging black jacket-and-skirt suit with the nipped-in waist because it emphasized her greatest assets—her legs. Corinne had great legs and a great ass, everybody said so. And the short tight skirt, sheer black stockings, and high heels she had chosen today served to accentuate and lengthen every seductive line and curve. She knew what the two guards would be saying the minute she was out of earshot. Normally it might cause her a moment's irritation.

Today she savored the sensation. At thirty-six and still single, Corinne understood that her best days were strictly rationed. Despite her legs and ass she knew she was not beautiful. Her face was a little too long and thin, her features too severe, and her sallow complexion always needed skillful makeup. But she had learned to do the best with what she had. Her dull brown hair was cut in a flattering pageboy and gleamed with expensive rinses and conditioners. Mostly, however, the secret of her new-found allure could be found in the way she felt. Corinne had a new man in her life. Only an hour ago they had been making love in her tiny Soho apartment. That was what had put the bloom in her cheeks today.

His name was Brian. A soft-spoken Anglo-Irishman with blue eyes, corn silk hair, starkly contrasting dark eyebrows, and a devastating accent. She had met him at a fake English pub on the Lower East Side only two months earlier. He had promised to see her at work later today. To Corinne it could only mean one thing: their own kind of hot lunch. She wondered where he would take her this time. That was the reason for the sexy outfit—it was for Brian. But she enjoyed the effect it had on other men, too.

Corinne had almost forgotten how it felt, that raw, hormonal current that could charge the air between the sexes like sheet lightning. Then the sure and tantalizing thrill of knowing that men were getting turned on just by looking at her.

"Whooee." Pete smirked and cocked his ear theatrically in Corinne's direction as she disappeared from view, leaving only the echo of her footsteps. "Her ass is so tight I can still hear it squeakin'."

Henry shrugged. "Looks good today," he said. "The lady's tryin'."

Pete shot him a sly look. "You like to fuck that?"

Henry hesitated, looked uncomfortable for a moment; then a

slow, salacious grin unfolded across his big ugly-friendly face. "Yeah . . ." he conceded finally. "But I'd only be practicin'."

Corinne heard their muffled laughter down the corridor as she reached her office. She stepped inside her own private sanctuary, leaned back gratefully against the closed door, and thought of the day ahead. It had the potential for spectacular and sustained disaster.

Jack Halloran, president of Standard Transport Charter, America's twenty-seventh-largest corporation, was due on one of his rare visits to the company's East Coast headquarters. Which was why Corinne had come in earlier than usual. It was a little before eight, but she could already hear her boss—Dick Hemmings, vice president, Eastern Division—working in his office next door. It was Hemmings who ran the company during Halloran's long and, Corinne thought, self-indulgent absences. It was Hemmings who would be kept busy upstairs all day answering Halloran's questions.

The entire forty-sixth floor was reserved for Halloran and operated behind a permanent security shield. No one visited the forty-sixth floor without triple-A security clearance. To work on the floors immediately above and below took double-A clearance, and even then the staff had to be known to the specially selected, uniformed security guards. All the staff and uniformed guards on the top three executive floors were subjected to rigorous and repeated security checks, which were updated at random. It was a nuisance and an intrusion but it was all too necessary in the age of terrorism. To complain was to be seen as disloyal. Besides, STC was a hard company to crack and jobs there were highly prized because salaries were 20 percent higher than anywhere else. In New York, an extra 20 percent buys a lot of extra loyalty.

Apart from his position as president of a high-profile, multinational corporation, Jack Halloran was known to be friend and confidant to senior administration officials in Washington and to be a frequent guest at the White House. He had to be considered a target.

Corinne had heard rumors that, in the event of a terrorist attack or kidnap attempt, the entire forty-sixth floor could be sealed off from the rest of the building until the threat had been neutralized. Even the windows on the top four floors of the STC Building were armored.

In her five years as Dick Hemmings's secretary, Corinne had seen Halloran only half a dozen times. On each occasion she had been accompanied upstairs every step of the way by one of Halloran's goons.

"Harvard-educated goons," she had told her lover, "but goons nonetheless."

Brian had seemed curious about the elusive American tycoon, but Corinne was used to that, too. Everybody was intrigued by America's superrich, even the cool, controlled, and allegedly aloof British. As many people did, Corinne sometimes liked to bathe in the reflected glory that shines its warming, golden rays on those who live or work close to power and celebrity. But eventually she'd exhausted her meager supply of gossip and Brian's interest had dwindled away.

Corinne heard more footsteps scurrying along the corridor outside and knew that the whole floor would soon be humming with activity as the rest of Halloran's New York staff arrived and went about their work with conspicuous diligence in deference to their master's temporary presence upstairs, even though it was highly unlikely that anyone but Dick Hemmings would catch more than a glimpse of the company chief. The first anyone would know of Halloran's presence would be when his personal bodyguards swept the floors above and below the forty-sixth floor just prior to his arrival. When Halloran arrived it would be either by chopper to the rooftop helipad or by armored limo to the basement garage and then his own private elevator straight to the forty-sixth floor.

Corinne hurried to her desk and began rechecking the papers her boss had asked her to prepare for his meeting with Halloran. If she could give Hemmings everything now, she knew, there was a chance she wouldn't be called upstairs at all during the day and she would be able to slip away with an easy conscience to enjoy her midday dalliance with Brian. Just the thought of it made Corinne's cheeks burn with anticipation.

It was extraordinary how a chance meeting with Brian had transformed her life in such a short space of time. She felt safe

and secure with him, unexpectedly elevated above the aggra-
vations and disappointments of ordinary life in New York.
Maybe, Corinne thought, in her most vulnerable, hopeful moments, maybe a plain-Jane career girl from New Jersey, who had
made it across the Hudson on ability and hard work alone, could
pull everything together after all. Career, success, and romance,
too. Maybe, she dreamed, she could have it all.

The intercom on her desk beeped. "You there, Corinne?"

"Yes, Mr. Hemmings."

"Could you come in for a minute please?"

"Yes, Mr. Hemmings."

Corinne pushed all thoughts of romance from her head and
stood up. She noticed her skirt was riding a little too high for
a business meeting with her boss and briskly smoothed it down.
She fussed with the prim white collar of her blouse for a moment
and straightened her jacket, then scooped up the deskful of
papers, took a deep breath, and opened the connecting door to
Dick Hemmings's office.

It was Hemmings who noticed it first. He and Corinne had
been working for two solid hours and still there hadn't been any
summons from upstairs or an early-warning visit from Halloran's
security goons. The East Coast veep stopped in the middle of a
sentence and listened carefully. Corinne waited and listened,
too, but she couldn't hear anything unusual above the muted
rumble of city noise that floated up from the Manhattan streets
far below.

The silence lengthened and Corinne watched her boss curiously. He grinned back at her self-consciously and slowly shook
his head.

"Can't be," he said. Hemmings was about to continue dic-
tating the final alteration to his report on proposed marketing
strategies for the new fiscal year when he heard it again. This
time he got up from behind his desk, walked over to the window
that took up one wall of his office, and gazed out over the skyline,
at the gray ramparts of capitalism glinting with power in a hard,
wintry light. The view from the forty-fifth floor of the STC
tower at Columbus Circle swept south and west over a huge
expanse of city to the murky, industrial suburbs of Newark and

Jersey City beyond. Corinne waited patiently while her boss scanned the smog-hazed skyline. Then she heard it, too: the rhythmic thudding rotors of a helicopter.

Corinne frowned. Just another chopper, she thought. The skies of New York were full of them, like gnats in summer. News choppers, traffic report choppers, police choppers, VIP choppers, airline choppers ferrying passengers to and from JFK. Then she realized. It must be Halloran arriving by chopper; that was why Hemmings was so interested.

Corinne got up and walked over to the window to join her boss. Hemmings had been good-looking once but had let himself run to seed. Too much of the good life, she knew. It showed in his fleshy, roseate face and the gut that strained his pristine white shirt. Still, he hadn't lost any of his mental toughness, and that was what made him Halloran's right-hand man for STC on the East Coast.

Corinne also knew her boss had been a lieutenant with the air cavalry in Vietnam. He knew a thing or two about helicopters, and obviously something about this one had aroused his curiosity.

"I don't think it's the company chopper," he mumbled absently, answering her unspoken question.

She looked at him and again he seemed oddly self-conscious. That, too, was unusual for him.

"Something funny . . ." he mumbled again. "Something funny . . ." Then he turned to look directly at her as though noticing her for the first time since she had come into his office that morning. In the five years that Corinne had been his secretary Dick Hemmings had never before considered her especially desirable. Hemmings had been a bit of a player in his time and he was still inclined to indulge in the occasional episode of free-lance stickwork whenever the opportunity arose, but he'd always thought Corinne lacked a little something. Her face was a little too thin, her features a little too sharp. Shrewish almost. He didn't think she would age well. Still, he had to admit, she had great legs and a great little ass. And, he thought, discreetly eyeing her smart black outfit with the stockings, she knew how to dress to maximize what she had.

He had sensed something else about her these past few weeks.

Something different. Something that enhanced her innate femaleness a little more. Something that gave her an unexpected yet quite unmistakable sensuality. He noticed it even more now that she was standing close to him. He could smell her perfume and he sensed a certain kind of heat emanating from her. It made him uncomfortable and he jammed his hands deep into his pants pockets and grinned, embarrassed.

Corinne noticed and smiled back. Her face, Hemmings noticed, seemed full of new color and life. Her cheeks were flushed; her eyes had a mischievous sparkle he had never seen there before. Suddenly he knew what it was. Corinne was in love. Somebody, Hemmings realized, was fucking his secretary into a state of near-permanent ecstasy. Whoever it was, he decided, was doing her a world of good. Dick Hemmings was suddenly very happy for Corinne; immediately he became more relaxed and smiled openly back at her.

A sudden blast of noise swept across the face of the building as the elusive helicopter slid into view.

"Jesus Christ . . ." Hemmings breathed. "It *is* a Huey."

Corinne didn't know anything about helicopters although she guessed from the reaction of her boss that whatever she was looking at wasn't supposed to be there. All she could see was a helicopter bearing familiar red-and-white livery and with the words U.S. COAST GUARD printed boldly along the fuselage.

"What the hell would the Coast Guard be doing with a Huey?" Hemmings muttered to no one in particular.

Corinne looked at him. "What's a Huey?" she asked.

Hemmings shook his head in disbelief. "It's what we flew in Vietnam," he said without looking at her. "Bell Iroquois . . . the workhorse of the air cav. I can't believe the U.S. Coast Guard is so hard up they're using old Hueys . . . it doesn't make sense."

The Coast Guard chopper slid from view again and they both listened carefully, following the muffled thump of its rotors as it worked its way slowly around the building, circling the top few floors of the STC tower.

"What's a Coast Guard chopper doing hanging around here?" Corinne asked, voicing the obvious question. "What is he, lost or something?"

"That's what bothers me." Hemmings frowned. "He shouldn't be here. There's something else, too."

"What?" Corinne was becoming nervous. Hemmings's anxiety was contagious.

"Let's take a good look at him when he comes back," Hemmings stalled.

They waited for what seemed like ages as the noise of the chopper ebbed around the far side of the building and faded to nothing. Then it started to come back, just a low, sinister grumble at first, then an ugly mechanical growl. Then it grew rapidly in power and volume until it had reached a threatening, deafening roar and suddenly there it was again, closer this time, the deadly, spinning blades chopping dangerously close to the side of the building. Corinne and Hemmings both instinctively stepped back from the window and watched with an uneasy fascination. The armored glass in front of them began to tremble in the wash of the props.

"He's cutting it kind of close, isn't he?" Corinne asked, her voice faltering, seeking reassurance, betraying the bile of fear that soured her throat.

"Jesus God . . ." The words spilled from Hemmings's mouth but he seemed unable to move or do anything more than stare fixedly at the slow-moving chopper with its innocuous red-and-white Coast Guard markings.

The helicopter edged sideways across the face of the building, like a giant hungry bug looking for something to eat. Then it seemed to find what it was looking for. It came to a halt facing the window where Corinne and Dick Hemmings stood, the deadly, glittering tips of its rotor blades hacking the air only a few feet from the plate glass. Slowly it began to turn until it was parallel to the building. Then the chopper's side hatch slid open and a man appeared. He was wearing a full orange flight suit and helmet, but something about him seemed familiar to Corinne. The man waved and Corinne knew he could see her through the tinted glass and he was waving to her.

Then the realization hit her like a shock wave and a gasp of disbelief escaped her lips. It was Brian, the man who had made love to her so enthusiastically only a few hours ago. Fear and relief flooded through her in a giddy, intoxicating rush. The crazy limey bastard, she thought. This was the surprise visit he had hinted at in bed this morning. Somehow her lover had the pull to hitch a ride on a Coast Guard chopper and buzz the building where she worked. God, she thought, it was the most romantic thing any man had ever done for her—even though he could probably go to jail for something like this. Awkwardly she waved back, then flicked a nervous glance at her boss. Hemmings stared down at her, his face a mask of astonishment and horror. Corinne tried to tell him but her throat was too dry and she couldn't find the words even if she had been able to make herself heard over the roar of the hovering chopper. Then Hemmings grabbed her shoulder so hard it hurt. Corinne gasped and looked back at him and saw something in his eyes that turned her blood to ice.

He was stabbing wildly with his other hand at the helicopter, toward the skids underneath. She stared back at him, uncomprehendingly for a moment, until she realized what he was pointing at.

The chopper was armed. Corinne knew nothing about aircraft armament, but she had seen enough war footage on TV to know what rockets looked like. The chopper had what looked like a battery of rockets attached to each skid. There was something else, too: the slender, needlelike profiles of two lethal missiles attached to the underside of the fuselage. She looked back at Hemmings and for one eerie moment she seemed to see his whole face in unnatural detail. His mouth was working furiously; there was a trace of spittle in one of the skin crevices at the corner of his mouth; his eyes glistened with fear. But her ears were filled with an insane roaring sound and she couldn't hear anything he was saying. Desperately, Hemmings began dragging her away from the window, across the office, toward the door and the cool marble safety of the hallway.

Corinne resisted. She couldn't help herself. She struggled to turn around and look back through the window at the orange-suited man in the chopper hatch. Everything seemed to be happening in slow motion. She watched her lover as though in a dream.

Slowly, and with an absurd and deliberate grace, he raised a hand to his mouth and blew her a kiss. Then he disappeared back inside the helicopter and the hatch slid shut. Corinne felt Hemmings's hand leave her shoulder as he decided to save himself and scrambled desperately toward the door.

In that moment Corinne knew what she wanted to do. She took two deliberate steps back toward the window. The chopper rotated slowly again, altering its profile, turning its gleaming white face to stare directly back at her. The inky reflector glass of the cockpit windows looked like the empty black sockets of a skull. For a moment the helicopter seemed to have transformed itself into a giant death's-head suspended in the dirty white sky outside her window, watching her, claiming her. The chopper hovered only for another instant and then the rocket launchers on both sides blossomed with flame. The last thing Corinne saw was a wall of shimmering glass and fire rushing toward her as her lover took her in one last lethal embrace. A sudden, dissolving blast of heat . . . and then there was nothing.

Hemmings had made it to the hall and was running for the nearest fire door to the emergency stairs, his fleshy face stricken with the rictus of fear. If he could make it into the stairwell, he knew, he stood a chance. The stairwell was insulated against blast and fire. If he could just get on the other side of that damned red door and hurl himself down the stairs he would live. Dick Hemmings had faced death before, in another time, another place. That was different. He had been someone else then. Now he wanted to live. He needed to live. It wasn't fair to come so far only to die like this.

The words swirled around inside his head . . . it wasn't fair. He heard a ripple of fear spread through the offices along the hallway, incredulous shouts of alarm and panicky screams as other STC employees saw the chopper turn to fire. The unworn soles of his shoes skidded on the buffed marble floor and he almost fell.

He put a hand out to save himself. His fingernails bent backward against the marble. A sob of fear escaped his lips. A pretty blond secretary walking along the corridor toward him with a bundle of files in her arms froze and stared numbly at him. Farther down the corridor he saw Pete, the young security guard, amble curiously into view and stare at him in bewilderment. Hemmings had only a few more feet to the fire door. For an instant, he saw himself as the victim of a nightmare, one sole, stricken figure struggling through a frozen tableau of terror, his arms and legs feeling as though they were weighted down by some invisible leaden force while he fought to save his life. More screams. There was a sudden deafening crack as the first rockets hit and the whole floor shook. The shock threw Hemmings to the floor and he lay there, winded for a moment. Then he realized he was unhurt and began scrabbling on hands and knees across the slippery, polished marble, whimpering like a panic-stricken animal struggling the last few feet to the sanctuary of its lair, a red metal door marked FIRE—EMERGENCY EXIT ONLY. Hemmings heard a terrifying whooshing noise and instinctively looked behind him. His eyes widened in horror as a fireball burst through the walls of his shattered office and filled the corridor with the roar of a ravening wild beast. With nowhere else to go the trapped forces of the explosion boiled up the hallway toward him. The beast seemed to transform itself as it rushed at him, first into a giant fist and then an evil, burning claw.

Hemmings threw himself the last few inches, seized the cold steel handle of the door, and pushed. But the door was locked.

Locked for Jack Halloran's security.

The claw reached out and took him in its fiery grasp, and the scream that erupted from Dick Hemmings's burning body chilled the souls of all who heard it.

The helicopter reared back in the pale Manhattan sky as the first volley of rockets hit. The man in the orange flight suit let out a whoop of delight as he watched a whole corner of the forty-fifth floor explode in a fountain of glass and flame. The pilot banked the chopper around for a fresh approach while his companion stepped back into the cabin, kicked open the hatch, and pointed a bipod-mounted M60 through the door. He pulled the trigger and raked the side of the STC Building with a long, wicked burst.

The first salvo of bullets stitched a ragged pattern across the forty-fifth and forty-sixth floors, punching holes through armored glass designed to frustrate the random sniper, not to withstand the ferocious onslaught of a sustained stream of 7.62 mm shells. The murderous hail of bullets tore through busy offices, killing people where they worked, shredding flesh and bone, splintering desks and chairs, shattering computer terminals into deadly glittering fountains of glass and plastic shrapnel, turning the East Coast headquarters of STC into a slaughter-house.

Henry was in the staff kitchen on the other side of the floor, microwaving a couple of coffees, when he heard the first screams and then the sudden thunder of an explosion from the southwest corner of the building. For a moment he froze, too, and stared into the eyes of the frightened woman standing next to him. Then the policeman's reflex in him took over. His job was clear. In the event of a terrorist attack he had to raise the alarm and protect the lives of the staff. That's what he was paid for, not to look good in a tight uniform and exchange small talk with the boss's secretary.

Henry dropped the scalding coffees and hurried out of the staff kitchen, drawing his pistol as he went. He saw people wandering out of their offices, looking fearfully around at one another as he ran the length of the corridor.

"Get the fuck out," Henry heard himself screaming. "Use the stairs . . . drop everything and get the fuck outta here."

More people poured into the corridor behind him, yelling, jostling, on the brink of panic as they scrambled for the fire exits on the unscathed northern side of the building. He saw a dozen people milling frantically in front of a fire door, two men in suits struggling hopelessly to force it open.

"Damn." Henry had forgotten the doors had been locked the night before for Halloran's security. A few people broke away from the crowd and began running for the elevators.

"Don't use the elevators," Henry barked after them, the note of command in his voice reminding them that elevators could turn into death traps during a fire or explosion.

"Get out of the way," he yelled at the crowd in front of the door. They fell back obediently, their eyes on Henry, silently, desperately beseeching him to help. He glanced around and plucked a seat cushion from a nearby chair. He wrapped the cushion around the barrel of the automatic to stifle a ricochet in the crowded corridor and fired three shots into the lock at point-blank range. The lock disintegrated and Henry opened the door with a savage kick. The panicking crowd surged past him and began pouring down the stairwell. A man in a gray suit promised to recommend Henry for a pay raise and then was gone. Henry turned and began trotting back along the corridor toward the security desk.

He saw the first wisps of black smoke and smelled burning as he got closer to the main elevators. Instinct compelled him to slow down as he approached the security desk. There was no sign of Pete. He could hear Dave, the front-desk security guard downstairs, yelling through the mike, his voice urgent, demanding to know what was going on up there.

If only Henry knew. He bent low and crept around the edge of the security desk, his automatic poised in his right hand. He snatched a quick glance around the corner and saw two bodies, both badly burnt. One of them was a woman, he guessed, from what was left of her long blond hair. The other was Pete. Henry forgot about his own safety and hurried over. He knelt down and checked the woman first but she was gone. It was just as well, he thought. She wouldn't have wanted to go on living looking like that. He turned to look at Pete and winced. One of Pete's arms was fused to the molten flesh around the woman's middle. He must have been trying to pull her to safety when they were both hit. Henry looked down the hallway and saw that the whole corridor appeared to have been seared by a flame-thrower. There was another body halfway down, charred and smoldering.

"Shit!" he swore to himself. "What happened here?"

He heard people stumbling past him, sobbing, choking, fighting to get out. Then he heard a soft moan from Pete's burnt and blackened lips. Henry stood up. He had to call an ambulance for Pete. For everybody.

Before he could reach across the security desk to the emergency phone he heard gunfire. It seemed to be coming from outside the building.

Outside? That was impossible. They were forty-five stories above street level.

All around him the screaming flared to a new crescendo. Henry stood upright again and looked around, stunned by what was going on about him. Someone bumped into him, hard, but

he scarcely felt it. He forced himself to move toward the nearest
open door, pushing against the escaping crowds. He walked
through the door to marketing control and stepped into a scene
of almost unbelievable destruction. The room stretched for half
this side of the building and looked as though it had been torn
apart by an rampaging army. His toe dug into something soft
and he heard his shoe squelch on something wet in the carpet.
He looked down to see the body of a young man with most of
his left side missing. The man's eyes were open and seemed to
be staring at Henry with the same expression of shocked bewilderment Henry knew was on his own face. Henry swallowed,
fought down the urge to vomit, and stepped over the body. He
gazed the length of the office, dumbstruck.

There were bodies everywhere. He heard more moaning, a
woman this time. He couldn't see her but he could hear her,
calling weakly for someone to help. Henry was afraid to look.

"Sweet Jesus in heaven," he whispered disbelievingly to himself. "What is this? What could do something like this?"

A cold blast of air hit him in the face and Henry saw there
were gaping holes in the windows; a freezing, wintry wind was
blowing through the room. Whole sections of armor-plate glass
were missing.

Then he saw the chopper hovering lazily, no more than fifty
yards away, in the pale winter sunshine. Watching. Henry could
see a man in the side hatch with a heavy machine gun. The
man was firing into the building.

Henry ran to a shattered window, raised his automatic, and
fired every last shot in his eight-round magazine at the chopper.
The man in the chopper hardly seemed to notice. The pistol
clicked empty and Henry began fumbling frantically at his belt
for a fresh clip. The man in the chopper suddenly seemed to
catch sight of Henry's blue-and-gray uniformed figure in the
gaping window and fired a long, withering burst in his direction.

The bullets caught Henry squarely in the gut, and even though
he was a big man they hit him with such concentrated force
that they lifted him off his feet, flung him disdainfully across
the room like a doll, and dumped him in a blood-sodden heap
against the wall.

Henry was dead before he hit the ground.

The man in the chopper pulled the M60 back inside and slammed the hatch shut. Then he stepped into the cockpit and reached down to a new switch connected to a length of yellow cable leading out through a small hole cut in the cockpit floor.

They had rehearsed the maneuver half a dozen times in secret but this was the first and only time using live rounds, and now that the operation was under way they had only two more minutes to discharge all their armament before making their escape.

"Pull her back and we'll put the Sidewinders through the forty-sixth floor," the man yelled through the helmet mike. "If he's home, that's where the bastard will be."

The pilot obeyed without a murmur. He pulled the chopper five hundred feet back from the STC tower, then circled around again to give his passenger a clear shot. The pilot risked a quick glance at the man sitting next to him in the copilot's seat, a man with whom he had worked for eight months and still only knew by his second name: Hennessy. An Irish name. Yet there was no trace of an Irish accent. Just flawless, cultivated British. And in the treacherous world of the mercenary the accent and the name were probably both fake anyway.

In seventeen years of taking mercenary pay in Africa and South America Ted Brackman had known many social misfits, but he had never met a true psychopath before. He had never known anyone who took as much pleasure in killing as this man. The bastard had actually enjoyed looking for the woman and had jeopardized the success of the operation until he was sure he had found her and paid his bizarre last respects . . . just so he could enjoy the perverse thrill of intimate murder.

Hennessy's pale, bland face wore a strange smile as he lined up the Sidewinder on the forty-sixth floor of the building at point-blank range. The sun burst momentarily through milky clouds and caught the steely gleam of the letters: STC, the company logo atop the great skyscraper.

The first shards of broken glass and shattered masonry had already tumbled into the streets far below, sending screaming people running for cover. A lump of cement the size of a refrigerator exploded on impact as it hit the pavement, filling the street with stone shrapnel, killing and maiming half a dozen passersby.

An elderly couple were mutilated by falling glass and lay dying on the ground, their bodies surrounded by a slowly expanding puddle of blood. A young man fifty yards down the busy street lay writhing and screaming on the sidewalk with a jagged splinter of stone embedded in his back. A wicked steel sliver pierced the yellow roof of a taxicab like a javelin and stuck in the seat next to a terrified woman passenger. Traffic stalled to a maddening, panic-stricken jam as drivers assumed a bomb had exploded or a plane had hit one of the city's skyscrapers. People ran, or cowered in doorways, searching the skyline for signs of catastrophe.

Only a few people on the street saw the red-and-white speck of the circling helicopter at first . . . and then the terrible realization spread through the crowds.

The chopper was the source of the carnage.

An armed helicopter had launched an assault on a New York City skyscraper in broad daylight. And there was nothing anyone could do to stop it.

Hennessy thumbed the button and the first Sidewinder missile leapt from its mountings, slicing the air between the chopper and the skyscraper with a fiery hiss. The helicopter bucked wildly but Brackman fought it back to an even keel, and Hennessy launched the second Sidewinder. The instant the second missile was free Brackman hauled back on the controls and the chopper arced steeply away from the skyscraper to escape the shock wave. The effect of the two missiles, each armed with fifty pounds of high explosive, was devastating.

For a moment nothing happened. The STC Building seemed to swallow both missiles without a ripple, presenting its blank, shining facade to the world unblemished except for the minor disfigurement of a single, smoking scar on the forty-fifth floor. Hennessy thought the air-to-air missiles might have passed right through the building . . . but he knew that was impossible. He had armed the warheads himself. Then the whole forty-sixth floor of the STC tower erupted with a gigantic gout of fire and destruction. It was followed an instant later by another massive explosion as the second Sidewinder detonated. From his safe perch in the sky, a thousand feet overhead, Hennessy could see a four-sided waterfall of flame and debris spewing out of the building and cascading down to the city streets far below. He saw bodies flapping like wounded birds as they were hurled out into the concrete chasms and thought he could hear their screams through the roar of sound in his helmet. For one breathtaking moment the entire building seemed to shudder. Hennessy and Brackman both held their breath, enthralled by the terrible spectacle and the enormity of what they had done. Hennessy waited, wondering if the building could withstand such devastation or if it would begin to crack, crumble, and tear asunder.

A huge plume of crimson-tinged smoke billowed up into the soiled Manhattan sky, obscuring the top six floors of the building. Hennessy couldn't tear his eyes away. At any moment he expected to see the first massive avalanche of debris sliding through the rolling, thickening clouds as story after shattered story began to crumble into the city streets.

Somehow the building held. As the smoke cleared he saw flames flickering from three devastated floors, forming a ragged, lurid fringe around the outside of the building.

"Down," Hennessy yelled. "Take her back down . . . we're not finished."

Brackman shook his head but did as he was told. The thudding red-and-white bird of prey swooped mercilessly back down on the stricken building.

"Circle around the top floors," Hennessy ordered. Brackman obediently swung the chopper around the building and steeled himself against the madness of the man sitting next to him. Hennessy picked up another set of switches and began firing salvo after salvo of rockets into the flame and smoke. Fresh new explosions ripped through the building as the rockets exploded, tearing gaping new wounds in its steel-and-glass skin. Finally all the rockets were gone. But still Hennessy hadn't finished.

"Take her right over the top one last time," he ordered.

Brackman took the chopper up and swooped past the building's summit, skirting the thick, choking clouds of smoke. Hennessy unclipped his seat belt, struggled into the back of the chopper, and slid open the hatch again.

"Keep her level, you bastard," he yelled. Brackman was tempted to decant Hennessy through the open hatch and into the inferno he had created but kept the thought to himself. If

Hennessy died, he would never see the final paycheck for this operation. Nor would he have the protection he needed to keep himself safe from the ruthless global manhunt that would be under way within hours of such an outrage.

Hennessy swung the M60 around, aimed it through the open hatch, and fired another long stream of bullets into the smoke and flames.

"Closer," Hennessy yelled. "I want to be sure."

Brackman suddenly understood what Hennessy wanted and swung the chopper closer in to the skyscraper's shattered, burning summit.

Hennessy fired a last concentrated burst and grunted with satisfaction as the bullets ripped across the big steel initials that spelled STC. The letters twisted, buckled, and tore apart as though writhing in pain under the torrent of bullets. For one brief and eerie moment the company emblem seemed silhouetted by a silver halo as glittering slivers of metal sprayed out into the sky. Then the bullets ran out and the STC logo was left a grotesque, charred sculpture of slashed and ruined scrap metal.

Hennessy indulged himself in one last cold smile. Then he yanked the M60 back into the cabin and kicked the hatch shut.

"Okay," he yelled. "Get us out."

Brackman yanked thankfully back on the controls. The chopper reared high in the sky and wheeled eastward. The turbines screamed as the pilot pushed the engines to the limit and the helicopter began a desperate flight east by northeast—out over the Atlantic.

Hennessy scrambled back into the copilot's seat, the small cold smile still on his face, pale blue eyes shining with excitement.

"Did you catch that stupid nigger with the popgun?" he grunted into the mike, without looking at Brackman.

The pilot said nothing.

"I enjoyed getting him," Hennessy added, almost to himself. He squirmed around for one last look at the burning STC Building receding behind them and grunted softly to himself again. Sated.

For the moment.

They were already over the ocean, streaking eastward into the deep Atlantic as fast as the chopper could go. Neither of them spoke.

At least Corinne's death had been quick, Hennessy thought. He owed the poor dumb bitch that much.

Half an hour after the attack, when the ferocity and the enormity of the assault on the STC Building had first become known, a squadron of F-18's scrambled from the joint United States Air Force/Air National Guard base at Trenton, New Jersey. It was already too late. The attack had thrown Manhattan into chaos. Police, ambulance, fire—every emergency service in the city was swamped with calls . . . and all were needed. There were no emergency procedures in place to deal with an outrage on such a scale. The New York Police Department's SWAT team responded in the belief that terrorists might still be in the building. The FBI was notified automatically and sent its own team. A blizzard of calls jammed telephone lines between New York and Washington. The CIA and the State Department were aware of the attack within ten minutes and immediately sought the whereabouts of the President. A Delta Force team on sixty-minute standby at Fort Bragg, North Carolina, was ordered to New York. National Guard units and state troopers throughout the New England states were ordered to mount road-blocks in case the attackers were making a dash for the Canadian border. It was only when the first confirmation of a helicopter attack reached Washington that the harassed State Department undersecretary called the commanding officer at Trenton on his own initiative and the CO agreed to order a squadron of F-18's into the air. Air traffic controllers at Kennedy International Airport were called by the air force radar operators at Trenton and confirmed the sighting of an unscheduled and unauthorized aircraft flying east by northeast out of Manhattan at around 220 miles per hour immediately after the attack. However, they said they had lost it moments later in the usual mass of air traffic. The men in the control tower at Trenton surmised the chopper had dropped to wave height to escape radar detection the moment it was clear of the mainland.

Hennessy and Brackman were already eighty miles out over

the Atlantic when the F-18's wheeled into the skies over Trenton and the formation leader adjusted his radar sweep and led his squadron eastward over the ocean in pursuit. Hennessy and Brackman knew what they were looking for. The F-18 flight leader didn't. By the time he was in the air all the information he had was that he was looking for a Huey painted in Coast Guard colors somewhere over Long Island Sound . . . and if he found it he was to keep it in sight and await further instructions.

"There she is," Hennessy shouted harshly into his helmet mike.

"I see her," Brackman confirmed. They had been wave-skipping for the last ten minutes and keeping to strict coordinates while they searched for their pickup vessel. They had ignored the supertankers and freighters of a hundred nations that cluttered the sea lanes with cargo going to and from the great Eastern Seaboard cities. The two men in the hunted chopper were looking for a battered ninety-foot, green-painted deep-sea trawler that waited patiently on a sea anchor for them, flying the orange, white, and green Irish tricolor. Now they both saw her, exactly where she was supposed to be.

"Good man, Liam," Hennessy muttered to himself as he spotted the black-clad figure of the skipper watching them through binoculars from the foredeck of the *Ceilidh Princess*. The pilot buzzed the trawler at sixty feet before wheeling back around in a tight circle and bringing the chopper into a hovering position about one hundred yards off the stern. The swells were running about six feet. Weather had been an important consideration for this job. High seas meant it would have had to be put off yet again. They had already waited two weeks for a spring day like this, calm enough to enable them to ditch the chopper and be picked up safely.

Hennessy ducked back into the cabin, dumped his flight helmet, kicked open the hatch for the last time, and hauled on the inflatable raft stowed in a corner. He waited until they were hovering about thirty feet above wave height, then yanked the ring on the inflation canister and kicked the raft out. The yellow raft began to inflate as it fell. Hennessy had already tied a rope from the raft to one of the struts inside the helicopter, and when the raft hit the water it trailed obediently behind them in waves flecked white by the rotor wash. He pulled in the slack, then hauled hard on the rope until the raft was almost exactly underneath them. Hennessy caught Brackman darting an anxious glance at him through the cockpit hatch. He responded with a reassuring thumbs-up and Brackman nodded. Hennessy turned away and smiled again. He knew what Brackman was thinking. Now that the pilot's role was almost over he was staring sudden obsolescence in the face. It was a dangerous moment in any operation.

Hennessy secured the last coil of rope inside the chopper before he turned and buckled himself to the rope leading down to the raft and stepped backward out of the helicopter. He slid smoothly down to the raft, unhooked himself, pulled a knife from a sheath in one of the leg pockets of his orange flight suit, and cut the rope linking him to the chopper. The raft immediately began to drift away under the force of the rotor wash. Hennessy pulled a small wooden paddle free of the raft and fought to get some control in the sloppy seas. He gave the okay signal to Brackman and the chopper wheeled obediently away. Hennessy covered his face against the renewed blast of wind and salt water and watched while the Huey executed a slow, ungainly hop a mere fifty yards away and began to settle again. He watched the rotor blades slow from a blur to a choppy stalling speed. The stubby tail prop kissed the waves first with a spurt of spray and the chopper wobbled. For a moment it looked as though Brackman might make a mess of it but then he caught it and steadied it again, bringing the helicopter down into a trough in a perfect ocean ditching. Hennessy watched as the rotors slowed to a dead stop and the Huey began to lean sickeningly over on one side.

Christ, Hennessy thought, he's not going to make it.

But Brackman had eased the chopper onto its starboard side. The open hatch was on the port side. A moment later Hennessy saw Brackman scramble awkwardly into the open hatch and jump. Hennessy grinned and began paddling toward the swimming figure. The pilot was wearing a life jacket so there was no panic. Hennessy kept his eye on the chopper, waiting for it to sink. But it wouldn't. It pitched and rolled heavily in the swells, settling lower and lower, taking in more water through the open hatch . . . but it wouldn't sink.

Hennessy frowned. This wasn't part of the plan. The fucking thing was supposed to sink almost immediately so there would be no danger of its being spotted by searching aircraft. That was why ditching in open ocean was such a precarious business. The pilot said he would only have seconds to get out before the chopper started to go down. Instead, here she was, rolling about like a great red-and-white fucking gin palace trying to attract attention to herself.

"Shit!" Hennessy swore. Brackman could have ditched her and had his fucking lunch before getting out.

Almost as soon as the thought passed through his mind the chopper pitched heavily forward, a big, sloppy breaker flooded in through the open hatch, and she nose-dived smoothly beneath the surface. The tail rotor was the last thing to disappear and then she was gone without a trace, starting her last journey two miles down to the chill, crushing blackness of the ocean floor.

Hennessy's smile was back. He had lost sight of the pilot but then saw him again, a small, orange figure, splashing in the open water maybe eighty yards away. Hennessy heard engines and looked around to see the *Ceilidh Princess*, with the mate at the wheel, chugging slowly around to pick them both up. He signaled McKee to pick him up first and waited.

"Throw me a line," Hennessy called as the trawler pulled up alongside the bobbing yellow life raft. "Tow me over to him."

McKee obeyed without a word. Didn't even ask how it went, Hennessy noted. He would find out soon enough. Another cold bastard. Another good man for the Cause.

With the trawler towing him Hennessy closed the gap to the chopper pilot in a few minutes.

"Thought we might leave you out here, didn't you?" Hennessy grinned cheerlessly as he helped the pilot onto the raft.

"The thought had crossed my mind," Brackman answered as he heaved himself out of the water. He slumped back against the side of the raft, pulled off his flight helmet, and wiped his streaming face. The *Ceilidh Princess* wallowed about twenty feet away. McKee began pulling the raft in by the tow rope. Hennessy reached up to grab on to the gunwale as they bumped alongside and McKee began securing the rope. Hennessy fumbled for a moment and it looked as though he was having difficulty making the leap from the raft. Then he turned and looked down at the pilot.

"You don't think much of me, do you?" he said, smiling.

Brackman looked back up at him and shrugged. "I don't have to like you," he said. "I only have to work with you."

Hennessy's smile broadened. The raft plunged and Hennessy clung to the trawler with his left hand.

"Yes," he said. "But I have to like the people I work with." He brought up his right hand holding a Colt automatic and fired. The first shot passed through the pilot's life jacket and hit him in the right side of the chest. Brackman began screaming with a mixture of pain and rage and hurled himself forward with arms outstretched, trying to get his hands on Hennessy. Only one thought rushed through his mind: he was going to die. But if he could just grab hold of Hennessy and pull him over the side, Brackman knew, he wouldn't let go. He would take the bastard down with him. Hennessy fired point-blank into the top of Brackman's charging head and the screaming stopped abruptly as the pilot fell in a heap at Hennessy's feet. Blood began spilling out into the seawater on the raft's undulating deck, making a lurid mess against the bright yellow rubber. Hennessy emptied the rest of the magazine into the sides of the life raft and heard the hiss of escaping air. Then he pulled himself nimbly up over the gunwale and onto the deck of the *Ceilidh Princess*. Hennessy watched as the limp yellow wings of the deflating raft slowly enfolded the pilot's corpse and began to sink.

Then he turned and looked into the dark, expressionless face of Liam McKee.

"I take it he's not comin' with us," McKee nodded at the corpse in the sinking life raft. The accent was pure Belfast and there wasn't a trace of irony in it.

Hennessy grinned and dropped the gun back into a flight suit pocket.

He preferred the company of men like McKee.

2 Memory of a Lifetime

"The entire top half of the building will have to be rebuilt," STC's chief architect, Jerry Fox, was saying. "The rest is still structurally sound—as far as we can tell. But it'll be a couple of weeks before we know for sure. Even using ultrasound. The whole thing is a mess . . . a helluva mess."

Jack Halloran barely heard the words. He was still trying to come to grips with the other information he'd been given: the latest casualty list. A woman called Dorothy Eldridge, from the accounts department on what had been the forty-fifth floor, had died overnight in the hospital from her burns. That took the death toll to 174. It would go higher, Halloran knew. There were nearly 200 people injured, many seriously. Some would be maimed for life. Others would succumb to the awfulness of their injuries: horrific burns, broken spines, shattered legs and arms. And there were still 11 people unaccounted for. That's what Halloran found hardest to come to terms with. Eleven people missing, vanished from the face of the earth. They hadn't been identified from the remains found on the streets far below or among the bodies retrieved from the building's ruined upper levels. Some of them could have just disappeared into the city and be hiding somewhere, catatonic with fear and shock. But that was unlikely. It had been twenty-four hours; if anyone had wandered off into the streets they would have been found by now. No, Halloran knew. It was worse than that. Those 11 people never would be found because there was nothing left to

find. They had been vaporized by heat and blast. Converted to
atoms by the exploding rockets or cremated to ash in the fires
that followed. It would take several more days to find out who
they were, even by process of elimination using company records.
Because not a fragment of bone, not even a tooth remained of
those who were missing. And some of the hospitalized victims
were still unconscious and too badly burnt to be seen by relatives.
They would all have to wait a few more days for the final list,
Halloran knew. And the news was only going to get worse.

They were standing on the forty-second floor. It was the
highest anyone could go in the shattered husk of the STC Building. The top six stories and the roof were missing. The city
engineers wouldn't guarantee the safety of the elevators beyond
the twenty-fourth floor, so they all had to walk up from there.
It was a hard climb for a man of sixty-one; Halloran felt he knew
every step of the last ten stories personally. He was sweating
when he walked out into the shattered remains of the forty-
second floor and the icy wind that howled through the naked,
fire-blackened girders cut through his heavy winter overcoat,
freezing the sweat on his body into a cold, clammy film.

"Don't go near the edges," the architect warned Halloran and
his escort of six armed bodyguards as they filed out onto the
floor. Halloran's personal security chief, Bob Becker, looked
uncomfortable. He put one man in the doorway while he and
another guard stuck close to Halloran. The other three men
fanned out through the gloomy, cavernous ruin looking suspi-
ciously at the half dozen city engineers and fire marshals picking
through a few scattered piles of rubble, some of whom stopped
what they were doing to stare curiously at Halloran when he
appeared.

"We've tested this floor as much as we can and we think it's
okay, but we still can't be a hundred percent—" The words
ended abruptly, as though snatched from Fox's lips by the wind.
The company architect was struck by the look of shock on the
old man's face. Funny, he thought. He had worked for Jack
Halloran for twenty years now, and even though he and many
other STC employees often referred to Halloran as the old man,
the president of STC had never really seemed old. Until now.
There had always been something ageless and indestructible

about the pugnacious old bastard. The tough, weatherbeaten face; the hard blue eyes; the thick gray hair, cut with military severity, exactly the way he had worn it since the days he served with the marines in Korea. But right at this moment Halloran looked older than his years. Old and tired. The lines on his face looked deeper, his jaw hung loose and slack, and there were heavy pouches of wrinkles under both eyes. It was as though his whole powerful, scheming, and violent life had finally turned on him and collapsed around him at precisely this moment.

In a way, it had.

Halloran viewed the devastation in silence. The whole floor was empty and open to the elements except for the steel supporting girders and their ragged concrete jackets. The walls and windows were gone. A man who strayed too close to the edge could easily be plucked out by a sudden malevolent gust of wind. This floor had been divided into offices, Halloran thought, plush, comfortable offices. People had worked here. Scores of people, innocent people: his employees. Now it was all bare. A few piles of rubble pushed untidily into the middle of the floor were all that remained of the interior dividing walls and office furnishings. Desks, telephones, computers, polished marble, paintings, expensive furniture . . . all obliterated. The floor was black from the fires and wet from the firemen's hoses; great pools of sooty water lay on the scorched cement. Here and there he could see a seared fragment of carpet, the coagulated plastic puddle of a power cable outlet in the floor, a shattered slab of marble.

Halloran looked up through six ruined stories to the open sky. A jagged rind of broken concrete clung to each level where there had once been a floor. Strands of frayed, useless steel cable hung down like cauterized nerves. Only the girders remained, and they had been stripped of their protective cement coats from the forty-fifth floor up. A couple of girders in the middle had yielded completely to the power of the two exploding missiles and ended now in ugly molten stumps. Others had twisted and warped in the vortex of the fire that followed, cracking the cement, tipping the burning contents of the floors above onto the floors below.

Six floors. All gone, Halloran thought. The whole building

evacuated and unfit for occupation for months. The human cost was still too much to comprehend. The economic cost would run into hundreds of millions of dollars. From the outside the summit of the once-proud STC Building looked like a ruin, a hideous blackened stump of a building. From the inside, it was worse. It wasn't just the ugliness, the nearness of the destruction, it was the smell. The stench of death and burning. It caught in Halloran's nose and throat and stayed there. He knew it would stay with him for a long time.

Some of the names started coming back to him. Dick Hemmings, his vice president, East Coast. Confirmed dead. Lauren Wilson, his personal assistant in New York. Still missing . . .

"Hell of a price to pay just for working for Jack Halloran, isn't it?"

Halloran looked around. A thin-faced man in his mid-thirties with well-trimmed black hair and wearing a long dark overcoat stood about ten yards away. As two of Halloran's bodyguards moved on him with guns drawn he obligingly took his hands from his coat pockets and held them up to show they were empty. Judging by the expression on the face of the guard at the stairwell door the man must already have been on the floor when they arrived, standing somewhere in the wintry gloom. Halloran's guards didn't look happy.

"Who are you?" Halloran asked. His voice was dead steady. Steadier than he felt.

"John Ritsczik. FBI, New York bureau chief," the man said. Neither Halloran nor his men looked impressed. Ritsczik stood quietly for the thorough search Halloran's men did on him. Bob Becker took Ritsczik's gun and checked his shield against his ID.

"Looks genuine," Becker said. He returned the shield, then took the clip from the FBI man's gun before handing it back.

Ritsczik eyed the mini-Uzis Halloran's men carried.

"Your guys don't fuck around, do they?" he said.

"Neither do my enemies," Halloran answered. "You have anything for me, Mr. Ritsczik?"

Ritsczik shrugged. "Like what?"

"Like who the hell did this?"

"I was hoping you might help me, Mr. Halloran. But you're a hard man to reach."

"Yeah," Halloran agreed. "Now, if you've got nothing for me maybe you'd like to get off my property, please. There may not be much of it left but what there is of it is still mine."

Ritsczik stood his ground. "This is an official FBI investigation, Mr. Halloran . . . and I've wanted to see you for some time."

"Have you, Mr. Ritsczik." Halloran answered with studied indifference and turned back to the exit. His bodyguards fell in around him, putting themselves between him and the FBI man.

"This is hardly a surprise, is it, Mr. Halloran?" Ritsczik called after the departing STC chief executive.

Halloran ignored him.

"Play with fire and you get burned," Ritsczik persisted. But Halloran kept walking.

"Pity so many people got burned with you."

Halloran whirled back at the door, his face gray, eyes glittering with anger.

"This is none of your business, Mr. Ritsczik," he said harshly. "You're out of your league. Stay out."

"Acts of terrorism inside the United States are my business, Mr. Halloran," Ritsczik called after him. But Halloran and his entourage were already on their way back down the stairs, leaving the FBI man alone on the forty-second floor with only the howling March wind for company.

"Time we were out of this fucking town, Bobby," Halloran told his grim-faced security chief as they stepped from the elevator in the basement garage and walked toward the armored limousine waiting nearby. "Let's go to Washington."

Becker looked relieved for the first time since they heard of the attack. They climbed into the car and the driver squealed out of the garage, up the ramp to street level, and out past the police barricades keeping the crowds and news crews back. The tinted windows of the limo prevented anyone from seeing who was in the back of the automobile. So far only a handful of people knew it was Jack Halloran. He wanted to keep it that way for a little longer.

The driver cut across the traffic jamming Columbus Circle and headed for the Triborough Bridge to La Guardia Airport. Halloran slumped back into the cream leather upholstery, closed his aching eyes, and let the thoughts tumble through his brain. He and his men were aware that whoever had mounted the attack had known enough about Halloran's movements to pin-point exactly where he was supposed to have been at ten o'clock the previous morning. If his private jet hadn't been uncharac-teristically held up by the control tower at Glenview, his de-parture from Chicago would have been on time and he would have been in his offices on the forty-sixth floor of the STC Building—as scheduled—when the missiles went in. Instead he was still in his limo, stuck in the traffic on FDR Drive when word came through on the radio that a helicopter had crashed into the STC Building and triggered a massive explosion. Hal-loran had promptly detoured to one of the company's secret town houses on Riverside Drive, where he had remained under tight guard for the past twenty-four hours.

He had hardly slept at all. Neither had Becker or any of the other guards who usually traveled with him. Halloran spent the rest of that day and most of the night in an upstairs bedroom watching news reports of the atrocity on television while his guards turned the house into a minifortress. He hadn't eaten at all, although he did drink a lot of coffee. He had watched all three TV sets in the bedroom with grim interest, using the remote to skip from one to the other as successive broadcasts struggled to fill in the blanks. It had been confirmed that a helicopter bearing fake Coast Guard colors and insignia had launched a rocket, machine-gun, and missile attack on the STC Building. The attack represented the worst single act of terrorism ever to take place on American soil. There were still no leads. International condemnation had been unanimous. On his return to Washington from a grain growers' convention in Omaha the President of the United States pledged that no effort would be spared to capture and bring the perpetrators to justice.

By prime time the networks had drummed up a small army of professors, pundits, and pretenders to expound a bewildering array of theories and propositions about who might be respon-sible, and why, and what it may or may not mean. Still, the

newscasters announced during successive bulletins, it could not
be confirmed whether Jack Halloran, the president of Standard
Transport Charter, was among the dead or missing. That un-
certainty didn't prevent their running a hastily assembled bi-
ography of Halloran's life and times. Halloran watched himself
age rapidly as one network anchorman narrated a series of pho-
tographs stretching from the 1950s to the mid-1970s. Most of
it was old newspaper and magazine stock, social pages, business
pages, routine stuff. Halloran was pleased to see that the pictures
stopped at 1976, though his appearance hadn't altered too much
since then. His face had become a little fleshier and his gut had
thickened up, but the head was unmistakable. He wasn't pleased
when he saw STC's national director of public relations, Bill
Douglas, giving a lengthy interview, airing his opinions on the
attack and speculating on the whereabouts of Jack Halloran and
the impact on the company. He decided to fire the bastard in
the morning. And he sat bolt upright when they screened a 9
mm color home movie of him with former President Kennedy
at the Kennedy compound in Hyannis Port. Halloran was visible
for only a fleeting moment among a group of casually dressed
friends sitting with Kennedy at a table on a sunny, manicured
lawn, but it was enough for them to freeze and hold, presenting
him full face and looking about as animated as Mount Rushmore,
as usual. And it was also enough to emphasize the point: Halloran
had been a power behind the American throne for a long time.

"Damn," Halloran swore from his position atop the bed cov-
ers. He wondered where the hell they could have obtained film
like that. He couldn't even remember it being photographed.
Not that it mattered particularly; at least that was ancient history. He had more urgent problems to worry about.

Halloran's natural instinct was to tell nobody, absolutely nobody, where he was for at least twenty-four hours. The phones
rang three times but Halloran let the answering machine deal
with them. One call was from the company's national vice president, Mike Cummings, at the head office in Albuquerque, New
Mexico, Halloran's home state and the nucleus of his corporate
empire. Cummings was one of the few people in Halloran's
organization to know of the existence of the New York town
house. The second call was from the secretary of state, person-

ally. He sounded agitated. Halloran let them both sweat. The third was a voice that had once had the power to make his pulse quicken. Now it made him smile bleakly. Janice Street, the woman who had once been closest to him and who was probably calling in the hope of confirming that he was dead after all. She would have to wait a little longer for the bad news, too. Two men had called at the front door around eight-thirty, but the house was in darkness and everyone inside ignored their knocking. They had left after ten minutes, looking dissatisfied. Halloran was certain they were FBI or State Department, but was in no mood to trust anyone. He wouldn't have put it past the secretary of state to have another unit mount an assassination attempt against him under the pretense of terrorist attack. It was a little messier than their usual style, but when the State Department fucked up they always managed to do it on a spectacular scale.

Jack Halloran had lived in the twilight world of secret intelligence long enough to know that at a time such as this he was on his own. He would fall back on the resources of his own carefully constructed world—the empire within an empire that he had built over thirty-five years as one of America's most successful corporate citizens.

In 1953, when Jack Halloran had returned as a Marine Corps sergeant to his hometown of Albuquerque, New Mexico, at the end of the Korean War, he knew exactly what he wanted to do. He wanted to be powerful. He had spent two years with the Marine Corps on the battlefields of Korea and had seen too many good men die because of weak and incompetent leadership. More times than he cared to remember, he had come close to being killed himself due to almost unbelievable stupidity on the part of senior officers. Luckily he survived the various episodes of short shelling, mistimed air strikes, uncoordinated attacks, and botched withdrawals. But while shivering in a slush-filled, rat-infested ditch just south of Tongyang on Christmas Eve, 1952, waiting for the Communist Chinese to attack, he made a solemn vow. If he survived the war, Halloran promised himself, he was never going to take orders from another powerful asshole again as long as he lived. Instead, he would *become* a powerful asshole.

Unlike most of his former comrades in the Corps, who blew their pay on whiskey and whores whenever they got the chance, Halloran went home with close to two years' pay saved up. Using the money to make a down payment on a ramshackle little supermarket on the outskirts of Albuquerque, he set out to make himself rich. Within two years he had rejuvenated the supermarket, paid off his loan, and borrowed money to expand. Within five years he owned the shopping mall around his store and had opened two more supermarkets in burgeoning new suburbs. He had picked the right time to expand: America was awash with money; consumerism was the new religion. It was Halloran's constant boast that if a man was willing to sweat a little during the 1950s he couldn't help but get rich.

By the end of the decade he was a millionaire, with shopping centers throughout the Southwest, and he was moving rapidly into interstate trucking, cattle, and real estate. He brought his thriving empire under the corporate umbrella of a single company structure he called Standard Transport Charter because it gave him the two things he craved: power and anonymity. By 1960 Jack Halloran wasn't taking orders from anybody anymore. But he had discovered that when you gave big checks to the Republican Party you got to tell a lot of greedy and ambitious politicians how to behave, and no one ever knew who was really pulling the strings.

Halloran had first been introduced to President Dwight D. Eisenhower at a thousand-dollar-a-plate Republican fund-raising dinner in Washington, D.C., in 1958. They liked each other immediately. A former general who had become isolated among White House advisers and sycophants, Eisenhower found it refreshing to meet an influential man like Halloran who still possessed the foot soldier's talent for common sense and would voice an honest opinion in language everyone understood.

By 1959 Ike was playing golf with Halloran half a dozen times a year and calling him regularly to solicit his opinion on a wide range of issues. Halloran had a good gut feeling for politics and a genius for finding simple solutions to problems that had become needlessly complicated. It was Halloran whom Ike called in early 1960 when he had a problem with a prominent Republican senator from Halloran's neighboring state of Arizona. The man was married with a family but had been investigated by the FBI and found to be a practicing homosexual with links to a child prostitution racket.

Ike thought FBI Director J. Edgar Hoover might be a little too heavy-handed if he was left to handle the case—especially with an election looming later that year and a threat to the GOP in the form of a charismatic Catholic upstart Democrat from Boston called Kennedy. The Eisenhower Administration simply couldn't afford the embarrassment of a sordid homosexual scandal so close to the White House. Halloran promised to take care of it. Within two weeks the senator from Arizona had resigned, citing failing health. Ike never asked how Halloran had accomplished exactly what was needed with such swiftness and discretion but it immediately earned Halloran a reputation in the Republican Party as a formidable Mr. Fix-it.

In the end Kennedy won the election anyway and Halloran never expected to see the inside of the White House again. He concentrated on building up his business, opened his first office in New York in early 1961, and listed STC on Wall Street. But he was wrong about not seeing the inside of the White House again. Lyndon Johnson, an acquaintance from Texas, had been elected vice president of the United States and was well aware of Halloran's growing reputation throughout the Southwest. John Kennedy decided he needed more allies in the Sun Belt and elected to court Halloran by inviting him for the occasional weekend to the Kennedy summer compound at Hyannis Port.

Halloran discovered that Kennedy was a rabid James Bond fan. The President had an almost schoolboyish love of melodrama and was fascinated by the world of secret agents, treachery, and counterespionage. Kennedy, for his part, became convinced that Halloran lived according to the purest of patriotic principles, principles that transcended politics and party lines. Halloran's patriotism was in fact bipartisan. He would give his loyalty to the office of the President, no matter who the occupant of that office happened to be. Kennedy could trust Halloran as long as Kennedy was the President of the United States; Halloran told him as much, and that was good enough for Kennedy.

One afternoon, on the veranda of the house at Hyannis Port, during one of those long summer days full of innocence and perfection, while the kids and the other guests were playing down by the water's edge and the Secret Service men were patrolling the background like scowling blackbirds, Kennedy confided to Halloran that he had need of his own Mr. Fix-it. It was only a few months since the Bay of Pigs fiasco, the failed attempt by the CIA to initiate an invasion of Castro's Cuba by Cuban exiles. In the interim Kennedy had formed the opinion that he could not entirely trust the intelligence services already at his disposal. He needed some insurance. Another small, independent intelligence agency operating with the utmost discretion outside the established parameters of government, to inform and advise the President on a select range of domestic and international issues.

At first Halloran wasn't sure if the idea stemmed from the President's paranoia or an overdeveloped sense of the theatrical. But it appeared to Halloran that Kennedy might actually be afraid of his own intelligence services, that he needed someone else, someone independent and objective, to advise him on issues of national security. Halloran was neither flattered nor alarmed. He merely saw the opportunity to acquire more power.

Kennedy said he could not contribute federal funds but promised Halloran access to all the massive resources of government—buildings, matériel, manpower, transportation—all over the world. Halloran picked and chose as he saw fit. The word he cherished most was *independent.* He began building his own private security force, men and women recruited to serve him and him alone, people whose loyalty was beyond question. Like many ex-marines he favored Corps veterans. Like them, he'd been through the mill. So he knew how they thought. He could talk to them. They were loyal; they knew about security; they followed orders. His bodyguards, engineers, pilots, communications people, and clerical workers—almost everyone who worked close to him—were recruited exclusively from the ranks of the Marine Corps and the U.S. Navy.

On the outside STC was a legitimate corporate empire, which employed some of the finest talent in the country and competed annually with all the other major American corporations for the brightest stars from the business schools of Harvard and Yale. But at its core, at the secret humming nucleus that surrounded

Halloran, STC ran like a military machine. It was a dual system that enabled Halloran to groom talent on the business side of his empire and then recruit those of special merit to his inner circle.

Halloran had just reached the point where he felt his private intelligence-gathering agency was ready to meet any demand the President might make of it when Kennedy was assassinated in Dallas. Halloran's first reaction was that he had failed the first and greatest requirement that the Chief Executive had placed upon him. Halloran had failed to detect any hint of a plot against Kennedy.

Halloran brooded for days on the President's implied mistrust of his own intelligence services and speculated privately that Kennedy might have had just cause, that the CIA could have been behind the President's assassin, Lee Harvey Oswald. Once again, Halloran decided, events had conspired to remove him from the innermost circle of power in America. He wondered when he should begin to dismantle the new, untested intelligence agency. Lyndon Johnson had other ideas. It was LBJ who gave Halloran the authority to proceed. Now, more than ever, Johnson decided, an independent intelligence agency was essential to the welfare of the President.

The corporate growth of STC was matched by the growth of Jack Halloran's secret powers throughout the sixties. Halloran arranged his first foreign assassination in 1968. A South Vietnamese army general working for the CIA in Saigon was believed to be selling secrets to the North Vietnamese. The Company —as the CIA was known—refused to terminate him on the grounds that they could use him as an unwitting double agent. The Tet offensive of 1968 proved to Johnson that the CIA was nowhere near as efficient as they claimed to be at running anyone as a double agent. The President couldn't ask any other branch of government to get rid of the general and so he turned to Halloran.

Halloran assured the President he would take care of the matter and there would be nothing to connect it to the White House. He was grateful for the opportunity to send the CIA a message of his own, that they weren't omnipotent. Halloran flew to Saigon by himself, made a simple pipe bomb, which was something he had learned in the Marine Corps, and paid a couple of Vietnamese hoods two hundred dollars to plant it in the general's apartment. The CIA double agent was terminated. From then on, Halloran was in the assassination business. The jobs increased in complexity, involving everyone from drug kingpins in Central America to Middle Eastern terror groups. And all the while Halloran gained more and more experience and became more and more dangerous.

By the time LBJ left office Jack Halloran was too powerful and knew too much about too many people to be shut out in the cold by any administration. He was also aware that he, too, was now a target for assassination, from friend and foe alike. He retreated into his own armor-plated world, answerable only to the President. Meanwhile, official and rival government intelligence agencies like the CIA, the FBI, the Drug Enforcement Authority, the National Intelligence Service, and the State Department lobbied constantly against Halloran's unsanctioned powers and for the dissolution of his organization. When that failed they worked ceaselessly to undermine his influence at the White House.

His bleakest period came during the Carter years. When he offered his services during the hostage crisis in Tehran he was rebuffed at the insistence of the military. Following the subsequent debacle of the bungled hostage rescue attempt at Desert One, Halloran was reinstated to a position of major influence at the White House, a position that was consolidated during the Reagan era. The implementation of Executive Order 12333 gave Halloran the imprimatur of the President to organize clandestine operations abroad on behalf of the United States government.

Despite all his wealth and power, Halloran remained alone. He had never married; to marry was to risk vulnerability. Yet, he had never been without the companionship of beautiful women. At one point, during the sybaritic sixties, he had kept half a dozen mistresses in cities around the world. Occasionally he favored one more than the others, but he never let them get close to him. As far as Halloran was concerned, bought sex was the best sex. He liked to keep it impersonal. Now, he was paying the price. Now, he was the loneliest man in all the world.

In twenty-four hours he had allowed one crucial contact with

the outside world. He had ordered one of his guards to visit the
mayor's office and then to call at every city hospital, as a representative of STC, to confirm to the families of the dead and
injured that the company would pick up the tab for everything.
It was close to dawn before exhaustion had imposed a couple of
hours' sleep. Then, about eight, he had showered, shaved, put
on a fresh change of clothes, and left the town house to visit
his shattered building, much against the wishes of his bodyguards. It was Becker who noticed the two guys who had called
at the door the previous evening still watching from a brown
Chevrolet Impala parked across the street. When the limo pulled
out the Chevy followed them, all the way to the cordoned-off
building at Columbus Circle.

It wasn't morbidity, guilt, or even masochism that had compelled Halloran to go and see the damage for himself. He had
to see it. It had been intended for him. He already thought he
knew who was behind it. He'd wanted to see, close up, what
his enemies were capable of. He wanted to hate them. He needed
to hate them with every atom of his being, to fill the void inside
with the kind of rage he required to fight back.

He had been pleased to see Jerry Fox, the company architect,
already at the scene with the city engineers. God, he thought
for the millionth time, he had some good people working for
him. They deserved better than this. He thought about the FBI
man, Ritsczik. Halloran wasn't happy about him. But the FBI
was the least of his worries at a time like this. He would get
that stupid, overzealous New York bastard off his back later.

The limo pulled up in front of the gates to the private hangars
at La Guardia and Becker opened his window to speak to the
cops on duty there. Halloran grunted with displeasure when he
saw a couple of news vans with reporters standing around by the
gates, too. The news crews scrambled toward the limo as it
slowed briefly to get through the gates; then they were through,
leaving the reporters in their wake. The Chevy Impala that had
followed them from the town house pulled over to the side of
the road and stopped outside the gates. The guy on the passenger
side got out and watched them drive onto the airport tarmac.
Becker saw him duck back inside the car and talk into a radio
handset. Almost certainly federal agents, he decided, though

from which department was anybody's guess. Halloran was relieved that the airport police had been able to keep the TV crews well away from the company hangar; the limo hissed across the tarmac and was soon out of sight of the frustrated reporters. Halloran saw his plane was already on the jet apron guarded by two more of his men and a couple of cops. The pilot was in the cockpit of the nine-seater Beechcraft and Halloran could see the heat waves rippling the air behind the tail-mounted jet engines. The limo sighed to a halt and Halloran's men had him in the plane in less than three seconds. Becker's heart almost stopped when he heard the thudding rotors of a helicopter over the whine of the Beechcraft's engines. He looked up to see a Live Eye news chopper thudding toward them from the direction of the city.

"Jesus," he swore. The fucking thing deserved to be blown out of the sky, pulling a stunt like that. But the news chopper was too late—Halloran was out of sight and in the plane. Half an hour later they were airborne.

It was only when the pilot confirmed they were at twenty-eight thousand feet and on course for Andrews Air Force Base, outside of Washington, that Halloran seemed to relax. Andrews was the high-security military airfield used by the President, the Cabinet, the Joint Chiefs, visiting heads of state, and other VIPS whose business was considered of national importance. Halloran's special status had assured his private aircraft landing rights at most military installations inside the United States. His aircraft and pilots were all assigned military recognition codes, which guaranteed him access to airspace and airfields normally prohibited to civilian air traffic.

He unbuttoned his heavy winter coat, leaned back in the seat, closed his eyes, and lay still for a long time. Becker and the others watched him in silence. He was breathing deeply and looked as though he had fallen asleep. Becker wouldn't have been surprised. They had all been awake for nearly thirty-six hours and they had another long day ahead of them. But that was part of their job . . . and Halloran had thirty years on Becker.

The old man heaved a sigh of pure exhaustion, forced his eyes open, and looked blearily around him. He checked his watch. Five minutes. That was all he'd needed: a power nap, a trick he'd learned in the Marine Corps when he could sleep in a cold, wet, mud-encrusted uniform in a waterlogged foxhole if he had to. The long, healing sleeps of another lifetime may have been denied him but a power nap would get him through the next four or five hours.

"Give me the phone," he ordered Becker.

The first call was to the President of the United States. It only took a minute, once he'd given his priority access code to the White House switchboard operator, and he was through. Halloran listened to the solicitous words of sympathy from the President in his familiar aging-Yalie voice and then confirmed that he was tired but unhurt. He smiled thinly when the President told him that the secretary of state hadn't slept all night because he'd been worrying about what in the hell might have happened to the coordinator of their most effective top secret counterterrorist combat unit. Halloran said he would be arriving in Washington in forty-five minutes and needed to see the President before the day's end. The President agreed.

"I don't think it's a good idea for me to be seen arriving at the White House at this time, sir," Halloran said. The President was the only man in the world whom Halloran addressed as "sir."

"I intend to take the chopper direct from Andrews to Chesapeake," Halloran continued. "I think it would be better if we met there aboard my yacht this evening."

One of the privileges of being considered indispensable to the office of the President of the United States was the power that went with such status. Jack Halloran had survived seven presidents because of his many rare and precious qualities. The first was his great wealth, which, in itself, carried great power. The second was his unwavering patriotism. The third was his discretion. And the fourth was most important of all: Jack Halloran got things done. It was perhaps his greatest gift. He was a manipulative organizational genius who got results, however dirty the job. Political assassination, sabotage, hostage rescue. And because he operated outside the United States, independent of any government agency, he was unaccountable to any arm of government, including Congress. Under Executive Order 12333 Halloran was answerable only to the President of the United

States. That made him one of the most powerful men in the world. It also gave him a lot of enemies, at home and abroad. It generated a groundswell of resentment among the government agencies—such as the State Department, the CIA, and the Secret Service—who didn't enjoy the same degree of freedom and who occasionally had to give him logistical support. But power always came at a price; Halloran knew that better now than ever before.

Power also came with its privileges. One of them was a yacht berth in the waterside compound reserved for the President's official yacht in the Chesapeake Bay, the great ocean inlet seventy miles southeast of the nation's capital. Halloran's private oceangoing yacht, the seventy-six-meter, twenty-two-hundred-ton *American Endeavor*, was anchored there now.

The President confirmed he could be there.

"We have an official dinner for the prime minister of Australia at the White House tonight, but if we can keep him off the subject of himself we ought to have him out by eleven."

The President paused for a moment, then added: "I'll have the secretary with me too, Jack. I want to get things moving on this one. We've got all our intelligence services working on it. What I told the news media last night wasn't only for public consumption. I want the people who did this, too. Whatever it takes, Jack . . . whatever it takes."

Halloran smiled faintly. "Thank you, Mr. President."

"Jack," the President added, "I know you prefer to use your own people—but are you sure you won't let the Secret Service assign a few extra agents to your protection till this is over?"

"Thank you, but no, sir," Halloran answered firmly. "My people are trained to work with me and they're familiar with all my . . . peculiarities."

He didn't add that fewer contacts with government agencies meant fewer leaks.

The President expressed his sympathy to Halloran once more and hung up. Halloran waited for a moment before punching another number into the handset. This time he called somebody who was more important to him than the President of the United States. He called the only man in the world who could save his life.

STOWE, VERMONT, MARCH 21

The man on the other end of the line listened in silence. When Halloran had finished the man gave a curt "okay" and hung up. Then he turned back to the woman curled comfortably in front of the fireplace, nursing an empty coffee cup.

"When do you go?" she asked, without looking at him.

"Tomorrow."

She nodded but said nothing. He crossed the room and sat down on the rug beside her and they both looked into the open fire without speaking or touching each other. The heat from the flames didn't quite take the chill off the air in the lodge. The atmosphere inside was as cold as the winter landscape outside. The sky was overcast, the temperature hovered around freezing, and the mud-streaked slush on the track in front of the lodge was beginning to freeze hard again.

"It's good it's started," he said after a while.

The woman gave a soft, resigned laugh and looked at him.

"I know you're happy," she said. "It's only at times like this that you come back to life." Then she shivered. He moved closer, put his arm around her; he felt the tension in her but she didn't pull away.

"Who would have thought it would start like this?" she said. "Who would have dreamed . . ."

Janice Street had fled her New York apartment within an hour of the attack on the STC Building. As Halloran's former mistress, and the woman who had been closest to his center of operations, she had to be considered a target, too—if only as a way of getting to Halloran. But the scale and ferocity of the assault on Halloran's New York office had shocked her. She had known some of the people who died. No one expected anything like that, not even Halloran. As a man whose job it was to mastermind the demise of some of the world's most rabid terrorist organizations, Halloran was always at risk—from a sniper's bullet perhaps, a bomb under his car or in his plane, a machine-gun attack from a passing car on the highway. They were occupational hazards in Halloran's violent world. They came with the territory—and they could be anticipated, guarded against, avoided. But something like this, the wanton sacrifice of so many

innocent lives, the callous destruction just to get at one man
. . . it was so evil it defied belief.

It had taken her hours to get out of New York because of
the traffic snarl that followed the attack. She had only made
it to Northampton, Massachusetts, by nightfall and had spent
the night at the Howard Johnson's because she didn't like the
idea of navigating the icy mountain roads to Stowe in the dark
in her little silver BMW. She had tried calling all the confidential numbers she had for Halloran from the motel, without
success. But she wasn't worried. Something told her Jack Halloran wasn't dead. If Halloran had been in the building someone would have known. The news reports said his plane had
arrived at La Guardia half an hour before the attack and he
hadn't been seen since. But no one could confirm seeing him
enter the building. There had been no chopper flight scheduled
from the airport to the STC rooftop helipad, and the front-
door security guards hadn't seen him enter the building. There
was only silence, an impenetrable wall of secrecy surrounding
Halloran's whereabouts. And that was exactly the way it should
be. That was Jack, she knew. He would have gone into hiding
somewhere, unscathed, untouched by the bullets and exploding
rockets that had slaughtered so many of his innocent employees. No one would know where he was until he was ready.
And already he would be plotting his plan of retaliation. Soon
he would emerge to put that plan into action. And whatever
that plan was, it would hinge upon the man who was holding
her—the only man she had ever believed was strong enough
to keep her free of Halloran's reach. And now, the ultimate
irony. They both depended on Halloran for their own survival. They had both lingered a little too long in his dirty
world.

"I should have let you kill the bastard in Tel Aviv," she said,
casting her mind back almost a year. "It would have saved a lot
of lives worth more than his."

Colin James Lynch, formerly Lieutenant Lynch of the Royal
Navy's elite Special Boat Squadron, formerly of Britain's Counter
Terrorist Command, looked at her with skeptical amusement.

"Halloran may be a bastard," he said, "but he's the only
bastard who can help us get out of this."

She sighed a sigh of deepest resignation. "If only you'd said no the last time . . ." she said.

Lynch shook his head.

"There are no guarantees," he said. "There are at least half a dozen Middle Eastern terror groups who want us dead. Tuckey and his wife were killed before we even went into Lebanon on that last hostage rescue job. This has been coming for a long time. Somebody has been playing a very nasty little long-term strategy . . . and so far I'd say he's doing pretty bloody well at it."

"Little . . . ?" Her words ended in exasperated silence. Sometimes the British penchant for understatement left Janice cold.

Emmet Tuckey had served with Lynch in the first mercenary operation Lynch had ever performed for Halloran, an ugly assassination job in Libya. The tall, amiable blond ex–USN SEAL had left the mercenary game after that to run a small ocean-salvage business in Panama City, Florida, under a new name. Lynch had approached Tuckey last year on Halloran's behalf, inviting him to join a new mission to rescue American hostages in Lebanon. Tuckey had declined. Only days later Tuckey and his pregnant wife, Luisa, were incinerated in a huge dockside gasoline explosion. It was weeks before the explosion was confirmed as a deliberate act of murder. Lynch had suspected Halloran; anything was possible in their world—and there was only one sure way of keeping people quiet. The operation to rescue the hostages had been costly in lives but successful. Afterward, Lynch had come close to wasting Halloran on the tarmac at Lod Airport in Tel Aviv. Only Janice's intervention had prevented him. Halloran had desperately denied that he was to blame for the death of Emmet Tuckey. He told Lynch the murder had almost certainly been carried out by a foreign-based terrorist organization, an organization dedicated to the destruction of the elite team Halloran had created with Lynch to engage in high-priority foreign assassination jobs and hostage rescues. Tuckey was just the beginning. Someone was stalking them all, Halloran and everyone close to him. And whoever it was didn't seem to care how many people got killed to get the job done.

"We could just disappear," Janice said now, turning to look Lynch in the eye. "We've got enough money. You know how to do it. You know all the places. We could do it."

"And leave Halloran to fight them off on his own?"

"He's a big boy. He wouldn't hesitate to sacrifice any of us if it suited him. You know what he's like."

Lynch nodded. He stared back into the face of the woman he'd met in London two years earlier. The beautiful, knowing face of a woman who, though only in her late twenties, already knew the horrors of which men could be capable. Thick, dark hair covered her shoulders and framed a face of startling sensuality, a face with huge brown eyes and full lips against skin made pale by the winter's weak light and made taut by fear. Janice Street had been just another one of Halloran's plans, a device to snare Lynch in the mercenary net and keep an eye on him until Halloran was satisfied he was trustworthy. It hadn't been part of the plan for them to fall in love. She had seduced other men as part of Halloran's power games. The Radcliffe-educated daughter of a small-town Maine doctor, it had suited her to be Halloran's mistress and then to play the part of his whore until she had amassed the money she thought would give her real freedom. But when she was ready to leave, she found she couldn't. Halloran wouldn't let her go. And she had fallen in love with a man who knew only one world: Halloran's world.

She looked back into Lynch's face. His thick brown hair had been cut short again since she'd last seen him. She thought it made him look older. The tiny wrinkles around his stone gray eyes had grown a little deeper, too. Still, she thought, he looked fit and well. His color was good, and his body had felt hard and strong when he held her. He seemed to be thriving on his life in the snow-clad hills of Vermont.

It had been three months since she had last seen him. He had come down to New York for the week before Christmas and stayed with her in her apartment again. But she had spent Christmas Day with her mom and dad and her sister's family at the house where she grew up in Maine. She had spoken to Lynch on the phone. He was alone. Twenty years of military service had taught him to live without Christmas, he told her. He had spent the day skiing. A year earlier they had been almost inseparable. Lately they had begun spending more time apart. The distance between them grew with the understanding that no matter how much they were attracted to each other, her expectations and the accumulated psychological baggage of his past life were too much for them to overcome.

"I happen to think Halloran is right," Lynch said. "There's no point in running. I can't run. People like you and me can't hide. The only way to beat this thing is to hit it back. Rob it of its momentum, outmaneuver it—then step on it." ·

"You talk about it like it was some kind of giant bug," she said.

"It is . . . and the only man who can give me everything I need to squash it is Halloran. Till then, we haven't got a future."

"Does he have any idea yet who's behind it?"

Lynch shrugged. "No."

"Nothing?"

"Nothing."

"So, where do you start?"

"We decide that tomorrow," he said flatly. Then he steered the conversation back to her. "Halloran said you shouldn't stay here or at your apartment. I agree. We have to assume your apartment is known." He paused and looked around the brick-and-timber lodge he'd hoped would make a perfect retreat. "This place would be too easy to hit. I'm not even happy about us spending tonight here. Whoever wants us seems to know a helluva lot about us."

She followed his eyes around the lodge she had helped furnish. The wildlife prints; the sturdy, American colonial furniture; the brilliantly patterned throw rugs on the polished pinewood floor; the pretty cushions on the couch and chairs; the huge bed in the balcony upstairs: it had been nearly all her doing. Lynch could have lived happily in a barracks.

"Does it have to be this cold?" she asked, shivering again.

"No." He smiled and stood up. "I'll switch the central heating on."

Later that night, when the house had been warmed through, they curled up again in front of the fire and made love with a comfortable familiarity. Afterward, when they lay quietly together, he savored the patterns the firelight made on the curves and hollows of her body. The way he looked at her excited Janice and she turned to him again.

"Maybe love doesn't last forever," she said softly, teasing his earlobe with her tongue. "But the memory of a great fuck will last a lifetime."

3 A Whore
in Velvet Drawers

Tom O'Donnell threw another dun-colored slab of peat onto the fire and stepped back as a shower of sparks and a gust of foul brown smoke belched out of the fireplace, thickening the air in the tiny living room. His wife looked at him disapprovingly while she finished setting the dinner table.

"For heaven's sake, man," she chided him, "do you have to bank the fire up like that? Why can't we use the gas heater like normal people? That stuff's still damp . . . it stinks the whole house out."

O'Donnell glanced reproachfully at her. "Ye've no sentiment in ye at all, have ye, Mavour?" he grumbled. "If God wanted us to waste good money heating our houses with gas, he wouldn't have carpeted the whole bloody country with fuel that costs nothin'."

His wife stood her ground and glared back at him. Her real name was Margaret, but O'Donnell had called her Mavour since their courting days thirty-three years ago. Mavour was a shortened version of *mavourneen*, the Irish word for *darling*. Mavour O'Donnell was fifty-seven, with a fresh pink face that showed the lingering prettiness of her youth, though she wore her long gray hair the old-fashioned way, plaited into a thick rope, coiled and pinned neatly above the nape of her neck. She looked like a kindly grandmother who wouldn't use a harsh word against anyone.

"It smells like burnin' shite," she protested. Then she shrugged and turned back into the kitchen. "I'm glad it's you and your pals eatin' in here tonight and not me."

O'Donnell shook his head resignedly, as though his wife were immune to logic, and took his pipe down from the cluttered mantelpiece to add even more fumes to the suffocating air inside the cottage. Once he'd got it going he stood with his back to the fire, savored the strong taste of the tobacco, and felt the warmth of the smoldering peat seep through his heavy brown corduroy trousers. Mavour had done a good job, he thought, glancing around the room. He always felt at his most comfortable in this room, with its homely old furniture, the armchair near the fireplace that had molded itself to his shape over twenty years. The whitewashed walls were crowded with memories—a wedding picture taken in front of Saint Thomas's in Dublin, christening pictures of their four children, all married now and long gone from Ireland. Caitlin, the last of his three daughters, lived in Manchester, married to an English policeman. O'Donnell could hardly bring himself to speak to her. Mavour did all the writing and always sent his love, anyway. It was Mavour who kept a statue of Jesus on a small table in a corner with a gorily exposed heart and lurid droplets of crimson plaster blood streaming down its blue-and-white robe. Pride of place, over the mantelshelf, was reserved for a painting of Wolfe Tone, the founding father of Irish nationalism who cut his own throat rather than be shot by a British firing squad in 1798. An elegantly written scroll, painted onto the bottom of the picture, summed up Tone's aim: "To unite the whole people of Ireland, to abolish the memory of all past dissensions, and to substitute the common name of Irishmen in place of the denomination of Protestant, Catholic, and Dissenter."

Tom O'Donnell could not have put it better himself. He rocked gently on the heels of his shoes and relished the moment. The room was exactly the way he liked it: a warm fire, supper cooking in the kitchen. The cottage filled with a pungent mixture of fire smoke and cooking smells—the simple pleasures of home and hearth.

A thickset man of middle height with a friendly, open face and soft brown eyes, Tom O'Donnell's most distinctive feature was his hair. Originally glossy black, it had started going gray when he was twenty-one. By the time he was forty it had turned completely gray. Now, in his fifty-eighth year, it was the color of sun-bleached cotton. He liked to wear it long and brushed back with a calculated effect of utter carelessness so that it covered most of his ears and hung thickly around his collar. It wasn't only vanity that compelled him to keep it that way. O'Donnell understood that any man who aspired to leadership would be assisted greatly if he could cultivate some distinguishing physical feature, something that made him stand out from the crowd. Something people would remember and remark upon. With him, it was his hair. He thought his mane of thick white hair gave him a certain nobility and made him look gentle and scholarly. That alone stood him apart from his fellows in the Irish Republican Army.

The table was set for four. He and his pals, as Mavour called them, would be eating in the living room. It was the biggest room in the squat, five-room fisherman's cottage, which stood alone on a windswept, rising headland overlooking the slate-colored waters of Donegal Bay. O'Donnell had moved from Dublin to Donegal with his wife in 1982, bought the run-down stone fisherman's cottage and a few bleak acres on the outskirts of town for seven thousand pounds, and done it up. He viewed his move to Donegal as a kind of spiritual homecoming because the old fortress seaport on the northwestern shores of the Republic had been the ancestral home of the O'Donnells, the last Gaelic clan to be expelled from Ireland by the first Queen Elizabeth in the late 1500s.

The O'Donnells had been the most enduring of the original Irish clans. For four hundred years after the Norman invasion of England and Ireland they alone defended and preserved intact their northwestern kingdom against all enemies. But it wasn't only their military prowess that distinguished the O'Donnells. They were also the most civilized of the Gaelic clans. It was Red Hugh O'Donnell and his wife, Nuala, who founded the Donegal friary in 1474, a monastic school that attracted the finest scholars in all Europe. The O'Donnells were sponsors of the first chronology of Ireland, the *Annals of the Four Masters*, which started as a history of the saints and evolved into the definitive history of Ireland and an affirmation of the brilliance, the uniqueness, and the integrity of medieval Irish literature.

Tom O'Donnell had no idea whether he was a descendant, though it was most unlikely. The original O'Donnells had been exiled to Spain and Austria and their ancestors still survived there, assimilated and unrecognizable. But it suited O'Donnell to let others think he might be descended from one of the greatest Gaelic dynasties.

If Ireland had a true cultural home, Tom O'Donnell knew, it was Donegal. Not that overblown ford on the Liffey known as Dublin, which had been given its eminence and its name by other foreigners, the Norsemen who preceded the Normans by a mere 150 years. In O'Donnell's eyes, Donegal was the only true and worthy custodian of Irish integrity. It was the most Irish of the counties in the free state. The home of more Gaelic speakers, or *Gaeltachtai*, than any other county. And O'Donnell was proud of his rekindled fluency in the language. Donegal was a sacred place, he believed, the place selected by destiny to be the crucible for the forging of a new movement: the revival of an uncorrupted, undiluted Gaelic spirit—a spirit that would be the catalyst needed to subdue all the dissenters and heal all the differences that continued to plague the Cause; a spirit to unite all the factions behind him and reunite Ireland at last under the banner of pure nationalist pride. It was also the safest and most convenient place for O'Donnell to make his base following the violence of his disagreement with his former IRA colleagues in Dublin and Belfast.

Like many Irishmen, O'Donnell had been seduced by the romance of the IRA when still a young man. He had trained as a draftsman in the Dublin City Planning Department but had been easily lured from the challenge of designing council houses in the austere environs of Corporation Hall to spend most of his time in the smoky city pubs listening to the beer bards and whiskey poets who filled the bars back then. He had bought Guinness by the keg for Brendan Behan at McDaid's on Harry Street in 1958 and eventually got himself sacked for his trouble. Behan had laughed uproariously when O'Donnell told him.

"To hell with 'em, boyo," Brendan had roared. "They begrudge you your independence of mind. Fuck 'em. Fuck all the begrudgers." And O'Donnell gladly admitted it had been worth it. Behan at full throttle was worth hearing. True, it was mostly blarney. But what magnificent, impassioned, lyrical blarney it was.

It was Behan who introduced O'Donnell to a few of "the boys" from the Irish Republican Army. At that time the IRA was nothing more than a geriatric shadow of its former self. The troubles in the North had yet to flare anew, the Easter Uprising was ancient history, and the Second World War had changed nothing. The Cause existed in theory only, celebrated by reminiscence and romance. There was something quaint and comic about it back then. Belonging was a harmless enough commitment for a young man to make as a declaration of his Irishness.

It was about then that O'Donnell had become seriously interested in Irish history and had begun writing long, meandering articles about politics and the Celtic heritage for the official IRA newspaper, the *United Irishman*. That lasted until 1962, when the newspaper was hijacked by Denis Foley, a Communist hardliner who threw out all the Celtic typefaces and gave the paper a strident, modern politicism. Longtime IRA subscribers in the country were shocked into incomprehension.

O'Donnell drifted, hanging around the pubs, drowning in Guinness and republican polemics, writing unread political pamphlets, picking up a few quid doing odd jobs for IRA mates. It was Mavour who supported him most of those years, on her paltry nurse's wages. Charmed by the good looks and innocent enthusiasms of the young man she'd met at an IRA fund-raising party, she had soon moved in with him and was paying most of the rent on their poky bed-sitter in Baggot Street. He repaid her by getting her pregnant, and they were married in September 1963. The priest was a pragmatic man, a veteran IRA sympathizer who didn't mind Mavour's wearing white. O'Donnell borrowed a suit and got married with safety pins holding up the cuffs of his trousers. An IRA mate with his own photographic studio did the pictures as a wedding present.

Times were hard until 1966, when O'Donnell went to one of the many big, boozy parties held after the march through Dublin to celebrate the fiftieth anniversary of the Easter Uprising. A new mood was apparent within the IRA. Battle lines were being drawn as the long-predicted split between the old and the new guard looked as though it was becoming reality. A new generation of firebrands was hungry for action. After years of stagnation there was talk again of direct action to free the six northern countries from British colonial rule. The old-timers were all for a political solution, but the younger, hard left Catholics believed they were letting down their coreligionists in the North. Both sides were counting numbers. Soon, O'Donnell would have to choose. Instinct told him it was the young radicals who were in tune with the temper of the times; it was they, he felt, who would emerge strongest from any split. Three years of poverty and neglect had eroded his loyalty to the old guard and convinced him that the young bloods were right.

O'Donnell was badly in need of a sense of direction, too, a purpose to his life. He wasn't getting any younger. Like a good Catholic, in three years of marriage he had produced three children. He was getting tired of living on principle and black pudding. If he was going to dedicate himself to the Cause at all then it would have to be with a view to getting things done, to changing the bleak realities of his own insignificant life. To hell with the idea of eternal struggle, he decided. He wanted results within his lifetime. And Tom O'Donnell was not content to be just another foot soldier for the Cause. He had ambitions of his own. He had learned something about the nature of the power struggles within the IRA. He knew the kind of pedantic, polemical maneuvering that could drag on for months, even years in the IRA—and then there would be a sudden violent explosion and everything would change in the fallout. In the gathering storm clouds O'Donnell saw the opportunity to seize some power of his own, to turn it to his advantage.

It was an ambitious man called Sean McStiofan, a member of the IRA's twenty-man army council, who tipped the scales for O'Donnell. McStiofan had acquired a sizable following within the IRA, a following intoxicated by his passionate philosophic brew of socialism and Irish traditionalism. O'Donnell didn't much care for socialists—he thought them the most humorless of people—but he decided he could live with McStiofan's faction. For a time.

When McStiofan offered him a job as driver and courier between Dublin and Belfast, O'Donnell took it gladly. It was a job that suited O'Donnell because it gave him the opportunity to learn about the power structure within McStiofan's movement, to make vital contacts, and to build a few loyalties of his own.

The catalyst for the split came in August 1969 with the eruption of bloody Catholic riots in Belfast and Londonderry against rule from Stormont, Britain's puppet Ulster parliament. The riots were followed by the reintroduction of British troops . . . which was just the spark McStiofan needed to ignite his own fire. The IRA old guard wanted to apply pressure by becoming a political party. The new guard wanted to kill British soldiers. McStiofan chose the IRA national convention in October that year to denounce the old leadership and remove his followers from the hall, O'Donnell among them. By Christmas, McStiofan had announced the formation of the Provisional IRA—the notorious Provos.

What followed was two years of bloody murder between the Provos and the old, official IRA—or the Officials as they became known. Both organizations claimed to represent the cause of national unity and both fought for the right. When they weren't fighting the British they were fighting each other. And, as the Provos discovered to their cost, the gunmen of the old IRA could be coldly efficient killers. Dozens died on both sides in bomb blasts and bloody ambushes before the Provos and the Officials forged an uneasy truce. After 1971 the Provos were virtually left alone to carry the war against the British in the northern counties—which they did with murderous enthusiasm. All of McStiofan's patient efforts had paid off; Ulster had become an unassailable power base for the Provos. It was a lesson O'Donnell learned well.

In 1972 Tom O'Donnell killed a man for the first time. Terry Rooney, a cabdriver in Belfast, had been suspected of passing information to the Royal Ulster Constabulary's Special Branch. O'Donnell was sent to pick him up for interrogation and almost certain execution. It had been after eleven at night when O'Donnell and a loyal but brutal Provo thug called Kevin Bourke called at Rooney's house. The cabdriver had been in bed asleep with his wife. It hadn't been easy for O'Donnell to convince Rooney that all the Provo army council wanted him for was a little chat. Rooney's wife had started crying and pleading at the front door and their two kids had woken up and come to the top of the stairs, screaming in terror when they saw two strange men come to take their dad away. O'Donnell and Bourke had been forced to bundle Rooney a little too roughly into the car and drive away before the whole street woke up.

Rooney panicked during the drive down the Shankhill Road, tore himself free of Bourke, and threw himself out of the back of the car and onto the road. O'Donnell's orders were clear. If Rooney made a bolt for it he was to be shot. O'Donnell had been given a pistol just in case, a six-round Ruger. But he didn't need the gun. Rooney had staggered to his feet on the wet road and tried to get away across an empty building site, a pathetic figure in bare feet with a raincoat over his pajamas. O'Donnell swore, spun the stolen black Granada into a U-turn, mounted the sidewalk, and chased Rooney across the open site. It was close to midnight but there were still a few people about, mostly gangs of youths coming home from the shebeens, idling, looking for trouble. O'Donnell wasn't worried about them. They wouldn't interfere. It was just another show for them in the black theater of Belfast. He was most worried about a British army patrol. It was important to do a quick and efficient job on Rooney. Not only for security reasons, but because his stock would rise among the Provos. Killing a man made you different. Especially when you did it like this, in cold blood. It showed you were a serious man. It earned respect.

O'Donnell caught him with the right fender little more than halfway across the site. Rooney screamed and disappeared in a flurry of arms and legs so that O'Donnell lost sight of him for a moment. He bumped down off the building site back onto the road and turned around. With the headlights raking the open space he saw Rooney lying on his side in a puddle of black water, his right leg broken. O'Donnell could see the glint of blood-streaked bone protruding from the luckless informer's thigh.

Steeling himself, O'Donnell stamped on the gas pedal and bounced back up onto the building site toward Rooney. The doomed man raised his hand in a feeble self-protective gesture and screamed as the car roared down on him. The car bounced again as a wheel went over Rooney's head and shoulders, and the screaming stopped. O'Donnell backed the car over Rooney's still form one last time to make absolutely sure, then accelerated away, toward Andersontown and safety. It was an ugly, squalid killing, but O'Donnell had expected it to be—there was precious little romance left in the IRA that he had joined in a haze of stout and patriotism in Dublin seventeen years earlier. And it had been different after Rooney's death. Everyone had treated him with respect. People had paid him greater heed.

O'Donnell rose steadily through Provo ranks during the terrible attrition of the mid-1970s. He was involved in the kidnapping, interrogation, and execution of two more men, both informers. In 1974 he attended an extraordinary meeting in Belfast, involving some of the most feared terrorist organizations in the world. A meeting that included the PLO. It was during this conference of terrorists that he met a man called Abu Musa. Musa was a powerful and influential figure within the PLO and was to prove an invaluable contact for O'Donnell in the years to come. A man who, O'Donnell believed, would help him to fulfill his historic destiny one day.

Most of O'Donnell's work required him to crisscross the border almost weekly, smuggling arms and men, planning attacks, raising funds, somehow avoiding capture and the hospitality of Long Kesh. In 1975 he orchestrated the robbery of the Ballymena branch of Barclays Bank and boosted the Provos' coffers by nearly seventy thousand pounds. It also marked the first time that O'Donnell had broken one of the Provisionals' strictest rules— by keeping twelve thousand pounds for "personal expenses." If the army council had found out he would have been kneecapped, but O'Donnell was already enjoying the protection of his own small, loyal following.

In 1976 he was elected to the Provisional army council and flew to New York to speak on behalf of Noraid, the IRA's American fund-raising agency. He proved so effective a communicator that the next year he represented the Provos at another meeting of terrorist organizations in Spain. Once again the PLO was there and once again it was represented by Abu Musa. The difference this time was that O'Donnell had some new ideas of his own, ideas that he wanted to discuss with his new friend. When the conference ended O'Donnell and Musa spent several days lounging in the sun at Alicante on the Costa del Sol, like any couple of vacationing conventioneers with time to spare. Between drinks and exchanges of mutual flattery they were able to cement their relationship, a relationship based on mutual need that one day might benefit both. At the time, however, neither man was able to forecast exactly how.

When O'Donnell returned to Northern Ireland he helped develop new strategies for Sinn Féin, the political wing of the Provisional IRA, and quickly earned a reputation for tactical cunning. All the time he worked on his own political theories and preached his own gospel about putting the sanctity of Celtic identity above the mindless anonymity of socialism. It annoyed some of his socialist comrades-in-arms but he found a few sympathetic listeners. Tom O'Donnell began to acquire a following of his own.

By 1981 he was tired of socialism and the Provo vision of a united, socialist Ireland. Dedicated socialist and longtime IRA mouthpiece Gerry Adams had made Sinn Féin his own and was supported through sheer force of arms by the Provo army council. O'Donnell believed it was time to make his move. He believed he had enough support to engineer a split of his own. A few years earlier he had noticed how much Londonderry had been left to its own devices by the Provos and had made a point of cultivating the brigades there. The Derry brigades were indifferent to the Belfast brigades, proving receptive to O'Donnell's antisocialist rhetoric and his ideas on Gaelic unity. O'Donnell decided to assume a greater role in the leadership of the Derry brigades and to turn them into a power base of his own. In late 1981 he assumed command of the Bogside army council. The Bogside and the Creggan Estate were the two biggest Catholic ghettos in Londonderry and had become almost unassailable strongpoints for the Provos. With most of the original Provo leadership dead, in jail, or otherwise occupied, it was left to a Provo hard-liner called Callum O'Brien to challenge O'Donnell's authority. O'Brien simply disappeared from the face of the earth. No one doubted that O'Donnell was responsible for O'Brien's mysterious disappearance, and his reputation as a man not to be crossed increased accordingly.

The Provo command in Belfast responded by ordering O'Donnell to step aside and to present himself for a disciplinary hearing. O'Donnell knew well enough what that might entail and preferred to hang on to his kneecaps a little longer. He refused point-blank and the army council issued an execution order. It almost succeeded. Six months later O'Donnell was ambushed and shot four times as he drove through Armagh on the A5 from Derry to Dublin, where he planned to see Mavour. The bullets were from an Armalite M14. O'Donnell had probably helped bring it in. Two of the 7.62 mm slugs passed through his right shoulder, breaking his collarbone. Another severed a rib and deflected through the upper part of his right lung. The last sliced his right kidney in half. His life was saved by one of those bizarre twists that happen only in Northern Ireland. He was rescued by a British army patrol and taken to a hospital in Belfast, where British intelligence put a guard on him, hoping he would turn informer. They were soon disappointed. Two weeks later O'Donnell discharged himself and Mavour drove him through the night to an old friend's farm near Cork, where she nursed him for six months. He was never the same again.

The ambush and the long, painful recuperation that followed proved to be the turning point in Tom O'Donnell's life. A different man emerged through the curtain of pain. His political passions had been corrupted by a lifetime of violence, cruelty, and deceit. His long-cherished ambitions were hardened by bitterness into obsession. Mavour lamented quietly that she had lost the man she married. As soon as he was fit O'Donnell ignored her pleadings and left for Belfast on his own mission of revenge. His first stop was at a flat in the Markets where he played his own kind of roulette with a gun pressed to the left kneecap of George Cleary, the Provos' Belfast armorer, until Cleary told him who had ordered the ambush and who had carried it out. By the end of the night two of the three men who ambushed him were dead. The third was safe only because he was doing seventeen years in Long Kesh for his part in the murder of an RUC man. O'Donnell's next step was to plant a bomb in Jimmy Keenan's car. Keenan was the army council chief who had issued O'Donnell's execution order. The bomb blew off both Keenan's legs. The Provos, who weren't prepared for another protracted, self-destructive feud, were canny enough to figure that they were only adding to the legend of O'Donnell as indestructible. With this in mind they offered him a deal. If he stayed out of Northern Ireland and promised not to meddle in IRA business they would call off the execution order. O'Donnell agreed. It was close enough to what he wanted. He already had another plan—and he couldn't put it into effect if he had to spend every day looking over his shoulder for a Provo hit man. He agreed to the new deal with the Provos. For a time.

Now, here he was, all these years later, in his warm, cozy cottage on the shores of Donegal Bay, about to put the final stages of his plan into effect. It was a plan that would wipe out the entire leadership of the Provisional IRA at a stroke—and put him in its place as the head of an organization destined to represent the legitimate interests of the Irish people at the triumphal moment of their historic battle for unity and identity.

Tonight was an important meeting. A difficult meeting, considering the news from New York. It had been worse, much worse, than he expected. Secrecy was vital, even from Mavour. She had already put the portable TV in the kitchen; she'd sit in there, watch television, and do a bit of knitting while he and his pals talked business. It was better for her if she didn't know everything, O'Donnell believed. Mavour was inclined to agree. Although lately, he thought, he had detected a change in his wife. She had tended to display an unusual degree of intolerance with him. Him! Who once could do no wrong in her eyes. And it was about the most piffling little things, too. O'Donnell slowly shook his head. It wasn't normal for her, not after all they had been through together. Tom O'Donnell made up his mind to talk to Mavour about whatever it was that was bothering her. Soon. Just as soon as this bit of business was finished.

A banner of light splashed suddenly across the windows and he heard cars coming up the drive. O'Donnell stepped to the window and looked out through a misty curtain of drizzle drifting in from the gray Atlantic as two cars pulled up in front of the cottage. The first was a white Datsun. It was followed by a small blue van marked GARDA, the name of the Irish Republican police. A small man climbed apprehensively out of the Datsun and waited while a much bigger man wearing the black uniform of a sergeant in the Garda got out of the van and approached him.

"Ah." O'Donnell smiled to himself. "The boys."

They warmed themselves in front of the fire while O'Donnell produced a fresh bottle of Bushmills from a kitchen cupboard.

"Ye'll be needing this after your drive, boys," he said, handing the first two of his guests a glass of whiskey each.

The man in the uniform of a Garda sergeant took his drink and smiled apologetically. "I'm sorry I didn't have time to change," he said. "I was already runnin' late when I left the station. An' it's been a prick of a day."

Eamonn Docherty was the sergeant of the Garda at Lifford, a little town thirty kilometers northeast of Donegal on the republican side of the border, opposite the Ulster town of Strabane. One of many sympathizers in the Garda, Docherty's commitment to the Cause and his loyalty to O'Donnell sprang from a friendship that went back to Dublin in 1961 when he joined the IRA six years before he joined the Garda. Eamonn had been an enthusiastic brawler during the Dublin pub days and made a few extra pounds for himself fighting for bets. He was an amiable enough man and an effective policeman, but there was an undeniable brutishness about him that meant he had gone as far as he was ever likely to go in the Garda. For a man who had no idea how dumb he was and whose ambitions far exceeded his limited abilities, it wasn't enough. Eamonn Docherty intended to play a far more important role in the united Ireland he saw conjured up by Tom O'Donnell's grand vision. In the meantime, O'Donnell was happy to use him as a crude but effective tool.

"I nearly pooped myself when I saw him get out of the van," Billy McCormack declared with a frown. "I've never seen him in uniform before. I don't like uniforms."

Billy was a man who had always seemed old—old and mean. He had the shrunken face and build of a jockey and had been known around the Derry brigades by his nickname, "the Jockey," for nearly twenty years. He had been O'Donnell's staunchest ally when O'Donnell had staged his short-lived take-over of the Bogside command. His loyalty sprang from a shared loathing of socialism and a belief that O'Donnell's vision of the IRA was the right vision. The IRA should be an honorable, populist militia, not just another terrorist branch of the international socialist movement.

"Drink up, boys," O'Donnell coaxed them both, raising his glass first to the portrait of Wolfe Tone and then to his guests. "To the Cause."

Echoing his toast, they savored the smooth malt burn of the whiskey for a moment.

"Slides down easier than a whore's velvet drawers," McCormack pronounced, and held out his empty glass.

"Thirsty, Billy?" O'Donnell splashed another three fingers of whiskey into the glass. Despite his size McCormack had been known to drink bigger men under the table and still keep his wits about him. O'Donnell said it was because God had forgotten to give him a heart and had given him a second liver instead.

"How are the boys in Derry?" O'Donnell asked. It sounded like light conversation. Nothing could have been further from the truth. O'Donnell needed to know that his support in the Derry brigades was still intact. They were to be his springboard to Belfast. He had been elected to the command virtually by acclamation back in '81, and the events that followed only served to make him more of a hero. But in reality the Provo army council had regained control and loyalty to O'Donnell had gone underground. He made frequent visits to ensure the fires still burned on his behalf . . . but it had been a long time. His stature may have grown with time but his presence had shrunk. O'Donnell's supporters needed something big. He had promised it six months earlier on his last visit to Derry.

"Be patient, boys," he'd told them. "Another year at most . . . and we'll make history together." But he needed to be sure.

"The Bogside's still yours," McCormack now reassured him. "We had another visit from Gerry Adams last week. He's got his head so far up his arse he thinks he's looking at Karl Marx. Every time he gives a talk in Derry the boys move a bit further to the right."

McCormack took another sip of his whiskey. "They'll fight for a united Ireland, right enough," he added. "But they'll be buggered if they're going to fight for a Marxist Ireland. And that's what's on the agenda."

O'Donnell smiled. It was what he wanted to hear. There was another splash of light through the rain-spattered windows, followed by the sound of another car. A few minutes later Danny Locke stepped into the room looking even paler and thinner than usual. He nodded to each of the three men in turn, then stretched and stamped his feet to shake the cramps out of his skinny legs after the three-hour drive from Belfast.

"God love you, Daniel, you look like you haven't slept or eaten properly for a week," Mavour scolded him, taking his soiled blue raincoat.

It was true, O'Donnell thought. Danny looked bad. His black trousers and sweater appeared slept in, with perhaps a crust of dried snot on one sleeve. His black curly hair was greasy and unwashed. There were dark shadows under his eyes and his skin had a sickly, etiolated sheen. With his dark hair and eyes Locke seemed more Latin than Celtic; undoubtedly some Mediterranean blood flowed in his veins from the days when the troops of Philip of Spain's vanquished armada were marooned on Ireland's shores. When Locke lit a cigarette his movements seemed quicker, jerkier than usual. O'Donnell wondered if he was on smack. There was a lot of that shit around Belfast these days.

"Would ye like a small malt to settle you, Danny?" O'Donnell offered.

Locke shook his head. "Don't touch it anymore," he said. "Fockin' ulcers."

"Ah." The Jockey nodded sagely. "We live in stressful times." His words seemed devoid of all sympathy.

Locke believed he had a right to be stressed. O'Donnell had met him in Belfast after the split, where he'd been a snotty-nosed street kid from the Unity Flats who'd graduated to IRA gunman only to discover that he, too, had doubts about his political masters. But it was too late, he realized. He was in too deep. He wouldn't be allowed simply to walk away. The Provos didn't deal kindly with those they considered to be deserters. It could mean a kneecapping or a bullet through the back of the neck. The only hope for Danny Locke was a massive change in the Provo leadership—nothing less than the annihilation of the Provisional IRA council. That would require a carefully orchestrated, ruthlessly executed purge of the entire socialist leadership. And that meant Tom O'Donnell. Which was how Locke became a spy for O'Donnell, keeping him supplied with a steady flow of intelligence about the power plays and shifting alliances inside the Provos: who was on the way up, who was on the way out, who had been meeting with whom and why. Locke had also proved invaluable in buying time for O'Donnell by spreading disinformation about him, how bad his health was, how his old bullet wounds plagued him, and what a quiet, harmless retirement he was living in Donegal. If anybody deserved ulcers, it was Danny Locke.

"Here, get this into you, boys." Mavour bustled into the room with a plate of hot greasy food in each hand. "You too, Danny. You can have a glass of milk with your supper."

Danny eyed the food and grimaced.

"Mixed grill," Docherty grunted when he saw the plates piled high with steak, lamb chop, kidney, fried black pudding, and chips. The big Garda sergeant wasn't a man whose stomach was likely to be denied by oversensitivity and he took a seat at the table without waiting to be asked. Mavour arrived with two more plates and the others joined Docherty at the table. O'Donnell kept a keg of Smithwick's in the kitchen and all but Locke had a pint glass of the strong dark beer with supper. Mavour latched the door to the kitchen and left them to it.

Locke picked at a few chips between sips of milk but quickly gave up and lit another cigarette. O'Donnell eyed him closely and decided it wasn't only ulcers that were bothering Danny. There was something else, and he had a good idea what it was. Docherty finished his own meal, then Locke's, and began tapping his knife absently against the rim of his plate while he watched the Jockey's progress. McCormack ignored him and plodded through his supper, methodically chewing every bite. The talk meandered through all of Ireland's troubles, past and present, with O'Donnell dominating the table, recalling old speeches, quotations, and occasional snatches of poetry, which he liked to recite in the Gaelic, and ended with them slipping into the same, comforting old hates and prejudices. It wasn't till after Mavour had interrupted briefly to clear the plates, top off their empty glasses, and leave them with a slab of homemade fruit cake and a wedge of cheddar that they were able to get down to business.

"I need three men to do a job for me," O'Donnell said, leaning back in his chair and lighting his pipe. "Three hard men, Billy. What do ye think?"

"Sure." McCormack nodded and lit a cigarette. "What's the job?"

"I want them to go to the States for me," O'Donnell said. "Score needs settlin'."

The Jockey almost dropped his cigarette.

"Shit, Tommy," he stammered. "I don't know. How long would they be gone? Carson would get suspicious, y'know. Our fellers can't just disappear for weeks at a time."

Ronnie Carson was the Provo's battalion commander in the Bogside. O'Donnell knew the Jockey was right; he couldn't pull three men out of Derry for more than a week without their being missed. Somebody like Carson would be sure to ask a few hard questions. Even then the timing had to be perfect.

"It'll take a week at most," O'Donnell reassured him. "They could be in and out in three, four days. There'll be a few extra quid in it for their trouble."

McCormack took a drag on his cigarette but didn't look any calmer.

"It's risky, Tommy," he said. "A day, two days . . . no problem. But a week. We've never done anything like that before. Are you sure it's essential?"

O'Donnell smiled his friendliest smile at the Jockey. Inside he was getting annoyed. He didn't want any arguments, any complications. Not now. McCormack had his uses—he'd been a loyal lieutenant and a good courier—but there were times when he could carry on like a bloody old woman. He would have to go when the business was done, O'Donnell decided. In the meantime, he was needed.

"I wouldn't ask ye, Billy, if it wasn't important," O'Donnell said, with disarming gentleness.

"Fockin' hell," McCormack sniffed. He still missed the point.

Docherty and Locke looked on in silence. They knew that when Tom O'Donnell was at his gentlest he could be at his most dangerous.

"It's risky stuff doin' a job in the States," McCormack went on. "We've a bad enough PR problem there as it is, y'know. The money from Noraid isn't half what it used to be. And that business in New York the other day, what about that? If our fellers got connected with that, even accidentally . . ." He let the words dangle in the air for a moment. "If there's a fock-up and any of our fellers get caught over there we'll all be in the shite. All of us . . ."

O'Donnell nodded. "I've got a good man over there already," he added patiently. "He knows the ground. He'll look after our boys. It's a straightforward house job, Billy. One man. They go in, knock him over . . . and the next plane home. As easy as knockin' over a grass in the Creggan, for Christ's sake. Easier . . . no British army patrols, nothin'."

McCormack smoked his cigarette in silence.

O'Donnell got tired of waiting.

"I'm not askin' ye to like it, Billy," he said, leaning forward, his voice silky with menace. "I'm tellin' ye to do it. I want three good men to come and see me here. I'll give them all they need, Irish passports, money, the lot. They'll fly out of Shannon. My man in New York will have the guns and everythin' else they need. All they supply is the manpower. You just pick the men and send them to me. Now, if ye can't fockin' organize that much for me, what fockin' good are ye?"

Looking up, McCormack caught the cold glint of controlled anger in O'Donnell's eyes for the first time, and he blanched.

"Okay, Tom," he answered softly. "I guess it'll be all right. I can keep Carson out of the picture for a week. Gettin' the men won't be a problem."

With a satisfied look, O'Donnell leaned back and pulled deeply on his pipe again. From his handsome, blunt-featured face, to his great shock of white hair, to his brown corduroys and baggy cardigan with the cracked leather patches on the elbows, he was the very picture of the kindly Irish uncle.

Docherty looked on and smiled. Locke fidgeted and looked at his watch.

The evening ended a little after one o'clock in the morning in a haze of blurry bonhomie after they had finished the Bushmills. Mavour had long since gone to bed. Docherty buttoned up his sergeant's tunic and walked unsteadily to his blue Garda van. He drunkenly offered the Jockey a safe escort to the border but McCormack wisely declined in case it gave him a bad name. Only Locke hung back, as if there was unfinished business. O'Donnell closed the door against the damp night air and hurried back into the fume-laden warmth of the living room.

"Now, Danny," he said, planting himself with his back to the fire again. "What's eatin' you, boy?"

Locke pushed his hands into his trousers and paced nervously back and forth across the tiny room.

"I don't fockin' know where to start," he said. He was stone-cold sober. He glanced at the old man's face and was met with eyes that were equally sober but infinitely more calculating. O'Donnell had shrugged off the pretense of alcoholic merriment as easily as he might shrug off an old coat. Locke realized that O'Donnell had been careful to keep the others so full of drink they hadn't noticed that their host had stuck to one glass of beer and two, perhaps three whiskeys all night. He jerked his head at the door, in the direction of O'Donnell's two departed guests.

"They don't know, do they?" he said. "Haven't got a fockin' clue what's really goin' on, have they?"

O'Donnell studied Locke for a moment, still unsure whether the man he'd cultivated these past fifteen years was strung out on dope . . . or just plain fear. Whatever it was, it wasn't doing him much good. Locke looked much older than his twenty-nine years.

"Losin' your nerve, Danny?"

Locke stopped pacing and stared hard at O'Donnell with bright, glistening eyes. "I lost my fockin' nerve a long time ago," he hissed. "I've been gettin' by on cigarettes and milk of fockin' magnesia for the last two years." He stopped and looked at the ceiling for a moment.

"Jesus Christ, Tommy . . . a hundred and seventy-odd people dead?" His voice seemed ready to break. "What the fock is that all about in New York? What sort of fockin' monster have you turned loose over there?" Fear and hopelessness overwhelmed him and robbed him of all words. He shook his head furiously to clear the tangle of thoughts.

"If the others knew, they'd shite," he went on, struggling to keep control. "I bet they don't even know about Hennessy, do they? Never heard of him. He's your secret weapon, isn't he, Tommy? He's the one who's goin' to make it all happen for you . . . an' you don't give a fock how many people get topped along the way, do you? What's the deal, Tommy? What's the fockin' deal here?"

Apart from O'Donnell and Hennessy himself, Locke was the only other man in the O'Donnell faction who knew all there was to know about Hennessy. Aware that Hennessy was working for O'Donnell in the States, he was certain he recognized Hennessy's handiwork in New York when he saw the news flashes on TV. Only Hennessy killed like that. Men, women, children, it didn't matter. There was nothing Hennessy wouldn't do for O'Donnell. In return, O'Donnell seemed happy to give Hennessy a cause to vent his psychosis. Not just any cause . . . The Cause. The bomb outrage at Saint Justin's in Dundalk, where twenty-three innocent people had been killed while attending a memorial service to the victims of an earlier atrocity, had been engineered by Hennessy on O'Donnell's orders—to discredit the Provos. Locke was more than familiar with the evil Hennessy could do. Ironically, he owed his life to Hennessy.

O'Donnell's pipe had gone out. He cleaned it slowly and methodically, then pulled a new wad of Condor Slice out of his tobacco pouch, thumbed it into the bowl, and lit it again with deliberate slowness.

"How many people have you killed, Danny?" he asked eventually.

Locke sat down on the green-covered couch, put his head in his hands, and stayed silent.

"How many, Danny?"

Locke looked up. Anger had replaced the fear in his eyes.

"It's hard to know, isn't it?" he said, sarcasm and defiance creeping back into his voice.

"How many?"

Locke shrugged. "There's four that I can be sure of."

"How many of your own kind?"

"What do you mean?"

"Catholics? Your comrades-in-arms in the Provos?"

"Informers are shite, you know that."

"Yes, Danny." O'Donnell paused. "But some of them aren't informers at all, are they? Some are just former members who have become a little inconvenient to the gentlemen on the army council, aren't they?"

"I never killed nobody who didn't know what he was into."

"What about the two women and the baby who were killed by the Woolworth's bomb?"

Locke glared back. "I didn't plant that bomb."

"You stole the car. You drove Eddie Egan into Belfast with the bomb. You played a big fockin' part in it, Danny."

A hostile silence descended between the two men.

Finally Locke spoke. His voice sounded hoarser than before, but it was steady.

"What's up, Tommy?" he asked. "What's the deal?"

O'Donnell flexed his right shoulder a little and grimaced. The rheumatism and arthritis from the muscle and bone ravaged by Provo bullets were always worse in the winter. Thank God the spring wasn't too far away, he thought.

"We're in the last year of a long campaign, Danny," he said. "It all comes down to the next few months. We can't afford to get queasy about some of the things that have gone wrong. Innocent people always get killed in war. We live with it, Danny. We live with the pain and the madness and all the bloody awful things that go wrong. Besides, those people who got killed in New York weren't entirely innocent. They were working for a bastard. One of the biggest bastards in the U.S. military-industrial complex. A man who thinks nothin' of meddlin' in the internal affairs of other countries. They paid the price for his arrogance."

"What's it got to do with us, Tommy?" Locke looked anguished. "What are we doin' over there? What's Hennessy doin' over there? We lose our American support and we'll never win in the North."

O'Donnell took a deep breath and decided it was time to give Locke another scrap of information. Just enough for him to cling to and keep him loyal for a little longer. Long enough to do his job like everybody else O'Donnell needed.

"In a couple of months we won't need the Americans at all," O'Donnell said, speaking with exaggerated slowness, as though explaining something serious and complicated to a child.

"The ones we're hurting have always been hostile to us, anyway. I've been working on this for more than ten years. And when it's over we'll have the arms to get rid of those red bastards on the army council and take the North in a bloody fortnight. Hennessy is over there doin' a job of work for me . . . and a few friends. Important friends. Friends of ours. Friends of the Cause. In return, I get the biggest arms shipment ever to come into the country. I'm not just talkin' about the little stuff, Danny. I'm not talkin' about a few dozen Armalites and a thousand rounds of ammunition here. I'm talkin' about M16s, M60s, anti-tank rockets, and the like. I'm talkin' about tons of ammunition. I'm talkin' about missiles. Stingers. Five hundred of the bastards. I'm talkin' about antipersonnel mines, grenades, launchers, and enough Semtex to blow Stormont right across the fockin' Irish Sea into Maggie Thatcher's lap. The Brits and the Proddies won't know what hit them. There'll be general uprisings in Derry and Belfast. We'll extend the no-go areas to both city centers. The Brits won't be able to move fast enough to stop us. And they wouldn't risk the destruction of both cities to put the uprising down—not with the whole world watching them. And we'll be too strong for them to do it any other way. Either way, they're buggered. All we have to do is take both city centers and hold them for two or three weeks. We'll have food and resources to hold out longer but I don't think we'll have to. We'll demand a UN-negotiated peace settlement and UN peacekeeping troops. The Brits will have to negotiate a pullout. We'll get a real timetable for withdrawal. It's that big. The men are ready and the shipment I'm talkin' about is big enough and powerful enough to change the course of the struggle . . . within the year. Within the year, Danny."

O'Donnell watched as a look of disbelief spread slowly across Danny Locke's face. He crouched down and looked into the younger man's eyes and tried to inject just the right, reverential tone into his voice, a tone that would convince Danny Locke that he was being made privy to something momentous, something sacred and historic.

"You've kept faith with me this far, Danny," he said. "I need you to keep the army council lookin' the other way for just a little bit longer. We're nearly there, for Christ's sake. Don't go to pieces now. Six months from tonight we'll both have what we want. You'll be free of the Provos and we'll be setting the timetable for the reunification of Ireland. It's that close . . ."

Locke looked back at the white-haired old man and saw the fire blazing in his eyes and realized that every word O'Donnell had spoken was the truth. The tired, worn-out, prematurely old street-kid-turned-gunman lowered his head. He would do what was expected. He had no choice; he owed his life to O'Donnell . . . and to Hennessy.

A few minutes later, as he walked outside to his car for the long drive through the night back to Belfast, Locke turned to look at the old IRA man silhouetted against the light shining out the back door of the cottage.

"Jesus Christ," he said tiredly. "All the pain and the dyin,' Tommy? Is it worth it?"

"It's been a long war," O'Donnell said. "But it's comin' to a head."

A few kilometers down the road Locke felt the bile surge into his throat. He stopped the car, flung open the door, and leaned into the cold, clammy night to dry-retch into the hedgerow for ten minutes as all the acid and turmoil and self-loathing in his guts boiled out of him. He sat upright again and wiped his chin with the sleeve of his raincoat, his hand shaking. Then, Danny Locke leaned forward over the steering wheel and cried like a child. At last he understood. He was still trapped. Tommy O'Donnell was mad. Completely bloody mad. Just as mad as the rest of them.

CHESAPEAKE BAY, MARCH 22

"Jesus H. Christ. Will you get a whiff of that."

Bob Becker sniffed at the night air and grimaced.

The late night tide was out in Chesapeake Bay and the pungent aromas of the great East Coast tidal basin were drifting inland on a dank inshore breeze.

"Well . . ." Becker glanced at the guard on the fantail of Halloran's huge private yacht. "Either the tide's out . . . or Jo-Beth Steiner from Berkeley is out there somewhere, looking for a gang bang."

The guard snickered and went back to scanning the cold black waters of the inlet. From their heavily guarded berth on the York River they could just see the lights of Cape Charles blinking twenty miles away, across the bay. To the south flickered the lights of Hampton Roads and, beyond that, they knew, lay the Norfolk Naval Base, the biggest naval base in the world and home port to the U.S. Navy Atlantic Fleet.

It was hardly necessary for Becker to put his guards on watch aboard the *American Endeavor.* Half a dozen Secret Service agents had been there since Halloran had arrived a little after midday, and the rules were that nobody but Secret Service carried weapons around the President. Becker and his men had stowed their weaponry in the ship's armory an hour earlier but still they remained on watch. Becker thought it good for discipline, especially in front of other professionals. Besides, it was easy duty. There were half a million soldiers, sailors, and airmen armed with the most advanced weapons systems in the world within a fifty-mile radius.

It was unlikely that Halloran could ever be any safer than in the berth adjoining the President's mothballed yacht, the *Liberty.* They were protected on three sides by military installations: Fort Eustis immediately to the west, the Yorktown Naval Weapons Station to the north, and the NASA Research Center and Langley Air Force Base to the south. Fort Monroe, Fort Storey, and Oceana Naval Air Station were all minutes away on the southern reaches of the bay. Their waterside compound was a fortress within a fortress. A navy patrol boat was anchored just outside the entrance to the inlet, half a mile away, with a couple of Secret Service men on board with the crew. The mouth of the inlet was floodlit and sealed with a heavy boom, which was festooned with underwater sensors and cameras to detect anything mechanical that might be interpreted as a threat. Armed marines guarded the only road into the compound, and more Secret Service agents were spread out through the woods flanking the inlet. All were in constant radio contact with the President's chief security officer in the skipper's chair on the bridge of the *American Endeavor*.

Halloran's skipper, Captain Penny, should have gone to bed hours earlier, but he wouldn't leave the bridge on such a vital occasion—and with so many strangers on board—even if it killed him. It annoyed the former minesweeper skipper that the President's security men seemed able to work around him with such apparent indifference, but he stayed silently in the background, a dignified man with white hair and neatly trimmed mustache, bristling with nonchalance.

The President's security officer tensed as new information chirruped through his earpiece. He flicked on the ship's transmitter, tuned to the new security wave band, and spoke in a low, clear voice.

"All right everybody," he said, "Eagle One is on the way. Everybody pay attention."

Twenty minutes later they heard the heavy thudding of a big helicopter. Becker and his guard on the fantail scanned the northwestern horizon and saw the first Super Stallion hover into view a couple of miles to the north over the high-security naval weapons station. There was a sudden blaze of white light from inside the station as the landing lights were switched on. A moment later two more choppers thrummed into view and, one by one, all three descended below the distant tree line.

"I better tell the old man," Becker decided and set off belowdecks to the main stateroom, where the STC chief was waiting for his guests. Halloran had caught up on some sleep during the day and felt better fortified for his meeting with the President and the secretary of state. He took off his glasses and put down the statement he was drafting for the stock exchange. Halloran had woken up a little after nine o'clock earlier that night to the news that the markets had murdered STC's stock following the destruction of his New York headquarters and the lack of confirmation that he was alive and well and still running the company. What had been blue chip shares had plummeted from $37.50 to a little under $22. A disaster. He had called his national veep, Mike Cummings, in Albuquerque to confirm that he was safe and that a statement would be following for release before the markets opened in the morning.

"Oh, and by the way Mike," he had told his much relieved senior executive, "fire that cocksucker, Douglas, in public relations. That ought to put five dollars back on the stock before noon tomorrow."

After putting the draft statement in a desk drawer in his office adjoining the stateroom, Halloran pulled on a windbreaker to go up on deck and meet his VIP guests. He was already on deck with Becker, Penny, the President's security chief, and a cluster of Secret Service men when they saw the lights of the motorcade filtering through the beechwoods. The motorcade pulled up alongside the *American Endeavor* with a flurry of opening doors and black suits. The President climbed out of the second car and hurried up the gangway with the energy of a much younger man.

"Hello, Jack," he said, taking Halloran's hand. "Sorry we have to see each other again under such awful circumstances."

"I'm afraid, sir, that it's almost always awful circumstances when we see each other these days," Halloran responded.

He noticed the President was still wearing a dinner jacket and bow tie under his long black overcoat. Obviously he hadn't wasted much time after leaving his state dinner. Halloran quickly introduced Captain Penny and Becker. The secretary of state came on board next, carrying an attaché case. He was followed closely by another man.

Halloran knew Clayton Powell, the secretary of state, but he hadn't had the opportunity yet to get acquainted with Wesley Hatten, the new director of the FBI. Powell was an old colleague and adversary, the kind of political animal Halloran knew well. But all he knew of Hatten was what he'd read in confidential reports. A union-busting Chicago lawyer renowned for his love of work, lack of vices, and total absence of humor, Hatten was only thirty-seven, the youngest man to be director of the FBI since J. Edgar Hoover.

Halloran shook hands with them both, noticing only that Hatten had a soft but firm handshake, a delicate, almost feminine face, and was unusually bald for a young man. Their breath misted in the cold morning air and Halloran abruptly shepherded everyone belowdecks.

"What can I get you to drink, sir?" Halloran asked the President, once the four of them were settled in the stateroom and the door was closed.

"You know what I'd like, Jack? I mean really like?" the President said, sitting down heavily in a burgundy leather chesterfield nearest the open fire.

Halloran waited.

"Coffee. That's all. I'm not supposed to drink it. I like it. I miss it . . . and you serve the best damn coffee I've tasted anywhere."

Halloran ordered the coffee from the galley and turned to the others.

"Bourbon, Clayton?"

Halloran could tell by the look in Powell's eyes and the smell on his breath that the secretary wanted more of what he'd been drinking all night.

"That'd be fine, Jack," Powell said, looking agreeably surprised. "And just a splash of water."

Shit, Halloran thought to himself. The corrupt Texan bastard was smooth. Clayton Powell was a former congressman from the Lone Star State, a lifelong Republican with a reputation for making shrewd deals and keeping few friends. A tough, vain man who favored expensive suits, dyed his hair, and cheated on his wife, Powell gave his loyalty to no one but himself, only renting it to anyone else. If it suited him to see Halloran go, then Halloran would go. But at least Halloran knew where he stood with Powell; the fourth man in the room was still an unknown quantity.

"Mr. Hatten?"

"Mineral water, please."

"Oh yeah?" Halloran arched an eyebrow. It wasn't that he objected to nondrinkers. He'd simply found he could trust them better if they'd gone through a few barrooms first. In Halloran's opinion, a man wasn't properly rounded off by life until he had a bit of heavy drinking behind him.

Hatten didn't respond. Instead he glanced around the huge cabin, taking in the lavish furnishings, the antiques and paintings, absorbing the details of Halloran's wealth.

"Wesley is one of the more disciplined people in my administration," the President remarked.

"My father died of a heart attack when he was forty-one," Hatten explained blandly. "His cholesterol was three-twenty."

Powell carried his bourbon to the chesterfield opposite the President and sat down. "I'm fifty-three years old," he said. "I like my steak rare. Baked potato with sour cream and chives on the side. Corn on the cob with butter . . . salted butter. I enjoy good whiskey and cigars. The only exercise I get is when my secretary goes under my desk, and yet my doctor says my cholesterol is one-fifty. Tell me, Wesley, what am I doing wrong?"

Hatten shrugged. "You're lucky," he said.

"Good health is like youth, huh, Wesley?" Powell winked over the rim of his glass at the President, enjoying his little moment of showing off. "Wasted on some people."

The coffee arrived a moment later and the President took off his jacket, loosened his bow tie, and generally made himself comfortable.

Halloran poured himself a small scotch on the rocks and sat down on a third couch with Hatten and waited. They had been making small talk long enough, he decided. Protocol demanded that he defer to the President of the United States, his Commander in Chief, but it was plain Halloran wanted to talk business.

The President took the cue. "I think Clayton has some news, Jack," he said.

Powell looked up in genuine surprise. The bastard had settled in for the night, Halloran realized. The secretary leaned forward with a grunt, picked his attaché case up from the side of the couch, and opened it on his knee. It took him a minute to find the right papers. The first he produced was a State Department memo.

"This came in around four-thirty yesterday afternoon. I'll read it the way I got it, Jack," he said finally. "Then you'll know as much as the rest of us."

Powell took a pair of glasses out of the attaché case and put them on.

"It's from our office in New York. At 1337 hours, March 21, a Navy Nimrod engaged in the search of the quadrant bordered by longtitudes forty and forty-one and latitudes seventy-one and seventy-two reported wreckage believed to be a life raft containing one person. USS *Lansing* ordered to intercept."

Powell put the memo down and looked at Halloran. "That's about one hundred ten nautical miles due east of New York in the Atlantic Ocean," he said. Then he picked up a new memo. "This came in around seven o'clock last night.

"USS *Lansing* confirmed intercept at 1709 hours. Life raft picked up containing one white male, deceased. Bullet wounds to head and chest. No further identification at that time. Life raft was partially submerged due to damage believed caused by gunfire. No sign of any other wreckage."

Powell glanced back at Halloran. "That still doesn't tell us a lot," he said. "If it's connected to our suspect helicopter it had nearly twenty-four hours to drift from wherever it was put in the water."

Halloran stared at him. "That's it?"

Powell shook his head.

"We had the stiff picked up by chopper and taken to Trenton where we ran a few checks off its fingerprints and dental records." He produced his last memo with a flourish. "This came in less than two hours ago."

Halloran leaned forward.

"Deceased identified as Edward Anthony Brackman," Powell read. "Born Knoxville, Tennessee, 1951. Enlisted in the Marine Corps, 1969. Assigned Marine Corps air wing 1970. Served Vietnam 1971 to '72. Two Purple Hearts, two citations for valor. Discharged medically unfit, 1973." Powell paused and looked up. "Now it gets interesting," he said. "Exited U.S. 1974 . . . no record of reentry. Then we have a couple of military intelligence reports of Brackman popping up again in a few interesting places. First, Rhodesia, 1974 to '76. Chopper pilot for the army until the Smith government folded its hand. Then Mr. Brackman drops out of sight for a while and does who knows what?

A little dope, a little gunrunning maybe? Doesn't surface again until Angola and Namibia, 1981 to '83. Chopper pilot again. For the South Africans. Then, last thing we hear—and I really like this—the bastard turns up in Honduras." Powell paused for effect. "Flying for the CIA. From 1984 to '86 he was back working for Uncle Sam . . . on the Company payroll."

Halloran snorted. "Must have been running out of luck."

A sly smile tugged at a corner of Powell's mouth. "Sounds like just the kind of guy you might have used, Jack," he said.

Halloran feigned pure indifference. Powell's smile broadened.

"That's a good report, Clayton," the President interrupted. "Don't cheapen it with distasteful remarks." The President pinched the bridge of his nose and closed his eyes. He was getting tired.

"I'm afraid that's all we've got for the moment, Jack," he said, opening his eyes to look at Halloran. "Unless Wesley here has anything to add."

The director of the FBI sat with his legs crossed primly in the corner of the couch. He nodded gently to the room at large and when he spoke it was in the same strange, toneless, expressionless voice.

"We have nothing to add to that at this time," he said. "We're going through a process of elimination that tells us who it isn't rather than who it is. We'll know where to focus more of our attention in a few days. According to the Port Authority of New York and civil aviation control, the chopper was first sighted on radar coming in from the northeast. Radio contact was made by the Port Authority and someone aboard the chopper knew enough about Coast Guard procedure to claim it was an unscheduled mercy flight with an injured seaman on board, even though they weren't on the Coast Guard wave band. By the time anybody thought to check it out, it was all over. New York is a busy place. These matters don't get addressed as promptly as they should. We've got men working with local police units, checking all the countryside between New York and Providence to see if anybody knows anything. But"—he paused—"it doesn't look promising at this stage. It's an easy matter to hide a helicopter in a barn some place and give it a new paint job—and it could have taken off from anywhere. Where it went down, we just don't know. Our best information says there were eight hundred forty-seven vessels from a total of sixty-three separate nations in the coastal approaches yesterday. Some were outbound from Boston and New York, some were inbound. We can't search them all. Some of the bigger vessels were large enough to accommodate a helicopter on the deck, and then it could have been concealed or pushed over the side. The body and the life raft are our best clues so far, but there's nothing from them yet to show us the way." He shrugged. "And it's possible, just possible, that they're not even connected with this incident. Nevertheless, it is my opinion that this was not a domestically planned operation. Somebody came in from outside, somebody who knows the country. Brackman fits that picture. He was part of the hit team and he hadn't been into the States, that we know of, for many years. Certainly, given Mr. Halloran's past activities, logic would indicate that a strike against him would most likely be made from one of six or seven terrorist organizations based in the Middle East . . . with some local assistance."

"So what the fuck are you doing here, Wesley?" Halloran asked. He glanced apologetically at the President. "Excuse me, sir."

The President smiled wanly. Hatten appeared unruffled.

"I said 'some local assistance,' Mr. Halloran. That concerns us. That is why we have begun investigating the backgrounds of all your employees—"

"What?" Halloran leaned forward, undisguised anger in his voice.

Hatten shrugged. "We have to do it. STC and its subsidiaries employ in excess of twelve thousand people. Include former employees going back ten years and you have the population of a medium-sized town. Any one of them could hold a grudge. Any one of them could have helped the perpetrators plan and carry out the attack, voluntarily or against their will. Blackmail, threats, bribery—there's any number of possibilities. It's going to take a while but if we put all the bureau's computers on it for a week we should see some interesting facts emerging. It's called police work, Mr. Halloran. Routine, dull, effective . . . police work."

Halloran studied the FBI director in silence. It was easy to see him as a policeman. A bald little policeman suddenly handed one of the most powerful jobs in the country. In the world.

Clayton Powell smiled again. Halloran could see that the secretary of state was enjoying his discomfiture.

"Naturally," Hatten continued, "we will expect full and free access to all your computer records." He paused and then repeated the words with unmistakable emphasis. "All your computer records . . ."

Halloran nodded, smiling his most congenial smile. "Certainly," he said. "Anything I can do to help."

Powell knew Halloran was lying, but neither the President nor Hatten appeared to notice. The President had his eyes closed again and was rubbing the bridge of his nose between the thumb and forefinger of one hand. There were heavy bags under his eyes. Halloran wondered if he was going to sleep.

"I understand that some employees on your payroll are of an . . . extraordinary nature," Hatten said. "We will expect full disclosure there, too. As I said, we intend to cover all the possibilities. We can assure you complete discretion."

"Sure," Halloran agreed with a sip of his scotch. He had transformed himself into an agreeable, unperturbable wall.

Hatten realized what Halloran was doing. "Mr. Halloran," he persisted in his official monotone. "Given your past pattern of behavior it does concern us that you might want to operate on your own in resolving this incident."

Halloran smiled grimly to himself. *Resolving.* He liked that. The FBI director had a talent for euphemism, too.

The President stirred. "I know this is difficult for you, Jack," he said. "But you must realize . . . this is no longer confined to your sphere of operations. It is a national outrage. I have the assurances of the secretary and the director that our agencies will proceed with the utmost prudence where the more sensitive areas of your operations are concerned."

"Thank you, sir," Halloran deadpanned. At the same time he was wondering how in hell the President thought he could make such a guarantee for even one second. Obviously, his influence in the Oval Office was slipping. The President had been listening to Hatten and Powell for a little too long.

"I can assure you all that I will reciprocate with equal prudence."

Halloran saw the brief flicker of a nerve in the President's jawline. He had made his point. It was time to flex a little muscle back. He may have taken a bloody nose but he still had immense resources—and the capacity to embarrass them all if he felt the investigation threatened his survival.

Hatten spoke first. "We have one major concern," he said.

"Yes?" Halloran inquired ingenuously.

"The bureau doesn't want any more incidents like this on American soil. The foreign policy alternatives can be debated in the appropriate places when we have concluded the investigation. So"—he paused for emphasis—"we don't want you sending any of your fucking hit squads after whoever you think is responsible." This time it was Hatten's turn to glance apologetically at the President.

Halloran smiled. So, he thought, the little policeman had teeth. He began to appreciate how Hatten had gotten into the director's chair at such a young age. He was a lot tougher than he looked. More important, he wasn't easily diverted.

"I suppose you're behind that, whatsisname . . . dipstick . . . ripshit guy in New York?" Halloran huffed.

"Mr. Ritsczik is one of the finest executive officers we have in the bureau," Hatten said. "He's in charge of the New York end of the investigation and he has my full confidence. You would do well to cooperate with him."

"Jack." The President sounded concerned. "I want you to cooperate with Wesley and the bureau until we're sure we know who is behind this. We have to give a broadly considered response. It isn't only terrorism . . . it could well be interpreted as an act of war. I've never seen such uproar on the Hill as there was yesterday when this was announced in Congress. They're always at me to play it cool, to stay my hand. After the censure motion went though I had Democrats demanding to know who we should be bombing. That's our problem—we really have no idea where that helicopter came from. Or where it went to after the attack. We don't know who else was involved at this stage. There was a second man in the chopper. We don't know what happened to him or what nationality he is. He may well have been picked up by submarine after killing Brackman and ditching the chopper. God knows there are still plenty of Soviet submarines outside the two-hundred-mile limit and a few of them have been known to come in a lot closer than that."

Halloran looked shocked.

"You can't believe the Soviets would get involved in something like this," he said.

The President shook his head. "No. I don't think the Soviets are involved," he said. "But if their submarines can get in close, so can someone else. There are vessels from several unfriendly nations out there, Jack. China, North Korea, Syria, Iraq . . . they've all got close links to the Libyans, the Iranians, the PLO. We have to know who is behind it."

The President leaned forward in the couch and looked earnestly at Halloran. "Believe me, Jack, I know the temptation to strike back is almost irresistible. Especially when you have the men and the resources to do it on your own. But I'm asking you as a friend . . ." He hesitated for a moment. "And I'm ordering you as your Commander in Chief to do nothing for the time being. Cooperate with the bureau and Clayton here. As I told you yesterday, Jack, I've committed all our resources to discovering who's behind this. It may take a while but we'll find out, and when we know for sure we'll hit them hard. Try to look at the big picture, Jack. We know they were after you but this isn't only a crime against you—it's a crime against the whole United States."

Halloran stayed silent for a long time. He had already made up his mind but he felt he owed them all a minute's deliberation out of courtesy to the President. His shoulders drooped and he gave a huge sigh. Finally he nodded his head.

"Thank you, Jack," the President said. Then he looked at his watch and stood up. His entourage followed suit and prepared to depart. Halloran helped the President back on with his jacket while Powell finished his bourbon and Hatten signaled to the Secret Service man outside the stateroom door that they were about to leave.

"Try to take care of business for a while, Jack," the President said, as Halloran's aide arrived with the guests' overcoats. "Your company needs you. Your own people need you. We'll find out who's behind this . . . and when we do we'll nail 'em. You have my word."

"Thank you, sir."

Halloran said good night to Hatten and remained expressionless when Powell passed him with a wink that could have meant anything. He watched from the deck rail as his guests climbed into their black, armored limos followed by another mini-opera of fluttering black suits and slamming doors. Then the motorcade pulled away and disappeared through the trees toward the waiting choppers from the 89th Military Airlift Wing, which, among other things, acted as the President's own flight wing. When the last taillights had vanished into the trees Halloran went back to the warmth of his stateroom and the task of finishing his company statement for a 9:00 A.M. release.

First pouring himself another small scotch, he settled himself at his desk with pen and paper. He started to write but his thoughts kept straying back to the meeting that had just ended. He knew Powell was using this catastrophe as a means to rob him of his extraordinary power and to undermine his privileged position so close to the President. It was just part of the old game, he knew. Nothing personal. Powell was a career politician; diminishing Halloran's power would enhance his own and rid the State Department of a burdensome rival. Hatten, the young, tough, and ambitious new director of the FBI, was a more than convenient pawn in the wily old Texan's strategy. And to hell with the best interests of the country, Halloran thought.

He pushed the notepaper away and drained the glass of scotch. He'd enjoyed a helluva run, he knew. More than thirty years and seven presidents. He'd made a lot of enemies along the way; perhaps it was his turn to fall. Everywhere he looked there was disaster. At least 174 people dead. His New York headquarters destroyed. Even with insurance payouts the eventual cost would be staggering. It would take the company years to recover. STC stock had almost halved in value. The jackals were already gathering in the dying light of the flames. He could already see the beginning of the erosion of his political power and his independence. War on all fronts.

So this was how it started, he thought, hardly tasting the scotch as it went down. This is what they meant by the beginning of the end.

SIASCONSET, NANTUCKET ISLAND, MARCH 22

It took Brian Hennessy all night to run the Zodiac the thirty miles from where the *Ceilidh Princess* had dropped him to the beach at Siasconset on the southwest corner of Nantucket Island, the old New England whaling haven just south of Cape Cod. McKee had taken Hennessy as close as he dared, close enough to see the sweep of the Nantucket lighthouse on the horizon, and then chugged off back into the night before the Coast Guard arrived. The *Ceilidh Princess* would show up on radar but the Zodiac wouldn't. By the time the Coast Guard had investigated, the Irish trawler would be back in international waters and Hennessy would be ashore. From the aircraft activity and the radio traffic they overheard they knew the search was concentrating on an arc spreading east. Nobody was looking for terrorists who were crazy enough to be coming back.

Hennessy cut the outboard half a mile from shore and snapped a pair of fins over his wet suit boots. The last thing he did before sliding over the side was to slash the Zodiac with his dive knife; then he kicked himself away as the rubber dinghy went down. It took him less than half an hour to swim to the beach and crawl ashore unnoticed into the sand hills a mile along the shore from the half-empty vacation resort of Siasconset. It was almost dawn as he struggled out of the wet suit and pulled a thin sweater and pair of pants out of the runner's pouch tied to the small of his back. He pulled them on quickly over his thermal underwear, then hacked the wet suit and fins into unrecognizable rubber strips and scattered them into the surf. The wet suit boots looked a little odd compared to the rest of his clothes but it was late winter, early spring, and they wouldn't attract any attention until he'd bought a pair of sneakers in town. The last thing he did was to check the ten hundred-dollar bills he'd kept folded inside the rubber-lined jogger's pouch. That would get him on the ferry from Nantucket to Woods Hole on the mainland and from there he could take a Greyhound back to New York, where his own small apartment still waited for him. Hennessy wiped the sand from his trousers, pushed his thick blond hair back off his forehead, and started walking back up the road through Siasconset toward Nantucket, the island's county seat. It would take him a couple of hours, he calculated, looking at his watch. Just in time for breakfast. The sun was almost completely over the horizon, bringing with it what looked like a beautiful spring day. Hennessy began to whistle contentedly as he walked. An Irish song, "The Rose of Tralee." He'd be ready for a good breakfast when he got to Nantucket, he thought. He still had work to do. There was a lot of unfinished business in New York.

4 Finger Lickin' Good

"Fuck! Shit! Piss!"

He jammed his forefinger into his mouth and tasted blood and gasoline. The gasoline was concentrated into jelly and even the tiny smear on the tip of his finger started to sear the inside of his mouth.

"Pith . . . muck . . . thit!" he swore again, and stood up, cracking his head against an overhanging tree branch. The swearing ended abruptly and vaulted the anger scale to a full-blooded scream of rage. The big, granite-faced man in army surplus winter greens stumbled out of the tree line with one hand clenched to his skull and shook the forefinger of the other as though it were ablaze. A squat brown dog followed him at a safe distance. He staggered a few short steps to the gray rind of a melting snow drift and stuck his burned and bleeding finger into the snow. When the pain eased he sat down in the drift with a grunt and slapped a handful of snow on the cut on top of his head. Then he broke off a piece of the drift's icy crust and sucked at it to ease the scalding inside his mouth.

The dog sat down a few feet away and looked at him curiously.

"Uck oth," the big man grumbled resentfully through a mouthful of dirty snow. The dog, a nondescript mongrel, appeared not to understand. The man squirmed forward and tried to kick the dog in the head. The dog understood this and leaped nimbly out of the way, circled back a couple of feet, sat down, and stared balefully at his master again. The man said something about a gun and settled down to a soothing mumble.

Former U.S. Marine Corps Private Samuel J. Bono was not a good-humored man. Nor was he a safe man to be around. He regarded the world through the hostile eyes of one who always expects the worst from people and is rarely disappointed. And when he wasn't a threat to those around him, he was a threat to himself. It was an unfortunate trait for a man who worked in military demolitions. He had been working in the slushy, winter-hardened fields around the farm for several hours and was sweating heavily. He could smell it wafting up dense and acrid through the thick clothing and the mat of red hair that covered his body. By contrast the snow felt cool and soothing. He lay back in it and watched the steam pour from the open neck of his shirt.

Bono's natural demeanor demanded that he spend much of his time alone. It was the way he liked it. He was not someone who conservative people might find appealing. He had few male friends and no women friends. When he wanted sex he paid for it, and not always with whores. He was often amused at how many women would fuck for money. Women in bars, in stores, in shopping malls—anywhere. It was one of those little anomalies of human nature that provided him with ceaseless entertainment. Even the wives of friends would do the most perverse things for a couple hundred dollars and a promise of silence. Sometimes there was more pleasure in the game than in the sex. When he was nineteen and in boot camp at Parris Island he had fucked an officer's wife—but he suspected she was just into ugly men.

A big, powerfully built man entering his mid-thirties, he was starting to carry a little too much flab. It led certain unwise men in bars to assume he was unfit as well as large and ugly. He always enjoyed educating them to the contrary. Bono had gone bald early in life and now only a few filmy wisps of sparse red hair clung to a head like a granite slab. He was unshaven and his breath smelled bad. His mouth was an ugly wet gash and his nose was thickly clotted with red hair, in which a few tiny flakes of dried snot fluttered like wind chimes as he lay in the snow, breathing heavily, looking at the sky and waiting for the pain to go away. The sun had shone most of the morning but then the clouds had moved in and now it looked as though it might snow again. That was alright by him. It would help disguise most of his handiwork. Not that it would have been visible anyway in a farm that appeared to be dying of neglect; Bono was not the kind of man to spend much time on housework.

The cut on his head had stopped hurting and the pain in his finger had settled to a dull throb. His mouth still felt a little tender where he had accidentally smeared a little of the napalm. He sucked on another sliver of ice and then propped himself up on one elbow and looked around. The ramshackle two-story farmhouse was typical of the homes that dotted this part of the Midwest. All flaking timber and rust streaks from eighty years of merciless winters. It might have been attractive once upon a time but that time had passed long ago. Now it was a rural slum. And Bono liked it that way. It attracted very little attention.

A noise floated to him on the chill, winter breeze. A faint ringing sound. The dog jumped up and started barking. Bono got up awkwardly and lumbered toward the house to answer the phone. As the dog ran across his path, Bono swore and caught it with a glancing kick across the rump. The dog yelped and snapped at his foot, then seemed to think better of it. Bono stamped into the house and picked up the phone.

"Fuckin' what?"

"Bono?"

"Yeah?"

"Lynch."

"Yeah?"

"It's started."

"I saw the news on TV."

"Can you cover yourself for a few days?"

"Yeah."

"I've been trying to reach you since it happened."

"I've been outside doin' some stuff. Where are you?"

"With Halloran. On the ship."

"What now?"

"Nothing yet. I just got here. Drove down from Vermont this morning and caught the first plane."

"Any ideas who's doin' this?"

"We think we know. Nobody was expecting a hit like this."

"I know who it is."

Lynch waited.

"Fuckin' Ayrabs, man. That's who. Them Islamic Yahoo Red September Black Tuesday Pink Sunday Purple Jesus fuckin' Ayrabs."

"Probably. We have to be a little more specific."

"Fuck 'em man. Fuck 'em all. I'd like to get my hands on some nuclear fuckin' ordnance and lay a big black radioactive stripe between Paris and fuckin' Bangkok. That's what I think of fuckin' Ayrabs. How's the old man takin' it?"

"He's okay."

Lynch's voice gave away nothing and everything.

There was a pause and then Bono's thick, phlegmy chuckle rumbled all the way down the phone line from Hibbing, Minnesota. "Harder to move than skidmarks on a biker's underwear, huh?"

Lynch smiled and glanced at Halloran, who was standing next to him in the communications room of the *American Endeavor*, listening to everything on the conference line.

"Something like that. You going to be okay there another few days?"

"You think they know where to find me?"

"They knew where Jack Halloran was supposed to be."

After a pause Bono answered, "They want to try for me . . . it may as well be here."

"How are you holding up?"

Bono knew what Lynch was worried about. Even his callused soul had been scarred by the death of his partner, Henry Reece, on their last mission into Lebanon. Bono and Reece had been buddies for eleven years, ever since they had met in the Marine Corps and formed an unlikely team based on rough humor and hard living. They had bought the ramshackle farm on 220 acres outside Hibbing as a refuge between mercenary jobs for Halloran.

"I'm okay," Bono answered. "I got a dog. Mean, ugly little motherfucker. Think it's a cross between a pit bull and a rat . . . just like Reece."

From the corner of his eye Lynch caught Halloran's half smile.

"I'll call you as soon as we're ready to move," he told Bono and hung up.

The moment Lynch put the phone down Halloran stepped forward. "Okay, it's around nine-thirty in London. Let's see if Porter's at his desk yet." He punched the numbers into the phone and waited.

Sir Malcolm Porter was the controlling officer of Britain's Counter Terrorist Command, the elite air and seaport security network where Lynch had been a squad leader before going to work for Halloran. Sir Malcolm was a career army officer and had been commanding officer of the SAS before he resigned to start CTC, created to detect, deter, and destroy terrorists at the nation's gateways. Lynch had never been comfortable in a purely defensive role. Halloran had given him the chance to project the power of ultimate retribution anywhere in the world. And revenge was the purest form of justice Lynch knew. Sir Malcolm Porter had helped him go. Both Porter and Halloran shared information and resources whenever it suited them.

"Glad to hear you're safe and well, Jack." Porter's cultivated English voice chimed clearly over the line. "Nasty bit of business. What can we do to help?"

Lynch could see Porter clearly. Medium height, compact, exceptionally fit, in his late fifties with crinkly brown hair graying discreetly at the temples. He would be impeccably dressed in the jacket and stripes of a Whitehall warrior and perched on a corner of his desk in the third floor office of "C" Wing with its view of the plane trees along the Mall. He was astonished at how affected and strange Porter's accent sounded after all this time. Obviously, Lynch realized, his ear had become attuned to American speech.

Halloran was in no mood to waste time. "We think Red Jihad is behind it, Malcolm," he said. "We'd appreciate it if you could see what your people can turn up . . . and the sooner the better."

"Red Jihad," Porter echoed. "Yes, we know a little about them. Unpleasant bunch of people. Led by a former PLO chap, if my memory serves me correctly. What's his name . . . Musa, I think? Yes, Abu Musa. Kicked out of the PLO for trying to bump off Arafat. I take it he isn't a particular friend of yours either?"

"You could say that," Halloran answered with equal irony.

"Last I heard he had camps in Tripoli and Damascus. We've hurt him and his sponsors pretty badly over the years. I think this is an all-out effort to destroy us. Me, my people, my whole organization. You saw what happened in New York. They're not playing around. If it is them I want to know fast so I can nail the sons of bitches."

"Yes, quite," Porter drawled. "Are your own people aware of this?"

"Yes," Halloran lied. "But our intelligence agencies don't know the Middle East the way your people do. I want something fast on this one, Malcolm. You can name your price."

"Oh, don't worry about that, old chap," Porter answered breezily. "At a time like this we're only too happy to do all we can. You'd do the same for us."

Halloran smiled at the implied obligation. "Thank you, Malcolm," was all he said.

Porter said good-bye and the line went dead. Halloran led the way out of the communications room back into his office.

"You dropped Janice at the safe house okay?"

Lynch nodded. "Before I went to the airport. We went to her place first. She wanted to get a few more clothes."

Halloran shook his head. "Crazy broad. Somebody wants to blow her away so she wants to make sure she looks good."

Lynch ignored it. He and Halloran had been forced to declare a truce in their dealings with each other over Janice. It was a price they had to pay for both having loved her.

"Were my guys there?"

Lynch nodded again. "They seem okay."

"They are," Halloran assured him. He paused. "Maybe not in your league."

"What league are the guys in that we're playing against?"

Halloran frowned. "I'll send Becker up tomorrow," he decided. "He's the best I've got and I need you here with me—"

"To watch your back?"

Halloran looked back at him, stung. "To move against these bastards the moment we know who they are." He breathed deeply.

Lynch noticed an unexpected shadow flicker across the old man's eyes. Guilt, perhaps, though he doubted it.

"We'll keep moving her," Halloran said, trying in vain to reassure him. "Whoever wants us will have to be fucking psychic . . . and they can't watch all of us all the time."

Lynch didn't seem entirely convinced. "What do we do?"

Halloran looked uncomfortable. "There's nothing we can do for now." He shrugged. "The intelligence services of both our countries are humming on this one. They have to turn something up." He went behind the bar and pulled the first beer of the day out of the refrigerator.

"Want a drink?"

Lynch shook his head, then turned and wandered restlessly over to a window. Thick columns of gray, low-bellied clouds moved sluggishly in from the ocean and broke up along the shoreline, leaving a few misty trails clinging to the tops of the winter-bare beech trees. He was getting that feeling about Halloran again, the feeling that he wasn't being told everything. The feeling that his life depended on people and events that were beyond his control.

"You think these are the same guys who took out Tuckey and his wife?" he asked without turning around.

"I'd say there's every likelihood," Halloran replied from across the room.

Lynch breathed deeply. He felt dead inside. Dead and old. The only emotions he seemed to feel anymore were all bad. Anger. Hate. Revenge. He stopped thinking about it. He preferred to act.

"I don't like this, Jack," he warned. "I don't like it when the other guy is making all the moves."

Halloran eyed Lynch warily. He knew about Lynch's slow fuse. And he knew what happened when Lynch went off.

"Hold on to it, Lynch," he said. "Whatever it is we're up against . . . it's going to take everything we've got."

HIBBING, MINNESOTA, MARCH 27

They arrived shortly after midnight. There were four of them: Tom O'Donnell's old pal, the brutish Kevin Bourke, from the early days with the Provos in Belfast, and two others—Terry O'Laughlin and Del Morris. And Hennessy.

Bourke had been driving for the past four hours with O'Laughlin beside him. Morris and Hennessy were in the backseat. Hennessy had been asleep for a couple of hours. They all noticed that he made no sound when he slept. It was eerie, almost as if he had stopped breathing. But if something odd happened, like the time Bourke wandered across the center line, Hennessy's eyes blinked open and took in everything at a glance. Then he went back to sleep.

Everything about this job, it turned out, was unsettling. Despite the nature of their work the three IRA gunmen were a long way from home. They weren't sophisticated men; alien surroundings made them nervous. Instead of reassuring them, Hennessy's presence only served to unnerve them more. There was something unpleasant and sinister about him. Something about the half smile that always seemed to be on his lips. A cross between a smile and a sneer. And that accent, that upper-class Irish lilt that sounded so English to them with their coarse street dialect. That was bad enough. But there was worse. He seemed to take pleasure in keeping them on edge, telling them strange and shocking things about himself that may or may not have been true. That he was a Protestant. That he had once served with the British army in Northern Ireland. And then, most shocking of all, that he had been an officer in the parachute regiment, the most loathed British soldiers to serve on Irish soil since the Black and Tans. That had stunned them all. Even Bourke had wanted to throw his hand in then. But then Hennessy had laughed and turned on the charm and they had found themselves wondering whether it was only his bizarre sense of humor and they had failed to pick up the joke.

They had been in the States for five days. After meeting O'Donnell they had flown from Shannon to Amsterdam on Aer Lingus and then caught a Canadian Airlines flight to Toronto. Hennessy met them in Toronto and drove them across the border at Niagara Falls. There had been a couple of days to rest and plan the job in Hennessy's New York apartment and then he had bought a secondhand Chevy sedan for the drive to northern Minnesota. It had taken them three days to reach Hibbing.

When the job was done they would cross the border into Canada within the hour and drive through the night back to Toronto. In twenty-four hours they would be on another Canadian Airlines flight back to Amsterdam.

The job was simple, Hennessy promised. He wanted it to be fast, hard, and effective. There would be no time for finesse. He had checked the farm out a few months earlier and was satisfied Bono lived there alone. They would go in across the fields on three sides, under cover of night. They would hose the farmhouse with crossfire and then put half a dozen grenades into it. Anybody who came out would be shot. When they left, the house and everything in it would be dead and burning. It sounded simple enough . . . but Bourke and his pals weren't entirely convinced. They were violent men who had lived their lives in a violent city, but something about Hennessy disturbed them. Perhaps it was his twisted sense of humor.

"We just got to Hibbing," Bourke announced softly as he drove the Chevy slowly down the deserted main street.

"I know," Hennessy answered out of the darkness in the backseat. "Follow the main road out of town. Then pull over and I'll take the wheel."

The mood in the car grew as bleak as the night outside when the three newcomers realized the moment was coming soon when they would have to do murder. It wasn't the first time. There was a way of dealing with it. You did it and you didn't dwell on it. Bourke had long since learned that it didn't pay to think too much about some of the things that were done in the name of the Cause. Somewhere, he knew, there was a grand design. He was happy to be part of it, even as a mere soldier. He didn't have to understand it all. But he would be happy when this job was done and he was on that safe, warm plane back to Ireland.

Hennessy followed State Highway 37 until he was satisfied he was getting close; then he killed the lights and slowed the car to a crawl for the last couple of miles. If some suspicious highway patrolman found them now, they all knew, he would be shit out of luck, because they wouldn't hesitate to blow him away and complete the job now that they were this close. The car muttered softly up to a gravel turnoff near a stand of poplars. Hennessy gently turned off the road, bumped softly behind the tree cover, and cut the engine. For a moment they all sat in the silent darkness, hearing only the ebbing sounds of three days of travel in their ears.

"Right, boys?" Hennessy asked. It wasn't really a question. It was an order. The kind of order army officers give. The four men climbed quietly out of the car and winced as the freezing night wind cut through their cheap, quilted winter jackets. Hennessy opened the trunk and pushed aside a couple of half-filled bags of groceries and a few cheap items of clothing. He flicked back a piece of carpet and then slid out a canvas bag. Amid the jumble of tools there were four Armalites, a dozen clips of ammunition for each, and a satchel containing six Czech-made hand grenades. Hennessy passed each man a rifle and shouldered the satchel himself.

"Okay?" he whispered.

The other three nodded.

"Bourke and Morris, go in from the southwest over there. Take your time, like I said. Wait till you hear my shot, then get down and put everything you've got into the farmhouse. You'll cease fire after exactly one minute and I'll do the rest." He pointed them in the right direction and watched as they scurried into the wintry blackness. He turned to O'Laughlin, who waited apprehensively beside him.

"Go in from the northeast, over that way." He gestured. "I'll give you five minutes, then I'll circle right around and come in from due west. Direct all your fire eastward through the farmhouse. Got it?"

With a quick nod, O'Laughlin stumbled obediently off into the night.

Hennessy watched him disappear and then smiled quietly to himself. Cannon fodder, he was thinking. That's all these gun-toting bog-Irish clods were. Cannon fodder to the Cause.

He waited five more minutes before he set off at a brisk trot across the frozen ground. Somewhere ahead in the darkness, he knew, a man was waiting to die.

Morris was the first to be killed. He and Bourke had fanned out to put a hundred meters between them as they covered the last kilometer to the house. The moon was new and sickly but there was enough starlight between the high, scudding clouds to see the black silhouette of the farmhouse and the nearby barn. He had forgotten about the barn. He would have to put a burst through that too, as Hennessy had ordered. Hennessy, he thought. The bastard had even used their second names like they were soldiers. Something tugged at his trouser leg and he heard a slight pinging sound. A few meters away something about the size of a hubcap sprang out of the ground in a shower of pretty, sparkling ice crystals and glinted dully in the chill starlight. Morris knew instantly what it was but the deafening clap of the exploding Claymore mine, triggered by the tripwire at his feet, drowned the scream of terror on his lips. White-hot shrapnel, as lethal as a scythe, sprayed out for 360 degrees and hit Morris at waist height, cutting him almost in half.

Bono was already awake. Ever since the attack on Halloran's building in New York he had been living in anticipation of this night. He no longer used any rooms in the house above ground level. He had moved everything he needed down into the one-room, brick-lined storm cellar that he had set up as a bunker and command post. He had spent most of the past week laying a network of booby traps around the farmhouse. He had 250 ground sensors scattered in a wide circle in the surrounding fields. Each sensor was tuned to a computerized map grid in his bunker. It had made for a few false alarms, but small animals made different sounds than men.

Now he listened carefully and heard the faint, muffled crunch of footsteps treading warily across the distant fields. He checked his homemade electronic security map and saw that his assailants were coming in from the north, south, and west. Bono grunted. He slid out of his bunk and put on army pants, shirt, and jersey in the dim red glow of a small safety light. He pulled on a pair of boots, grabbed a couple of radio transmitters he had tucked away in a wall niche, and crept silently upstairs to watch. The dog stirred from its blanket and followed him, curiously. Upstairs in the abandoned living room, with the musty unused furniture that had come with the house, he glanced through one of the narrow eye slits he'd cut in each wall but saw nothing. For a moment he almost felt sorry for the men outside. There was a lot of pain waiting out there. But it was their play. They dared to come and try to kill him while he slept. They deserved everything they got. He had been waiting almost ten minutes when he heard the first Claymore go off. There was a short, terrified scream, an ugly thud, and then nothing. Bono shook his head. "Nasty," he grunted. The dog started barking. He lunged swiftly across the floor, seized the dog by the collar, slung it down the cellar steps, and kicked the door shut. Then he turned back to the task at hand. They would come quickly now, he guessed.

Bono decided it was time to light up their lives. He unhooked one of the transmitters from his belt and thumbed the button. There was the short, sharp crack of an ignition charge detonating somewhere outside, followed by a vivid flare of light, which grew rapidly in intensity. Bono smiled to himself. There were twenty-two kilometers of polymer pipe out there, all filled with napalm jelly and laid out in a series of interconnected circles radiating outward from the house. It had taken him the best part of a week to lay them out and pump in the jelly. Now, anybody walking within the network of pipes was going to get burned. And anybody who saw it was going to be seriously disheartened. If that didn't work, Bono had another nineteen Claymores out there, which he could detonate en masse if he wanted. And that was in addition to a half dozen other lethally innovative booby traps of his own invention. It was enough to stop anything but an air strike. Still, after New York, Bono wasn't sure it would be enough. He waited and watched as a livid red glow lit up the fields around his house.

O'Laughlin stood, transfixed, as a long finger of brilliant white flame snaked out across the black, frozen ground toward him just as though it knew where he was . . . reaching out to touch him.

"Move, ye eedjit," someone screamed at him from the distant blackness. "Move . . ."

He turned to run but the finger seemed to twist and split and then there were more, spreading out across the fields now like a burning spider's web. O'Laughlin had dropped his rifle and was running back toward the road. For a moment he thought he caught a sharp gust of petrol fumes on the night air and then one of the burning fingers reached out like lightning and touched him. In a moment he was ablaze from head to foot. O'Laughlin's cry was a heartrending scream of agony and despair, the scream of a man who knew he was finished and who could not face the unbearable pain of his dying. He ran and ran for what seemed like an eternity, his clothes and his skin and his hair on fire until finally the flames seemed to rush down into his lungs and burn away the very breath of his body. Bourke watched in horror as O'Laughlin hit the ground and lay still, his body still burning furiously. The sudden, sickening stench of cooked meat caught Bourke's nostrils, carried perversely to him on the night air through the stink of napalm. The napalm was burning out and the flames were dying, leaving a smoldering patchwork quilt on the frozen ground.

Kevin Bourke looked around in mute shock. He was alone on a battlefield in a strange country and around him his pals were dying. In an instant he lost all his brittle self-control and with it he lost his fear. Two men were dead. Comrades-in-arms in the struggle, the only life he'd ever known. A lifetime of hate and indoctrination. The years of IRA conditioning on the streets of Belfast spilled over; he began running toward the farmhouse, firing from the hip. The first volley went wild. A few bullets splintered the rotting timber of the farmhouse and hummed across the darkened rooms. Bono wormed his way back across the floor, pulled open the cellar door, and slid down the stairs on his backside, slamming the door behind him. He and Reece had lined the door with sheet steel eighteen months earlier. The house could be razed to the ground and nothing would touch Bono in his bunker. Except he wasn't prepared to sit and wait. At the far end of the cellar was a short passageway leading to a set of steel-lined storm doors covered with a layer of dirt and slush on the outside and invisible to anyone aboveground who didn't know they were there. Bono grabbed the Heckler and Koch MP5 submachine gun Lynch had given him after their last job and padded up the passageway leading to the storm doors. He opened one door a fraction and looked out. Somebody was still firing wildly from the other side of the building. He could hear the bullets smacking and howling through the house overhead, shattering and smashing woodwork, furniture, and crockery. During a sudden lull Bono slipped out and scurried down the side of the barn into the dark fields. Behind him the dog began barking again. Bono was the only man who knew precisely where and how he had set every booby trap. He was the only man who could move around outside with impunity.

On the other side of the house Bourke had put a fresh clip into the Armalite and was stumbling forward, firing blindly and yelling. There was no sign of Hennessy. Bourke was yelling for Hennessy to come to his aid, to come and finish the job they were here to do. But Hennessy was still waiting two kilometers away. He had seen what had happened to Morris and O'Laughlin; he had no intention of joining them or that madman, Bourke. He realized now that the whole place had been expertly booby-trapped in preparation for them. He had been wise to send in the others first to probe the defenses. Obviously their target was a professional, and one who must have been forewarned. Hennessy swore softly to himself in the dark, feeling at the same time a glimmer of admiration for the man they had come to kill. He could hear a dog barking inside the house. He would wait and watch a little longer.

The words floated to him over the winter fields. "Hennessy . . . where are you . . . you fockin' coward . . ." Bourke sounded enraged, like a man who had lost his reason. Hennessy smiled. A moment later there was a brilliant white flash from the direction of the house, followed by a thin-sounding crack. Bourke's yelling came to an abrupt halt. Hennessy waited for fifteen long minutes but there was only silence. Carefully, using years of training in one of the world's elite fighting units, the parachute regiment of the British army, Hennessy began picking his way across the fields toward another stand of trees halfway between him and the house. His eyes searched the ground for tripwires. It was going to take a little longer than he thought. But the job would be done. There were a few more hours and a few more surprises left in this night, Hennessy knew. And before morning, Samuel J. Bono would be dead.

When Bono left his bunker he dashed for a patch of scrub on the eastern side of the house, the only area where his security grid told him there were no intruders. Once he had made the cover of a thin strand of low brambles that masked an old broken-down fence, he began inching his way toward the front of the house to try to get a visual fix on his attackers. He needed to get some idea of their numbers to determine the level of his own response. If it all went bad, he knew, he could thumb the button on the transmitter attached to his belt and detonate every remaining Claymore with a master signal. The fields around him would erupt in a maelstrom of exploding, flying metal, annihilating any living thing within a one-kilometer radius of the house. Including him. A few wisps of smoke from the smoldering traces of napalm drifted through the night air, making it harder for Bono to see anything. Eyes could play tricks in conditions like this. Wisps of smoke had an unsettling way of assuming human form to wary eyes, and he didn't want to betray his position with an untimely burst of fire.

He needn't have worried. Bourke had thrown his senses, along with his caution, to the wind. Bono watched the man as he staggered clumsily across the fields, firing burst after burst of automatic fire into the impassive face of the farmhouse. He was yelling something as he ran. Bono couldn't make out what it was. The guy didn't seem to be speaking English. It only confirmed Bono's suspicions. Somehow the man had avoided two more tripwires in his wild run across the open fields and now he emerged into the open space around the house. Just at that moment his gun went dead again and Bono watched in disbelief as the man took an age to produce a fresh ammunition clip and replace it in the M16. Bono could have wasted him at his leisure. Instead he waited. It would help if he could get a few words out of the guy.

Bourke slammed in the fresh clip and resumed his charge on the house. Again, unbelievably, he ran straight toward the front door.

Bono shook his head. This guy was a serious asshole. Bourke stumbled up the steps on the porch, his breath coming in great wounded gulps and his voice painfully hoarse. Confronted by the closed front door the man seemed unsure of what to do for a moment. Then he lowered the Armalite, blew away the lock, and kicked opened the door.

"Very good," Bono mumbled under his breath. The guy should have been dead half a dozen times by now. Obviously Bono was meant to get his hands on him.

Bourke rushed through the open door to find himself in a small, enclosed room, the kind of cloakroom used in most northern farmhouses to hang bulky winter clothing and park muddy boots. Bourke seemed bewildered for a moment and then he kicked the inside door off its hinges. The grenade obediently slid out of its bean can hiding place and exploded a foot and a half above and in front of Bourke's face.

Stun grenades contain thousands of particles of magnesium and fulminate of mercury. When a stun grenade goes off it creates an ear-splitting explosion and a blinding flash of light with an intensity of fifty thousand watts. Anyone in the near vicinity is deafened, blinded, and thoroughly disoriented for at least seven seconds.

When the grenade went off Bourke believed he had been killed.

Bono covered the distance between the edge of the clearing and the front porch in nine seconds.

Bourke sprawled on his back, half in and half out of the cloakroom, moaning with both hands over his head. The Armalite lay at his side. He was just coming around to the notion that perhaps he wasn't dead after all when Bono leaped over him, snatched up the rifle, opened the cellar door, and threw it into the darkness. Next, Bono grabbed him by both feet, hauled him roughly across the floor, and dragged him down the cellar stairs, cracking his head on every step. The dog went for Bourke when they reached the bottom and Bono had to kick him again and warn him off. Bono quickly secured the cellar door and the storm doors, flicked on the red safety light, and bent down to get his first good look at his prisoner. What he saw was a middle-aged, heavyset man with greasy skin and thinning black hair. He could have been Arab or Mediterranean but there was nothing to say for sure. Bono quickly pulled the man's jacket off and went through the pockets. There was nothing. The rest of his pockets were empty, too. The clothing was all new—new and cheap, the nondescript kind of stuff for sale in any low-rent department store.

Kevin Bourke lay on the cold cellar floor wondering how bad his injuries were. He knew he had been hit by an explosion. There had been a terrible flash of light and a deafening bang and he had been thrown heavily onto his back. At the same time he had felt things hitting him, as though the house had collapsed on top of him after the explosion. His throat was parched and sore, his ears still echoed to a tinny ringing sound that wouldn't go away, the back of his head ached, and he still couldn't see anything through the neon blizzard that swirled in front of his eyes. He blinked furiously and his eyes watered. He began rubbing at them and trying to focus. The snowflakes were melting into a pit of blackness. Bourke grunted and propped himself up on one elbow. The blizzard was slowly fading, but only to be replaced by a terrible darkness—a darkness that smelled of damp and body odor and excrement. He heard something scuttle nearby with a low threatening growl. Bourke flinched and blinked his eyes harder. The snowflakes had all but gone and the darkness seemed to be assuming an eerie red haze. An insane thought leaped into his mind: he was in hell. He had died in the explosion and he was waking up in hell. For all his crimes, Kevin Bourke knew, he deserved to go to hell. Despite the absolution given by the IRA priests, two thousand years of Catholic superstition were hard to erase. Part of Kevin Bourke had always suspected that hell was a real place. He moved his hands and legs a little and that only confirmed that he had died and gone to hell. He knew what explosions could do. He'd seen enough of them. His mortal body would be in pieces by now. This was his body for the afterlife, a body given to him only to endure the eternal torments of hell. To be reborn and reborn again as he was punished through eternity for his sins.

"Hey . . . Einstein."

Bourke blinked. The voice sounded low and threatening and close. He looked fearfully around and the red haze seemed to strengthen and brighten. And then he saw a face. A huge red face leering demonically out of the haze toward him. Bourke recoiled and whimpered despite himself.

"Don't worry," the face reassured him. "I'm not gonna fuck ya."

A moment later Bourke felt himself lifted off the floor and thrown into a chair as though he weighed nothing. The battered back of his head hit the brick wall and he screamed. He felt something cold and metallic clamp around his ankle and then click tight. A sudden, vicious tug and another click told him he'd just been handcuffed or manacled to something. The pain was real enough, he decided. Everything else felt real. Maybe he wasn't dead. Maybe it was worse than that.

A flashlight snapped on suddenly, confirming his worst fears. Bono set the flashlight on a small folding metal table and studied Bourke. Bono didn't really like the extra light but he needed it to intimidate and question his prisoner. Besides, the cellar was so secure that hardly any light would escape to alert the others who were almost certainly still outside.

The two men stared at each other for a long time. Bourke looked around and saw that his whole world had been reduced to a hostile puddle of light in a cold and darkened room. He was seated on an old wooden chair and cuffed at the ankle to a water pipe. There was a green metal table in front of him and a man sitting on the other side—a big, ugly, dangerous-looking man. The man they had come to kill. Bourke heard a growl again and saw a small homely dog pad menacingly across the pool of light near his unmanacled foot.

"Down, Liddy," Bono commanded. "Not yet." The dog disappeared back into the shadows.

Instead of frightening Bourke, as they had been intended, Bono's words had the oddest and quite opposite effect. They reassured him. This was a situation he had been preparing for all his adult life. He had been told about it, trained for it, spent hours, days thinking about it. It had to happen sometime to an IRA man. There was nothing unusual about it at all. Uncomfortable maybe, painful almost certainly. But survivable. That was what had been drummed into him most of all. All interrogations were survivable. He already knew that. He'd lived through two informal sessions with the Ulster Defence Force and one prolonged attempt to break him in isolation at the Maze. Every IRA man knew how to withstand interrogation. It was part of the job. There was nothing this big ugly bastard could show him that was new.

Bono seemed to read his prisoner's thoughts and sighed heavily.

"Ain't life funny?" he said in a voice resonant with armor-plated irony. "A couple of hours ago, you and your pals were out there in the dark thinking about how you were going to

come in here, in the middle of nowhere, pretty as you please
. . . and blow me away. You figured it would take you, what—
half an hour? Just walk in, hose the place down, put a couple
extra into me to make sure, and then you'd be on your merry
way. Maybe stop off on the way back into town and have a
coupla beers. Right?"

Bourke said nothing.

"Now . . . here we are . . ." Bono's eyebrows arched in
feigned surprise. "One of your pals is hamburger . . . the other
one is baked Alaska . . . and you're chained to a cellar wall with
a guy who has every reason in the world to be very, very angry
with you."

If there was one lesson Bourke remembered above all others,
it was never to break silence. If you didn't break your silence,
his IRA masters had told him, the bastards couldn't find a way
into you. They couldn't start breaking you down, tripping you
up, trapping you. Bourke was good at keeping quiet. If you had
to break silence to ask for food or water, keep the conversation
to just that. Admit nothing. Deny everything. Bourke's teachers
frequently held up the example of the IRA man who had been
arrested on the evidence of a single British army officer. When
the officer died weeks later in a bomb blast they had to let the
IRA man go because he had kept his silence. He had never
admitted to anything even though the arresting army officer had
him cold.

Bourke's body cried out for a drink of water but it would be
a long time yet before he opened his mouth to ask. Nor would
he ask to go to the lavatory. He would rather piss and shit himself
where he sat than show an atom of weakness. See how this
bastard dealt with that, he thought. Bourke wasn't a particularly
clever man, as much of his recent behavior attested. But he had
a certain rat cunning, a street smartness honed to a hard edge
on the mean streets of Belfast. There might even have been a
little of the masochist in him, too, if he'd only known. Because
there was something about these games that he enjoyed. And
sometimes, if it went on long enough, the strangest thing happened. The roles became reversed. The prisoner would assume
a strange kind of superiority over his interrogator through his
refusal to crack. And the interrogator would crack first. A pure

demonstration of the triumph of the will. If Bourke understood only one thing in his life it was that interrogation was a blunt contest of wills in which the interrogator held all the aces— and yet he could still lose.

"Tell you what I'm going to do," Bono went on, emphasizing his words with the same menacing undercurrent of sarcasm. "Seeing as we don't have a whole lot of time available to us to get to know each other properly, I'm going to make you a little deal." He unfastened his wristwatch and propped it up on the table where they could both see the face.

Bourke was trying to feign indifference but Bono caught the glimmer of curiosity in his eyes. Apart from the incoherent yelling when Bourke had charged the house, Bono hadn't heard another word out of him. Until now he hadn't even been sure whether the man understood English.

"See, on my watch there," Bono continued. "The big hand is at two. The little hand is at one. That means it's ten minutes past one. In the morning."

Bourke remained impassive. Bono reached down to his right leg, slowly withdrew a Bowie knife from a leg sheath, and laid it heavily on the table in front of him. The big hunting knife rocked hypnotically for a moment and then stopped. The blade was scarred and scratched from years of use but its long, curved edge had been honed to razor sharpness and the hooked tip glinted wickedly in the beam of the flashlight. Bono noted that from the moment he produced the knife the man opposite had been unable to take his eyes off it.

"It's called an Arkansas toothpick," Bono said softly. In that moment he changed the whole tone of his voice and pitched his delivery so that the words glimmered with an unmistakable threat.

"I want to know how many more of you are out there. I want to know what weapons you have. And I want to know who sent you," he said.

The knife had shaken him, but now, for the first time, Bourke felt that he'd been given the upper hand. Time was on his side. His captor was desperate for information. Bourke only had to hang on for another hour, perhaps two at most. Then Hennessy would come. Hennessy would be out there now, Bourke knew, picking his way across the fields toward the house. Fresh, un-harmed, deadly.

Hennessy was indeed moving forward toward the farmhouse in a low crouch and at a sure, steady pace. He held the Armalite easily in one hand and the satchel of a half dozen grenades hung at his hip. It had been slow going and he had already crossed three tripwires. White nylon fishing line, invisible against the frozen snow. Each line hooked to the trigger of a Claymore mine a few inches under the snow. He had less than three hundred meters to go before he reached the house, and he had stopped to catch his breath amid a small stand of pines. He looked around carefully but saw nothing unusual, and so he stepped cautiously forward. As he did his foot skidded on something hard and metallic, and he froze.

A pressure plate. It had to be—the pressure plate on a mine. His weight had set the trigger and the moment he took his foot away the mine would go up with it and blow away the bottom half of his body. If he was unlucky he might live, like the soldier in his unit who stepped on a similar mine during a patrol in Armagh and survived the loss of everything below the rib cage. Hennessy would put a bullet in his own brain before he surrendered to a life like that. He forced himself into an icy calm and looked around. Nothing. He looked up. The lowest branches of the nearest pine tree swooped to within a meter of his head. If he reached up his fingertips were only a few centimeters short of the lowest branch. He smiled. That was his way out.

It took him five painstaking minutes to put down the rifle, take the satchel off his shoulder, and unfasten the satchel strap. All this he did without altering his weight too much on the pressure plate. The next stage would decide whether he lived or died. He had to throw one end of the strap over the lowest tree branch and make a loop—without disturbing the plate. It took him five attempts. On the fourth attempt he could have sworn his right foot inadvertently lifted off the plate, and he shut his eyes and grimaced. But there was nothing. On the fifth attempt the buckled end of the strap finally slid into view on the other side of the branch, by which time his face and body were covered in a sheen of sweat. It was a few more minutes before he secured the ends of the strap around both wrists.

Then he braced himself. He would only have one chance to get it right, he knew. When his foot lifted off the plate the explosion would be almost immediate. Almost. There was a whole world of possibilities between that "almost" and the explosion. The experts said there was slightly less than a second between the release of pressure and the detonation of the half-kilo explosive charge inside the mine. That was something like half a beat to get clear. The force of the explosion would go upward and outward. If he could put something between himself and the radiating force of the explosion, Hennessy knew he could survive. The rest would depend on what else was inside the mine—whether it was packed with something nasty, like ball bearings that would shred everything within five meters. Even so, he persuaded himself, that was a thick tree branch and a good-sized trunk. If he swung his body up fast enough and put as much of the tree between himself and the exploding mine as he could . . .

Hennessy was a strong and fit man. He knew the maneuver was well within his capabilities. But he would only get one chance. His whole nervous system tingled in anticipation. He smiled grimly to himself, took one last deep breath, then leaped upward and pulled hard on the strap at the same time with every grain of strength in his body. He flew up into the tree like a shadow. The moment he felt his legs hook on to a smaller branch beside the tree trunk he let go of the strap and used his momentum to grab on to the nearest small branches and pull himself around to the other side of the tree. It felt as though it had taken only a second.

Hennessy clung to the tree and waited. But there was nothing. No explosion, no sudden rush of sound and flame, no searing blast to strip the tree of its spiny needles, its pine cones, and its bark. Nothing. Then he heard something unexpected from the direction of the other tree. A strange rushing noise that made his skin prickle. He peered forward into the darkness and watched in amazement as a great curved blade swung out of the lowest branches of the tree opposite and hissed across the steel plate where he had been standing only a moment ago. An instant later there was the mighty thunk of metal biting deep into soft wood and Hennessy felt the whole tree shudder beneath him.

Then everything was still and quiet again. When he was sure it was safe Hennessy shinnied back down to the ground and carefully picked up his Armalite and the satchel filled with grenades.

He walked back to the tree and examined the metal object that would have cut him in half if he had not cleared the plate so quickly. When he saw it he smiled. The man they were hunting was an inventive bastard, he thought. Bono had hooked an old plowshare onto a length of rope and secured it in the opposite tree, held only by a bent branch that would have been connected with a length of wire to the hair trigger beneath the pressure plate. The mines had been reserved for the open air where they could do the most damage. Bono had spiked the trees with a few other surprises. Hennessy skirted the remaining trees and began moving purposefully toward the house again. He had lost precious time. He decided he would take his chances in the open with the tripwires.

"I want you to tell me now," Bono was saying. Bourke had been staring fixedly into the blackness over the big man's head but now he glared defiantly into his small, piggy eyes and allowed just the hint of a smirk to play across his face.

"Because if you don't," Bono persisted softly, "when that watch says one-thirty . . . you are going to be dead."

It was the smirk that did it. If there was one thing Bono demanded from the world it was respect for his word. He never bluffed. Never. When he threatened a man it was real. And the surest and fastest way to force his temper was to scorn his word.

Bono's left hand flashed across the table, seized the man's right wrist, and slammed his hand palm down on the table. The smirk was still on Bourke's face until he saw the big knife in Bono's other hand and then it disappeared in a blur of fear and disbelief as the great blade flashed down toward the table. There was a short, sickening chopping sound as the blade sliced through the little finger on Bourke's hand and then screeched against the table's metal top. Bourke's eyes widened in horror as he watched bright crimson blood spurt from the stump of his severed finger and puddle onto the table. His little finger, complete with grime and bitten fingernail, rolled a few inches across the tabletop and then stopped. Bourke screamed and gasped in shock but forced himself to block out the pain. Bono let his hand go but

Bourke left it there on the table and stared at it in horrified disbelief.

What happened next threatened his sanity.

Bono leaned forward, picked up the severed finger, and twirled it briefly in the beam of the flashlight.

"Shouldn't bite your nails, pal," he said. "It's a very nasty habit."

Then he turned sideways in his chair and looked into the shadows.

"Here, Liddy," he called. The dog trotted back into the pool of light. Bono studied the severed finger for one moment more. With just a glance at the man opposite he casually threw the finger onto the cellar floor in front of the dog. The dog pounced and there was a sickening crunching and grinding sound as it seized the finger in its jaws and chewed.

Bourke could hear himself screaming from a very long way away. He was floating somewhere close to the ceiling, looking down on the disgusting spectacle below, watching the dog swallow his finger and watching himself screaming.

Bono leaned across the table and smacked him hard across the face. The blow stung him back to horrific reality and he found himself staring into the big man's face again. The stump of his little finger was still bleeding heavily and he could feel his heart pounding in his chest as though it were about to explode. Then he fell forward and vomited the contents of his stomach across the table and floor.

He must have blacked out for an instant. It wasn't long. He felt Bono take a fistful of hair and jerk him upright again.

"Sixteen minutes to one-thirty, asshole," the big man said. Then he grabbed Bourke's other hand, slammed it down on the table, and raised the knife.

The words spilled out of Bourke's mouth in a torrent of fear and shock. They poured out so quickly they held no form or meaning. To Bono it sounded like gibberish, the fevered ravings of a man driven to madness. He grabbed the man's hair again and pulled his face up.

"Make sense asshole . . . how many men . . . what kind of weapons . . . who sent you?"

Bourke was panting as though he'd run a marathon. The words came in meaningless, unconnected bursts.

Bono caught a few of the words and guessed that the man was trying to speak English. Or a kind of English. But it was the weirdest-sounding English he'd ever heard.

Without warning the storm-cellar doors burst inward with an almighty explosion and the room was swept with machine-gun fire. Bono hurled himself into the sheltering darkness in the farthest corner away from the doors. The green metal table toppled sideways and threw the flashlight on the floor. The flashlight beam danced crazily around the room and Bono caught a series of bizarre, terrifying strobed images. His prisoner had leaped to his feet and was screaming. His head disintegrated in a sudden welter of blood and then he was gone. The dog scurried yelping under Bono's bunk. There was the briefest glimpse of a man standing in the gaping hole where the storm-cellar doors had been. He had long blond hair that was fluttering in the cold night breeze and he was smiling while he emptied his rifle into the cellar. Bullets cracked and ricocheted around the confined space of the cellar, filling it with a hail of splintered wood and shattered brick and turning the bunker into a tomb.

The firing seemed to last forever. Bono clawed desperately across the cellar floor trying to get to safety. There was one last place of refuge, if he could make it. The house had been coal-heated before the oil furnace was installed and there were still the foundations of the original chimney in the cellar. Inside it was a big cast iron ash box, big enough for a man. Bono knew he needed a diversion or he would never make it. He reached down to the transmitter still hooked to his belt and pushed the button. Two seconds later nineteen assorted mines detonated in the fields surrounding the farmhouse. The ragged roar of the explosions split the night like the crack of doom and Bono felt the whole building tremble. The firing stopped. Bono's ears screamed with pain. He scrambled for the safety of the ash box and chanced one quick glance over his shoulder. There was only night sky. The explosions had stopped and Bono was tempted to grab his gun and go after the bastard. Suddenly, the blond man was there again, silhouetted against the skyline. The man swung his arm in a casual underarm throw and Bono caught the briefest glimpse of a small satchel as it dropped into the cellar. Then the man was gone.

A moment later the farmhouse erupted in a fountain of flame as the five remaining grenades in the satchel exploded. The blast reached up from the bowels of the old building with the force of a giant fist and punched a great fiery hole in the roof, sending a huge spout of flames and sparks high into the sky. The whole house shuddered under the impact, as if gutted from within. For a second it seemed as though the decrepit old ruin was sturdier than it looked, that it might withstand the power of the explosion. But then slowly, pathetically, it began to sag and fold until finally it collapsed on itself in a great shower of sparks like the facade of an old western storefront that had suddenly had its flimsy foundations ripped away.

Hennessy lay still on the ground as the first shower of debris rained around him. Then he got up and began running toward the car. At least the mad bastard in the house had obligingly cleared the minefield for him. The land was cratered and smoking like something from a World War I battlefield, Hennessy thought as he zigzagged across the open ground, stopping only to pick up the dead men's rifles. Minutes later, after he hurled the retrieved weapons into the trunk of the car, Hennessy turned to see that the burning farmhouse was now a vivid red glow against the night sky. Somebody would be here soon. He started the car and drove slowly back toward Hibbing. There was no longer any need for him to cross the Canadian border.

He had just made the city line when he saw the flashing lights of the first oncoming police cruisers and fire trucks, their sirens a grating symphony of bad news. Some hayseed had finally woken up to the mayhem on his neighbor's property and raised the alarm. The screaming, flashing convoy passed without seeming to notice him. Hennessy drove slowly through town, until he was sure he was well clear of any lingering patrol cars, then stepped on the gas. Those cops and firemen were in for a few ugly surprises when they reached that little farm outside Hibbing. Until then he had at least a couple of hours to put some serious distance between them and him.

He glanced at the dashboard clock. Just coming up to 3:00 A.M. He yawned and switched on the radio for company. His stomach growled. He hadn't eaten for nearly twelve hours. Chicago was a good town for breakfast, he decided.

5 Irish Eyes

Deep in thought, Jack Halloran sat in the skipper's chair, alone on the bridge of the *American Endeavor*. It was a little before dawn and he had come up to the bridge from his grand and cheerless stateroom, pouring himself a cup of coffee and telling the officer on watch to take an early mark. The officer had hesitated, fearing that Captain Penny, his autocratic skipper, would disapprove. But Halloran made it clear that he wanted some time alone on the bridge and the young man had gone gratefully below.

The hydraulic suspension of the skipper's chair wheezed softly as Halloran shifted in an attempt to ease the dull aches and pains in his lower back. The older he got, Halloran found, the less sleep he seemed to need. Perhaps he had trained himself so well to get by on naps that he had adjusted to going without much sleep at all. Certainly, he had grown accustomed to feeling tired. There were days when he felt as though he'd been old and tired all his life and that he would go blissfully to his grave in anticipation of a long and uninterrupted sleep. In the meantime he had come to savor these quiet, peaceful moments before the dawn, when the day felt fresh and clean and full of promise. It was as though, for a few fleeting moments, he could borrow some of the youth and hope of the morning.

The sky was already lightening in the east and he could see a heavy spring dew glimmering wetly on the sleek white superstructure of his ship. The *American Endeavor* was one of the most beautiful privately owned vessels in the world and the object of his greatest material pride. But today it gave him little joy. Halloran sipped at his coffee and thought about the events of the past six days since he had met with the President, Secretary of State Powell, and the new FBI director, Wesley Hatten. There had been no word at all, from any of the government intelligence agencies, or from Porter in London. Even though he needed their assistance, Halloran begrudged the loss of independence it had cost him so far. He felt particularly uneasy about the FBI's involvement in the case. The bureau was obsessive about its authority on home ground. The FBI and the CIA had clashed many times in the past on that issue and the CIA had always lost, confining itself to ruining the internal affairs of other countries. Halloran had never known the bureau to relinquish control of an investigation once it had moved in. He intended to play the bureau along just as long as he needed it and then pull back.

So far, the FBI had gotten the better end of the deal. He'd already given as much as he felt he could afford, and maybe more. They had taken it all and given nothing in return. With each passing day Halloran believed he would be better served by pulling out of the formal investigation and going it alone—despite the express wishes of the President. It would be a radical, renegade step that would put him and all his covert-operations people outside the protection of the United States and the western alliance. And such a move would certainly strengthen Clayton Powell's hand against him and alienate the President. It could even result in the armed forces and the intelligence services of the United States turning against him to prevent his executing his own strategy with its attendant risk of embarrassment to the administration. And yet, Halloran knew, to go it alone would merely be to acknowledge a harsh, long-term reality: Halloran had always operated outside the protection of the United States; if any of his previous clandestine operations on behalf of the White House had been exposed, Halloran and his people would have been abandoned to their fates, however ugly. Not a finger would have been raised to assist them. Halloran's commitment to this kind of work sprang from his own old-fashioned, die-hard brand of patriotism, the kind of patriotism that didn't accommodate diplomatic terms like "expedience" and "compromise." And he did it because it suited him and whoever happened to be occupying the Oval Office at the time. Sometimes, the selective application of blunt force in certain areas was the only way of imposing reasonable solutions on unreasonable people. It was simply the best way of getting things done. Often the only way.

Halloran had always understood that he was useful to the office of the President as long as he could get things done. As long as there was a confluence of interest. Suddenly, there was no confluence of interest anymore. Instead there was an acute divergence of interest, a difference of views on the appropriate strategy to be employed in resolving the present crisis. It just so happened that Halloran was at the center of the crisis and it was he and his people who were going to be the biggest losers. It no longer counted with anyone that he had run seventeen high-risk, government-deniable operations for the various occupants of the White House over the past thirty years—and that all had been successful. Every situation was different; this was a new situation and it called for a new approach. Halloran had hoped that the backup he wanted from the President, the authority to resolve the situation his way, would have been readily forthcoming. But, instead of having the nation's intelligence services put at his disposal, he had been put at theirs. He wasn't overly surprised that the support he needed had been withdrawn. Politics was politics. This was a political problem as well as a security problem. There could be serious international consequences, depending on whose hand was found to have held the smoking gun.

Halloran heard a door open and looked around to see Lynch stepping onto the bridge.

"Not a lot of sleep at times like this, is there?" Halloran remarked as he finished the strong, sour coffee and put the mug down on the bulkhead.

Lynch didn't answer. Instead he poured himself a cup of the same overstewed brew and climbed up into the first mate's chair next to Halloran. He sipped the coffee with a grimace and looked out at the rapidly retreating night. The clock on the bridge said five minutes to six.

"I want to bring Bono in," Lynch said abruptly, without looking at Halloran.

Halloran sniffed. He wasn't surprised. The wait had been testing him, so he knew it must have been killing Lynch. Colin Lynch was, perhaps, the most dangerous man Halloran had ever taken into his employ. A quiet, self-contained, and most civilized man, he was, nevertheless, capable of the most extreme and devastating violence.

There were times when even Lynch was afraid of the anger that had simmered inside him all his adult life. He had no idea when it started or where it came from. It seemed to him that it had always been there, like molten magma seething in the belly of a volcano, needing only the first big tremor for it to spew forth in a white-hot torrent of violence and destruction. He had never been able to explain it to himself, let alone anyone on the outside. And it had led to the slow destruction of his first and only marriage, fifteen years earlier.

His wife had known him better than any woman, and yet she told him one night after making love that she was afraid of him, afraid of what he might do one day. It shocked him, because he had never raised a finger to harm her. And because he thought he kept his anger suppressed and hidden successfully deep inside, where no one would ever see its real ugliness—except him. She left him while he was serving at sea with the Royal Navy. A long, thoughtful letter arrived in which she wrote that she feared she would never grow close to him if they lived together for a hundred years because of all the volatile emotions he kept suppressed inside him. Yes, she told him, there was another man. And she wouldn't tell him where they were going because she was afraid of what he might do. He had never heard from her again and as far as he was aware they were still married. He had not bothered to file for divorce on the grounds of her desertion. It struck him as ridiculous. Besides, he didn't intend to marry again.

Lynch had been born in Dumfries on the west coast of Scotland some thirty-eight years earlier. He had grown up loving the mountains and the sea, a natural athlete hardened by years of play on the windswept moors and in the cold deep waters of the Scottish lochs. It was a childhood that equipped him for a life of adventure.

He was the younger of two sons; his much-favored elder brother had squandered a university education and now ran a market garden near Carlisle. His father was a railway guard who devoted his life to beer, dominoes, and stewardship of the railway social club. His mother had been dutiful but distant. When he was older Lynch had put it down to exhaustion from a lifetime of drudgery. But as a boy he had believed he was merely the less loved of two sons. Lynch had been a bright student at school but his parents had spent their meager savings on their favorite and had nothing left to give their younger son, who craved their love and struggled vainly for their recognition of his best efforts. And now he hadn't seen any of them for ten years.

On his own initiative Lynch had taken the examination for officer entry into the Royal Navy and was accepted. He trained at Dartmouth Naval College and was commissioned to the rank of lieutenant. He spent twelve years at sea, serving on mine-sweepers, missile cruisers, and the aircraft carrier HMS *Invincible*. When he realized he could advance no further in a navy that had many more captains than ships he applied for the Special Boat Squadron. The SBS was the Royal Navy's special force, an elite unit of highly trained men skilled in the art of coastal surveillance, espionage, sabotage, assassination, and covert warfare. Most SBS men were drawn from the ranks of the Royal Marines. Only the toughest and the brightest Royal Marine commandos were accepted for SBS training, and only a fraction of those who applied were successful. Lynch was widely expected to fail. He emerged from the selection process the leader of his squad. Focused anger could be an irresistible force.

The Falklands War gave him battle experience. In 1984 Lynch led an SBS team onto the Argentine-occupied island of South Georgia. It was an operation that could have ended in disaster. He led his men to the cliff-ringed island through heavy seas at night in the midst of a blizzard, navigated his way through a minefield, and took the entire Argentine garrison prisoner without taking a single casualty. He was decorated and came home a war hero. Except there was no home and there was no one waiting for him, no one to be proud of him.

A career in civilian life held no appeal to him, and he hadn't the stomach for mercenary employment. He had cast around and just when he saw himself consigned to a new life as a rich man's bodyguard the British government had set up the Counter Terrorist Command network. The CTC was a highly specialized combat force, which drew on men from all branches of the armed forces and the police and was formed expressly to safeguard Britain's air- and seaports against terrorist attack. Its commanding officer, Sir Malcolm Porter, was a former commanding officer of the Special Air Service, the British army's elite special forces regiment.

Lynch had been a CTC squad leader at London's Heathrow Airport, the busiest airport in Europe. None of his training or experience, however, had equipped him to deal emotionally with the Christmas Eve massacre at Heathrow that claimed forty-seven lives and ended his career with CTC. The subsequent official inquiry exonerated him from blame but Lynch was sick and tired of reactive strategies to campaigns of terror. Brimming over with anger, he drank heavily for a while to drown the frustration. He needed to take the initiative. Halloran gave him the opportunity.

Jack Halloran recruited Lynch in London. The STC chief was broadening the scope of his organization in response to the shifting menace of the times; he needed foreign nationals with special skills to help undertake an assassination inside Libya. Colin Lynch came highly recommended by Sir Malcolm Porter. The special forces of Great Britain had always maintained close links with the special forces of the United States, frequently sharing training, techniques, matériel, intelligence, and manpower. Lynch was too dangerous a man to let loose in the world without close monitoring from Britain's intelligence services. Porter knew he could keep an eye on Lynch if he could steer the former CTC man into Halloran's employ. Janice Street had been an unwitting partner in that strategy. She worked for Halloran, too. That Lynch and Janice would fall in love had never been part of anyone's strategy.

Lynch never understood how thoroughly he had been manipulated until he returned from the Libyan operation. The operation had been a success but Lynch had been seriously wounded and needed months of hospitalization to recover. It was Janice who helped nurse him back to good health. It was Janice who left Halloran's employ and tried to take Lynch with her. It was Janice who discovered that even the most patient love could not reclaim Lynch from the prison of his own anger. And it was Janice who lost when Halloran persuaded Lynch to lead one more operation, an operation that took him into the maelstrom of Lebanon to rescue American hostages from a terrorist militia fortress deep in the Beqaa Valley.

Janice knew that the only reason Lynch had agreed to the mission was because Halloran could give him a focus for his anger. She could not. The anger inside Lynch ran deeper than his love. All the wrongs in the world weighed on him personally and all he lived for was the opportunity to strike back, to find a catharsis for his terrible rage. As though righting a single, great wrong could somehow exorcise all the small wrongs that had accumulated inside him over a lifetime. He had been clever enough to keep his anger hidden from every navy, SBS, and CTC psychologist who interviewed him to assess his mental fitness for his work, but he couldn't keep it secret from the woman who made love to him. She had only to look into the coals of his blue-gray eyes to feel the anger inside him with every thrust of his passion.

The only time Lynch felt any real sense of calm was when he was embarked on some clear-cut mission of retribution. There was a dreadful simplicity about war and the destruction of evil men. It gave him clarity of purpose. It justified his anger.

When he had returned from Lebanon, Lynch had withdrawn to his hideaway in Vermont to await the backlash of the monster he knew he and Halloran had unleashed. Now it had begun. The monster had reached out to claim them all. One by one. And the only reason Lynch was back aboard the *American Endeavor* was because Halloran could provide him with the tools, the resources, and the opportunity to hack off the monster's head. To give him the fleeting peace he craved. Then Lynch would return to the shadows and try to disappear.

Halloran had observed the changes in Lynch over the past couple of years. This was a different man from the man he'd recruited in that hotel in London. His eyes had seen too much. This was a man who had evolved through a dreadful process of self-revelation and who did not like what he saw. Consequently, he had withdrawn from everyone around him, including Halloran and Janice. Because Halloran reminded Lynch too much of himself. And because Janice reminded Lynch of his inability to return love.

Halloran betrayed none of his thoughts to Lynch. The tough Briton sat silently nearby, waiting.

"Okay." Halloran made up his mind. "It's been long enough. To hell with 'em. To hell with Powell. To hell with Hatten and the FBI. To hell with the President of the United States. We're on our own. We'll do what we've always done. We'll do what's right. Bring Mr. Bono in. It's our business—we'll take care of it."

Lynch glanced at his watch. A few minutes past six. It would be four o'clock in the morning in Hibbing. It didn't matter, he decided. He picked up the bridge phone and gave Bono's number to the communications officer. There was no direct dialing aboard Halloran's ship. Everything went through the communications room and was logged by the duty officer as well as the computer. No calls could be made in or out without somebody knowing the name and number.

The minutes ticked ominously past. The bridge phone beeped and Lynch picked it up. It wasn't Bono.

"I'm sorry, sir," the communications officer said. "That number seems to be out of order."

An apprehensive tremor ran through Lynch's body.

"Check it," he said.

"I have checked it, sir," the young officer persisted politely. "The number is out of order."

"Jesus . . ."

"Pardon me, sir?"

"Get me the telephone operator in Hibbing."

A woman's voice came on the line a moment later. It was the phone company's regional supervisor in Duluth, the nearest control exchange to Hibbing. Lynch gave her the number and asked her to check how long it had been down. She came back in a minute.

"That line has been out of service for twenty-four hours, sir," she said. "There seems to be a serious fault. Our people are aware of it but we haven't been told the nature of the service breakdown yet, sir."

Lynch asked her for the number of the Hibbing police department.

Halloran was on his feet, watching, his stony face masking his emotions. Jack Halloran had never been accused of excessive displays of sentiment in his life. He had never married. He was the only surviving member of his family and he often claimed the Marine Corps was the only family he had ever given a damn about. All of which was part of the reason he harbored a sizable affection for Sam Bono, a man who had served nine years in the Marine Corps and never made it above the rank of grunt.

The Hibbing police department came on the line.

"I have an emergency," Lynch said, his voice carefully neutral. "I'm trying to contact a friend of mine." He gave Bono's phony name and his real address off State Highway 37. There was a long pause at the other end of the line, filled only with the sound of muffled voices as the officer held his hand over the mouthpiece while he conferred with someone nearby.

"Can I have your name please, sir?" the officer finally asked.

Lynch gave his name as Robert Prentiss, the counterfeit green card ID Halloran had given him that was supposed to provide him anonymity.

There was another pause. Lynch was getting angry.

"I said that this is an emergency, for Christ's sake. I have reason to believe my friend is in some danger . . ."

A new voice came on the line.

"This is John Ritsczik of the FBI," it said. "Is that you, Mr. Lynch?"

Until that moment Lynch had believed there were only half a dozen people in the whole world who knew his cover name was Robert Prentiss. He hung up and swore.

Halloran looked at him questioningly.

Lynch stared at the deck for a moment and shook his head. Then he looked hard into Halloran's eyes.

"Do you know somebody called Ritsczik?" he asked. "John Ritsczik from the FBI?"

NEW YORK CITY, MARCH 28

"Look, sweetheart, it's a job. I do my job. Sometimes I don't like it, but I do it. When I get off duty I'll probably get changed and I'll be on the other side of the fuckin' line with the demonstrators. Does that tell you how I feel?"

Victor Flannery turned his back on the young woman from the *Post* and joined his colleagues in the New York City Police Department keeping back the chanting mob of demonstrators on the other side of the riot barriers outside the United Nations. It was a small demonstration by usual standards, but then Northern Ireland had been out of the news for a while. No British outrages to decry, no more dirty protests or hunger strikes to support. Just the usual terrible bloody war of attrition, with England and Ireland determined to go down through history with their fingers clenched firmly around each other's throats.

The demonstration had been organized by Noraid, the North American fund-raising arm of the IRA, to protest the visit to the United Nations of the British secretary for Northern Ireland. Not that he had any new answers to what the British called "the Irish Question." Nobody did. He was simply expected to review Britain's longstanding position on Ulster and reaffirm his country's refusal to negotiate with terrorist organizations, like the IRA, as Whitehall's contribution to the Security Council's scheduled debate on Northern Ireland.

Officer Flannery drew a few smiles from his fellow policemen with his remarks to the reporter from the *New York Post*. The stocky, burgundy-faced forty-seven-year-old, a veteran of twenty-six years with the department, had never been known for his diplomatic language when asked for his opinion on anything concerning Northern Ireland. In point of fact, he had been positively reticent. Victor Flannery's real views about Northern Ireland far exceeded anything he was prepared to admit publicly. His Irish roots were no secret, and the occasional copy of the *Irish Weekly*, the pro-IRA newspaper published by Noraid, had been seen poking out of his locker at the station. He had also been known to attend Noraid fund-raisers and march in the Saint Patrick's Day parade under the Republican tricolor. But so did a lot of other people, including a lot of cops. Nearly 30 percent of the New York City Police Department could still be traced back to Irish stock. And in New York City a man's Irishness was something to be proud of. It had stamped Officer Flannery for life.

A fifth-generation New Yorker, Victor Flannery grew up in a house dominated by the twin Irish religions, Catholicism and Republicanism. His family had migrated from Sligo during the worst of the potato famine of the 1840s. His childhood had been filled with vivid, melodramatic reminiscences of Ireland, passed on by relatives. His grandfather had a collection of sacred 78 rpm records of songs by the great Irish tenor, John McCormack. They had been passed on to Victor's father, the first policeman in a dynasty of laborers. Victor remembered many a sweltering night at his parents' old apartment in Brooklyn. His father would sit at the kitchen table with his uniform unbuttoned and his collar loose, a beer in his hand as he listened to crackly, haunting ballads, tears joining the sweat streaming down his great red face as he drowned in maudlin homesickness for a land he'd never seen. Victor had learned from his own family all there was worth knowing about Ireland. About its history, its beauty, and its tragedy.

And the greatest tragedy ever to befall old Ireland was the British, Victor Flannery knew. He had grown up with a deep and abiding contempt for all things British. He had even learned to loathe them on sight or when he saw them on TV. Especially their politicians with their fat pink faces and their preposterous, phony, fluty accents. Victor had never really questioned why he hated them so much. He simply accepted it as part of his birthright as an Irishman born on American soil. And none of that was a secret.

What *was* a secret about Victor Flannery was the real extent of his involvement with some of Noraid's more illegal activities, including buying and smuggling guns, sheltering fugitive IRA gunmen, and assisting visiting IRA dignitaries. Such as Brian Hennessy. Now there was a man to be admired, Victor believed. The quintessential Irish gentleman. Educated, well spoken, gentle, and charming.

The first Victor had heard of Hennessy had been eighteen months earlier when he received a call from Tom O'Donnell in

Donegal. Like its transatlantic parent, Noraid was a reflection of all the differences and disputes that racked the IRA. The same factions and political groupings that formed, split, and re-formed in the IRA were mirrored almost perfectly within Noraid. When the split finally happened, Victor Flannery came down on the side of the Provisionals. They were the true custodians of the struggle, he believed. And there were many a broken nose and black eye in the Celtic Club to demonstrate the strength of his convictions—and his right arm.

Then, the Provos had turned commie and it had been a trying time for Victor. He had found himself torn between hatreds and unable to decide whom he hated most—the Communists or the British.

Tom O'Donnell helped him make up his mind. Victor and his wife had visited Ireland twice. Pilgrimages, he called them. On the second visit he had met Tom O'Donnell at an IRA night in Dublin. The two men had become instant pals. Their wives got along together, too. Tom had gone out of his way to show Victor and his wife a lot of kindness, and Victor had been moved. Later, when Tom was ambushed on the orders of the Provo army council, Victor had sent his sympathy and an open offer of assistance. It put him in direct conflict with the hard-line Provos in Noraid and Victor had to weather a trying year before Tom got back to him.

Even then, Tom had a plan. He was taking an enormous gamble on Flannery, but Victor listened and agreed. He would continue his good work for Noraid, as usual, and heal the dif-ferences between himself and the Provos. In due course Tom would call upon his assistance. O'Donnell had no idea what form that assistance might take at the time he secured Victor's prom-ise, but he had cultivated the Irish-American cop carefully, knowing that one day he would prove useful. That day had come eighteen months earlier when Tom phoned out of the blue to tell Victor that a man would be contacting him soon and it would be appreciated if Victor could assist him in every way. That man was Brian Hennessy.

Victor still had no idea what Hennessy was doing in the United States. He understood that there were plenty of reasons for him not to know. No doubt, he believed, he would be told more in the passage of time. In the meantime, he was happy to do anything Hennessy asked of him. A couple of times he had found Hennessy apartments where he could meet people, although he had never been asked to sit in on the meetings. He had acted as liaison between Hennessy and Liam McKee, the skipper of the *Ceilidh Princess*. Most surprisingly, he had never been asked to provide Hennessy with arms or money.

If there was one thing Victor had learned about Hennessy in the time they had known each other, it was that Hennessy never gave away anything he didn't want to give away. Victor found the tall, elegant man with the sandy blond hair a compelling figure, and so had many of the regulars at the Celtic Club—especially the women. Although there had been a bit of trouble when one of his female admirers turned up at the club early one afternoon with a bruised and puffy face and claimed that Hennessy had given her a hiding. Victor had shut her up with a few dollars from the emergency fund and sent her down to Atlantic City for the week. He had been concerned enough to raise the issue with Hennessy, though not entirely because he disapproved of men hitting women.

Sometimes, Victor believed, women had no comprehension of the extremes to which they could drive a man. As a child Victor had seen his father belt his mother a few times, especially after the old man had been drinking on Thursday and Friday nights. Oh, there were plenty of remorseful tears afterward and his father would wink at him and tell him that making up was the grandest part of all, and Victor had thought he understood. He had even given his own wife, Maureen, the occasional backhander. But only when she deserved it, he reminded himself. Only when she deserved it. And he was concerned that Hennessy should be a little more discreet and not draw attention to himself by the carping of a silly girl. It had surprised Victor that a worldly man like Hennessy didn't realize that. Hennessy had given Victor his most elegant and roguish grin and Victor knew that they understood each other. As men.

Victor hadn't seen Hennessy for a while. That wasn't unusual. Hennessy came and went without notice. Sometimes he would be around for weeks at a time, living an apparently normal life. Never flashy or conspicuous but never short of a dollar either.

Occasionally he ate supper at Victor's home with Maureen and the two girls and charmed them all. Then, he would disappear, for a few days, for a few weeks. When he turned up again he never told Victor where he had been. And Victor had finally learned not to ask.

It was extraordinary, Victor often thought to himself. Extraordinary how easy it was to switch off being a cop. The bluff Irish-American policeman looked at his watch and saw that it was almost three o'clock. It would soon be time for him to go off duty. Then maybe, he thought, maybe just now that he'd thought about it—maybe he would go back to the precinct and change and come back and join the demonstrators and give all his pals on the force a big laugh.

On the opposite tip of Manhattan, Janice Street gazed through a dirt-smeared bedroom window at a blank brick wall two feet opposite. She hadn't eaten since breakfast and was just starting to feel hungry. She put down the book she was reading, climbed off the bed, and checked herself quickly in the wardrobe mirror. Her hair was pulled straight back from her forehead and pinned into a prim but practical bun. She wore a bottle-green sweater and jeans. Her feet were bare. She smiled at herself briefly. It wasn't an image calculated to drive men into a frenzy of desire.

And that was just as well, she felt. She had been confined with the same three guys for almost a week. First to an apartment on the Upper East Side and now to a tiny town house in the Village. She wondered where the hell Halloran found these places. Whether he owned them or whether they belonged to certain of his employees. She glanced around at furniture that looked as if it had been supplied by Holiday Inns of America. She decided it must belong to Halloran. She unlocked the door to her bedroom and shuffled down the dark, narrow hallway to the kitchen. On the way she passed two of the guards Halloran had assigned to her protection, sitting on the couch in the living room. One of them had an Uzi in his lap and was toying absently with the breech mechanism. They were watching Phil Donahue on television. Great, she thought. Sensitive, caring goons.

When she reached the kitchen she found Bob Becker perched on a stool with a sandwich and a glass of milk on the counter in front of him. He was reading the sports pages of the *New York Times*. A thinking jock, she had noted, at the beginning of the week. Under any other circumstances she might have found Becker attractive. He was young, good-looking, well built, smart, and—most important—he had a finely tuned dirty mind. He looked up as she came in and let his eyes linger on her a little too long.

"Hi," he said blandly, and went back to the sports pages. "Everything okay?"

She wasn't deceived. She had seen the look in his eyes. He might be acting cool but she suspected a week in close confinement with her was having a certain effect on him too, no matter how cool and professional he wanted to be. Human nature was human nature. Lock men and women up together for any length of time and thoughts inevitably start turning to . . . certain possibilities. Janice smiled, pushed those thoughts out of her mind, and opened the refrigerator door. There had been no muffled knocks at her bedroom door during the night. No head poking around the door to inquire if she had everything she needed. He had been very much the professional. Besides, Janice speculated while she surveyed the dozen different brands of sliced meats her guards had stocked the fridge with, these were only the mischievous wanderings of a restless mind.

Colin Lynch had been the only lover she'd had in more than two years. So strong had been the intensity of her feeling for him that, even now, when there was no expectation, no need of commitment, she could not imagine herself with another man. Plainly she wasn't ready. Not yet. Fidelity had been a new and enlightening experience for her. She had found it surprisingly easy to accept. Comforting, even . . . for a while. Now it seemed as though it was only a matter of time before it ended for both of them. She knew the signs from a long time ago and didn't particularly like them. She was all for the clean break. And God knew she had tried. But part of her, a big part of her, was still reluctant to let Lynch go. There was just enough New England stubbornness left in her that said it wasn't all over yet.

"Do you guys eat anything except salami?" she asked, poking in a desultory manner through the packages on the shelves.

Becker glanced across and saw the way Janice's jeans molded

themselves to her buttocks when she was bent over. He suppressed an involuntary sigh and looked back at the pages of the
newspaper.

"There are twenty varieties in there," he said, forcing himself
to concentrate on the hockey stats. "It keeps forever. Whaddaya
want?"

The Rangers had done well all year but seemed to have run
out of steam in the playoffs. As usual, Philadelphia posed the
biggest threat. Only the Montreal Canadiens were certs for the
final of the Stanley Cup.

"How about something fresh . . . like a salad maybe? Or do
you want us all to die of scurvy before the bad guys get us?"

Becker took his eyes off the columns of figures again and
looked at her. She had closed the refrigerator door and turned
to face him. He couldn't help but notice the way her breasts
seemed to tug her sweater up a little at the front. She had pushed
the sleeves of the pullover up to her elbows and was standing
with her right hand on her hip. It made her look tough. Tough
and sexy. Everything the damn woman did seemed to be sexy.
She must have been lying down before she came into the
kitchen, he thought, because her jeans had crept up her legs
slightly and seemed to emphasize every line and curve of her
crotch. Even the center seam of the jeans . . .

"I'll have one of the guys go out and get you some stuff," he
said with a nonchalance he didn't feel. "Make a little list. We'll
get everything you want."

She smiled and began to hunt around for a pencil and paper.
Jesus, Becker said to himself. He was thirty-three years old. He
had a wife and two kids. He was Jack Halloran's chief of security
because he was the best damn private security man in the United
States. The only reason he was here with this woman in a town
house in Greenwich Village was because she was important to
the old man. Becker was there to guard her with his own life if
necessary. He sniffed and drank some milk. Becker was no angel
but all through his career he had stuck to one golden rule: Never
dip your nib in the boss's inkwell. He might enjoy looking, and
nobody could blame him for what he was thinking. But that was
where it ended. Becker prided himself on his professionalism.
Janice Street was safe. He would bet his life on it.

MINNEAPOLIS, MARCH 30

It took Lynch the best part of two days to cover the fourteen hundred kilometers from Chesapeake to Minneapolis. The flight from Andrews Air Force Base, aboard Halloran's Beechcraft, took only three and a half hours. Before that, it had taken a long day and an even longer night just to cover the one hundred kilometers of open road from Chesapeake to Andrews. It was only then that Lynch and Halloran realized how isolated they were. They weren't exactly prisoners aboard the big luxury yacht in the presidential compound. But, as the hours had crawled by with infuriating slowness, they both understood that they were damn close to it.

The moment Lynch mentioned the name of John Ritsczik, Halloran had grabbed the phone and roused Wesley Hatten from his bed. The FBI director seemed surprisingly unperturbed for a man so rudely awakened. He told Halloran that he still had no word yet on Bono's condition but confirmed that John Ritsczik had flown to Hibbing following another violent incident. All Ritsczik had reported so far was that there had been a major explosion at Bono's house and there were several dead. It had been impossible to say how many because some of the bodies had been dismembered by the blast. Hatten was waiting to hear more himself. He promised to keep Halloran informed as word came in.

The first thing Lynch wanted to know when Halloran hung up was how badly their cover had been blown. Hearing his real name from a stranger on the other end of a telephone had unsettled him. Halloran quickly reviewed his meeting with Hatten, Powell, and the President a week earlier.

"I gave the bureau access to our computer files," Halloran admitted. "I have to play ball long enough to get something back."

"All of them?" Lynch knew that Halloran had files within files, codes within codes, and computer systems the FBI would never know about. He also knew that Halloran was too shrewd a poker player to give everything away. Especially now that he was playing for his survival.

"I gave them enough to convince them that I was cooperating

fully," Halloran confirmed. "Enough to keep them busy for a week or two. Our cover is already blown—that's the least of our problems."

Lynch looked grim. "So," he said, "all we've got so far is another man down and precious little to show in return for your generosity with our lives."

A rare shadow of doubt flickered across Halloran's eyes.

"I'm going up there now," Lynch decided. "If Bono's alive, if he can walk . . . I'm bringing him back."

"I'll arrange it," Halloran said. He picked up the phone and ordered his personal jet readied at Andrews to take Lynch to Minneapolis. But Lynch got only as far as the perimeter gate that separated the presidential yacht compound from the rest of Fort Eustis. The marine sergeant was polite when Lynch pulled up in the Lincoln but insisted that his orders meant no one was to leave or enter the compound without the express permission of the base commander. Lynch was incredulous. He had been allowed in on a single phone call from Halloran to the base commander and now he couldn't get out. It sounded like military bureaucracy at its worst. Or perhaps it was evidence of something more sinister. Perhaps Halloran's special powers were being stripped from him, one by one, without his knowledge.

He returned to the ship to find Halloran and Captain Penny conferring over a scroll of maps laid out on the chart table. Again Halloran picked up the phone. The base commander wasn't in his office, but yes, his executive officer confirmed, their orders were to keep the compound 100 percent secure. Special authorization, above and beyond the usual security clearance, was needed before anyone could leave or enter. The authorization had to come from the commander's office, and was to be issued on an individual basis after checking with Washington.

And where was the base commander now? Halloran demanded.

The executive officer hesitated. General Drewe was playing his morning round of golf, he apologized, sounding embarrassed. He would be back in his office by ten.

Halloran pulled almost every string he could before the red figures on the twenty-four-hour digital bridge clock signaled 1000 hours. But still he had been unable to get Lynch off the base. Wesley Hatten was unreachable. Clayton Powell was returning from a visit to his home in Texas but Mr. Halloran's urgent message would be given to him the moment he arrived in Washington. Halloran tried calling in favors from people he hadn't spoken to in years. Mysteriously, inexplicably, they were all unavailable.

The base commander called Halloran back at six minutes past ten. His orders came direct from the Pentagon, he said, from the office of General Barrie, commanding officer of the U.S. Marine Corps. They could not and would not be countermanded, except by a higher authority. That meant the secretary of state, Halloran thought. Or . . . his last big ace.

He placed a call to the White House.

The President was unavailable.

Halloran put the handset back in its cradle with an air of resignation. Captain Penny, in his proper white uniform and with his dignified white hair and impeccably trimmed, pencil-thin mustache, appeared bemused. Halloran and Lynch looked at each other. It could all mean nothing. It could be one enormous coincidence. But surely, irrevocably, and with an ominous silence, they could feel massive steel walls closing in around them.

Lynch nodded to himself but remained silent. He could get out, he knew. He would have to wait until dark, but he would get out. Four years with the Special Boat Squadron assured him of that. He'd already had plenty of time to survey his surroundings in the York River inlet. Force of habit had told him its weak points. And there were many. The *American Endeavor* carried wet suits and full scuba gear. The boom at the mouth of the inlet presented no real hazard. He would be in for a long night's swim in cold water, but compared to the work he'd done in the Falklands it would be easy exercise. Lynch left the bridge and went below to wait for nightfall.

Wesley Hatten called a little after three-thirty. Sam Bono was alive, he said. Injured but alive. He'd been trapped in the rubble of the farmhouse at Hibbing for eleven hours before rescuers could get to him. He had been treated in Hibbing first and then transferred by air ambulance to a small private hospital in Min-

neapolis, where he was now under FBI protection. John Ritsczik
had spoken to him briefly and found him uncooperative, Hatten
said. Ritsczik hoped to resume his questioning the following day,
assuming Mr. Bono was strong enough.

Halloran buzzed Lynch in his stateroom with the information.
It was the first of a run of good news. Lynch had returned to
the bridge to discuss their next moves when Clayton Powell's
call came through.

As usual, Powell had been all Texan charm and bluster.

"Of course you're not a prisoner, you ornery old bastard,"
Powell assured Halloran. "You and your people can come and
go as you like. My instructions to General Barrie, which I'm
certain he passed on in the only way the marines know how,
were to ensure your complete protection. That meant no visitors
without this office knowing about it. I'm sure you understand
our concerns, Jack. It doesn't mean you can't go outside and
take a piss if you want . . ."

Halloran smiled thinly.

"I'll call General Drewe down there at Eustis personally and
tell him you and your people are free to come and go on your
own authority."

Halloran thanked him coolly and was about to hang up when
Powell mentioned there was just one last small point.

"There's no need to go bothering the President with any of
this, Jack," he said. "Any other problems, call me—the department is here to help . . . like always."

Halloran put the phone down.

"Slimy Texan sonofabitch," he growled. Halloran had been
born and raised in New Mexico, and like many of his drier,
more reserved kinsmen, he had grown up with the feeling that
their Texan neighbors to the east had always been a little too
loud and showy to be entirely trustworthy. Then again, maybe
this situation had just been a big coincidence after all; sometimes
people weren't always there just when you needed them. Especially the busiest and most powerful people in the land. Certainly Powell had been edgy about Halloran's call to the
President. Somebody in the White House had tipped him off
about that. Maybe Powell had been trying to help. Maybe he
had overstepped the line a little for his own political purposes

and didn't want the President to know. Maybe the President had been unavailable for genuine reasons. It was a lot of maybes.

Halloran was further mollified when the President finally returned his call an hour later.

"I'm sorry it took so long, Jack," he said in his reassuring preppy drawl. "I've been in Cabinet meetings all day. Is anything wrong?"

The temptation to drop Powell in a little of his own shit was almost irresistible, but Halloran held back. Perhaps a little latitude was called for, he decided. A favor granted, a favor returned.

"Another one of my people has been hurt," Halloran said. "One of my operational people. I believe he's in the hospital in Minneapolis now, under FBI protection."

"Yes, I heard," the President said. "Your situation was a major part of our agenda today. I've got a lot of new hawks in the Cabinet as a result of that outrage in New York, Jack. This business in the Midwest didn't do anything to smooth their feathers, either. They want to know what the hell it is that we're dealing with here so we can hit back at it. This is a time for cool heads, I believe, Jack. I'm sure the bureau will provide a breakthrough soon. Then we can plan a considered response."

Sure, Halloran thought, and then we can give whoever it is a stern talking-to and tell them not to do it again. In the meantime . . .

"I need a small favor, sir."

"Go ahead, Jack."

"I want to send one of my people to Minneapolis. I don't mind the FBI talking to our man there but I need to protect our interests. I also believe it would be in the best interests of the investigation, because my people have all been conditioned not to yield any information to anyone. I think the injured man would be reassured by the presence of someone from the same operational unit. I'm sure you understand . . ."

Halloran hoped that the President didn't understand at all. He waited.

"Okay, Jack. I don't see anything wrong with that. As long as your people understand that they are to cooperate fully with the bureau. I appreciate your concerns, and we don't want the

bureau straying into any . . . inappropriate areas. I trust your
people are sophisticated enough to know the difference, and that
they will do nothing that might impede the progress of this
particular investigation. We're all working on the same side on
this one, Jack."

For a change, Halloran thought.

"Yes, sir," he answered. "I trust someone from your office will
advise the bureau accordingly."

"I'll see to it right away."

"Thank you, sir."

It had been a long day for Halloran and Lynch, and it was to
be a longer night. The situation had changed several times in
several hours. Their emotions had risen and fallen with the
fortunes of the day. They needed time to plan. Most of all, they
decided, they could no longer afford to put themselves at the
mercy of maneuvering, self-serving politicians. And that included the President, who had given only qualified support and
whose limited loyalty could not be guaranteed indefinitely. Both
Halloran and Lynch felt as if they had won a temporary victory.
Halloran's costly cooperation had bought them something after
all. But, as soon as they were able, as soon as Bono was safe,
they would pull out of the investigation. They would pull out
of the United States and move to a secret location offshore,
from which they could run their own counterterrorism strategy.
It was time, they decided, to seize the initiative.

Lynch had finally fallen into bed around four in the morning.
He was up at seven and this time the armored Lincoln was waved
courteously through the perimeter gate. He made it to Andrews
in less than an hour and was airborne by nine-thirty. By one in
the afternoon he was touching down at Minneapolis–St. Paul
and forty-five minutes later he had parked his rented Chrysler
in the parking lot of the Frobisher Private Hospital.

"Shit, you look worse than I do."

Lynch grinned.

Bono was sitting up in bed in a second-floor room at the end
of the south wing of the exclusive, two-story, sixty-two-room private hospital on an exclusive leafy street where the trees looked
as though they'd been cultivated by Gucci. The hospital's usual

clientele were rich old men with sagging prostates and rich old women with ballooning varicose veins. When the director had been told by the nice firm man from the FBI that the bureau wanted the whole top floor of the south wing, he had been hesitant to inconvenience his regular patients—until Ritsczik had said something about payment in advance and the personal gratitude of the President.

"I believe you've got half a dozen nurses on this floor with nothing better to do than look after you?" Lynch said.

"Sour bitches," the big man rumbled. "Except that one out there." He nodded through the open door in the direction of three young women in pristine pink-and-white uniforms at the nurses' station.

"Which one?"

"That one."

"Which . . ."

"Her . . . the one with the cocksucker lips."

"Oh . . . that one."

"Yeah. She's okay. Offered her fifty bucks for a hand job yesterday. Said she could keep the rubber glove on. She said she'd think about it. I think she's holding out for more money."

Lynch nodded. "It's never been the same since affirmative action, has it?"

Bono looked bigger and uglier than usual propped up against the snowy hospital pillows. He had been bathed but his face and head were badly discolored by livid violet bruises and an archipelago of swollen, blood-encrusted lacerations. A couple of the cuts had been stitched. He was sitting on top of the bedclothes, wearing a hospital gown, and Lynch saw that both his forearms and his lower right leg were patched with burn dressings.

"What's the final score?" Lynch asked.

Bono shrugged and then grimaced. "The old body took some hammering," he conceded with an ugly leer that might have been an attempt at a devil-may-care grin. "Few burns . . . few bruises. The X rays they took yesterday showed nothin'. Might be some internal damage. Sure as hell feels like it. That's why I asked Nurse Dicklicker if she'd mind takin' the wang out for a trial run."

Lynch smiled. If Bono's humor was intact, Bono was intact. "What happened?"

Bono flicked a wary look in the direction of the door. Lynch got up and closed it.

"FBI's been buggin' my ass since they dug me outta the house," he grunted.

"I know," Lynch said. "The corridor is crawling with them."

"They want to know everything, man. Fuckin' everything." Bono frowned and looked hard at Lynch. "They already know a lot of stuff they shouldn't. Somebody been talkin'?"

"Halloran."

"What?"

Lynch looked uncomfortable. "Halloran had to give them a lot of material he didn't want to give. By order of the President. He gave them enough . . . but he didn't give them everything."

"Pleased to hear it," Bono huffed. "Who gave the fuckin' panzer division my address?"

Lynch shook his head. "Somebody got some good information a while ago. Our cover has been blown for a long time. Tuckey . . . Halloran . . . now you."

"Any ideas?"

Lynch shook his head. "Some Middle Eastern terror group. Take your pick."

"Yeah, maybe . . ." Bono let the words trail away.

"What do you mean?"

"I got one of them. I talked to him."

"You what?"

"Yeah," Bono rumbled. "He looked kinda like a Ayrab. Black hair, greasy, hadn't shaved in a few days. But he didn't sound like any Ayrab I ever heard. When they talk they sound to me like they got somethin' stuck in the back of their throats. This guy sounded like he was drunk, like he was slurrin' everything together."

Lynch took a deep breath.

"Okay, tell me . . . from the beginning."

Bono told Lynch everything, including the moment when he fed his would-be assassin's finger to the dog.

"You what?"

Bono shrugged. "I was under a lot of pressure, man. I was in a hurry." I figured nobody wants to see himself fed to a dog a piece at a time. I thought two or three fingers would do it. He started singin' after just one."

Lynch sat in stunned silence.

"What did he tell you?" he asked finally.

Bono hesitated.

"I don't know . . . somethin' . . . nothin'."

"What?"

"He kinda went into shock, y'know. All this stuff, this gobbledygook, started comin' out of him. He was shittin' himself, man."

"Jesus . . ." Lynch took a deep breath. "Was it English? Did he have an accent? What did it sound like, for Christ's sake?"

"Yeah, it sounded like . . . some kind of English."

"What? What did it sound like?"

Bono paused, and the pause seemed to go on forever.

"Irish . . . I think he was an Irishman."

Lynch sat back in his chair.

"Irish?"

Bono nodded, and winced at the pain of the sudden movement.

"You're sure . . . it was Irish?"

"No, man. I'm not fuckin' sure at all, okay? I was buried up to my asshole in brick and shit for the best part of a night and a day. Right now I'm still not sure of anything. But I thought about it. I've tried to remember. I don't know what else it coulda been. He used a coupla words that sounded like Connor or Donnor or somethin'. And he said Jesus an' Mary a few times, some of that Hail Mary Catholic shit, y'know?"

Lynch looked skeptical, and neither man spoke for a while.

"Oh yeah," Bono added, "there was somethin' else made me think he was Irish."

"What?"

"He kept yellin' another name. It sounded like Tennessee or somethin' like that and it didn't make a lot of sense. But when I thought about it afterwards, it sounded more like Hennessy than Tennessee and then it made more sense, right? Because

Hennessy's an Irish name and it's a kind of booze and I guess an Irishman would figure he needed a drink in a situation like that, right?"

Lynch sat and thought in silence. Much of what Bono had said sounded muddled and contradictory. And it just didn't add up. What business would the IRA have with them? Halloran had never taken a contract against the IRA. And Lynch, through all his years in service, had never once set foot in Ireland. It didn't make a lot of sense. He knew the IRA had links to some Middle Eastern terror groups . . .

The door flew open and a tall, dark-haired man with bad skin and a severe expression walked into the room.

"Hi," he said by way of introduction, "I'm John Ritsczik. I've been looking forward to meeting you both."

DONEGAL, REPUBLIC OF IRELAND, MARCH 30

It was almost midnight when the telephone rang at Tom O'Donnell's cottage. Tom and Mavour had been in bed and asleep since ten o'clock. O'Donnell always slept well. A man with his profound sense of destiny could never be troubled by conscience. Over the years Mavour had grown accustomed to the phone calls at all hours.

"Business, darlin'," Tom would tell her gently. "Only business."

She knew well enough what sort of business it was and preferred not to know the details. In her troubled heart, Margaret O'Donnell knew that her husband was not the man she had married; had not been, in fact, for many years. Instead of the clever, passionate, bright-eyed young nationalist she had loved, a man brimming with ideals and confidence in his ability to influence the future for the betterment of Ireland, someone else had taken his place—an obsessive, embittered, vindictive old man whose natural charm had long been overtaken by a transparent and manipulative guile. Such guile might have fooled his pals, dimwits like Eamonn Docherty and Billy McCormack and pathetic misfits like Danny Locke, but it didn't fool her. And lately, she had been more disturbed than ever by her husband's behavior. In the past two years something else had happened. For the first time since the shooting, Tom had regained some of the vigor of his youth. But instead of youthful ideals his eyes now shone with an eerie, manic brightness. Mavour feared he had embarked on some terrible, squalid scheme in a final, desperate bid to carve a place for himself in the bloody history of Ireland.

It wasn't the life her husband had given her that fed Mavour's gathering disenchantment. She could live with that. Her father had been an IRA supporter all his life; her two younger brothers had served with the Officials before the split. If anyone had bothered to inquire, Margaret O'Donnell believed in a united Ireland as passionately as any IRA man—and for her own reasons. But no one had ever asked her. Not her father, her brothers, or her husband. Like all Irishmen of his generation, and those of generations before him, Tom O'Donnell had simply assumed that his wife would take his lead and support him in all things, including his political views. He had taken her unswerving loyalty of thirty-three years for granted. Which was no more than his due, Mavour acknowledged. She was an old-fashioned Catholic. She believed in her wedding vows. She believed that if she left her husband she would be committing a mortal sin.

There was one other reason why Mavour could not bring herself to leave him, despite the way her love had become a shriveled and exhausted thing. Somewhere, in the deepest recesses of her heart, there glowed a last feeble ember of hope. Perhaps—if she waited long enough, if she was patient enough, if she was strong enough, if she prayed enough—perhaps the man she had once loved so much would soften with time and somehow reemerge and take the place of the frightening, familiar stranger with whom she presently shared her home.

Mavour pretended to be asleep as her husband got out of bed, pulled on his dressing gown, and hurried downstairs. A chilling mist had crept in from Donegal Bay and the house felt cold and damp. O'Donnell forgot to latch the bedroom door behind him and it swung open with a soft creak. A cold and insistent draft rushed up the stairs from the kitchen and through the open door and Mavour reluctantly got out of bed to close the door. Downstairs she heard her husband raise his voice a level. The call must have been long distance.

"Looks like we missed the bastard," O'Donnell said, turning to look at the curtained windows. Beyond those curtains, beyond those windows, beyond the thick wet grass that rushed down to the bay, beyond the ocean mist and the three thousand miles of cold, gray Atlantic, Brian Hennessy in his Manhattan apartment turned to face O'Donnell.

"So it would seem," he answered softly.

It was coming up to eight o'clock in the evening in Manhattan. Apart from a couple of meals and rest stops, Hennessy had driven nonstop from Hibbing to New York. He was tired and dirty but he had cleaned the rented car thoroughly, replaced the fake license plates with the originals, and returned it to the girl at the rental agency with a smile. He was calling from a midtown serviced apartment Victor Flannery had rented for him. He hadn't spoken to O'Donnell since the attack on the STC Building ten days earlier.

"Do you think you did better with Mr. Bono?" O'Donnell inquired dryly.

"I shot him, bombed him, buried him, and burned what was left," Hennessy answered in a matter-of-fact tone. "Unless you believe in reincarnation. I don't think he'll be back."

There was a slight delay as Hennessy's words crossed the Atlantic and filtered through the electronic scrambler O'Donnell had fitted to his phone. The scrambler had been supplied by a pal who ran an electronics-import business in Dublin. Each month he visited O'Donnell's cottage, swept the line for bugs, and recoded the scrambler. They had never found a bug but it was a precaution O'Donnell insisted upon, even though the Provos, the Officials, the Garda, the Irish Special Branch, the British army, and MI6 had considered him inactive for years. Eamonn Docherty had been able to tell him that much.

"What about the boys?" O'Donnell asked with a chuckle. "Did they enjoy themselves?"

"No," Hennessy answered without a hint of emotion. "I think you can save yourself some airfare where they're concerned."

O'Donnell hesitated. He was shocked, but when he spoke again his voice was calm.

"All three?"

"All three."

"I thought you said it went all right."

"It did. It was just a little expensive. The guy made a fight of it. They don't all lie down and take it in the neck, you know."

O'Donnell's mind was racing. Despite Hennessy's coolness, his news constituted a disaster. A minor disaster, set against the grand strategy O'Donnell had devised, perhaps. But still, it had the potential to wreck everything O'Donnell had planned for two long years and that was due to come to fruition within two to three months. The Jockey would be hysterical with fear when he discovered that "the boys" wouldn't be back within the week, as O'Donnell had promised. The Provo brigade commander in Derry, Ronnie Carson, would become suspicious, just as Billy had predicted. He would start asking questions. The men's families would grow anxious. First the spotlight would fall on Billy. O'Donnell could keep a lid on things for a couple of weeks, a month at most; Billy could be shut up—one way or another. But nobody could disguise the disappearance of three serving IRA men for any longer than that. Even if the Jockey could withstand the first wave of inquiries. The men on the army council weren't stupid; they would know something was up. They would start looking around. O'Donnell could use Danny Locke to sow some disinformation about a British army plot, but it would only buy a little time, and it would expose Danny. No, O'Donnell realized, there were too many strands to unravel. Once the army council became suspicious they would sweat Danny and the Jockey and then they would know O'Donnell was plotting against them. And, shortly afterward, O'Donnell could expect some visitors to his innocuous little fisherman's cottage on the shores of Donegal Bay.

The instant Hennessy mentioned the deaths of the three IRA men, O'Donnell knew his entire strategy would have to be committed to a new and urgent timetable if it was to have any chance of success. It took him only a moment to run through the alternatives and to confirm in his mind that they all led to exposure and catastrophe if he tried to delay more than two weeks. He was confident he could stall things for that long, and then he would have to begin pulling men out. The Provo army council would know something was up, but they wouldn't know what or from which direction it was coming. Two weeks after that, O'Donnell would launch a series of assassinations against the entire Provo army council. Then, while the North was reeling and the Provos' loyal gunmen were leaderless, while the British army and the British government were struggling to make sense of it all, he would launch his offensive in the cities. The attacks would be a catalyst for the remaining, undecided IRA active service members; they would be compelled by sheer weight of events to accept O'Donnell's leadership. But now, he knew, he had to move everything forward. It was already something of a miracle that he had been able to maintain secrecy this long. It had only been possible by keeping all the different components of his plan and all the major players separate from one another. He alone was aware of the grand strategy behind it all, the central, unifying thread that would pull it all together. No one else knew. Not Hennessy. Not even his old friend from the PLO, Abu Musa, who had helped to make it all possible.

With the loss of Bourke, O'Laughlin, and Morris, O'Donnell saw his master plan thrown into jeopardy. But then, before he could feel a pang of fear, before the first scrabblings of panic could begin clawing at his gut, he felt something else. Something calm and soothing settled over him and gave everything a vivid and indelible clarity. A strange electricity seemed to permeate the room, and everything, even the most ordinary household objects, took on a sharper, clearer definition. O'Donnell would tell others about it later, he knew, and they would listen to him, enthralled. Uncanny as it might seem, he would tell them, it was at that moment that he felt destiny touch his shoulder. It was this phone call from a loyal lieutenant in the dead of night that set the whole grand strategy irrevocably in motion.

Tom O'Donnell felt a thrill of excitement surge through his old and tired body. History was being made at this moment, he knew. He could see it. He could feel it. And one day, this modest little cottage in Donegal, the place where it all began, would be a shrine, a monument to the man who orchestrated the unification of Ireland. And if he could trace it all back to the one moment when his destiny acquired its final, glorious momentum, then this would be it.

" . . . you still there . . . O'Donnell . . . can you hear me?" Hennessy's voice hummed over the line from New York.

"Yes, Brian." The odd, reverential tone had crept back into his voice. "I want you to move everything forward," he said. "We have to proceed with some urgency now, Brian. Do you understand me?"

"Yes," Hennessy said. His voice was clipped but he still sounded pleased. He had been wondering when it would all start coming together and when he would return to Ireland, where he knew the final act had yet to be played. He had been following O'Donnell's orders in the United States for eighteen months without really knowing where it would all lead. Eighteen months applying the deadly skills he had learned in nine years of service with the parachute regiment. He had enlisted in the British army within a year of leaving school in Liverpool, a city devastated by unemployment and devoid of opportunity for anyone without qualifications. When the recruiting officer asked him which unit was his first preference he instinctively asked for the paras. If pressed at the time for a reason he would have been reluctant to give an honest answer. He simply thought they looked like the toughest bastards he had ever seen, and he wanted to be one of them.

Hennessy was a born warrior, a man for whom peacetime held little meaning. Or opportunity. Remarkably, the army granted him his first choice. The paras gave him everything he needed to blossom. His natural fitness, keen intelligence, and unrestrained enthusiasm made him a superb soldier, despite his lack of formal education. When the Falklands War came and 3rd Para were dispatched with the rest of the British task force to help dislodge the Argentine invaders, it was all the opportunity Hennessy needed. The dirtier it got, the better he liked it. To the officers and men of his unit he seemed both tireless and fearless. At the storming of Goose Green he led a charge on an Argentine bunker, which killed eleven enemy soldiers and helped turn the Argentine flank. When the war started he was just another capable young corporal in the paras. Six weeks, one Military Cross, and one battlefield promotion later, he was a sergeant and a hero.

Within six months of the task force's triumphant return to Britain, Hennessy was recommended for officer training. That was when it had all started to go wrong. Sandhurst, the British army's officer training academy, proved a nightmare for him. He had no difficulty absorbing the information. Indeed, he had excelled at the work and he had a natural flair for leadership and tactical thinking. His greatest obstacle was his classmates. Younger, better educated, better connected, they had seemed to him to come from another planet. In everyday military life, and on a one-to-one basis, he got along well with officers. Most officers. But thrust abruptly into the alien social milieu of Sandhurst, he suddenly found himself alone. His peers were no longer his peers; they made that abundantly clear. War hero or not, Brian Hennessy's classmates at Sandhurst were snobs. Not all, but most. It wasn't anything overt. If anything, it was the exquisite subtlety of their disdain that enraged him most. Because it was there, subtle and yet as deadly as any bullet. His working-class scouse accent, his manners, his attitudes, his views, even the way he dressed when he was off duty . . . they were all unacceptable.

Stung by their snobbery, he moderated his accent, polished the rough edges, copied many of his classmates' mannerisms, watched the way they dressed and ate; but it was little use. He could copy them but he couldn't *be* one of them. Inevitably he found that he spent time off on his own or with the few other men at Sandhurst who were like himself, men from working-class backgrounds who had been commissioned from the ranks and were doing it the hard way—on guts and raw ability, without the privilege of class. In that entire year Brian Hennessy was not invited once to spend a weekend with any of his classmates at any of their grand country homes, nor was he ever invited to the parties up in London where so many of his classmates went to carouse with their debutante girlfriends. Still, he survived. He did well. But at the end of the year he emerged from Sandhurst with a deep and violent loathing of the British upper class.

Ironically, Brian Hennessy had learned something else, in

addition to his military studies. Despite his hatred for the British upper class, he had learned how to behave like them. Not well enough to pass close inspection at any Sloane Square party— he just didn't have the right connections, and never would— but well enough to fool strangers. Particularly Americans, who thought all middle-class English people sounded like BBC announcers, and who wouldn't detect the fraudulent nuances underneath that would expose Hennessy in the eyes of the astute social observer.

Sandhurst was the beginning of his disaffection from all things British. His tour of duty with the paras in Northern Ireland the following year cemented that disaffection. It was a dangerous place to send a man like Brian Hennessy, his superior officers knew. They also believed that it would be the making of him or the breaking of him. They never knew how wrong they were. Because Brian Hennessy had been born in Belfast, in a Catholic ghetto of Catholic parents. That hadn't helped him at Sandhurst, either. It didn't matter that his parents had left Belfast for Liverpool when Hennessy was only six years old. He was a mick and a Catholic and a working-class upstart: a nobody. Hennessy had only the dimmest recollections of Belfast from his early childhood, but like all childish memories they were heavily romanticized. Daily, as the weeks and months progressed, he was angered by the devastation he saw wrought on the city of his birth. And daily he listened to the casual contempt of his fellow soldiers for the local population. Especially the Taigs— the Catholics. The longer he studied the situation the more he saw British repression rather than Irish intransigence. And he saw the way in which the IRA held a modern army at bay. How a few hundred determined men and women kept one of the best-equipped and most disciplined military forces in the world neutralized by terror and cunning and dumb Irish stubbornness. Gradually, irredeemably, he lost the last vestiges of regard for anything British and transferred his sympathy and his allegiance to the people of his birthplace. And now, only a few years later, he was chafing to return, to assume the vital role O'Donnell had promised him in the final liberation of Ireland. To claim his birthright.

"What do you want me to do?" he asked.

MINNEAPOLIS, MARCH 30

As Brian Hennessy hung up the phone in New York it was a little past six o'clock in Minneapolis. After four hours of skilled and determined questioning in Bono's room at the Frobisher Private Hospital, John Ritsczik had gotten nowhere. All he had learned from Bono was that there had been an attack by unknown armed men on the farm and there had been casualties. When Ritsczik asked Bono what his occupation was, Bono had replied, "Sportsman." When Ritsczik had produced two plastic-wrapped files bearing Lynch's and Bono's names both men had calmly expressed their surprise and reservations at some of the information they contained. Secretly, Lynch was much relieved. A lot of information had already been purged from the software before the FBI had obtained their printouts. But Ritsczik's patience was beginning to wear thin.

"Listen to me," he said coldly. His words were for the benefit of both men but he kept his eyes on Bono. "Under federal law I have the authority to hold you for days, weeks if necessary, until I get the cooperation I need. If you still want to play smart I can go to a federal judge and get a rubber stamp to hold you in the interests of national security. I don't even have to bring charges. And I can keep doing it till you're an old man, if that's what you want. In a couple of days you're going to be well enough to be moved from here. Unless you decide to be a little more forthcoming I'm going to have you transferred from these luxurious surroundings to the isolation block at the federal penitentiary in New York State where I can keep you on ice indefinitely. Do you understand me?"

"I have a headache," Bono answered feebly. "It's been a hard day. So many questions."

Lynch had been studying Ritsczik as much as the FBI man had been studying them. In any other circumstances, Lynch concluded, Ritsczik was a man he could like. Tough, smart, and persistent—a good cop. Except fate had cast them as adversaries. He suspected Ritsczik was bluffing about the federal penitentiary, but he had no doubt the FBI man could make life hard for them. He reached a conclusion.

"I'll tell you what you need to know," he said, and stood up. "Let's cut a deal."

All Lynch wanted was to buy a few more days until Bono had recovered sufficiently to make the journey from Minneapolis to the sanctuary of the *American Endeavor* at Chesapeake. Until then, Lynch decided, he could afford a trade-off with Ritsczik. The agent might even come in useful. And they could use some friends.

"On the way in here I saw a nice little coffee shop downstairs," he continued. "Let's go and have a little chat, shall we? Perhaps I can make you an offer you can't refuse."

A small smile tugged at Ritsczik's lips although his eyes betrayed a healthy skepticism. Still, the FBI man conceded, it was a beginning. It might be the way into this investigation that he had been looking for.

"We'll hear what you have to say," was all he offered in reply, and got up to follow Lynch.

"By the way." He turned back to look at Bono. "How did you survive all those hours buried in that shit? I saw that place. It looked like an atom bomb hit it."

The tension in the room eased palpably. Now that Lynch had taken the spotlight off him Bono mysteriously seemed to have regained much of his strength.

"Little number my pal showed me," he said, nodding at Lynch. "Had a couple of cave-diving cylinders in the cellar with me. They built the chimneys in those old places big and strong. The foundations were good. The iron plating on the ash box kept the heavy stuff off me. All I had to do was keep takin' little sucks on those air tanks and I could have stayed down there another twelve hours. The hard part was the heat. But I guess the worst of the fire was kept way over my head after that bastard caved in the cellar on top of me. Funny thing, ain't it? Hidin' in a fireplace to get away from a fire?"

The two men walked out of the room and then Lynch popped his head fleetingly back around the door.

"What happened to the dog?"

Bono shrugged. "Maybe he pissed off to Canada when things got hot." Then something resembling a smile crossed the cut and swollen lips. "Or maybe," he added slyly, "he's in heaven with Colonel Sanders."

The two men left Bono to heal and walked without speaking along the corridor toward the elevators. Lynch had just pressed the button when they both heard a long and dire croak echoing down the hallway from Bono's room.

"Yoohooo . . ." the voice crooned with a hoarse and plaintive urgency. "Are you there, Nurse Bonesnacker . . . did you bring your rubber glove today . . . ?"

6 The Skorpion's Song

Janice Street awakened to the sound of persistent, heavy banging at the front door of the town house. She looked at the bedside clock and saw that it was 2:38 in the morning. The door to her bedroom opened and Becker padded softly in on bare feet, wearing only his black suit pants and a T-shirt. His right hand held an Uzi.

"Get under the bed," he said. "Pull all the blankets around you. Whatever happens, stay there."

Janice began to do as he said and then decided that whatever was happening, she'd rather it happened with her wearing more than panties and undershirt. She started to hunt for her jeans and sweater in the dark. The banging had stopped and she could hear a man's voice speaking urgently from outside. Becker and the two guards had arranged themselves in rooms leading off the hallway. The younger, fair-haired man stood alongside the living room window with its view of the brick wall next door. The other, bigger man knelt in the doorway to the living room, which allowed him to cover the hallway leading to Janice's bedroom. Becker crouched in the kitchen door to the hallway with a clear view of the front door but without exposing himself to any line of fire that might come from that direction.

The town house was bordered on three sides by other buildings—another, bigger town house on one side, a small bistro on the other, and a thirty-two-story office block in the rear. The only way in, apart from the front door, was through the walls, the roof, or down a narrow, deadly sliver of space between the two town houses that would leave no room for anybody to maneuver.

"Open the door, for Christ's sake," the voice was demanding from the other side of the door with an increasing note of desperation. "I know you're in there, Becker. Halloran sent me. There's been another hit. We've got to move the girl."

Becker glanced across at the guard in the living room door and shook his head. They waited.

"Come on guys, will ya open the door? It's Chris Wilson from STC Albuquerque. I got my orders, too. We have to move the girl. Check with the old man via security central, Albuquerque, if you want, but do it fast."

Becker covered the options quickly. He didn't recognize the name, but that meant nothing. Halloran had thirteen hundred private security personnel protecting STC's business empire. Either the guy was telling the truth or he knew enough about STC security to run a good bluff. Either way he wasn't coming in. Becker decided there was one safe way to find out.

"We just put a radio call through to NYPD, pal," he yelled through the front door. "They'll be here in five minutes. You can stand there and take your chances or you can go home. But you're not comin' in."

He nodded at his colleague across the hall and the man picked up the radio from a nearby coffee table. It was already tuned to the New York Police Department's emergency call wave band. He pressed the transmit button and had just begun to speak when the front door exploded inward under a withering storm of machine-gun fire.

The hallway filled with bullets and broken masonry and deadly flying splinters of hard, polished wood. Becker flinched but emptied the magazine of his Uzi back in the direction of the disintegrating door. The guard opposite was knocked onto his backside by the shock of the onslaught, and the radio slid out of his grasp and across the wooden floor, under a chair. He ignored it and opened fire from an undignified sitting position, his legs splayed out into the hallway. The fair-haired man at the window hurried across the room and bent down to recover the radio. There was a deafening explosion and then another

and another until his eardrums erupted with pain and he involuntarily dropped his Uzi and covered his ears. The explosions
were accompanied by a series of blinding flashes, and for a
moment Becker thought they had been fire-bombed. Reflexively
and with his eyes shut he threw himself backward across the
shiny kitchen floor, his right fist still clamped firmly around the
Uzi, the other holding a fresh clip. The roar of gunfire flared to
a crescendo inside the town house, the muffled stutter of his
men's Uzis drowned by the harsh answering bark of what Becker
realized had to be a Skorpion. The Czech-made Skorpion isn't
the most sophisticated submachine gun in the world. It takes
only a twenty-round clip compared to the Uzi's thirty-two, and
when switched to automatic it shudders so dramatically it is
impossible to aim with pinpoint accuracy. Its best feature is that
it has a greater cyclic firing rate of 840 rounds per minute and
assumes a devastating swath. At close-quarters, room-to-room
fighting it is one of the most effective weapons in the world.
Suddenly Becker heard his men scream and the Uzis stopped.
The screams descended to a low, pitiful moan. There were two
ugly, businesslike bursts from the Skorpion and then there was
nothing. For one fleeting moment the house filled with an eerie,
terrifying silence. Becker forced himself to open his eyes but all
he saw was another blinding white flash and the world disappeared in a flare of brilliant reds and blues. He felt himself slam
into the wall. He knew the second doorway from the kitchen
into the hallway was to his right and that the door to Janice's
room would be outside and second on the left, past the toilet.
He bent forward, slammed the fresh clip into the Uzi, felt for
the doorjamb, and fired a couple of short, three-round bursts
down the hallway in the direction of the front door. Then he
took a deep breath and lunged into the hallway. Flailing with
his free hand, he fumbled wildly for Janice's door. The answering
torrent of 7.65 mm slugs from the Skorpion opened him up on
the right side of his body in a zigzag pattern that reached from
head to toe. Bob Becker was dead before his Uzi clattered to
the floor.

Hennessy stepped over Becker's body, kicked open the door
to Janice's room, lobbed in his last stun grenade, and waited for
the seven explosions and seven accompanying flashes to com-

plete their terrifying percussion. He slapped a fresh twenty-round clip into the Skorpion, then swiveled around and down on one knee and raked the room with a sustained burst.

Based on Becker's behavior, Hennessy figured Janice Street would be in this room. He also figured that she would be on the floor and that anyone assigned to guard her would have to be at least above knee height in order to discharge his own weapon efficiently. When there was no answering fire Hennessy pulled the welder's protective goggles from his eyes, removed his rubber earplugs, and braced himself; then he threw himself in a forward roll across the full width of the room. If there had been another guard in any condition to react after the stun grenade had gone off, Hennessy wouldn't have made it. But Becker had been told to expect a hit, not a kidnap. He had put all his resources into stopping the attack at the front door.

The bedroom was narrower than Hennessy anticipated and, as he completed his roll, his feet hit the opposite wall with a loud smack, throwing him off balance. He was forced to scramble into an awkward crouch to meet any threat. But there was nothing. Only the terrified yelp of a woman hiding under the bed. Hennessy lifted the bed with one hand and hurled it on its side against the wall. Then he wrenched the blankets from Janice's trembling body and pressed the Skorpion to her head. When he saw that her hands were empty he reached down with a black-gloved hand, seized her roughly by the elbow, and yanked her to her feet.

Janice Street had kept her eyes shut tight and her hands over her ears while she cowered beneath her flimsy nest of blankets under the bed, and so when the stun grenade detonated it did no more than add to her terror. Physically she was unhurt. She could still hear and she could still see—perfectly. When she was pulled to her feet, she saw a blond-haired man in his early thirties with a face flushed from his exertions and a terrifying light in his hard blue eyes. He wore a long, navy blue raincoat that was far too big for him; underneath, she saw, he was wearing some kind of body armor, the kind policemen wear.

As he hauled Janice to her feet she did what she had always promised herself she would do in this kind of situation. She fumbled for the pocket screwdriver she had hidden in the waistband of her jeans, clenched it in her right fist, and swung it upward at his face with every ounce of power she could muster. The screwdriver had a red plastic handle and a short steel shaft, the chisel tip of which had been sharpened to a lethal edge. Janice usually carried it in her purse, and had never before needed it. Now that she needed it she tried to kill with it. Hennessy saw it coming, but too late. The tip of the screwdriver pierced his cheek just below the left eye. He was lucky. When it hit the cheekbone it didn't break the bone or skid upward into his eye. Instead it grated down and along his upper jaw until Janice could push no more and the handle slammed against his face.

Hennessy dropped the submachine gun, clasped both hands to his face, and staggered backward with an agonized roar of rage. Janice made a dash for the door but he saw her and lashed out viciously with his foot, catching her on the right hip and sending her crashing against the dresser where her suitcase still lay, half-full. She gasped in pain but it wasn't enough to stop her. She grabbed hold of the suitcase, hurled it at his head, and dived full length toward the hallway. Hennessy instinctively swatted the suitcase away with one hand, took one step forward, and, with a sadistic grunt, kicked her hard in the side of the head.

Janice screamed as the force of the kick slammed her against the bedroom door, and she blacked out. It must only have been for a moment, she thought when she came to, because she looked up to see him standing over her, watching her, one foot on her chest. The fingers of his left hand were spread around the shaft of the screwdriver. He had taken the glove off his right hand to feel along the line of the shaft under his skin. Then he took the handle in his right hand and carefully pulled the screwdriver from his face. When it slid free he glanced at it disdainfully and threw it across the room. There was a large ugly puncture wound where it had gone in and the blood poured out in a torrent, streaming down his neck and spreading in a dark stain on his blue body armor.

"You've fuckin' marked me, you bitch," he swore at her.

Janice cursed herself. She hadn't hit an artery or an eye and there was no exit wound. Next time she'd get a screwdriver with a longer shaft. Hennessy glanced briefly around. Then he stepped away, picked up one of her T-shirts off the floor, and dabbed his streaming cheek.

"Get up," he ordered.

She lay still and said nothing.

He snatched the Skorpion off the floor and jabbed the barrel against the side of her face.

"Get up, bitch," he spat. "Or I'll waste you here."

Janice lay still and didn't utter a word. She knew he wouldn't kill her now. She was the only person he'd come for. She wasn't going to make it easy for him. It had only been a couple of minutes, but surely, she thought, surely in the name of God somebody on the street must have noticed by now. Somebody must have called the cops. Even in New York . . . Almost the instant the thought entered her head she heard sirens. They could have been no more than a couple of blocks away. It was the last clear thought she was to have for some time. Without another word, Hennessy turned just a fraction, lifted his right foot up, and slammed the heel of his shoe against her right temple. Her head snapped sideways like a rag doll and her body went limp.

Hennessy threw the Skorpion into the pile of bedclothes on the floor, bent down, and felt her carotid artery with the fingertips of his right hand. There was still a pulse. A good, strong pulse. She was a tough little bitch, he thought. Grabbing her around the waist, he picked her up and hefted her across his shoulder. As Hennessy walked from the ruined town house he ignored the bleeding wound on his face and fished in the inside pocket of his raincoat with his left hand. When he emerged from the narrow darkened porch into the tiny courtyard in front of the town house, there was a crowd of about half a dozen people gathered on the opposite pavement in their nightclothes. Lights were flashing on in the surrounding houses and there were more people watching from the safe confines of their homes.

What they saw was a dark blue Chevy with a magnetic police lamp oscillating on the roof and a man in a raincoat carrying a badly injured girl down the steps of the town house to the car. Hennessy waved a genuine NYPD detective sergeant's badge at the stunned and hesitant onlookers.

"Sergeant Blainey, police department," he called out to them, breathlessly, like a man in shock. "Somebody call an ambulance. There are more hurt people in there."

Nobody moved. Hennessy opened the rear door of the Chevy, laid Janice across the backseat, climbed behind the wheel, and threw the car into a fast U-turn. As he drove out of the courtyard he plucked the magnetic police lamp from the roof of the car and slipped smoothly into the light nighttime traffic. A moment later he saw the flashing lights of a police cruiser screaming toward him from the direction of Washington Square. Back in front of the town house a few of the local residents moved forward to peer through the shattered front door into the darkened interior, muttering apprehensively to one another.

"Crack," pronounced Mrs. Trenheath, who had lived on the quiet Greenwich Village courtyard for forty-seven years. "Who'd have thought it in this part of town . . . a crack house? I'm glad they got the bastards."

As Hennessy drove north along Sixth Avenue, then out of Manhattan and onto the New York State Thruway through Yonkers and toward Danbury, Colin Lynch and John Ritsczik were arriving at Newark International Airport on an FBI Gulfstream charter from Minneapolis. Ritsczik had a car and driver waiting and they drove directly to the FBI's New York office at 26 Federal Plaza in Manhattan. They had two leads. For seventy-two hours, at least, they were going to work together. That was the deal Lynch had made in the coffee shop at Frobisher Private Hospital. He'd pointed out that the assistance had all been running along a one-way street, so far. From Halloran to the FBI. They had been given nothing in return, except more bad news. Meanwhile, their talents were being wasted and they were still taking casualties. It had seemed to strike a chord with the FBI man; Ritsczik bought the proposition that if they pooled their resources and their initiatives for a few days at least, they might all move forward a little faster. Lynch had then told him what Bono had said about one of his attackers having an Irish accent. Ritsczik had been as skeptical as Lynch. But Lynch had had time to think about it, and he knew that Bono wouldn't have passed on the information unless he thought it was useful, however unlikely or outlandish it might seem.

"If that's the case," Ritsczik had conceded, "then we'd have to switch the entire focus of our investigation. We've been concentrating on known contacts of Middle Eastern terror organizations."

"Don't go changing direction yet," Lynch had cautioned him. "We can run a few checks of our own first to see if there's anything to this. The IRA has had dealings with the PLO and other Middle Eastern terror groups for a long time. They've been getting most of their arms from Libya for the past fifteen years and Iran for the past ten years. The PLO has sent them arms and explosives from time to time. Occasionally they get a freelance consignment of Semtex. Eastern Europe may have kissed and made up with the rest of the world but the Czechs made a lot of Semtex when they were following orders from the KGB and there's an awful lot of it still floating loose somewhere in the world. And, oh yes, I almost forgot," he'd added innocently. "They get all their M16's and M60's from the American army, thanks to the healthy illegal trade in firearms here."

Ritsczik had sniffed. "We put five guys away for a total of two hundred fifteen years last year for illegal arms dealing. Your government sent the bureau a letter of appreciation."

"And you made a deal with one of them and let him go and you've never heard from him since, have you?"

From the look in Ritsczik's eyes Lynch had seen that the FBI man wasn't pleased that he knew.

"Just consider that an ongoing investigation, Mr. Lynch," he'd huffed. "In our line of work we are required to deal with a number of unreliable sources."

Lynch had only smiled, ignoring the gibe. Ritsczik was cool but he couldn't be pushed indefinitely.

"It could just be that the IRA is doing somebody a favor by taking a contract out on us. Somebody in the Middle East who isn't very happy with some of our activities," Lynch had suggested. Then he'd paused; he wasn't exactly sure yet how much the FBI knew of their past activities. Ritsczik remained impassive. Lynch went on. "A favors-for-arms deal, maybe. Middle Eastern terrorists can't move as freely in Western countries as they once did. They look different. They get noticed. The one lasting consequence of the export of Middle Eastern terrorism is that nobody in the West trusts Arabs anymore. But the IRA can move men and women anywhere in the Western world without attracting suspicion. Especially if they're virgins—not known to the security forces. False passports are no problem. Any decent terrorist group can produce a British or an American passport. Most of them have genuine passports from the Irish Republic anyway, and an Irish accent doesn't arouse suspicion. They're a very charming race, the Irish. People still smile when they meet them. Most of the time."

Ritsczik had thought about it.

"How reliable is your Mr. Bono?" he had asked after a while.

Lynch had smiled. "He's a blunt instrument. Crude but effective. But don't underestimate him. He's not dumb. If he says the guy had an Irish accent then he's probably right, or he's close to it. He knows what's at stake here . . . more than anybody else."

Ritsczik had nodded slowly. "Favors for arms, huh?"

"I think we must consider it a possibility," Lynch had added. "In the meantime, I'll talk to our people in London. You start running a few new names through your computers. See what we come up with."

Before closing the deal Lynch had imposed one final condition.

"Bono is free to go?" He'd made it sound more like a statement of fact than a question.

Laughing wryly, Ritsczik had shaken his head.

"I've given you everything he gave me," Lynch had said evenly. And it was the truth.

He'd gone on, "You're going to find it a lot easier working with me than with him. And he needs to be resting under ironclad security. He's not going to get that here. If he's on the yacht, you'll know where he is and he'll be safe. I think you'll find your director will agree to it."

An hour after closing the deal, Lynch had been in the Hyatt and sleeping the sleep of exhaustion, with two FBI men patrolling the corridor all night. Two more had spent the night in the stairwells. The following day he'd visited Bono again with Ritsczik and this time the three of them had carefully gone over Bono's recollections of the tortured man's words in the farmhouse cellar. Bono had taken his cues from Lynch and omitted the business about the finger. Before leaving Lynch had told the big man that in twenty-four hours he would be expected aboard the STC jet to fly on to Washington where a car would be waiting to take him to Halloran, aboard the *American Endeavor*. Bono had expressed regret at leaving his favorite nurse.

"I think she's startin' to crack," he'd said.

The next day Lynch and Ritsczik had flown to Chicago and spent the rest of the day at the bureau's Midwest headquarters, feeding names into the computer and examining the feedback. It hadn't been encouraging. Lynch had called Halloran to explain what was happening and then he'd called Sir Malcolm Porter, controlling officer of CTC, in London, but Porter was unavailable. By midnight there was still nothing in any of the information the computers spat back at them to keep them in Chicago. Both men had agreed that their hit man was probably long gone. They'd decided it was time to move the investigation back to New York. By the time they arrived at the New York office it was nearly three-thirty in the morning. Both men were starting to feel the strain and both men were determined not to show it.

Lynch calculated that the time in London would be 8:30 A.M. Sir Malcolm was an early riser and ought to be at his desk. The moment they reached Ritsczik's office Lynch picked up the phone and dialed. Ritsczik leaned forward and flicked the conference button on so he could hear, too.

Less than a minute later Sir Malcolm's cultivated voice floated into the room.

"My dear Colin," he said. "How are you?"

"Fine, sir."

Conditioning left its mark. Sir Malcolm was no longer Lynch's boss, and hadn't been for more than two years, but Lynch still called him "sir."

He went straight to the point.

"We may be getting somewhere in our investigation. We think there could be an Irish connection to this one, the IRA, INLA . . . somebody with links to Middle Eastern terror groups."

"The IRA?" Sir Malcolm echoed. "I'll be damned. All right, just as well. We're getting nowhere fast with our other inquiries.

There is nothing to suggest that any Middle Eastern group is active in the United States at this point."

"That could mean we're on to something," Lynch replied. "We have a few names we'd like you to check at your end."

"Fire away."

"They aren't full names," Lynch explained. "They're the usual thing, bits of names, similarities. We need you to check out anybody with similar names who has connections to the IRA, the INLA, or any other Irish terror group. Starting at the present and going back, say . . . ten years."

Lynch knew that every call on Sir Malcolm's line was recorded and he would simply have his secretary, the efficient Jean Hamilton, transcribe them in a few moments. Then a CTC clerical officer would run them through CTC's computers. And if that failed to produce anything interesting, permission would be sought to process them through the computers at MI5, MI6, and at Scotland Yard's Special Branch.

"The first name is Hennessy, like the brandy," Lynch said, spelling it out carefully. "We assume it's the name of an individual. We have nothing more, no first name. We don't know whether it is the name of a male or a female. We would lean toward male. The second name would be something like Connor or O'Connor, Connell or O'Connell, Donnell or O'Donnell. That's it."

"Yes, all right," Sir Malcolm said. "Not much, is it? Still, we've worked wonders with less. How soon do you need to know?"

"Anything you get, as it comes in please . . . sir."

"We'll see what we can do, Colin. I'll be back to you as soon as I can."

Lynch hung up and looked at Ritsczik. That was when the FBI agent dropped his bombshell.

"We may already have something," he said.

Lynch stared silently at Ritsczik and waited.

The FBI man looked uncomfortable. He turned and stuck his hands in his suit pockets and stared out the window at the spectacular nighttime Manhattan skyline for a long time.

Lynch was growing impatient. "I thought the deal was we shared everything. Two-way street? We're all on the same side, remember?"

"Yeah." Ritsczik nodded. "It's not part of this investigation but when you said there could be some Irish connection the other day I started thinking back about some of the guys we've pulled in, some of the people we've watched over the last few years."

"And . . . ?"

"Most of 'em are assholes. They think Ireland is a Disney movie full of Darby O'Gill and the little people. They've never been there. They have no idea what it's like and they think it's the done thing to give money to Noraid . . . to send arms to Ireland. Some of them get a little too caught up in the romance. They get vulnerable and they get used and then they get involved in really dumb things. Breaking into National Guard armories, bribing army quartermasters, driving truckloads of guns and shit to ships in Boston, Portland, Montreal, Halifax, Saint John, hiding wanted men . . . That's when we come in. We tell 'em they should stick to marching in the Saint Patrick's Day parade and waving placards. Sometimes they listen. Sometimes they don't, and so they go to jail."

Lynch was tired. He sat down in Ritsczik's chair and waited. The FBI's New York director began pacing slowly back and forth across his office.

"Every now and again we get something different," he went on. "Something that makes us look a little closer, usually because of the status or the sensitive nature of the person involved. It might be a Teddy Kennedy, a Tip O'Neill, a Senator Daniel Patrick Moynihan, or a Hugh Carey, the former New York governor . . . all good Irish-American Catholics. Sometimes they let their passions or their political aspirations run away with their mouths."

He stopped pacing and turned to look at Lynch. "You have to remember, there's a lot of latent anti-British sentiment in this country. A lot of respect and admiration but a lot of suspicion and resentment, too. There's always been political capital to be made in blaming the British for all the ills of Ireland, especially in New York and Boston. Don't forget, we fought two wars against your people. We took our independence from you. A lot of Americans still believe it was British skulduggery that maneuvered us into two world wars to save your skins."

"You know," Lynch sighed. "I always suspected it was the RAF that bombed Pearl Harbor. But I just never have been able to work out how they got all those camouflaged Spitfires back to London in time to finish the Battle of Britain."

"Yeah." Ritsczik smiled. "Anyway, like it or not, there's always an audience for somebody who wants to knock the Brits. Like I said, sometimes politicians and other public figures find themselves giving aid and comfort to somebody they shouldn't. It's sensitive because of their position in public life . . . you understand?"

Lynch nodded.

"We might check them out, discreetly, make sure it's just ignorance of the real situation, which nine times out of ten is what it is. Somebody from the bureau checks with the White House and then has a quiet word in the ear of this important public person suggesting that he or she might no longer want to be seen meeting with so and so, or appearing at fund-raising dinners for the Irish-American Association with so and so, because so and so just happens to be the local treasurer for the IRA, which used the money to buy the explosives that blew away half a dozen innocent shoppers outside Harrods in London."

Ritsczik pulled up a chair and sat on the visitor's side of his own desk, facing Lynch.

"And then, every now and again, we get somebody who doesn't fit neatly into either category. Somebody who really perks up our interest."

"Like?"

"There's a cop we've been interested in for a little while. Guy called Victor Flannery. Twenty-six-year man, works out of the Battery."

"There's a lot of New York cops with Irish names," Lynch said. "And he wouldn't be the first cop to sling a few bucks into the IRA's coffers. What's special about him?"

"Until three months ago, nothing. Then he suddenly comes into a little extra money. Not a lot, just enough to spend on short-term apartment rentals all around the place. But there's no explanation for the money. He's in Noraid, so it could be interesting. Maybe Noraid wants the apartments for something, or somebody. Then again, maybe he's tickling the cash register. Maybe he wants the apartments himself, for something dirty."

Lynch leaned forward in his chair.

"After a while my guys think he's just on the take. We think, maybe it's a matter for NYPD internal affairs. He's got a bimbo on the side. He needs a little love nest, that's all. Because none of these places he's renting are anything fancy."

"What changed your mind?"

"He never used any of them."

"Come again?"

"He rented them and then he never went near them again. Must have done it three, four times."

"Who did use them?"

"We don't know."

"Come on."

"I know . . . but it's true. I'm not holding back. We watched him. Not the apartments. We figured if he rented the apartments he must go back to do some business sooner or later and we'd find out what it was. It just seemed to fizzle out. We thought maybe he had a broad and then she changed her mind. Manpower's always tight here. We had one man keeping an eye on him, that's all."

"Jesus," Lynch breathed. "Taps?"

"No phone taps. No need. We were fishing."

"Do you still have the addresses of those apartments?"

"I can get them."

"Now?"

"Give me a minute to wake my man up. He'll tell me where they are."

"Good." Lynch glanced at his watch. It was approaching 4:00 A.M. "Feel up to a little driving?"

LONDONDERRY, NORTHERN IRELAND, APRIL 2

The Jockey was a very worried man. A week had passed since the three men he'd recruited to do Tom O'Donnell's dirty work in the United States had left, and there was still no word when they'd be back. It was already pitch dark at six o'clock as he hurried home through the mean gray streets of the Creggan Estate after an afternoon at one of the Provo shebeens, an illegal drinking club called Brennan's, in the Bogside.

Billy McCormack toured the pubs and clubs every day, from ten till the last horse galloped home at the last race meeting, taking the small bets that were the bread and butter of his existence. Ronnie Carson, the Derry battalion commander, had been at Brennan's, drinking heavily, and his presence had added to McCormack's nervousness. The Jockey made it a rule never to take a drink until he'd closed his book for the day, and then he'd usually idle a couple of hours away over a few whiskeys till he felt it was time to go home. He had been badly shaken when Carson had invited him to sit awhile, but Carson seemed to have nothing much on his mind except racing form.

Somebody had cracked a joke about kidnapping another race-horse, and the table had exploded in laughter. Only Carson didn't seem to appreciate the humor. But then, he'd been in-volved in the last one and it had been pure farce from beginning to end. It had ended with the horse being accidentally shot by one of its kidnappers before the ransom could be collected. Apparently the gunman had been showing off a few pistol twirls to a pal, the sort of thing he'd seen in cowboy movies as a kid, and the pistol had gone off and shot the million-dollar racehorse through the neck.

Billy had a couple of small whiskeys but they failed to soothe his nerves, and so after what he considered a respectable length of time at Ronnie's table he had taken his leave, thankful that nobody had asked after Kevin Bourke, Terry O'Laughlin, or Del Morris. McCormack wasn't sure he would have been able to keep the fear and guilt off his face. And Carson had a nose for treachery. Amazingly, nobody seemed to have noticed that the three men hadn't been around for a while. It couldn't last, McCormack knew. The questions would start soon. Another few days, another week at most, and people would start asking. Bourke's wife would wonder aloud to someone when her husband would be getting back from his latest job and Ronnie Carson's suspicions would flare because he had no one on active service at the moment.

McCormack wasn't sure his nerves would hold out for another week. He damned Tom O'Donnell more than a dozen times on his walk from Bishop's Gate, where he parked his car. He wouldn't leave his car in the street near his poky little flat in one of the gray concrete monoliths that dotted the bleak wastelands of the Creggan. It wasn't so much that the local yobs might steal it or burn it if there was trouble; the property of a Provo man was sacrosanct in the Catholic ghetto. The Jockey had lost his first car to the British army bomb squad, who proclaimed it to be booby-trapped and blew it up for him with profuse apologies. It was one of the quasilegal tricks the army used to harass known IRA men whom they couldn't link to anything that would hold up in court. Ever since he had bought the new car he'd taken to detouring into the city each night and parking it on a quiet, respectable street. Derry is a small, compact city and it is only a twenty-minute walk from the world of the city center to the netherworld of the Creggan Estate. McCormack's only real danger was that he could be picked up by a couple of the boys from the Ulster Defence Association, the Ulster Volunteer Force, or one of the other Protestant vigilante forces who might spot him before he could reach the safety of the Creggan and pull him in for a bit of a chat and a thump.

The Jockey had phoned O'Donnell two days earlier and had been assured that all was well and the boys would be back just a little later than anticipated. Another three or four days at most, O'Donnell had promised. The Jockey wasn't sure he could last that long. He crossed an open stretch of wasteland to his block of flats, passing beneath the tiered balconies from where plastic bags of excrement and urine and volleys of used tampons rained down on British army patrols whenever they ventured into the area. As usual there were a half dozen youths loitering in the entrance, smoking dope, passing a bottle, and listening to something loud and incomprehensible on a ghetto blaster. The lobby, the broken lifts, the corridors, and the stairwells in all the blocks of flats on the estate smelled and looked the same. They all stank of urine, they were all daubed with the same lurid and cretinous graffiti, they were all clogged with plastic foam fast-food rubbish and disposable hypodermic syringes. All the joys of America's exported ghetto culture to the world, Mc-Cormack reflected sourly.

He trudged up the six flights of stairs to his floor and gratefully unlocked the door to his one-bedroom flat with a shaking hand. He wasn't sure if it was the climb or his nerves that made his hand tremble so much that it took him a full minute to fit the key in the lock. He stepped inside, put the light on, and took off his overcoat. He put the TV in the living room on for company and then checked the budgerigar's cage to see that his pet bird was adequately provided with millet. It was the only other living creature that shared Billy McCormack's private life. He had never married and he saw nothing of his elder brother and two younger sisters. The Cause was all he'd ever had, all he would ever have. Even though he hadn't eaten since breakfast he wasn't hungry. He was looking forward to something that would give him far more comfort than food. He went to a cupboard over the kitchen and pulled out an unopened bottle of Bushmills. He opened it, poured himself half a tumbler, and drank it like water. The whiskey seemed to transfuse him with warmth and strength. He leaned back against the kitchen sink and closed his eyes.

"Irish penicillin," he mumbled. "God bless ye."

After a moment he began to feel better. He poured the tumbler half-full again, sat down at the kitchen table, took out his glasses, a pad and pencil, a form guide, and a copy of that day's paper, and began to calculate the odds on the next day's race meetings in the Republic.

It was a little after six when he heard a knock at the door and got up. He wasn't expecting anyone but visitors weren't that unusual. It could well be the woman from next door wanting him to put a quid each way on the favorite at Antrim for her the next day. Then again, he realized with a tremor, it could be bad news. Something might be up after all. It could be one of Ronnie Carson's boys come to ask him a few questions about some matters that had been puzzling them lately. McCormack took a deep breath and opened the door. For a moment he was surprised and then flooded with relief . . . and then the relief evaporated in a dreadful, chilling realization. There could only be one reason on earth why Eamonn Docherty had driven all the way from Lifford to see him without warning. McCormack began to back slowly up the hall toward the kitchen.

Docherty saw the shock of comprehension on the Jockey's face and hurriedly stepped inside, closed the door behind him, and pulled the Colt automatic from his overcoat pocket.

"Ah, no Eamonn . . . no," McCormack whispered in disbelief as he retreated down the hall.

Docherty almost felt sorry for the poor old bugger. Wanting to get it over with, he pulled the trigger three times. The reports in the small flat sounded like cannon fire. The first shot hit the Jockey in the chest and threw him against the back wall of the hallway. Slowly and with a strange, soft sigh he crumpled to the floor and settled into a pathetic cross-legged huddle with his head lolling forward on his chest. Just like an Indian holy man taking a nap, Docherty thought as he moved forward. The second bullet had followed the first, almost immediately, but it had missed the Jockey and gouged a fist-sized crater in the plaster behind the pale blue floral wallpaper instead. Docherty leaned forward, put the muzzle of the automatic to the back of Mc-Cormack's head, looked away, and fired.

Nobody came out to see what the noise was about as he hurried back along the balcony to the stairwell. The kids in the lobby had vanished with their ghetto blaster, and he hurried around to the back of the building, unchallenged, to where he'd parked his green Ford Escort. By the time the police came to investigate an hour later, accompanied by British troops in two armored Land Rovers, Eamonn Docherty was across the border and back in the Irish Republic. And no matter how hard the police pressed their inquiries, nobody saw or heard anything. Which was why they didn't press their inquiries very hard at all. A crowd was starting to gather. The mood was growing hostile. The first few filthy missiles from the upper balconies had begun to patter down toward the soldiers on the ground. Besides, Detective Sergeant McFarlane of the Royal Ulster Constabulary decided, as his men carried McCormack's body downstairs, it was probably only a bit of IRA housecleaning. Billy McCormack would not be mourned by many.

NEW YORK CITY, APRIL 2

The Algonquin Furnished Apartments in Englewood, New Jersey, on the western shore of the Hudson River, bore no relation to the legendary literary watering hole, the Algonquin Hotel in Manhattan. It was highly unlikely that the regulars at one would ever meet the regulars of the other at the same social gatherings. And the superintendent of the Algonquin Furnished Apartments was conspicuously lacking in charm when he was awakened from his bed at a quarter to five in the morning by two unshaven men in a hurry. One was tall and dark with bad skin, and his dark blue suit looked as though it had been slept in. The other was slightly shorter with a more athletic build, and wore gray pants, a black crew neck sweater, and a nice herringbone sports jacket. The superintendent knew cops when he saw them.

"Fuck off," he said, and closed the door.

The door almost hit him in the back when it opened again under the impact of a kick from the guy in the sports jacket.

The superintendent turned to face them with renewed interest. Perhaps they weren't cops at all.

Half an hour later he'd helped them all he could. It wasn't much. A lot of people with funny names and funny accents took apartments in his building. Sometimes for a couple of weeks, sometimes for a couple of months. He had one tenant who'd been there twenty-eight years. He had others who rented for a week, stayed a night, and disappeared. The terms were cash in advance. No references required.

By midday Lynch and Ritsczik had covered every address where Victor Flannery had rented apartments. Three people recognized his picture. Nobody remembered who used the apartments.

"I'll put a team on it," Ritsczik promised as they drove through the Holland Tunnel back into Manhattan after questioning the superintendent at the last address in Jersey City. The buildings were always the same. Big enough and cheap enough to guarantee anonymity and complete disinterest by the neighbors.

"It'll be days before we can talk to enough people to see if anybody remembers any guys with broad Irish accents and if there was anything funny about them. It's the dull part of the job. Straight police work."

Lynch grunted. It had been almost thirty-six hours since he had last slept and his eyes felt as if they'd been rinsed in vinegar.

"I think it's time for a little chat with Mr. Flannery," he said.

Ritsczik hesitated. "I think it's too early," he said. "I'd like to have a bit more to hit him with when we bring him in. If we do it now and he knows how little we've got he can laugh at us and walk out any time he likes. Give it another coupla days. I've got somebody on him. He's not going anywhere."

"I wasn't thinking about anything formal," Lynch said. "Just a quiet little chat somewhere . . . informal."

Ritsczik shook his head. "If we bring him in I want to charge him and I want charges that will stick. All we've got now is a lot of circumstantial bullshit and a lot of suspicion."

"I don't care about charges," Lynch persisted. "You can charge him with treason, you can charge him with picking his nose on duty . . . I just want some information. What I do doesn't have to affect what you do."

Ritsczik smiled dubiously. "Oh, yes it does," he said. "You get your information and walk and I get stuck with the shitty end of the stick. Any of his rights are violated and anything we have goes out the window. This is a federal operation, Lynch. We do it by the book."

"That's not what you told me in Minneapolis," Lynch said resignedly.

"Sometimes I lie."

"I know," Lynch added. "So do I."

They emerged from the tunnel and turned onto Canal Street, then drove north along Sixth Avenue and onto Eighth Street.

"Right now," Ritsczik said, "if I don't get some sleep, I am going to die."

Lynch nodded. A new plan was forming in his mind, and if he was going to be at all effective he needed some rest.

"Got a place to stay?"

"I'll call Halloran from your office if that's okay. Bring him up-to-date. He's got a couple of places scattered around New York." Lynch was thinking that it was time to check on Janice, to catch up on some sleep at the safe house where she was staying, and perhaps to engage in a different kind of therapy with her later in the day.

Ritsczik nodded. "I'll have to go with you."

The news had just come in to the FBI offices about Janice's kidnapping. Thoughts about sleep vanished for both men. They were at the safe house in Greenwich Village within twenty minutes.

"Sweet Jesus Christ . . ." Ritsczik breathed as he walked slowly through the shattered town house. "What kind of fucking rules do these people play by?"

The NYPD had cordoned off the house. Most of the immediate forensic work had been done and the bodies of Bob Becker and his two colleagues had been removed. It was only around mid-morning that the police had been able to trace the ownership of the town house back through a convoluted series of holding companies and, with this information, they had alerted the FBI. The assistant director of the New York office of the bureau had ordered the police to stop everything until an FBI forensic squad could get to the scene. He had been trying to raise his boss on the car radio just as Ritsczik and Lynch had stepped into the garage elevators.

Lynch followed Ritsczik carefully as they picked their way through the carnage. All that remained of the front door was a couple of shattered chunks of wood attached to the cast iron hinges. The hallway looked as though a bomb had exploded. Every square inch was pockmarked with bullet holes or scarred by shrapnel. In the doorway to the living room there was a large maroon patch on the beige carpet. There was another patch a couple of meters behind it. Farther down the hallway, in front of the door to what had been Janice's room, there was an even bigger puddle of dried blood. Her room was a shambles, with a ragged line of bullet holes leaving an ugly pattern around three walls. But there was no blood.

"We found three of these," said a small, wiry man with glasses and a dark suit. He was wearing transparent plastic gloves and holding what looked like a scorched aerosol container by a pair of long forceps.

"Stun grenade," Lynch said.

"Precisely," said the FBI forensic officer. "American made. Newer model. Repeater. Seven bangs, seven flashes."

"Whoever used these obviously knew what he was doing," Lynch said. "You've got seven seconds to go in and clean up while they're going off. The people inside have no idea what's happening. Two grenades to paralyze the opposition in the hallway, another to shut up anybody in the bedroom. Easy."

"Who the hell are we dealing with here?" There was a note of incredulity in Ritsczik's voice.

Lynch had lost count of the number of times he'd been asked that question in the past two weeks.

"People who work the same way we do," he said. "Maximum violence, minimum time."

"But," Ritsczik added, "they wanted the girl alive?"

"Oh yes," Lynch said softly. His face was stony except for the tiniest flutter of a nerve in his lower jaw to betray the tension building inside. "It isn't her they really want. It's me. They know I'll come after her. They're flushing me into the open. I'm next."

Ritsczik studied Lynch for a long time. The quiet, self-contained Briton seemed lost in another world.

"Excuse me," said the busy little man from forensics. "There's something else."

"What?" Ritsczik asked almost absently.

"This," said the man. He held up a small plastic bag containing a stubby screwdriver with a shiny red plastic handle and what looked like a smear of dried blood along the shaft.

"I think we have an excellent set of prints on this one," he said.

"Promise me you'll wait to see what the prints turn up?"

Lynch looked away. It was late afternoon and they were back in Ritsczik's office at Federal Plaza. The screwdriver handle was under examination as they spoke and the first prints were expected within hours. The moment they had the prints they would run them through the FBI's computer files, the most comprehensive police files of their kind in the world. A fax of the prints would be sent to Sir Malcolm Porter in London and to Interpol

within twenty-four hours. But none of that was any good to
Lynch. There was no guarantee that the prints came from a
convicted felon or anyone who had had even the vaguest brush
with the law. It was more precious time down the drain. The
kidnappers would get in touch at some point, he knew. In their
time, on their terms.

He needed an edge—he wanted Victor Flannery. He had
spent an hour running his tired eyes over the file the bureau
had compiled on Flannery so far, studying the pictures carefully.
The graduation shot from police college. The citation for bravery
in his role in disarming a holdup man. The more recent, grainier
shots taken by telephoto showing Flannery leaving his modest
house in Queens, then outside the Algonquin Furnished Apartments in Englewood, and all the others . . . Lynch had a feeling:
Flannery was a key. Maybe not the big key, but he would get
them through the first door.

"When we have an ID on the prints we'll have more to go
on," Ritsczik continued. "Hey, we're building a case. My guys
are going over all those rented apartments now. If we can es-
tablish a link between the past occupants of just one of those
apartments and the guy whose prints are on the screwdriver,
we've got something we can sweat Flannery with. If we can tie
Victor Flannery in with the town house, we've got him. Twenty-
four hours. Whaddaya say?"

After Lynch thought about it for a moment, he nodded. He
was exhausted and he wanted a night's sleep before he put his
new plan into action.

"We've got a place on Long Island," Ritsczik said. "I'll have
a couple of my guys go with you. Nobody will know you're there
except us."

Lynch shook his head.

"I work better on my own. Then I know there's no security
problem."

Ritsczik shrugged. "Where will you be?"

"Don't call me . . ." He left the rest unsaid.

Lynch left Federal Plaza on foot and walked half a block before
flagging a cab. He told the driver to take him to Bloomingdale's.
He walked in the main entrance on Lexington Avenue, took
an elevator up to the second floor, took an escalator back down

to the ground floor, and walked out the back door onto Third Avenue. He was sure Ritsczik would have him followed. He would have done the same. And New York City is one of the easiest places in the world to follow somebody. The crowds make it easy. There was no way Lynch could know who was following him and whether he'd shaken him loose. All he could do was try. There was one thing in his favor. Whoever was following him would have to be on foot. There was no way anybody could follow in a car with any degree of reliability. Not in Manhattan traffic.

As soon as he came out of Bloomingdale's he jumped on the first bus he saw stopped at the curbside and taking on passengers. He had no idea where it was going; it didn't matter. It was going uptown, to Riverdale. He counted eight stops, then got off, walked a block west until he could flag another cab, and headed back downtown. He got off at Times Square, walked quickly through the teeming crowds to Forty-second Street, and paid $7.50 to get into a porno theater called the Skin Bin. He took a seat at the back of the tiny, blackened auditorium and watched twenty minutes of something called *Porky Park*, a lurid, grainy film in which a series of young women passing through a small park obligingly engaged in sexual acts with a nude male statue that appeared unable to suppress its innate priapism. He was unable to detect any subplot because he was too busy watching the theater's two exits. Nobody followed.

When he left he walked slowly east toward Madison Avenue, stopping every few minutes and turning conspicuously to scan the faces behind him. A few people glanced at him strangely and gave him a wide berth as they passed, but nobody ducked for cover. Nobody's eyes flashed that tiny semaphore of concern that might give them away. Lynch decided he'd done enough. He walked another half dozen blocks along Madison Avenue, stopped at a pharmacy to pick up a few toiletries, then ducked over to Park Avenue and into the Drake Hotel, where he took a room for the night. The first thing Lynch did when he closed the door to his room was to call the Frobisher Private Hospital in Minneapolis and ask to speak to Bono. He was told that Mr. Bono had discharged himself that morning. Lynch smiled. That was all he'd wanted to know. He thought of calling Halloran but decided against it. If he had been followed they could put a tap on his phone within minutes of knowing his room number. Lynch took his jacket and shoes off, set the radio alarm, lay on the bed, and tried hard not to think about what might be happening to Janice right at that moment. Exhaustion overwhelmed him like a black tide.

If he'd only known, Lynch could have been asleep an hour earlier. The two agents who had followed him in relays sighed a joint sigh of relief and then called the information in to Ritsczik's office. Ritsczik was already in bed asleep at his apartment but the deputy director took the call. The agents settled themselves down for a long night, one in the fire stairs on Lynch's floor, the other in an office downstairs where the hotel detective brewed up a fresh pot of coffee, only too happy to assist the FBI. The tap went onto Lynch's room phone three minutes later, connected back to a tape recorder in a room at Federal Plaza. The recorder was one of four in operation that night, all monitored by a single agent. When Lynch next picked up the phone a red light would flash on the recorder. The agent would turn up the volume and then update the deputy director, who was under instructions to wake Ritsczik the moment Lynch started moving again.

Lynch didn't budge until the alarm went off at ten o'clock. It took him a minute to clear his head. His mouth tasted foul and he knew he smelled bad. He undressed, stepped into the bathroom, and stared with cold detachment at the sixty-year-old man who looked back at him. After a shave and a long hot shower he checked himself in the mirror again and estimated he'd got the age down to at least fifty. He dressed, left the unused toiletries in his room, stepped outside into the corridor, and walked to the elevators. Once downstairs he walked quickly across the lobby and had the doorman summon a cab.

"Flushing Meadow," he told the driver, and settled back for the ride.

"Got an address?" the cabbie asked as he pulled out into the pandemonium of Manhattan traffic.

"Yeah," Lynch said.

"Is it a secret?"

"Shea Stadium."

The cabbie drove in silence for a minute.

"What's on at Shea Stadium this time a'night?"

"Nothing, I hope."

"Oh."

The driver never said another word until he dropped Lynch off.

"Enjoy the game," he said, and drove away, leaving Lynch standing alone at the deserted gateway to the big blue and white bowl of Shea Stadium.

Lynch looked around but saw no one and nothing suspicious among the light passing traffic. There was a bitter wind blowing across College Point from Long Island. He turned up the collar of his jacket, jammed his hands in his pants pockets, and started walking briskly north toward the point. Across Flushing Bay on his left he could see the big jets landing and taking off at La Guardia Airport. Beyond that was the glamorous, glittering nighttime spectacle of Manhattan. One bawdy, jeweled phallus after another, competing to see which was the mightiest monument to capitalism. To his right was the Flushing Civic Airport, small, quiet, and deserted.

Lynch walked for half an hour, going deeper and deeper into the dark wasteland that flanked the neck of the bay. The streets got narrower, darker, and more threatening as he wound his way down to the waterside. The traffic thinned out until there were was only an occasional passing car. Lynch felt vulnerable. He wasn't carrying a gun or a weapon of any kind. Only his hands and feet. In a city where seventeen-year-old crack dealers have automatic weapons, it might not be enough. He felt not only vulnerable but exposed. That was the fatigue working against him, he knew. Seven hours' sleep in four days wasn't enough. He forced it out of his mind.

Since leaving Shea Stadium, Lynch hadn't passed another soul on foot. This wasn't a part of town where people took an after-dinner stroll. But he knew where he was going. After a few more minutes he came to a line of what looked like deserted, derelict warehouses. At the far end of the warehouses was a building that had once been the waterfront offices of the Polish-American Shipping Line. The shipping line had long since gone out of business and the warehouses and offices had served a variety of uses. Most recently the office block had been turned into a private club.

There was a big, potholed parking lot with a dozen cars at the side of the club. A single weak yellow light spilled onto the sidewalk. Lynch settled himself in the shadows of the warehouse opposite and waited. He could see a green-edged glass panel over the club door, lit from behind to display a crudely painted harp beneath an arch of block letters that said CELTIC ASSOCIATION. Underneath, in smaller letters, it said MEMBERS ONLY. Lynch knew the club was a favorite haunt for Noraid supporters. And every Thursday and Friday night, when he wasn't on duty, Victor Flannery could be found here. The FBI file had told Lynch everything he needed to know. Flannery would supply the rest.

It turned out to be a long, cold wait. The hours ticked slowly by, punctuated by the opening of the door as drinkers left the club in a haze of smoke and boozy bonhomie to go to their cars and drive home. It was almost three in the morning, there were only two cars left, and Lynch was bitterly cold. Even though it was early April, winter seemed reluctant to yield to spring. His tiredness only made it worse. No matter how much he rubbed his hands and jiggled his legs he couldn't keep the cold at bay. Somewhere behind that door, upstairs on the second floor where the lights and the occasional burst of laughter and raised voices spilled out into the dark, Flannery was warm and comfortable, full of beer and whiskey and sentiment. He could stay there till the sun came up. But so could Lynch. He had spent all his adult life in military service. He was used to waiting. All the cold and discomfort simply gave him a focus for the tension and anger that had been building inside him for two weeks. Victor Flannery would do nicely as the focus.

Lynch was beginning to wonder if the FBI had got it wrong and if Flannery was even there at all. He could have been on duty. It was a chance Lynch had elected to take. Around three-thirty the lights inside the club went out, the street door opened, and Flannery came out in the company of another man. The cop was wearing street clothes and a flat cap but Lynch recognised the blunt, broad features in the dim streetlight. The other man reached inside to switch off the stair light and set the security locks and the alarm system, then slammed the door with a solid metallic thud. The two walked across the parking lot together for security. Lynch assumed Flannery's pal was the barman and had the night's take on him. It would be the logical time and place for a snatch. The two men stood talking beside a green Toyota for ten minutes, their breath frosting the cold night air. Lynch could see the barman was impatient to leave but a long night's drinking had immunized Flannery from cold, fatigue, and any idea of polite suggestion; he wouldn't let the man go. Finally the barman decided he'd had enough and pulled his elbow free from Flannery's restraining hand.

"I gotta home to go to," Lynch heard the words of protest from across the street. "So do you. Be a good guy, go home to your wife and kids, Vic. Tell them who you are. Maybe they'll throw a reunion party." The barman climbed into the driver's seat and closed the door. Flannery looked bemused. The Toyota's engine started and the tailpipe belched a boiling cloud of fumes. Flannery tapped on the driver's window and leaned down to say something. The Toyota pulled away, bumped across the potholed asphalt, and turned up the street. Flannery watched it until the taillights disappeared and the sound of the engine faded into the distance. Still he stood there, as though expecting the barman to change his mind and turn around and come back. Finally Flannery seemed to realize he was alone. He shrugged, fumbled in his jacket pocket for his car keys, and wandered over to the last remaining car in the lot, a dark blue Mercury.

He felt only two hard blows before he blacked out. The first was the heel of Lynch's right hand as it hit him at the base of the skull. The second was the roof of the Mercury as it leaped up and hit him in the face. The impact of his face against the car roof broke his nose and split his upper dental plate in two. He was already unconscious as he slid down the side of the car, leaving thick streaks of blood and mucus on the car windows. Lynch grunted as he took Flannery's full weight. The cop was heavier than he looked. He wasn't a big man, only average height, but he must have weighed anywhere from 220 to 230 pounds. Then Lynch heard him choking.

"Shit." He let Flannery slump to the ground, then rolled him onto his side and began fishing out the bloody fragments of dental plate and teeth that were threatening to choke the cop to death before Lynch could talk to him. He cleared Flannery's mouth and throat as best he could and then the cop retched and disgorged the contents of his stomach over Lynch's hand and shoes. Everything Flannery had drunk and eaten in the past eight hours flooded onto the ground. The rank stench of warm vomit and stomach acid gusted into Lynch's face.

"Jesus Christ . . ." He stepped back and left Flannery to finish puking. After a moment the vomiting stopped and Flannery lay on the ground in his own mess, moaning softly. Lynch quickly went through his pockets, checked his wallet and police badge, and took the cumbersome .38 the cop carried in a shoulder holster beneath his brown winter coat. He looked around and found the car keys in a puddle of water beside the car, used them to open the trunk, then grabbed hold of Flannery's feet and dragged him roughly around to the back of the car. He reached down, grabbed the cop beneath the armpits, and hefted him up to roll him forward into the trunk.

Just as he started to roll forward Flannery grabbed on to the rim of the trunk with both hands and lashed out behind with both feet. The blow caught Lynch square in the crotch. The brutal, searing pain lanced up from his scrotum into the pit of his gut and took his breath away. Lynch staggered backward and fell. Flannery had been shamming about how badly hurt he was and had recovered enough to fight back. He rushed forward with the roar of an enraged animal and aimed a savage kick at Lynch's head. Lynch rolled and felt the cop's boot hiss past his ear. If the kick had connected, Lynch knew, it would have cracked his skull. He forced himself up onto one knee, swung up his right fist, and jammed the .38 into the cop's face.

"Sonovabitch." The cop stopped and patted his empty holster in dismay.

Lynch struggled to his feet.

"Get in the trunk," he gasped through the sickening waves of pain that kept flooding up from his groin, threatening to engulf him. "Or I'll blow your fucking head off where you stand."

The cop stood his ground. "Whaddaya want?"

Lynch heard more defiance than fear in the voice. He was getting some idea what a dangerous man Victor Flannery could be.

The Smith and Wesson .38-caliber revolver was one of the

older models and it had an unguarded hammer. He pulled the hammer back and pressed the muzzle against Flannery's forehead.

"Now!" The word came out like a bark and at the same time Lynch gave the gun a vicious jab, forcing Flannery's head to snap back.

It worked. Flannery knew his gun better than the man holding it. He knew that the slightest jolt could loosen the hammer and he began to edge backward toward the car.

"You want money?"

"Get in the trunk." Lynch managed to put just enough edge into his voice to convince Flannery that the man holding the gun was at the limit of his control.

"I can get twenty grand in an hour."

"Get in."

"Cocksucker . . ." The cop turned and climbed slowly into the trunk. Lynch slammed the lid hard down on top of him, glanced around to make sure they were still alone, then hurried around to the driver's seat and started the engine. He didn't have to worry that Flannery might suffocate. They weren't going far. He drove out of the parking lot, toward the wharves, and traveled the four blocks between the warehouses and the water-side before he saw what he was looking for. A single loading dock at the end of a disused jetty. He stopped the car, cut the engine, and went back around to the trunk to get Flannery. This time he didn't give the tough Irish-American cop any chances. He opened the trunk at arm's length and stepped back the moment he felt the lock turn.

"Get out."

He didn't have to say it twice. Flannery suffered from claus-trophobia. If he was going to die he wanted to die in the open. He got out of the trunk a little too quickly for Lynch's liking. Lynch cocked the gun again.

"You can walk away from here tonight," he said. "Or you can join the rest of the shit in the East River. It's up to you."

"Whaddaya want?" Flannery's voice sounded even stronger. Now he knew the man with the gun wanted to negotiate, there was still a chance . . .

"Who is Hennessy working for?"

Lynch saw from the look of shock on the cop's face that he

had hit a bull's-eye. It was a gamble and it didn't work. Instead of shaking the cop's tongue loose, it had exactly the opposite effect. Flannery knew now that he wasn't dealing with a mugger or some hood he'd put away for some petty crime or some thug working a revenge contract. He knew now that it was political. And he knew he wasn't going to give anything away. Even if it did cost him his life. Lynch had come up against the deepest, most unshakable loyalty Flannery possessed. A loyalty ingrained in him since birth and going back for generations. A loyalty that superseded everything else. There was no way Victor Flannery was going to betray the Cause.

"Who are you, where are you from?" the cop asked. His words sounded slurred and slushy through his smashed nose and bloodied mouth. But, Lynch noted, whether from fear or adrenaline or the emptying of his guts, Flannery wasn't drunk anymore. He was stone-cold sober and he wasn't going to give another inch.

"British intelligence," Lynch said. Another tack. Another gamble.

Flannery sniffed and wiped the blood off his chin with the back of his hand. He seemed to buy it. He nodded and looked around for a moment.

"Nice night huh? Still a bit cool though. Be nicer toward the end of the month.

"I thought you sounded different," Flannery continued. "British intelligence, huh? Imagine that. Big time. James Bond, huh?" He paused and looked around again. "Well," he added after a moment's reflection, "you can suck my dick before I tell you anything, Jimmy."

Lynch smiled grimly. There were times, he knew, when certain things had to be done . . . the old-fashioned way. He lowered the gun and stepped toward Flannery with deceptive slowness. Flannery tensed, but even though he knew it was coming he wasn't ready for it. Lynch turned slightly and his left foot caught Flannery just under the point of the chin. The cop reeled backward toward the water's edge and Lynch followed him and slammed the barrel of the pistol hard against the left side of his head. He grunted with pain and went down on all fours. Lynch hit him again, hard, on the back of the neck. Flannery fell to the ground, out cold.

When he regained consciousness some five minutes later, Victor Flannery was hanging by his feet in the dark, over the East River. He could feel the cold metal links from a length of chain biting into his ankles, and his hands were tied tightly behind his back with a rag. The skyline of Manhattan glimmered in the distance, upside down. A large aircraft with its red wing lights flew, upside down, into La Guardia. The pain around his ankles was excruciating. He tried to loosen the rag around his wrists but it only seemed to get tighter. A sudden wave of fear and nausea swept through him. He was going to die.

"You're a very boring man, Victor."

He could just make out a shadowy figure standing on the edge of the jetty, about two meters away. It sounded like the limey.

"Your friends think you're boring. I think you're boring. You're boring because you're stupid, Victor. You want to die for the Cause, don't you? You want to die for the Cause because you think it's a noble way to die, don't you, Victor? But there's nothing very noble about this . . . is there? This isn't a very noble way to die at all, is it, Victor?"

Flannery looked around. The chain reached up from his ankles to a hook in the end of a loading derrick and then disappeared.

"You're also very heavy Victor . . ." Suddenly he fell. It could only have been a few feet and then the chain bit into his ankles and held him again and he screamed with the pain.

"You see, I'm holding the other end of the chain, Victor," the voice resumed. There was silence for a moment while Flannery swung back and forth above the black, sluggish water.

Lynch wasn't a sadistic man. All his professional life he'd been schooled in the art of the quick kill: fast, ruthless, efficient. Maximum violence, minimum time. Then, there were times such as this, when it all reverted back to the most primitive of contests between two determined men. There was nothing noble in it. Nothing dignified. Just work. Dirty, bloody work.

"I'm sure you've heard the stories about the East River, eh, Victor? About all the acid and chemicals and toxic waste that's been dumped in there over the years. You've got a few cuts on you too. A few abrasions. Hate to think what might happen if you fall in the water. Some of those cuts might get infected, eh Victor?"

Flannery started screaming. He didn't intend to talk and so he knew he would have to die. So, he started screaming, in the vain, forlorn hope that somebody, somewhere, might hear him. He screamed with such force and such fear that his voice seemed to assume an eerie power and reverberate around the dark, empty warehouses and then carry right on across the river to bounce off the buildings on the other side.

Lynch let the chain go. Flannery plummeted into the water and the screaming stopped. Lynch grabbed on tight again and held. He didn't want Flannery going too deep and getting snagged on something down there. He counted to ten and then hauled on the chain. It was hard work without a pulley; the rusty links of the chain squeaked and scraped over the protesting steel hook one at a time until Flannery's head and shoulders emerged, streaming, from the filthy water. There was no shamming this time. Flannery was hurting. The water poured out of him in rivers and he choked and sobbed and flapped weakly at the end of the chain like a dying fish.

It wasn't just the chemical filth and gallons of human waste that made the East River deadly. It was the temperature. Winter had barely relaxed its grip. Six weeks earlier there had been ice on these wharves. The salt water would still only be a few degrees above freezing point. Flannery's whole body began to shudder as the icy wind buffeted in from the Sound, cutting through his sodden clothing, adding to his misery. Lynch knew Flannery could die from hypothermia at the end of the chain before he drowned. There wasn't much in it now. Another ten minutes and the shivering would be replaced by a deadly, creeping numbness that Flannery would welcome in place of the cold and pain.

"There won't be any funeral for you, Victor," Lynch went on, his voice as cold and dispassionate as the night wind. "No IRA gun salute over your coffin. They won't even find your body. There's enough chain on the end of your feet to keep you down there till the chemicals turn you to sludge. They'll never know what happened to you, Victor."

Lynch let him swing for two long minutes, then allowed the chain to slip a fraction.

Flannery let out a strangled cry of pure terror. The pain was beyond anything he had ever known. He had never dreamed that cold could cause so much pain. He could have faced a bullet, something quick. This was different.

"It's nearly time, Victor," Lynch went on. "I'm getting tired. I don't know if I could pull you in now, even if I wanted to. Do you want to die like this?"

Flannery started sobbing.

"Pull me in," he begged weakly. "Pull me in, for God's sake, I'll tell you, I'll tell you . . ."

"Tell me now, Victor," Lynch said.

"Brian Hennessy . . . his name is Brian . . . Hennessy . . . that's all I know." Flannery's breath came in painful, shuddering gasps. "You know how it works, for Christ's sake. We're only told what we need to know . . ."

It was something. It was the most Flannery thought he could trade to end his suffering. Hennessy was already out of the country, he knew. Hennessy was safe.

"I know his name," Lynch lied. "Who does he work for?"

"Jesus . . ." Flannery's voice was growing hoarse and weak. "I don't know . . . he came in . . . eighteen months ago . . . he's IRA active service . . . that's all I know . . . I swear to God . . ."

A voice barked out of the darkness.

"That's enough, Lynch, pull him in."

It was Ritsczik. A set of headlights clicked onto high beam and bathed Lynch and his tortured prisoner at the end of the jetty in a swath of brilliant light. Lynch saw three dark shapes get out of the car and hurry toward him. Another pair of headlights appeared between the warehouses and drove slowly toward the jetty. Though he didn't know it at the time, they had lost him en route to Shea Stadium and only found him again by staking out the Celtic Association club. They had followed him from there. Now, John Ritsczik had decided he'd let things go far enough.

"Ah sweet Jesus . . . get me down . . . for Christ's sake get me down . . . Jesus . . . Jesus . . . Jesus." A babbling stream of fear and relief poured out of Flannery's shivering, shaking body. He had no idea who the approaching men were but he knew they represented his salvation.

"Dammit Lynch, don't you ever sleep?" Ritsczik grumbled as

he hurried to the end of the jetty. Lynch waited till he was within touching distance, then let go of the chain. Flannery plummeted into the freezing black depths of the East River with a scream.

"Jesus . . ." Ritsczik gasped in stunned disbelief. He turned to the two agents behind him. "Go in after him," he bellowed. "Pull him out."

The two men hesitated. The river looked as cold and as evil as it was.

"Go in after him," Ritsczik yelled again, louder this time. He turned briefly toward the two men who had just arrived at the end of the jetty in the second car. "Bring lights . . ." he yelled. "Call the rescue squad, for Christ's sake." Then he tore off his overcoat, his jacket, and his shoes and began clambering down the jetty toward the spot where the ripples and bubbles still boiled. The two agents reluctantly followed his lead.

"Goddammit, Lynch," Ritsczik yelled back up at him. "If he dies I swear to God I'll have you on a murder charge." Then the director of the FBI's New York office turned and leaped into the water where the bubbles were just beginning to disperse.

Brave man, Lynch thought as he walked quickly back to the street and Victor Flannery's car. But then, it was exactly what he expected from John Ritsczik. He had counted on it.

There was one reason and one reason only why Lynch dropped Victor Flannery into the East River. He needed to keep the FBI occupied long enough to allow him to get back to Chesapeake and the *American Endeavor* and then the sanctuary of international waters. If that meant Victor Flannery had to be sacrificed then that was Flannery's bad luck. Besides, Flannery had revealed just enough. He had yielded the other half of a name. The crooked New York cop had elected to play the role of a pawn in a bigger, more dangerous game. He should have expected to be used by both sides.

"I don't think we're supposed to let you leave, sir."

It was one of the FBI agents who had stayed with the cars. Lynch had climbed behind the wheel of Flannery's Mercury and started the engine. The FBI man had rolled forward in his blue sedan to block Lynch's escape.

"What's your name, son?"

The agent had fair hair and freckles. He looked about nineteen. Lynch expected he was a little older.

"Beatty, sir . . . and you're still not leaving."

"Mr. Beatty, I'm sure you're a good man," Lynch said. "Don't die unnecessarily." He raised the .38 and fired a shot into the rear passenger window just behind the agent's head. It had the effect Lynch wanted. The agent ducked out of sight and then a second later the driver's door flew open as Beatty threw himself out and drew his own gun.

Lynch emptied the five-round revolver of its remaining four shells. Two went into the engine block of Agent Beatty's car. Two went into the engine block of the other car. The agent on the jetty trying to help his partners pull a drowning man out of the East River began running back toward the street with his gun drawn. Lynch threw the Mercury into a shrieking reverse and then slammed it into drive and stepped on the gas. The car catapulted forward, bumped heavily up onto the sidewalk, and scraped between the warehouse and the disabled FBI car. Lynch felt something snag on the front right fender and swore. The rear window disappeared in a blizzard of disintegrating glass as a bullet from an FBI gun smashed into the car. A millisecond later the windshield exploded outward as another bullet came though the back.

There was a screech of tearing metal as the car leaped free and accelerated up the street, the front bumper from the FBI car clattering and banging against the road as it trailed from the front of the Mercury. He heard another last volley of shots behind him, then nothing. He wrenched the car around the first corner, stopped, jumped out, tore the snagged bumper free, then jumped back into the car and drove fast toward Flushing Airport. At the airport he turned north again toward the Bronx-Whitestone Bridge and a few minutes later was cruising along the Cross Bronx Expressway, squinting with tearing eyes into the rushing wind as it howled through the shattered windshield.

Lynch prayed that he wouldn't pass a cop car. It was a little after four-thirty in the morning, traffic was at its lightest, and if a police cruiser saw him driving without front and rear windows they would pull him over. He passed Washington Heights and crossed the George Washington Bridge into Hackensack. A few minutes later he entered Passaic and decided he couldn't push his luck any further. He pulled into a quiet residential street, parked the Mercury, and hurried away on foot. Two blocks away he hot-wired a Dodge pickup and drove south toward Newark, looking for the New Jersey Turnpike and the fast lane to Washington.

Seven and a half hours later he stopped briefly at the main gate to Fort Eustis as the guard checked his authorization from General Drewe, the commanding officer, then waved him through. It was only when he arrived at the high-security entrance to the presidential marina that he realized something had changed. As soon as the marine sergeant had checked Lynch's authorization he signaled to his comrade in the gatehouse to get on the phone.

"Mr. Lynch, would you mind stepping out of the car for a moment please?"

"I'm sorry," Lynch answered amiably, "I'm a little tired. I've had . . . rather a busy week. I'm sure we can settle any questions later. Now, please . . ."

The marine sergeant wasn't about to be swayed. "Would you mind just stepping out of the car please, sir." Lynch saw the marine's hand go toward the flap on the pistol holster at his hip. He gunned the Dodge and, with a roar, the two-ton four-wheel-drive leaped forward into the steel mesh gates. The forged steel bar holding the gates shut was ripped free of its mountings, the gates flew open, and Lynch screamed down the narrow road that wound prettily between the beech trees toward the dockside. A rash of deafening clangs raked the back of the Dodge as the marine sergeant emptied his pistol.

By this time Lynch was close to utter exhaustion. The drive from New York to Chesapeake had been a nightmare. Every time he saw a highway patrol car or a state trooper he expected to be stopped. Now, he had only one immediate purpose and he was going to pursue it as long as there was breath in his body, whoever got in his way. If he could only make the safety of the *American Endeavor* they could hold off the military with threats and promises while Halloran made a few calls, and somehow . . . somehow they would pick up the pieces later.

The neat whitewashed stones at the roadside flashed past in a blur. The road forked. To the left was the road leading to the President's yacht and another security gate. He saw men running in the distance. Cars moving. In the rearview mirror he caught a glimpse of a jeep with armed men following him. He took the right fork and a moment later the Dodge screeched to a halt at the waterside and Lynch leaped out. He ran toward the edge of the dock, eyes staring wildly. Behind him he could hear the roar of approaching motor vehicles and men shouting at him to stop.

But the *American Endeavor* was gone. Her berth was empty. There was nowhere for him to go.

Lynch slowed to a few halting, exhausted steps and then abruptly sat down at the water's edge, put his head in his hands, and closed his aching eyes. All around him he could hear vehicles screeching to a halt and the thud of heavy boots running toward him. He was too tired even to raise his head, let alone his hands.

There was a rattle of automatic weapons being readied and then silence. Lynch took a deep breath. He would open his eyes in a minute, he thought. Just another minute. They ached so badly and it felt so good to keep them shut and look into benign, beautiful blackness. He thought of Janice for a moment and the noise around him faded like the whisper of a distant sea. He saw her face, and a smile tugged faintly at his lips.

He heard fresh footsteps approaching, crisp, smart, authoritative. They stopped just to one side. Lynch sighed and looked up into the handome face of a gray-haired man wearing the uniform of a two-star marine general.

"Mr. Lynch," he drawled. "I'm General Drewe, commanding officer of Fort Eustis . . . and you are under military arrest."

7 The President Requests

When Tom O'Donnell had hung up the phone after speaking with Brian Hennessy, four nights earlier, he had been so charged with adrenaline he was unable to sleep. Instead, he made himself a cup of tea, stiffened it with a splash of whiskey, and sat in his armchair and thought for a full hour before making two more phone calls. The first had been to Eamonn Docherty and concerned Billy McCormack. That had now been taken care of.

The second call had been to a number connected to a tape recorder in a tiny, windowless room inside the Iranian embassy in Helsinki, Finland. There was nothing else in the room except a desk, a chair, a telephone, and an answering machine that did nothing except tape incoming calls. Once a week a member of the embassy staff took the three-hour tape and replaced it with a fresh cassette. The tape went into a simple, bubble-pack envelope and then into the weekly diplomatic pouch to Tehran. Sometimes the tape would be blank. Sometimes there would be only one or two messages. Sometimes, especially during times of crisis, it would be almost full. The calls never lasted more than twenty or thirty seconds and could be in Farsi, Arabic, French, German, English, or any one of a dozen other languages.

When the tape arrived in Tehran the messages would be translated first into Farsi, the language of Iran, and then transcribed into Farsi first and Arabic second. The translation and transcribing processes were monitored at every stage by a uniformed officer of the Revolutionary Guards. When the transcript had been read by the mullah in charge of the ministry a call would be made and a courier would come to collect the tape and the Arabic copy of the transcript. The courier would carry both to his master, Abu Musa, in his villa at Qolhak in the pleasant, green northern suburbs of Tehran. Musa would read the transcript and then play back the tape, knowing that both had been scrutinized first by his hosts. It was part of the arrangement.

Musa had a dozen different telephone numbers connected to tape recorders in a dozen different cities around the world. Only three were in Iranian embassies: Helsinki, Prague, and Belgrade. The Iranians didn't even know about the other seven. Only Musa knew them all, and he changed numbers and locations frequently. This simple, flexible, and highly effective telephone network was an integral part of the terrorist organization he called Red Jihad, after the socialist-Islamic revolution. Musa had founded Red Jihad after breaking away from the PLO in 1983, following Yasir Arafat's expulsion from Lebanon by the Israeli army. Musa was one of many strong and charismatic PLO lieutenants disaffected by Arafat's leadership; when the PLO teetered on the verge of disintegration, with several lieutenants challenging Arafat's authority, Musa saw the opportunity to pursue his own ambitions and took it. When he left, he took two hundred followers with him, and in the two years that followed he was able to strengthen and streamline his organization, unmolested by Arafat, who had plenty of problems of his own within the PLO.

The name Musa assumed for his organization had never been more than a flag of convenience. When it suited him, he could change it. He had already mounted several operations under other names to confuse the intelligence services of the West. In the beginning he had found a sponsor in Assad of Syria, but Assad had proved a temperamental and unreliable host. Musa transferred Red Jihad's loyalties briefly to Hezbollah, and in 1985 and 1986 his organization was responsible for the shipment of 40 percent of the heroin produced in the Beqaa Valley to the streets of Europe and North America. But he had wearied of Hezbollah's fanaticism and had gradually drifted into the Iranian camp during the post-Khomeini era of rationalization. With

Hezbollah increasingly difficult to control, the new leadership in Iran saw the potential in Red Jihad to engage in a little arms-length mischief around the world.

If there was any one philosophy Musa and his disciples could have been said to follow faithfully, it was self-enrichment. The Palestinian cause came second, Islam third, and socialism a distant fourth. The only reason Musa paid lip service to socialism at all was because the Soviets were so generous with their supplies of arms. They had never been generous with money but, despite the era of *glasnost*, some of the diehards in the Kremlin still believed in the export of revolution to the Third World. And Mikhail Gorbachev couldn't know where every consignment of Kalashnikovs and SA-7's went when they left the Soviet Union.

The loyalties of Red Jihad operated very much according to the financial and political necessities of the day. Sponsorship by the Iranians didn't preclude Musa from taking other contracts, as long as his activities didn't directly prejudice Tehran's interests. Besides, Musa always had more than one fall-back position in case his current situation should prove unreliable. He had taken a leaf from Arafat's book and kept half a dozen houses scattered around the world, including one in Iraq, one in Egypt, one in Morocco, and another in Spain. It amused Musa that on one occasion his organization had even worked for their former master, Arafat, arranging the assassination of yet another mistrusted lieutenant within the PLO. It had been doubly ironic because the job for Arafat came a year after they had threatened to kill him as a traitor to the revolution. But that had been more for the benefit of the loony left in the Arab world; Arafat had never been a man to hold a grudge, when it suited him. Palestinians were, above all, pragmatists. They had acquired a genius for survival following their loss of statehood and displacement from their homeland. If necessary, they would survive for another two thousand years without a country to call their own. Indeed, as Musa had often reflected, Palestinians had much in common with their implacable enemies, the Jews.

There were only two items on the tape from Helsinki when Musa's courier arrived at the villa. As usual he read the transcript first and then played back the cassette. It was a beautiful day outside and so Musa walked out into a sunny courtyard with the cassette player and sat down at a picnic table to listen. He plucked a fat orange from a full fruit bowl, peeled it, and ate it quietly as he listened. The first call was from the leader of a three-man cell he had lying dormant in Copenhagen. They were running short of funds. Musa made a mental note to send another five thousand U.S. dollars with the instruction that it was to last the three of them another two months. Money was never a problem for Musa. Apart from the subsidy and the free accommodations he received from the Iranians, he had other income as well as several million U.S. dollars for his own use in half a dozen bank accounts around the world. The arms trade had developed into a lucrative sideline, especially considering the generous discounts the Soviets gave him, which he never passed on to his clients in Africa and Indochina. And he was always happy to act for the Saudis, the Iraqis, and the Jordanians in their purchase of British, French, and American arms, in exchange for a commission, which he took in cash or arms, according to his needs at the time.

The second call was from Tom O'Donnell. This was the call Musa had been waiting for although it would never have shown on his face. The call lasted two seconds and comprised four words.

"We have to meet."

That was all.

Musa nodded, stroking his dyed and impeccably trimmed beard. He was a thin, elegant man of forty-six with curly black hair worn long because it flattered him. It, too, was carefully dyed, just enough to keep the gray to a distinguished fleck at each temple. He wore a white shirt made from Italian silk, beautifully tailored cream trousers, and a pair of new espadrilles from France.

He nodded his head thoughtfully. The cartel had paid him a lot of money for this one. Five million dollars so far. Five million American dollars to wipe out Jack Halloran, every man in his unit, and anyone who was close to him. Another five million when the job was done. So far, he had been told, only two of Halloran's targeted top men had been killed, Tuckey and Bono. But the cartel had been pleased with the attack on the STC Building in New York, and its high loss of American lives. The members of the cartel were always gratified by the loss of American lives. Especially the Libyans.

The cartel consisted of three separate groups: the Libyans, the fanatical anti-American Iranian faction that supported the late Ayatollah's son, Khameini, and the Shiite militias of Lebanon. Three disparate groups united in a single, common cause. All had suffered at the hands of Jack Halloran and the activities of his special operations unit. All wanted Halloran dead and his squad stopped.

At whatever cost in American lives.

Above all else, that was the message they wanted sent to the administration in Washington. That . . . and revenge. So that even the Americans might decide it was in their national interest to disown Halloran and his squad and abandon them to their fate. And so far, their agents in the U.S. told them, it was working. Only Halloran and the Briton, Lynch, remained alive. And Halloran had been badly hurt by the deaths of so many friends and workers in his private company. Both men were in hiding, and Halloran seemed to be a hostage of his own government.

Musa congratulated himself once again on his skillful use of Tom O'Donnell. He had cultivated O'Donnell carefully over the years, in the belief that the Irish nationalist would prove useful one day. When he had called O'Donnell two years earlier and arranged a meeting in Milan, he had found the old man surprisingly receptive. O'Donnell had the men. He had dreams and plans of his own. But he had no arms and no way of getting anywhere near the amount he needed. Musa made it clear he could provide all the explosives and weaponry that O'Donnell would ever need to fulfill his ambitions. Musa understood ambition. All O'Donnell had to do in return was to provide the manpower; Musa would provide the money and the machinery.

And O'Donnell had kept his side of the bargain. Musa knew that O'Donnell had found a man, a very special kind of man. A man with a highly developed sense of purpose. A man with the skills to operate freely and effectively within the United States. A man who might appear quite ordinary and unexceptional on the surface and whose very ordinariness was his greatest weapon. That . . . and a passion for killing. A man who was not intimidated by the realities of death on the large scale. The kind of man who was at home on the battlefield, whatever form that battlefield might take. The kind of man Jack Halloran might have employed himself, Musa thought.

The four words on the tape told the Palestinian precisely what O'Donnell wanted, and Musa agreed. It was time. He decided to make a call to his people in the Sardinian port of Cagliari. It was time to release the boat. O'Donnell could have the first consignment of American arms and Czechoslovakian Semtex that had been assembled in Aden, in Southern Yemen, six months earlier. That would give Musa some good news to tell the Irishman when they met. Such a passionate, unpredictable people, the Irish. And with a surprising appetite for bloodshed. Musa smiled thinly. The British could expect a sudden, violent flare-up in the Troubles that had so long beset their little island neighbor to the west, he mused. The Palestinian sighed and finished the last segment of orange. There was still so much treachery and hatred in the world. Business was good.

BOSTON, MASSACHUSETTS, APRIL 3

This time Janice Street awakened to the stench of diesel fumes in her face. Her head pounded, inside and out. She could hear heavy machinery nearby but she couldn't see anything. Her mouth was gagged with a wad of leather held in place by a filthy piece of rag. She was lying flat on something cold and wet, she could tell that much. Her hands were pulled behind her head and when she tried to move she felt the painful tug of a pair of steel manacles around both wrists. She jiggled her hands back and forth and realized the cuffs had been fastened behind a metal pipe. She tried to pull herself up but something tugged at her ankles and she discovered there was something binding her by the feet too. She stopped struggling and waited.

She had no idea how long she had been unconscious. Her stomach felt empty and she was cold but that told her nothing. The floor swayed suddenly and she froze in terror. It swayed again. A boat, she realized. She was on a boat of some kind. She strained to hear something above the sound of thumping machinery that provided a painful syncopation to the pain in her head, but she heard nothing more. The deck moved again. A small boat, she guessed. It seemed to be susceptible to the swells. She tried to move her head and felt something rough scrape her cheek. It felt like sacking. She was tied up in the engine room of a small boat and covered from view with sacking and God knew what else.

She concentrated on breathing steadily through her nose and thought back. It was like trying to remember snatches of a nightmare. She could remember the struggle in the town house in New York. The blond bastard she had stabbed with the screwdriver. He had hit her. Twice. She remembered that much. Then there had been nothing for a long time. She thought she had been in a car at some point. She vaguely remembered trying to wake up and it was daylight and there were things moving past the windows and then somebody had shoved a pad of something medicinal in her face and she had blacked out again. Ether, she thought. Ether or chloroform. She wasn't an expert but something had been given her repeatedly to keep her unconscious while the blond bastard brought her to this boat. And now she had no sense of time and place. No sense of how many hours had passed, whether it was the middle of the day or the middle of the night. She could start to feel pins and needles in her arms. She hadn't been here that long then.

Voices. Muffled voices. Then the sound of heavy feet. They faded for a moment and suddenly they were right there, on top of her, in the room with her.

"Okay," she heard an American male voice say. "You guys are clear. Have a safe trip back to the Old Sod."

Janice struggled and tried to make a noise but she knew that nothing she could do would be heard above the noise of the engine room. The voices vanished abruptly and she heard the feet receding.

Up on deck the two men from customs and immigration clambered nimbly back onto the dockside. It had been a routine inspection. Nobody tried to smuggle drugs out of the United

States. The fishing trawler with the weathered, rust-streaked hull and flaky green-and-white superstructure checked out. Her registration papers were in order and her three-man crew had been in port three days, buying fresh fuel and supplies. The man from immigration handed back the three freshly stamped passports for Liam McKee, his first mate, and his deckhand, wished them bon voyage again, and followed his colleague from customs up the iron ladder. They could never have known that the vessel had left Ireland with only two crewmen aboard.

McKee stepped into the wheelhouse, took the wheel from Brian Hennessy, who knew nothing about boats, and revved the engines while his deckhand pulled in the bow and stern lines tossed to him by the longshoreman on the wharf. The trawler eased away from the dock and McKee brought her around and began heading past the big container ships for the main channel. It was a surprisingly warm spring evening in Boston and the harbor lights had just come on as McKee guided his craft carefully out to sea with eleven tons of Atlantic cod from the Dogger Bank in the freezer below. Neither customs nor immigration were to know that it had been there for almost a month and McKee had only been hanging around offshore awaiting further instructions from a man in Ireland. Hennessy waited till they were well clear of the harbor and had started to ride the big Atlantic swells before he decided they were safe.

"Next stop, Donegal," he said. Then he patted the thick dressing on his left cheek and thought of their passenger.

Janice heard the engine room door open. She waited. There was the sound of sliding timber and then the oily sacking was snatched from her face. She squinted up from her perch on a makeshift platform between the engine room deck and the bilges and saw the gaunt, blond-haired man she had tried to kill. He was unshaven and his eyes had an unpleasant gleam. She noted, with satisfaction, the thick gauze pad taped to his face. There was a dark red smudge at its center. She hoped she'd scarred the bastard for life.

"Welcome aboard the *Ceilidh Princess*," Hennessy said in a voice silky with menace. "Dinner will be at eight . . . and if you promise to be a good girl, you can eat at the captain's table."

WASHINGTON, D.C., APRIL 3

Lynch had never expected to see the inside of the White House. It came as a sudden and unexpected elevation from his accommodation in a holding cell inside the Fort Eustis stockade. Lynch had known somebody would come for him eventually. He had no idea how long it would be or what exactly his fate might be but he knew that his status was sensitive enough to warrant special handling. He suspected he would get a fast ride out of the country so that he would not prove too much of an embarrassment to Washington or Whitehall. That would suit him. It would enable him to rejoin the operation. Somewhere, somebody was holding Janice . . . and waiting for him. Then again, the United States was an unpredictable place. If the FBI wanted him he might have to stay and go through due process before he could be released. And that could mean a year or two in a federal penitentiary. And, of course, there was always the worst possible scenario. His sponsor, Jack Halloran, was perilously close to persona non grata with this new administration. They had tried to shut his clandestine operations unit down. The President and the secretary of state might simply decide Lynch was now an outsider who knew too much ever to be released. The FBI could be shut out and Lynch turned over to the Company for "disposal." The Company was the CIA and it would be very easy for one of their dirty tricks squads to take him on a little flight somewhere over the jungles of South America, during one of their irregular runs, and drop him off at twenty-eight thousand feet.

However, none of these thoughts bothered Lynch for the first twenty-four hours of his captivity because he was asleep. There is no place quite like a jail cell for a man who wants undisturbed rest, and Lynch was grateful to be left alone. Once he had been locked behind bars nobody seemed particularly interested in him. Nobody appeared to want to question him. He took off his jacket and shoes, lay down on the cement slab bed with a wooden bench for a mattress, made a pillow of his jacket, pulled the single gray army blanket over himself, and went to sleep as though he were in the presidential suite at the Ritz. When he woke up he had no idea what time it was. They had taken his

watch, along with everything else in his pockets, and his cell
had no windows. There was only a dim twenty-four-hour light
recessed into the ceiling. His only need was to use a toilet. There
was a lavatory bowl along with a wash basin, in a corner. He
felt a little hungry but ignored it, lay back down on the wooden
bench, and let his mind wander over the incredible events of
the past week. Always he came back to the same bleak image.
Himself, squatting at the end of an empty dock, looking for a
ship that had sailed without him. Should he be surprised? he
wondered. Why wouldn't Halloran feed Lynch to the wolves if
it meant he could save his own skin?

A metal door opened and he heard footsteps. A marine MP
appeared.

"Hungry?"

Lynch nodded. "I could use a little soap first. I'd like to clean
up."

"It can be arranged." The guard's voice was neutral. It gave
nothing away. At least they weren't hostile, he noted. That was
a promising sign. Half an hour later he was escorted to the
ablutions block where he showered under the watchful eye of
another MP and began to change back into his dirty clothes.

"We can get you some fresh skivvies," the MP offered suddenly.

"Yeah." Lynch nodded. "I'd appreciate it."

The MP disappeared for a moment and a few minutes later
another guard appeared with a pair of pale green marine shorts
and a T-shirt. They had estimated him a size too big but it didn't
matter. The sleep, the shower, and the clean underwear made
him feel rejuvenated.

After Lynch had been escorted back to his cell the MP disappeared and reappeared a few minutes later with a plate full of
hot dogs and beans, a couple of slices of buttered bread, and a
mug of lukewarm milky water with a tea bag in it. The food was
plain but filling and afterward Lynch lay down on the bench
and tried to rest. He must have dozed off again because the next
thing he knew he was being shaken by a new MP and the door
to his cell was open.

"Time to roll, mister. You're leaving."

Lynch was instantly wide awake.

"What time is it?"

"Quarter of ten," the MP said. There were two guards. They escorted him back down the corridor from the holding cells and down another long, featureless corridor to another metal door that opened out onto a garage. The garage contained half a dozen MP paddy wagons and a long, dark limousine with the engine running. Lynch couldn't see who waited behind the smoky, bulletproof glass. The two MPs escorted him to the limo, opened the door, and waited for him to get in. There were two men in the front, including the driver. The backseat was occupied by a man Lynch had never seen before, a young, bald man with surprisingly delicate features.

"Get in, please, Mr. Lynch," he said. "We haven't got all night. I'm Wesley Hatten, director of the FBI."

The drive from Fort Eustis, on the shores of the Chesapeake Bay, to the White House on Pennsylvania Avenue takes an hour. It was one of the most enlightening hours of Colin Lynch's life. It was only the beginning of what was to prove a more enlightening evening.

"The President wants to meet you, Mr. Lynch," the FBI director said. "I'm opposed to the idea but the President requests."

Lynch sat back in the plush leather upholstery and took a deep breath. From jail to the White House in an hour. Perhaps he ought to be in politics, he thought.

"What does the FBI want with me?" Lynch asked. There was a flurry of urgent questions in his mind but he kept his voice level and started with the most important.

"You may well ask," Hatten said. "I'm inclined to agree with Mr. Ritsczik and press charges against you."

"For what?"

Hatten looked at Lynch with what could have been amusement or contempt; Lynch couldn't tell which.

"Officer Flannery died," Hatten said. "It was three hours before they raised his body. Charming piece of work you did on him."

Lynch stared through the windshield at the headlights of oncoming cars.

"How will you handle it?"

Hatten's face folded briefly in an expression of distaste. "Of-

ficer Flannery fell into the East River while in a state of intox-
ication. The barman of the Celtic Association club says Flannery
was drunk but okay when he left him in the club parking lot
around three-thirty in the morning. It appears Mr. Flannery
tried to drive home, realized how drunk he was, stopped to go
for a little walk to clear his head, overbalanced, and fell into
the river. Maybe he was robbed and pushed. His wallet hasn't
been found. There'll be an open verdict at the coroner's inquiry.
The autopsy says death was due to heart attack caused by shock,
probably the massive invasion of cold water into his body. There
were some marks and abrasions to his head and body but they
could have occurred when he fell into the river. He didn't drown.
His lungs were still half-full of air."

Lynch nodded. "He wasn't exactly an innocent."

"That ought to be for a court of law to decide, Mr. Lynch.
Not you."

Lynch looked at him. What a sweet, old-fashioned kind of
cop Wesley Hatten was, for a young man.

"Well"—Lynch stifled a yawn—"somehow I suppose I'll just
have to learn to live with it."

"I'm sure you can, Mr. Lynch. I'm sure you can."

There was a long pause.

"Your guys okay?"

"Yes, thank you. John Ritsczik almost lost his life trying to
recover Flannery. He's suffering from hypothermia. He'll be
lucky to get away with pneumonia. They pumped his stomach
at the hospital. He's a little disappointed in you."

"We had different jobs to do . . . he's a good guy." Even to
Lynch it sounded lame. "What about the other guy . . . ?"

"Oh, Agent Beatty, the one you shot at?"

"I shot wide. I missed him by six feet. I wanted to stop their
cars, not them. They weren't trying to miss me."

"No," Hatten agreed. He didn't sound apologetic.

The limo entered the southern suburbs of the American
capital.

"So what does the FBI want with me now?"

"Tonight, we're running a limousine service. Seems the President trusts me to get you to the White House in one piece.

There are others who might not be so charitably disposed toward you."

Jesus, Lynch thought. He'd just heard how Wesley Hatten felt about him and Hatten was supposed to be an ally. The FBI director read Lynch's thoughts.

"The secretary of state was all for putting you through the system, Mr. Lynch. So was I. The President went past him and spoke to the secretary of defense to get you released without charges because that's the sort of thing Presidents can do."

Hatten sounded as though he didn't approve. "My job is simple," he added. "I deliver you to the White House . . . and then I intend to make sure that you never set foot on American soil again."

The FBI director shook his dainty bald head and looked puzzled. "You must have some kind of clout that I don't know about, Mr. Lynch. Whatever it is, you've used it all up. You're leaving the United States tonight. Your home in Vermont is a thing of the past. It will be compulsorily acquired by the bureau and you will be recompensed at market rates, once certain deductions have been made for expenses you have imposed on the bureau. Any remaining funds will be sent on to you . . . wherever you are. Your green card doesn't exist anymore. Within twenty-four hours your name will be a permanent fixture on the immigration department's shit list. If you are stupid enough to set foot in the United States again, I will have you arrested and charged. And if the President interferes again I will create a public stink that will, at least, guarantee he doesn't get reelected and could result in his impeachment for abuse of his powers under the Constitution. That's what I get out of this deal, Mr. Lynch. And I wanted to tell you that myself."

Lynch tried to keep the shock off his face. He suddenly realized what powerful forces had been at work through the past forty-eight hours concerning his fate. And by the note in Hatten's voice he could tell it had been a close-run thing. The lodge in Stowe didn't concern him. There was nothing there that he couldn't live without. Even so, he thought, when the door slammed shut . . . it shut with a mighty and resounding finality.

A half hour later the limo driver drove past the main entrance to the White House, the West Wing gate that the whole world sees on television. The driver didn't slow down until he'd driven another block to the Treasury Building, where he turned sharply through a pair of tall iron gates, under a grand Romanesque arch and into a courtyard closed in like a prison exercise yard. Two men in suits moved out of a nearby doorway and waited.

"You're in the hands of the Secret Service now, Mr. Lynch," Hatten said. "Good-bye."

Hatten opened his door and leaned out.

"This is he," was all he said. Then he closed his car door.

Lynch climbed out and waited while the two Secret Service men did a quick and expert search of his clothing. Lynch had nothing but the clothes he stood up in. Everything he carried before his arrest at Fort Eustis had gone and he wouldn't get it back. His wallet, his phony ID, his credit cards, his driver's license. His whole fake American identity, his life in the United States, had been vaporized. Lynch grinned. He'd just been mugged by Uncle Sam.

One of the agents noticed the smile but didn't comment. "Come with us please," he said curtly, and Lynch did as he was told, walking between the two men through the small entrance in the Treasury Building courtyard. They went through another door and down a short flight of steps to a long, bare, and well-lit underground corridor that seemed to stretch forever. Lynch estimated it had to be at least a block long. The thought had no sooner entered his head than he realized it was a tunnel to the White House. It took five minutes of walking before they reached the metal door at the other end. There was no lock, mechanical or electronic. Just a blank, green metal door and an intercom speaker with a button. One of the Secret Service men pressed the button.

"Yes?"

"We're back. We have our visitor."

"Code word?"

"Raven."

There was a pause while they ran a voice-print check. That was the only way this door would be opened, Lynch realized, through an agent's voice print, which, like his fingerprints, was

unique. The White House security computer processed the
agent's voice and matched it in nine seconds.

"Okay," said the voice on the intercom.

The door gave a barely audible *click*. One of the agents
pushed and it opened as smoothly and as easily as the door to
a bank vault. It was almost as thick, Lynch noticed as they
passed through. Bulletproof, blastproof, missileproof. They entered another short corridor and trotted briskly up a short flight
of stairs, Lynch in the middle. The open door at the top of
the stairs was an ordinary, Georgian-style door painted white;
it led directly into the main corridor of the West Wing of the
White House, where two more black-suited men were waiting.
Lynch glanced around, took in the neoclassic American furniture, the carpet on the highly polished floor, the wallpaper,
the several small chandeliers suspended from the arched ceiling. The hands of a grandfather clock told him it was nearing
ten to eleven.

"Good evening, Mr. Lynch," one of the men at the top of
the stairs said in greeting. "I'm Bill Simpson, chief of security.
Would you come with me, please?"

Simpson led Lynch and the other three agents no more than
twenty paces along the corridor before he opened one of a set
of double doors and ushered them all into a small sitting room.
Once inside, Simpson closed the door and gestured to Lynch to
wait in the center of the sparsely—though elegantly—furnished
room. Two camel-backed couches flanked a mahogany coffee
table; a pair of high-backed armchairs, three antique cherry side
tables, a burlwood Philadelphia Chippendale secretary, and a
screened fireplace with a marble surround completed the decor.
On the mantel sat an Eli Terry clock. There were also a couple
of portraits on the walls of serious men wearing long sideburns
and Victorian suits. He didn't recognize either of them, two of
the less distinguished former occupants of the White House, he
surmised. He knew he had been taken to a low-priority reception
room.

"I'm sure you've been through this once already. Would you
mind?"

It wasn't really a request. Simpson conducted the search himself. It was a demonstration in how thorough and fast such a search could be. Simpson felt the cuffs of Lynch's jacket and pants, the flaps of his pockets, and his lapels.

"They didn't give you your belt back?"

Lynch shook his head. Simpson smiled but said nothing more till he was finished.

"Okay, Mr. Lynch." He stepped back and looked him directly in the eye. "I understand you're a pro. I'm sure you know the protocols and you'll appreciate the few added security measures we've taken. The President wants to see you personally—otherwise you wouldn't be within a mile of this place. Nothing against you personally, you understand."

Lynch understood perfectly. None of it was personal. It never was. Especially the killing.

"The President will be along directly. When he arrives you will sit in that chair over there." Simpson nodded toward one of the armchairs, all on its own in a corner except for one of the small antique side tables and a brass lamp.

"You will remain seated until the President indicates the interview is over. You will not leave the room until I say so. I will be in the room throughout the interview. Understood?"

Lynch nodded.

Simpson asked again, more firmly. "Understood?"

"Yes."

"Good."

A thick silence descended on the room. Simpson walked over to the screened fireplace and leaned against the mantelshelf. One of the Secret Service men stood beside the double doors. The other two stood casually, hands behind their backs, and watched Lynch. Lynch put his hands in his pockets and looked around. The mantel clock seemed to have been carved from a piece of solid walnut. At eleven o'clock it chimed with a delightful, musical precision. Nobody moved.

There was no offer of refreshments, no inquiry as to whether he was hungry, thirsty, or needed to go to the bathroom.

"Mind if I sit down?" Lynch asked at a quarter past.

Simpson nodded assent.

Lynch walked over to his chair and sat down. The moment he made himself comfortable there was a knock at the door.

The Secret Service man opened it and another man whispered quickly.

Simpson straightened up.

"He's on the way. Would you mind standing over there?" The security chief nodded toward an open space in front of the heavily curtained window overlooking the West Lawn. Lynch got up again. Dry farce. It seemed to go hand in glove with awkward situations like this.

A moment later the door opened again. The President of the United States strode into the room, wearing a gray business suit and glasses.

"Mr. Lynch?"

Lynch shook the President's outstretched hand.

"Bill been giving you a hard time?" he asked.

"Just doing his job, sir," Lynch answered.

"Good." The President looked awkward for a moment, like a man made uncomfortable in his own house by the presence of an unwelcome visitor. Lynch noticed he must have cut himself shaving that morning because there was the tiniest crust of dried blood in the awkward little crook just above his Adam's apple. The three other Secret Service men faded noiselessly from the room.

"Please, sit down." The President gestured vaguely. Lynch obediently took his assigned chair. The President sat alone on a couch on the opposite side of the room. There seemed to be twenty feet of open carpet between them. Simpson remained standing, apparently idling near the cold fireplace. Lynch knew the security chief wouldn't take his eyes off him. And if he stood up suddenly or made some other untoward move, Simpson would have the mini-Uzi out of the holster nestling under his suit jacket in the small of his back and aimed at Lynch's head in a twinkling.

"Mr. Lynch, how well do you know Jack Halloran?"

Lynch paused.

"Well enough not to trust him."

The President smiled. Lynch caught the twitch of a smile on Simpson's face.

"What exactly does that mean, Mr. Lynch?"

"It means he'll do whatever he has to do to get the job

done—and he'll sacrifice anyone. Including me." Lynch was speaking from hard personal experience. And so far, he knew, he hadn't said anything the President wouldn't already know. The qualities he'd described were precisely the qualities that made men like Halloran valuable to men who occupied high office.

"Do you trust me?"

"You're a politician, sir."

The President nodded. "Yes, I am. And from the style of your answers so far, I would venture that so are you."

Lynch waited. He also knew he was dealing with a former director of the CIA.

"Do you have any idea why he would break his word to me and take his yacht out to sea?"

Lynch breathed deeply. "I think he's afraid that he no longer has the confidence of this office, sir. He's also afraid your judgment has been influenced against him by others . . . and I think he believes he has the most experience in dealing with this type of situation."

"Has he put to sea to organize his own operation from outside the jurisdiction of this government?"

Lynch hesitated. He knew that everything hinged on his answer.

"Yes sir." The instant the words left his lips he felt, instinctively, that he'd given the wrong answer.

The President nodded. "I thought so. Everything they told me about Jack Halloran seems to be true. He's either inside the tent pissing out, or outside pissing in."

Once again there was complete silence in the room. Bill Simpson's face revealed nothing. Lynch wondered if their conversation was being taped from hidden bugs. He doubted it. He got the distinct impression that his visit to the White House and this conversation were events that had never occurred.

"We've been tracking him since he left," the President said abruptly. "I could order the navy to intercept him on the high seas."

Lynch's stomach turned cold.

"He's a smart old bastard. He's skirting the coastline of Cuba, just outside their territorial waters but close enough that our ships can't go in without risking an incident. Nevertheless . . ."

He let the word hang in the air.

"My lord." The President sighed deeply and unexpectedly. "He must be in a desperate state of mind even to contemplate doing something like this."

Lynch waited.

"I want you to fly out to the *American Endeavor* tonight, Mr. Lynch," the President said suddenly. "We have a plane waiting at Andrews for you. I want you to take a message from me direct to Jack Halloran. I want you to tell him that he has my complete confidence. Your presence there should confirm that. Tell him I want to know if he's planning something, and I want to know before he moves. That's all. To make sure it doesn't conflict with anything else that may be in progress."

Lynch sighed internally. His instinct that the President would try to use him to bring back Halloran had been wrong. Or had it? Was the President only playing a new game now that Halloran had regained the initiative? Trying to ensure that Halloran kept him informed of his plans until the President could move to neutralize him permanently?

The President stood up, the signal that the interview was over. Lynch got up as well, and Simpson moved discreetly toward the center of the room.

"Mr. President?" Lynch was polite and deferential, but he seized the moment while he had it. "Would you mind if I asked you a question?"

The President waited.

"What changed your mind, sir?"

The tall, angular man with the patrician profile and the hayseed drawl smiled faintly. "Mr. Lynch," he said, "I may be a politician. And I may be surrounded by politicians. That is the nature of the business I am in. But I value my advisers. All my advisers. Jack Halloran is not a politician. He has been protecting the interests of the occupants of this office, and the greater interests of this country, since I was a freshman. And he's been good at it. Never once has he failed the presidency. Despite other influences—and yes, they have been considerable and not all ill intentioned—my instinct tells me to trust him now. But I want to be informed of his intentions. And, by God, tell him I will authorize the military to intervene if he moves without my approval."

"Thank you, sir." It made sense. Either it was the truth or it was a fine con; Lynch believed him.

"Thank *you*, Mr. Lynch. Good-bye . . . and good luck." The President turned to go but seemed to have a sudden afterthought. He turned and looked at Lynch over the top of his glasses, as a schoolmaster might while examining a bright but unruly boy.

"I spent an interesting hour reading your file last night, Mr. Lynch," he said. "That is one of the other reasons why I trust Jack to get it right. He knows people. He knows how to choose the right people and how to use them to the best effect. I admire and envy his gift. I enjoyed reading your file. Make a good book . . . one day."

Simpson opened the door and the President was gone.

An hour later Lynch sat in the copilot's seat of a navy F-14A Tomcat as it streaked down the runway at Andrews Air Force Base and climbed high into the skies above Washington, then headed south by southeast over the Atlantic Ocean. Within ninety minutes he was on the flight deck of the aircraft carrier USS *Saratoga*, cruising southward through the Caribbean to engage in war games off the coast of Panama. The navy didn't dally with him. A Sikorsky Super Stallion was waiting to take Lynch the short eighty-kilometer hop to the *American Endeavor*'s latest plotted position, north of Cuba in the Old Bahama Channel. Half an hour later, close to two-thirty in the morning, he was winched down to the deck of the big luxury yacht, and Jack Halloran knew he was back in the presidential fold.

STRASBOURG, FRANCE, APRIL 6

The elegant French city of Strasbourg is a convenient meeting place for terrorists. It sits on France's northeastern border with Germany, only an hour's drive along one of the most scenic stretches of the Rhine to the Swiss city of Basel. It is an easy border crossing for holders of Common Market country passports and, more important for Abu Musa, it is an elegant and comfortable city. Because O'Donnell was a Catholic, Musa thought it appropriate that they should meet, an hour before evening mass, in front of Strasbourg's beautiful Gothic cathedral. Neither man wanted to tarry in the open and, on Musa's nodded signal, they stepped quietly into the peaceful interior of the cathedral and talked murder.

O'Donnell had flown direct from Dublin to Paris on an Aer Lingus flight that morning and driven a rental car east to Strasbourg. Musa had flown Iranair from Tehran to the Romanian capital, Bucharest, where he had done a little business with the increasingly militant government opposition, which was interested in acquiring a consignment of new Beretta submachine guns from Italy. From there he had switched to a Greek passport and flown Air Romania to Munich where he, too, had rented a car for the pleasant drive to Strasbourg. Musa had little to fear when crossing the border. As a young man, at the PLO's expense, he had spent three years at the Sorbonne studying languages and political science. In addition to his native Arabic he spoke fluent French, English, and enough German and Italian to get by. The meeting would last only an hour; then Musa would drive back to Munich for supper. He had acquired a taste for German beer, but only a glass or two or it was bad for the figure. O'Donnell would return to Paris, stay overnight in a hotel near the airport, and be back in Dublin for breakfast the following day.

Musa wore an expensive Italian leather jacket over a light sweater, wool slacks, and handmade leather shoes. O'Donnell arrived wearing a plain black overcoat, his great shock of readily identifiable white hair uncovered by a hat. Musa thought he looked like an Irish peasant on holiday. He would make sure they left separately. The Palestinian waited in wry amusement while O'Donnell genuflected toward the altar and crossed himself. Then they sat down together in the same pew, bowed their heads, and talked softly. O'Donnell could barely contain his excitement. He had explosive news for Musa.

"We've got Halloran's tart," he said. "We're bringing her

home. Halloran and his man, Lynch, will have to come after her. We'll take them on home ground. It'll all be over in another week, mebbe two."

Musa nodded. "Good," he whispered. "My clients will be appreciative."

Now that O'Donnell had revealed his good news he felt bold enough to demand the long-promised payment. He'd received close to two hundred thousand U.S. dollars from Musa in the past eighteen months but it had all gone on expenses, and Musa knew it.

"Your cargo is on the way," Musa told him. "It's the *Nara Maru*. Japanese ship. Japanese registration. It will be off Donegal in one week. The skipper will wait four days. If he hasn't received any contact from you within that time he will turn around and go back."

"We'll be in touch, don't you worry," O'Donnell said. "My man, Hennessy, is taking care of it. We'll transfer to one of my people's boats at sea," he added. "What's in her?"

Musa smiled. "Sixty Armalites with twenty thousand rounds of ammunition. Six dozen Stinger missiles, fully armed. Two dozen automatic pistols, Soviet T33's. I couldn't get Colts . . . but the Tokarev is a good gun, very strong. Two thousand rounds of ammunition."

It was the next item that convinced O'Donnell he would have the strength to move.

"Fifty thousand pounds of Semtex . . ." Musa said.

O'Donnell silently clenched and unclenched his fists. It was enough to mine the city centers of Derry and Belfast. The British wouldn't dare move if they knew there were enough explosives primed to tear out the hearts of both cities and annihilate the hostages that would have been taken. Hennessy would run the show in Belfast and O'Donnell would take care of Derry. His hour of glory was approaching. He could see it clearly in his mind's eye.

"I put in something extra," Musa added. "Two dozen R22's."

"What are they?" O'Donnell tried to keep the tremor of excitement out of his voice but he wasn't fooling Musa.

"Land mines. Soviet land mines. Very effective. Blow up a tank."

"That's good," O'Donnell mumbled. "Very good . . ."

Musa smiled. "Very soon, Tom, we will both have what we want."

O'Donnell was ready to leave.

"Are you sure they'll come after the girl, Tom?"

"Of course they'll come after the bloody girl. She used to be Halloran's bit on the side. She's been sharin' Lynch's bed for the past two years. They'll come."

Musa looked skeptical. "Jack Halloran is a practical man. He may decide she's dispensable. Then what?"

"He won't. They'll come after her, I'm telling ye. I know how such people's minds work. You don't."

It was the first reference O'Donnell had made to the racial difference between them. The suggestion that Musa might not understand the Western mind rankled.

"We will see, Tom. We will see."

He put his hand reassuringly on O'Donnell's arm, then got up and walked quietly out of the cathedral. He turned right when he reached the street and walked down a dark, leafy boulevard bordering one of Strasbourg's quiet canals to where he'd parked his rented BMW. As he walked, Abu Musa reflected on one piece of intelligence he hadn't shared with Tom O'Donnell, a useful item from an old Palestinian school chum, a dedicated Marxist, who now lived in Havana. The man had emigrated to Cuba in the late sixties as a member of the starry-eyed international socialist youth movement that flocked to Castro's Marxist nirvana to slave for nothing in the cane fields to prove that communism did work. War in Lebanon had convinced the man there was nothing to come home for, but Musa had kept in touch. Once again, the benefits of maintaining one's contacts had paid off.

His friend had phoned one of Musa's offices in Amsterdam, an office with an answering machine that Musa had checked by long-distance phone every twenty-four hours. There was a big American yacht cruising back and forth along Cuba's northeast coast, the friend had said. Many people in Havana knew about it. One of Castro's gunboats had gone out to take a closer look and had confirmed that it was the *American Endeavor*, the yacht owned by Jack Halloran, the notorious American capitalist and enemy of communism who now seemed to have crossed his own government. Nobody knew what he was doing, cruising back and forth along the international boundary, twelve miles offshore. Wouldn't it be a joke if he had been found guilty of fraud like the other notorious American capitalist, Robert Vesco, who had escaped to wander the Caribbean aboard his luxury yacht a decade earlier? What if Halloran asked for political asylum? Wouldn't that be something? Anyway, the friend added, before hanging up, he only passed the information along in case it might prove useful.

Musa was still turning it over in his mind. He started the engine and drove the BMW back toward the border. The French waved him through and the Germans merely glanced at the passport, which described him as an Athens-based fashion buyer. By the time he reached Munich he had made up his mind. He had thought of a way to save himself a little money. Perhaps Tom O'Donnell was right. Perhaps Jack Halloran would act as he predicted. But, then again, perhaps not. Musa had been given good information. He knew where Halloran was now. He had an opportunity to finish the job, satisfy the cartel, get payment in full, and forget about the second shipload of armaments for his old "friend" Tom O'Donnell. It was too good to resist.

Tom O'Donnell had been thinking, too. After Musa left he had remained behind another half hour, meditating in the whispery silence of the great cathedral at Strasbourg. Perhaps Musa was right, he decided. Perhaps Halloran and Lynch wouldn't come as quickly as he wanted. Perhaps they needed a little incentive. Perhaps they needed to be shown the way a little more clearly. He got up from the pew with a grunt, genuflected and crossed himself again, and walked outside. He had made his decision. It was time to sacrifice another pawn. Or this time, perhaps, a rather worn and battered knight.

THE *AMERICAN ENDEAVOR*, WEST INDIES, APRIL 7

"He's serious," Jack Halloran confirmed, as he strode back into the master stateroom where Lynch and Bono waited. Halloran had just spent fifteen minutes in his office talking to the President of the United States.

"I told him I've considered a range of options and as soon as I decide on the best course of action we'll let him know . . . and then we'll proceed." He smiled broadly at the two men who sat at the huge satin oak dining table littered with maps and pads and pencils, calculators and scraps of paper scrawled with lists of names and places.

"Drinks, gentlemen?"

Lynch shook his head.

"Beer," Bono said.

Halloran plucked two cold Budweisers from the bar fridge, tossed one to Bono, and walked around to join them at the table.

This was more like the Halloran Lynch knew. Bursting with energy and purpose, radiating confidence, pushing, probing, demanding; and then, just when you thought you'd had enough . . . a cold beer and a pat on the head.

Halloran's spirits had picked up markedly with Lynch's dramatic arrival by USN helicopter three nights earlier. They had spent the rest of the night catching up—and there had been a lot of catching up to do.

"The first report I got was that they'd hit the safe house and wiped out everybody," Halloran had told him. "I thought they were all gone. Janice, Becker . . . everybody. I told the skipper we were putting to sea right then. We had Bono on board— he'd got in that afternoon—and I couldn't take the chance that they'd try to hold us. We were gone in two hours. I figured you could look after yourself."

"The secretary of state and the director of the Federal Bureau of Investigation wanted to put me away . . ."

"Clayton Powell's a treacherous sonofabitch," Halloran had growled. "When this is all over I'm going to look him up personally and punch his face through his asshole. Hatten's just a cop. He may be smart but he's still got a cop's brain."

He had attempted to reassure Lynch. "You wouldn't have gone to jail," he said. "You might have had to sit awhile but when things had cooled I figured the President would listen to me."

The subject had switched abruptly to the President's message. Did Lynch believe it? How had the President behaved? What exactly had he said?

Lynch had told Halloran he thought the President was on the level. He also mentioned the remark about pissing into the tent.

"Yeah," Halloran had grumbled. "I figure there's a little of that behind it, too. It pays to be a bastard sometimes, just so they know you've got it in you. Then, when a time like this comes around, they know you're not to be fucked with. Sure, he could send a destroyer out to pick us up. But what a fucking spectacular for the world media that would have created. I'd have seen to it. I'd have had every fax, wire machine, and phone line aboard this ship humming with shit straight into the newsrooms of CBS, NBC, ABC, the *Washington Post* and the *New York Times*, and anybody else I could think of. I'd be out there on the fantail with Dan Rather and that loudmouth from ABC, what'shisname—Donaldson? And I'd be singing for the cameras like a goddamned canary. The activities of this unit and the role of seven presidents going back to Eisenhower would have been blown wide open—and I'd have thrown in a few presidential peccadilloes for the *National Enquirer*, too. They'd have to sink us to shut me up."

Lynch had smiled. "The President told me he'd do that too—if you didn't keep him in the picture."

"Yeah?" Halloran had eyed Lynch skeptically.

It had been two full days before Halloran was prepared to talk to the President. He wanted to be armed with fresh information first. The only leads they had so far had come from Lynch's efforts. They had spent the two days sitting around the dining room table picking at the same information over and over again and trying to come up with a few answers. All they knew for certain was that the IRA was involved and that a man called Brian Hennessy had been behind the attacks. They had phoned his name through to Sir Malcolm Porter's office in London but still hadn't heard back. They had run his name through Halloran's computers but turned up nothing. All that had been confirmed was that Hennessy was not and never had been involved in any mercenary activity. The name was Irish but that alone meant little. The FBI, the CIA, the NIS, the Special

Branch at Scotland Yard, and Interpol had all drawn blanks. The only thing that told them was that Hennessy didn't have a police record. Anywhere.

The more Lynch thought about him, the more he tried to put together some kind of mental profile, the more convinced he became that Hennessy must have had formal military training. It could have been in the guerilla camps of the PLO or Hezbollah, he knew; the international terrorist fraternity operated highly efficient training camps for aspiring terrorists. More than one IRA man and woman had been trained in the use of arms and explosives in the Middle East. Hennessy could be one of them. Even so, Lynch had a hunch. The scale and efficiency that characterized the man's work; the chopper attack on the STC Building; the cold-blooded execution of the pilot; the military-style assault on Bono's farmhouse; the highly professional raid and kidnap at the Greenwich Village town house, using stun grenades: it all indicated a higher level of military training than the guerilla camps usually offered.

Lynch had a gut feeling . . . a feeling that they were up against one of their own.

Then he remembered. A funny, wiry little man in glasses at the town house, holding up the plastic bag containing the red-handled screwdriver. The FBI had found nothing, the world's best police forces and security services had found nothing. Perhaps it was because they were looking in the wrong places. They were all scouring the files for known terrorists, both Middle Eastern and European, crooks, and mercenaries—all the usual flotsam and jetsam of the terrorist and criminal worlds.

Lynch had placed another call to Sir Malcolm.

"Sorry, we don't seem to be having much luck," Porter had apologized. "I can assure you it's not because we aren't looking."

"Sir, I have a strange feeling about this one."

"Yes?" The voice was quite level, neither skeptical nor receptive. Sir Malcolm Porter knew enough about hunches to respect them according to their worth—once they'd been checked out.

"Have you run that name and those fingerprints through the army's records?"

"No." The voice sounded faintly curious.

"I think you should, sir. The army, the navy, air force, Royal Marines, SAS, SBS, CTC. Paras, Guards . . . anybody else you can think of."

"We've already checked the records for known mercenaries, you know."

"I'm aware of that, sir . . . but this man has never been a mercenary. He's not a gun for hire. He's a political. I think he could have been one of ours . . . and he's crossed over."

"A traitor? Good God, that . . . it's almost unheard of . . ."

"I know, sir. Doesn't mean it couldn't happen though, does it?"

That had been twenty-four hours ago and they were still waiting.

"So." Bono fidgeted in his chair. "What now?"

The big man was wearing familiar olive green pants and shirt, unbuttoned to reveal an army T-shirt spotted with beer. On his feet were a pair of new sneakers with the laces removed. They were already scuffed and aging rapidly. It had been more than a week since Bono's release from the hospital, and the stitches had come out, but there remained a latticework of small dressings around his head and neck, and Lynch could see fresh burn dressings on his arms. A few smaller burns hadn't needed bandages but they still looked raw and painful. Bono had been careful to keep out of the blazing sun ever since the yacht had left Chesapeake. Now, Lynch and Bono waited.

"Okay," Halloran announced. "We can use the yacht as a floating HQ indefinitely," he said. "I think we know enough now that it's worth our while to transfer operations to Europe. We'll have to pick up more fuel somewhere but I'll ask the skipper to plot a course. We'll leave in the morning."

The attack came just before dawn.

It had taken Lynch a long time to go to sleep because of his fears for Janice. When he finally drifted off it was into a deep and dreamless slumber until that hour before dawn when REM sleep is at its deepest. He was dreaming about Janice. They were together again, safe in her apartment. They were in bed, naked, and she was massaging his body with a frangipani-scented oil. He could feel the silken touch of her hands, the teasing way she traced the lines of his body with her fingertips. He felt himself begin to harden. Her hands reached down to his crotch and gently took hold of him . . . but then the doorbell started to ring. The dream began to fade and melt and he could see her slipping away. In that dark and eerie corridor between the conscious and the unconscious mind he knew he was dreaming and didn't want to let go. He fought vainly to hold on to it, to bring back the calm and erotic serenity that had given him his first real comfort in a week . . . and then he awoke to the brazen clamor of the ship's fire alarm just outside his stateroom. He had been jolted back to the harsh and ceaseless urgencies of the real world.

"Jesus Christ . . ." He stumbled groggily out of bed, all erotic stimuli banished by a new and unknown threat, pulled on pants and a sweater, and ran outside. On deck the alarm was deafening. He looked around and saw that first light was just creeping over the eastern horizon . . . but there was no sign of fire. Bono bumped into him from behind.

"Fuck . . . shit . . . piss . . ." The big man was healing well.

Lynch hurried forward, followed by Bono, and looked up to the bridge. They both saw Captain Penny in the bridge light, looking surprisingly disheveled. His white hair had been pushed carelessly back and his white skipper's tunic was unbuttoned. He was speaking rapidly to the first officer. A moment later he noticed Lynch and Bono below and motioned them up to the bridge.

"Keep well back," he ordered sharply. "It seems we've got company, gentlemen, and it could be hostile."

They heard the yacht's powerful engines grumble distantly into life and felt the vessel shudder as Penny brought it around with one hand on the wheel, the other fastidiously fastening his tunic buttons. A moment later Halloran appeared blearily on deck wearing sweat shirt and chinos.

"Are you sure?" Halloran asked Penny.

Lynch gathered Penny had already passed on the full extent of the alert by ship's intercom.

Penny's response was to flick on the line to the communications room and bark into the mike on the instrument panel in front of him.

"Mr. Halloran's on the bridge now," he said. "What's the situation?"

"Three aircraft approaching from west-southwest, sir. Bearing two-zero-two-niner. Six thousand yards and closing. They're still in formation. From their speed and profile I'd say they're choppers for sure."

Lynch looked in the direction the communications officer had given. It was still dark on the western horizon but he knew what was over there. Cuba.

Halloran looked around at the two men standing watchfully behind. And then he grinned. "Did I ever tell you that Jimmy Durante was a friend of mine?"

Lynch and Bono eyed each other as though Halloran had just gone quite mad.

"Yeah . . ." the old man went on. "Jimmy had an expression that I think is rather appropriate to our current situation: 'Everybody wants to get into the act.' " He turned back to gaze out of the bridge. "They think I'm down, and now they all want to kick me. Fine. I've been itching to kick some ass, too."

Lynch strained to pick out the first glimmer of reflected light from the approaching choppers but saw nothing in the predawn gloom.

Five nautical miles away in the darkness, closing in at a height of two thousand feet, Lieutenant Felipe Pascua throttled up for the first run. He'd had the big yacht on his radar since taking off with his comrades in the two flanking choppers ten minutes earlier. The Soviet-built Hind-D attack helicopters each carried two 12.7 mm cannon and eight air-to-surface rockets. With a top speed of 366 kilometers per hour they could have closed the twenty-kilometer gap between the coastline and the yacht in ten minutes. But Lieutenant Pascua and his comrades felt no sense of urgency. They intended to enjoy themselves. As their base commander had indicated when he asked for volunteers, it was going to be a piece of cake. A privately owned American cruiser had strayed into Cuban territorial waters. The government had decided it posed a threat and had to be sunk.

Everyone knew who owned the yacht. If it had been a cruise liner with passengers on board that had inadvertently strayed into Cuban waters they would have handled it differently. It would have been an opportunity for a little propaganda exercise. But this was a ship owned by an enemy of the proletariat, an enemy of the Cuban people, an enemy of all socialist nations. It deserved to be held up as an example. Fidel Castro himself had decided. And there was a precedent; the Russians had not hesitated to shoot down Korean Air Lines Flight 007 when it accidentally strayed into Soviet air space back in 1982.

Castro had been most sympathetic to the request from his Palestinian comrade when it was put to him the previous afternoon, especially when it was explained that the yacht and its owner were now persona non grata with the American administration. A fugitive, no less. It didn't matter that the yacht was in international waters, fully six nautical miles outside Cuban territory. Nobody would ever know for sure. Nobody would even care. Musa had closed the deal with a generous offer to cover all the costs of the operation with one million U.S. dollars in hard currency and to reciprocate in kind some day, whenever the Cuban revolutionary leader decided he needed some special favor.

Castro knew about Abu Musa. There wasn't much about the world revolutionary movement the Cuban president didn't know. There was no doubt in his mind at all that he could use a man like Abu Musa and his organization someday. Especially now that the Soviets were growing stingy with money and equipment. It was an easy enough operation, he decided. He had thirty thousand men from the International Brigade sitting idle in army camps around the island since their return from Angola. At least some of them might enjoy the exercise.

Lieutenant Pascua had been the first to volunteer. There had been a rush of candidates to join him but he had chosen his own men. Two comrades-in-arms who had flown with him on combat missions against the fascist-sponsored rebels in Angola and, on two occasions, in strikes against South African armored columns inside Namibia. They all deserved a little fun before breakfast, he decided. They had stayed up late planning the attack, enjoying the special kind of exhilaration that comes before combat. All three had grabbed a couple of hours' sleep, rising at four-thirty to check their aircraft and armament. They had passed a bottle back and forth and each savored a jolt of rum before takeoff. Thirty minutes at most, Pascua promised. The American pig's yacht would be finished in ten minutes. Their greatest concern was that they might not have enough flying time to watch it sink. Aviation fuel was strictly rationed in Cuba. They had each been given only enough for an hour in the air. But it would be more than enough to do the job.

Pascua got a visual fix on the *American Endeavor* through the Plexiglas dome of his cockpit, pushed the stick forward, and swooped low and fast. With his first pass he buzzed her at one thousand feet. The much-decorated veteran of the Angolan campaign wanted to make sure they were all awake down there. He wanted them to see what was coming.

Halloran, Lynch, Captain Penny, and Bono watched in fascination from the bridge. They had all ducked reflexively at the first pass but there had been no gun flashes from the approaching choppers, no sudden fluttering of cannon fire followed by twin columns of spray marching across the water toward them.

"Wait and see if they fire first," Halloran murmured. "They might just be giving us a look-see . . . but I don't think so."

Pascua opened fire on his second pass, coming in hard and low with the rising sun behind him. He waited until he was within a thousand meters and thumbed the firing buttons for both cannons. Twin bursts of shells streamed out of the sky toward the beautiful American yacht and beat a savage tattoo across her bow. Huge chunks of meticulously polished teak splintered and flew and a series of big metal gouges rippled across the bulwarks.

"Okay," Halloran yelled. "Waste the fuckers."

Penny calmly turned a small key in a box on the instrument panel and flipped open the lid. Inside was something that looked like a separate and entirely different instrument panel. It was. It was the control system for the ship's missile armament.

Lynch had known the *American Endeavor* was armed, forward and aft, with two batteries of Sea Wolf surface-to-air missiles. He watched the forward batteries materialize out of the deck as if by magic. Two large, square sections of teak planking suddenly elevated themselves above the deck and slid sideways, revealing dual hatches in the metal deck beneath. These hatches now opened smoothly outward and twin batteries of mounted and armed Sea Wolf missiles slid into view with sinister grace.

"Oh shit," Bono rumbled. "Those dumb fuckers don't know what they're in for."

There was another sudden storm of cannon fire and everyone ducked. The fusillade from the second chopper lashed across the fantail, twisting and ripping metal and filling the air with deadly flying shards. The third pilot unleashed a salvo of four rockets. The first two overshot by a thousand yards. The second two exploded on impact with the ocean, barely five hundred feet away. A moment later a curtain of fine spray drifted across the bridge.

Pascua wheeled sharply around to come in from the north and strafe the big yacht lengthwise. Someone chattered something in his headset about missiles. Pascua frowned. He couldn't be hearing properly. He brought the chopper down for his second run, thumbs poised over both cannon buttons. He thought the yacht looked rather beautiful as it sliced through a dark blue sea slashed with coppery flourishes from the rising sun. There was a dazzling flash of light as the full strength of the sun reflected off the sleek white hull of the ship for the first time. Lieutenant Pascua jammed his thumbs down on the firing buttons and a series of high white dashes marched in perfect parallel lines across the ocean toward the yacht.

"Got a fix?" Penny snapped into the phone line to the communications room. There was a pause. They all heard the staccato hammering of approaching cannon fire and tensed. Downstairs the communications officer had assumed his other role as weapons officer; the assistant communications officer had stepped into his traditional role. Their hands fluttered over the computerized keyboards in a deadly duet as they fed the altitude, distance, speed, and direction of the nearest chopper into the missile's electronic brain. Once the Sea Wolf was locked on the same altitude path as its target it would automatically home itself in and the destruction of the aircraft was only a matter of seconds. The eleven kilos of high explosive in the warhead would detonate on impact.

"Ready, sir," Penny said.

"Fire, for Christ's sake!" Halloran yelled. "Blow those bastards outta the sky."

Penny hit the launch button. An instant later the Sea Wolf snarled and leaped into the sky.

Lieutenant Pascua wasn't sure he could trust the evidence of his own eyes. There was a sudden spurt of smoke and flame from the forward deck of the yacht as it flashed below him, and he thought he saw the distinctive white sizzle of a surface-to-air missile. He put the chopper into a steep climb, banked around to get a clearer view of the yacht, and watched in horror as a tiny silver needle zigzagged through the sky toward him, leaving a pretty, furry white tail.

His own fear was the last sensation he felt on earth. The next moment Felipe Pascua, Cuban war hero, ceased to exist. The Sea Wolf bit and the chopper disintegrated in a boiling cloud of flame. Pascua's two comrades-in-arms had their throttles flat and were streaking back toward the safety of their revolutionary homeland as fast as the twin Isotov TV-3-117 turbos would take them. It wasn't fast enough.

"Don't let the fuckers get away," Bono protested in a low grumble.

"Don't worry," Halloran answered.

Penny got the confirmation on the second chopper and thumbed a second missile.

They all watched in silence from the bridge, hypnotized by the lethal beauty of missile warfare.

"Three hundred grand a pop," Halloran murmured. "I always wondered if they'd work when we needed 'em . . . fucking beautiful."

The Hind-D's top speed is 366 kilometers per hour. The Sea Wolf flies at Mach 2.6 and has a range of seven thousand meters. It is a very simple and very lethal mathematical equation.

From the bridge it looked as if the closest helicopter was being reeled backward on a long white piece of wool. There was a sudden, flaring fireball in the lightening sky and a moment later the thud of the explosion. Wreckage from the first chopper was already falling into the ocean in a ragged circle of amazingly small splashes. The last pilot might have made it to the limits of the Sea Wolf's range and escaped if he'd had another ninety seconds, but he didn't. The third missile leaped from its cradle on the forward deck and eight seconds later another fireball erupted in the distant gloom.

"Well." Halloran turned toward his colleagues on the bridge. "I think we just handed Mr. Castro an exploding cigar."

He turned to his skipper, Captain Penny, whose hair was still ruffled and whose elegant pink jowls were coated with a snowy stubble.

"Congratulations, Captain."

They shook hands. Rather formally, Lynch thought.

"Congratulations to you, sir," Penny returned.

"Not bad." Bono shambled forward and slapped the former USN minesweeper captain on the shoulder. "Not bad at all, Hornblower."

Lynch stepped forward last to add his congratulations, a trifle self-consciously.

"You saved your ship, Captain," he said.

"Thank you, Mr. Lynch," Penny replied impassively. And then, with the faintest sparkle in his eyes, he added, "Once a navy man, always a navy man, eh?"

TEHRAN, APRIL 8

The call came through a little after three o'clock in the morning, Tehran time. It took Abu Musa a few moments to wake up— he always slept deeply after an evening of satisfying sex. When the soft but insistent chimes of the bedside telephone finally stirred him from his slumber he hesitated for a second before picking up the handset. Calls at the darkest hour of the night always meant bad news. He waited. If the phone stopped ringing the bad news would have to wait. His lover stirred drowsily beside him and Musa reached out and put a comforting hand on the soft, feminine hip, letting his fingertips linger for just a moment, tracing the warm, inviting curves of the thighs and belly.

"Shh, my darling," Musa whispered tenderly, and reluctantly picked up the telephone. A man was yelling at him in Spanish even before he put the phone to his ear, but it was too rapid for Musa to understand. He began to grow irritated.

"Calm yourself, whoever you are," Musa answered in Spanish. "Speak slowly. I can't understand a word you're saying."

Either the caller hadn't heard him or he was too agitated to slow down. The words kept tumbling out in a hysterical, high-pitched jumble. Suddenly Musa recognized his caller. There were very few men in the world who had the current telephone number for his house in Tehran. It had to be Havana. Musa looked at his watch on the bedside table and did a quick calculation. It would be early afternoon in Cuba. Then a chill swept through his body as surely as if he had stepped into a bath filled with ice water.

Mixed in with the panic and the curses had been a few words he understood. "*American Endeavor* . . . disaster . . . heroes of the people's revolution dead . . ."

Suddenly Musa knew. The attack on Halloran, the attack he had personally arranged through his contacts in the Cuban government, had gone wrong. Terribly wrong. There had been loss of matériel and the loss of lives—the wrong lives. Halloran was still alive. Musa's irritation was suddenly replaced by an angry surge of temper.

"Take your time, you stupid man," Musa snapped into the mouthpiece. "Tell me properly, what happened."

All pretense of fraternity and brotherhood under the banner of international socialism had evaporated under the weight of fear and fury that gripped both men. But Musa's insult worked. Hector Enriquez, the Middle East liaison officer within the Cuban foreign ministry, struggled to get the words out without losing control again. Finally he was able to give Musa a coherent report of the full extent of the disaster that had followed the attack on the *American Endeavor*.

"Prime Minister Castro is . . ." Enriquez seemed unable to find the words again. "Prime Minister Castro is not . . . not happy with the result of this . . . this favor . . ." Enriquez let the words hang in the ether over the phone line.

Musa's face was black with repressed rage. It was all the more unbearable because he had nowhere to direct that rage. He had no one to blame but himself. And he knew that Enriquez had grossly understated the depth of Fidel Castro's reaction to the loss of three helicopters and their pilots. Especially when the Soviet Union was cutting military aid to Cuba and sophisticated hardware such as attack choppers would be difficult to replace. He had met Castro on half a dozen different occasions and had seen the Cuban leader in a fury. It was like watching a madman.

"All right, all right." Musa tried to calm the Cuban bureaucrat with an evenness in his voice that he did not feel. "I give you my word, I will make it up to Cuba. Tell Fidel from me personally . . . give him my condolences for the loss of life of three brave socialist airmen and tell him I will see to it myself that all his lost equipment is replaced."

Even as he said it, Musa had no idea how he would make good the losses. That kind of hardware was no longer easy even for him to obtain. And cash compensation would come close to nine million U.S. dollars, money he could not afford. Nor could he afford to make an enemy of a man like Castro.

Enriquez was not reassured and warned Musa that he would be hearing from the Cuban government directly through Tehran. Musa shivered. The world was running short of refuges for a devout socialist-turned-terrorist such as himself. He could not afford to antagonize two governments in one day.

Finally Musa was able to hang up the phone. He sat up in bed staring into the darkness and stroked his beard with a trembling hand.

His lover had been watching him apprehensively. An eleven-year-old Iranian boy with wide dark eyes, long lashes, and a beguiling feminine smile, he had been a perfect partner the night before. Intelligent, obedient, eager to please. Musa could easily see him becoming a favorite.

"Is there anything wrong, sir?" the child asked softly.

The timid inquiry acted as a trigger. Musa lashed out in blind fury, slapping and punching the screaming child, again and again and again.

8 Tears for a Princess

"Danny, I need ye to do a small job for me." It was eight-thirty in the morning and O'Donnell was standing in the living room of his cottage, with Danny Locke on the other end of the telephone line in Belfast. It wasn't the best time of day for Danny. He suffered from insomnia, went to bed late, and hated to be woken up after he'd finally gone to sleep. The anger in his voice tempered to quiet resentment when he heard O'Donnell. He knew it had to be bad news. It had been almost three weeks since that bizarre night at Donegal when O'Donnell had revealed his grand strategy for the liberation of Ulster and the repatriation of the six counties.

"What job?" Danny asked warily.

"I need a bit of money," O'Donnell lied. "Not much. Couple of thousand. Any small subbranch should do it. Or a post office."

"Shit, Tom." Danny Locke wasn't afraid of doing a small bank job. Lifting a couple of thousand pounds from some suburban post office, or a small branch of one of the big five British banks, was as easy for him as stealing milk cartons from doorsteps was for late-night drunks. What Danny was afraid of was the army council. The Provos frowned on free-lance fund-raising. If he was sprung he could be kneecapped.

"I know, Danny," O'Donnell snapped, injecting an uncompromising harshness into his voice. "Don't tell me how bloody hard it is for ye, all right? I'm not interested. It's hard for everybody. Just get the bloody money, will ye. I want it here within the week. Do ye understand me, now?"

There was a pause and then a sigh of resignation on the other end of the line. "All right, all right. I'll get you the money. I'll try and bring it down next weekend, all right?"

O'Donnell softened his voice a fraction. "That'll be fine, Danny. You're a good lad. I know it's hard but it won't be long now. I just have to slip a few pounds to a man in Dublin to look the other way for a bit." He paused. "I won't be here on the weekend. You'll have to come up to the farm. We're expecting a visitor. A nice American lady. That's all I'm going to tell ye now. You're a good lad. I'll see ye on the weekend." And he hung up before Danny had a chance to think up any more excuses.

The next phone call required a minor but essential piece of theater. He took out his pocket handkerchief and wrapped it over the mouthpiece. Then he dialed the number of the information hotline to the Royal Ulster Constabulary in Belfast. The informers' line. There was a recorded voice on the other end, calculated to engender a feeling of confidence in the informer. The line existed to receive any and all information that might help the police and the British government fight terrorism. Most of the calls consisted of foul language and abuse by street kids and drunks. There were dozens of hoax calls involving bombs in cars and buses and buildings. The police monitors had learned to screen out most of the rubbish but occasionally they recognized a genuine warning from the Officials, the Provos, or the Irish National Liberation Army. It required a fine and terrible judgment. If it was a convincing hoax they risked evacuating the city center at fifteen minutes' notice. Half a dozen times a day. If they guessed wrong and a bomb went off then innocent people were killed and maimed. Sometimes the IRA played cruel games and made two or three hoax calls before placing a genuine call. Later they would release a statement to the media that they had given a warning. It all added to the intolerable strain on ordinary policemen and women who found a single year with the RUC in Belfast worse than any tour of duty in Vietnam. At least, in Vietnam, the day came when you could leave and go home. In

Belfast you could never leave. You were home. You lived with
it. You were never off duty.

The voice said: "Police information line," and then there was
a small beep. If the message wasn't delivered within twenty
seconds the line automatically disconnected. O'Donnell had
edited the message down to three words; he said them only once.
The police and the army would have to work it out from there.

"Watch Danny Locke."

He was sweating and when he hung up he used the handkerchief to wipe his forehead. That would be enough, he knew.
Danny was a known IRA gunman. The RUC would tip off the
British and the army was certain to be interested. Even though
it was a setup the British couldn't ignore it. They would keep
an eye on Danny for the next few days and when Danny went
out to do the job they would pick him up. Danny was already
living on his nerves. He could be counted upon to crack under
interrogation. It might take a couple of days but he would crack.
And he would remember the bit about the farm and the "nice
American lady." That would be enough for army intelligence
to connect with the Americans, under joint intelligence-sharing
agreements, to see if they had anything going involving a woman
and the IRA. After that it was only a matter of time, days at
the most, before Halloran and Lynch took the bait.

They would have to hit the farm and they would have to do
it on their own. It was what they were good at. The Irish
government would not countenance any action by British troops
on Irish soil, and the British did not trust the Irish government,
riddled as it was with IRA sympathizers, to do the job for them.
It would have to be a covert operation. In and out. Hard and
fast. Government deniable. Exactly the sort of operation Halloran and Lynch specialized in, except this time they would be
limited in the amount of force they could use because they would
be afraid of hurting the girl. But Hennessy and the boys wouldn't
be limited in the amount of force they could use. They would
be expecting Mr. Lynch and his pals. They would be waiting.
They would wait until their visitors were well inside their trap
and then hit them with everything they had.

His plan was proceeding quite satisfactorily, O'Donnell

thought, with no small sense of satisfaction. Hennessy would be here soon, Hennessy and the girl. And somewhere else, he knew, Jack Halloran and Colin Lynch would be biding their time, working out who he was, where he was . . . and how they would come and get him. He would be ready. He and Brian Hennessy. Hennessy would take care of Lynch. There wasn't a man on earth Brian was afraid of. There was a certain symmetry about it all, O'Donnell thought. A rather beautiful kind of poetic justice.

He had chosen the place to spring his trap carefully. He and Eamonn Docherty had searched the rugged coastal country of northwestern Donegal, with its murderous Atlantic surf and soaring, terrifying cliffs, for a month until they found what they wanted: a small and isolated farmhouse on the northwestern tip of Donegal, bordered on three sides by cliffs and ocean. O'Donnell had liked it for its name as much as anything else. It was called Bloody Foreland, after a brutal massacre of the survivors of a grounded warship from the ill-fated Spanish armada, trying vainly to escape back to its homeland via the northern reaches of Ireland. At least one hundred shipwrecked and exhausted sailors and soldiers had been hacked to death, their bodies and their vessel plundered, by the wild local clansmen. O'Donnell thought it an appropriate and historic venue for another massacre, the bloody destruction of unwanted modern intruders.

"So this is how low you've sunk, Tom."

It was Mavour. Her voice was a weary blend of sorrow and contempt.

"Turning in your own pals to serve your filthy little schemes."

He swung around in surprise to see her there, standing in the doorway with her coat on and two small suitcases on the kitchen floor behind her.

Her face was as pale as the morning mist and her voice sounded close to breaking.

"Mavour . . ." he began, stepping toward her.

"Don't, Tom," she said, taking a small step back, as though afraid of him. "Don't come near me. Don't waste time. I've fought against this day for two years. But what I've seen and heard in this house these past few months has finished me. My husband is dead. I mourn for him. But I can't mourn for you. I should have accepted that he died years ago in that bloody business in Armagh. . . . That's when the Tom I loved died."

She took a deep, shaky breath to calm herself and stooped to pick up her bags.

"I called last night and booked a taxi for nine o'clock," she said. "I'll walk down to the road and wait."

Tom O'Donnell stared at his wife in disbelief.

"Mavour," he tried again. "What in the name of God . . ."

"It's too late for any of that, Tom," she said, the first tears glistening in the corners of her eyes. "You're not the man I married. You're all twisted up with your own hate and bitterness. I might have put up with that if I thought you were just sick . . . sick in the head. But you're sick at heart. You've done murder. There's been too much murder. You've lived bloody these past years, Tom. And I pray that almighty God takes pity on you . . . because as He is my witness, I know . . . you'll die bloody, Tom. You'll die bloody."

He watched her shuffle awkwardly out the back door and then listened while her footsteps faded on the gravel track down to the road.

Tom O'Donnell slumped down in his armchair and stared at the half-open kitchen door for a long time. There were no tears in his eyes. No pain on his face. Just disbelief. He had no idea how much time had passed, but when he finally got up, walked to the back door, and looked down the track to the road, she was gone. He stepped back inside and shut the door. He stood in the kitchen and stared at nothing for several minutes. After a while he went upstairs to their bedroom. She had made the bed and taken the pictures of the children from her bedside table. He went to the wardrobe and looked in puzzlement at the clothes she had left behind. There seemed to be too many. Then he realized they were mostly dresses and shoes from the early days of their marriage. Old. Long out of fashion. Clothes from another life. Another time. He trailed his rough hand lightly over them, feeling the fabric. He stopped at the pale green woolen dress with the voluminous skirt that he remembered her wearing at the Saint Patrick's Day Ball in Dublin in 1959. He pulled the dress to his face and smelled deeply to see if there were any traces of past innocence in there among the perfume. There was only the sharp smell of mothballs.

Thirty-three years, O'Donnell calculated. Thirty-three years of marriage. He went back downstairs to the kitchen, took out the Bushmills from the cupboard under the sink, picked up a glass in the other hand, walked back into the living room, sat down, and poured himself a drink. Thirty-three years, he thought. A man ought to feel something. There had been the sudden shock of the unexpected, but that was all. No pain. He knew he had loved her more than anything else in the world, once. What had happened? Perhaps she was right, perhaps he *was* sick at heart? He took a series of long, deep sips, like some kind of white-haired, cold-blooded reptile silently drinking from a pool. After a minute the whiskey seemed to put some warmth into his blood. He picked up the bottlecap, eyed the rest of the whiskey in the bottle, then screwed the cap back in place. He couldn't afford to get drunk. Tomorrow afternoon he would be meeting Eamonn in Strabane, just across the border in Ulster. They were both driving up to Derry to start pulling the boys out.

THE *AMERICAN ENDEAVOR*, MID-ATLANTIC, APRIL 9

"Jackpot!"

Sir Malcolm Porter's voice flooded into the communications room. Halloran and Lynch instinctively leaned closer to the speaker, even though the incoming radio call had been amplified to fill the cabin. Bono lounged attentively in the background.

"You were right, Colin," the chief of CTC complimented him. "Brian Hennessy served in the parachute regiment for nine years. I think we might be dealing with a bloody traitor after all."

Lynch smiled bleakly. Traitor? It had such an old-fashioned sound. It didn't seem to belong in a world where no one believed in anything anymore.

"I've got his file in front of me right now. Would you like me to give you the headlines?"

Lynch pictured Sir Malcolm in his Whitehall office with the window overlooking the plane trees on the Mall.

"Please, sir. We're all listening."

"Okay," the plummy English voice drawled. "Born in Belfast, 1961. One younger brother. Father a welder in the Belfast ship-yards. Family emigrated to England, 1967, settled in Wallasey, suburb of Liverpool. Left school at fifteen. Joined the army, 1978. Applied for the parachute regiment, accepted after basic training. Served with distinction. Outstanding athlete. Very capable soldier. Promoted lance corporal, 1981, corporal, 1982. Went to the Falklands . . ." Sir Malcolm paused.

"Wonder you two didn't run into each other, eh?"

Lynch didn't bite.

"Acquitted himself quite well according to this," Sir Malcolm went on. "Fought at Goose Green. Commended for bravery. Led a charge on an Argentine stronghold. Helped turn the enemy line. Awarded the Military Cross. Promoted sergeant. Commissioned from the ranks a year after his return to England. Seems things didn't go too well for him at Sandhurst, though. Did well on the academic side but some behavioral problems emerged. Couldn't get on with the other chaps. There were one or two complaints about him. Seems he was prone to issuing threats. Thumped a chap once in the local pub. He was inter-viewed about it and his version was that they were a bunch of Hooray Henrys. He was probably right, too. Got his lieutenant's pips all right though. I must say—" Sir Malcolm broke off his scanning of the file. "The psychological profile in here is piss poor. Very sketchy to say the least. Either his instructors were too bloody stupid to notice or too bloody lazy to care. Probably thought things would just magically sort themselves out, silly bastards."

"What's next?" Lynch asked.

"Year's tour of duty in Northern Ireland."

Lynch and Halloran exchanged glances.

"Yes?" Lynch waited.

"Getting interesting, isn't it?" Sir Malcolm said mildly. "Un-fortunately there isn't much after that. He was in line for a captaincy on return from Northern Ireland. Resigned his com-mission instead. Very odd. There's a record of interview with the regimental commanding officer here. Very briefly it looks as though they tried damned hard to persuade him to stay on but he wouldn't have any of it."

"Any reason given?" Lynch queried.

"Personal reasons. That's all it says. I've read the transcript. It's the most detailed part of the file. Seems they finally clued in that they were losing a good man. Bit too late though."

"What's next?"

"Very little. Virtually disappeared off the face of the earth."

"There must be something?"

"Only two records of his movements after resigning from the parachute regiment. Social security places him in Belfast, August 1989. Wherever he's been since, he hasn't had a job and he hasn't paid any tax."

"And?"

"This bit's interesting. Immigration department has a record of him reentering the country at Heathrow, November 1990. Recorded his port of embarkation as Ankara."

"Ankara?" Lynch echoed softly.

"Handy for a lot of places, Ankara, isn't it?" Sir Malcolm said.

"No other ports of call on his passport?" Halloran queried.

"Apparently not, Jack. He could have been anywhere. Beirut, Baghdad, Damascus . . ."

"Tehran . . ." Lynch interjected, thinking of the terrorist training camps sprinkled throughout northwestern Iran.

"Yes," Sir Malcolm concurred. "Tehran's a possibility too, if he's our boy."

"Why haven't we run into him before?" Halloran asked.

"Who knows?" Sir Malcolm answered. "Luck? Maybe he's just very good. He certainly came from the best military background in the world. You don't get much better than the paras."

"Or maybe he was being saved for something special," Lynch added quietly.

"Like?" Halloran stood up and faced him.

"Like taking care of us?"

The cabin was silent for a moment except the occasional hiss of static on the amplified radio phone.

"Sir, can you skip back to his time in Northern Ireland?" Lynch said. "Anything remarkable about his service there?"

There was a long pause. Finally a simple "No. Nothing."

"No bombings, shootings, clashes with the IRA in the border country? No nasty riot situations?" He paused. "Funny, isn't it?"

"What are you getting at?" Sir Malcolm's disembodied voice posed the question for them all.

"It's impossible . . . *almost* impossible for any unit in the British army to go to Northern Ireland and have a trouble-free tour of duty. Nobody gets a dream run. Every fresh unit transferred over there gets a baptism of fire at some point, the IRA guarantees it. That is especially true of the paras. The Catholics hate them more than any other unit in the British army. Not only for Bloody Sunday . . . but because they don't stuff around. You know when they're in town. They're always trouble to the IRA. They go out of their way to let the Provos and the Officials know who's in charge. Yet, here we have a lieutenant in the parachute regiment who spends a year in Northern Ireland and never gets involved in one serious incident? Odd, wouldn't you say?"

There was a pause.

"Yes," Sir Malcolm agreed. "It is odd."

Halloran watched Lynch carefully. The American realized he was entering a new and different kind of country. Northern Ireland had never been his area of concern. That was a problem for the British; he'd always thought they seemed to be doing a pretty good job of screwing it up on their own. But if that's where the murderous assault on his New York offices had originated, then he was going in. And, he knew, if they were going to launch an operation in Northern Ireland then he would have to put himself squarely in the hands of Lynch and his old friend and colleague, Sir Malcolm Porter.

"Who have we got in Ulster?" Lynch asked Porter.

"We?" Porter queried.

Lynch corrected himself. "Force of habit, sir."

"That's all right, Lieutenant Lynch," Sir Malcolm rejoined. Porter's use of Lynch's former naval rank was a subtle reference to his earlier role as a squad leader at Heathrow with CTC. Both men were well aware how hard Sir Malcolm had tried to persuade Lynch to stay active in the network after the Christmas Eve massacre at Heathrow. Each suddenly found himself wondering if Lynch's slip reflected a subliminal wish to come back to the fold. For Lynch, especially, it was an acute question. He was a man without a home.

"Is there anyone we can use in Ulster to pick up this Hennessy's track?"

"Well," Porter drawled maddeningly. "I believe your pal, Peter Gamble, is still on active service with the SAS over there."

Lynch smiled inwardly at the thought of the tough, swarthy, dry-humored SAS captain who had accompanied him on their last operation into Lebanon almost a year ago. He couldn't have asked for a better man to work with. Sometimes, he thought, you had to get lucky.

"Can we borrow him?"

"Depends," Porter answered.

"We have to squeeze the IRA, sir. We have to find out where this Hennessy fellow is now."

"I believe the regiment is squeezing the IRA pretty hard already," Porter added drolly. "I don't think Gamble's commanding officer will mind too much if we use him to squeeze from a new direction."

"Good." Lynch stood upright and stretched. "That settles it."

"What?" Bono inquired from the back of the room. It was the first time he'd contributed to the long-distance conference.

Lynch walked over to him and slapped him on the shoulder.

Bono winced. It had been nearly two weeks but the bigger burns were still tender.

"We're going to Belfast," Lynch said.

THE *CEILIDH PRINCESS*, NORTH ATLANTIC, APRIL 9

While the *American Endeavor* butted rhythmically through the mid-Atlantic rollers en route to Ireland, some two thousand nautical miles to the northeast the *Ceilidh Princess* had already dropped her sea anchor. Apart from two days of heavy weather, as they left the lee of Newfoundland and caught the dwindling fury of a storm scouring the wave tops out of Greenland, it had been an easy crossing from Boston to the coast of Ireland. Liam McKee had thrown out the sea anchor and they were wallowing in a light swell, forty nautical miles west of Rossan Point, the westernmost tip of the craggy headland that guards Donegal Bay. They were well out of sight of coastal traffic and any other prying eyes from the mainland.

Owen, the deckhand, was spread-eagled across the cargo hatch, rereading a grimy copy of *Mayfair*, a British girlie magazine. McKee was smoking a hand-rolled cigarette on the bridge, listening to the coastal radio traffic and the weather reports. Hennessy was dozing on one of the bunks in the galley. They had been at anchor for thirty-six hours, and apart from McKee's occasional navigational corrections to keep them in the right spot there had been little to do. A kind of torpor had settled over the trawler, punctuated only by mealtimes and sleep. Janice remained in her prison in the bow, lying awake on one of the two narrow bunks that flanked each wall of the tiny forward cabin.

She was tired, dirty, and close to the breaking point. Hennessy had offered her the run of the boat; he knew she couldn't go anywhere. But she had declined. She had decided she wanted no communication, no interaction, no conversation. Nothing that might humanize her captors. As Hennessy had amusedly pointed out, she only made it harder on herself. He was right. She was losing the battle of wills. She depended on her captors for everything. Every time she had to ask for something they won a minor victory. She had to ask for permission to use the head. When she was thirsty she had to ask for water. When she was hungry she had to ask for food. It stuck in her throat but she had to eat. Whenever she yielded enough to ask, Hennessy would grin and tell Owen to make her a cheese sandwich or give her a mug of soup. When she wanted to wash she had to ask for soap and a towel. She hated using anything with the stink of her captors on it. She couldn't bring herself to use the shower. She was afraid. She washed her face, hands, and feet, and rinsed her hair, but that was all. She washed her pants and bra quickly, wrung them out, and put them on wet.

She had been shocked when she saw the size of the bruise on her right hip where Hennessy had kicked her. It was crescent shaped, almost exactly the length of a man's foot, and a deep aubergine. When she looked in the tiny, circular mirror in the head and saw her face, she caught her breath. The side of her face was tender to the touch and she had felt the lump on her right temple, but nothing had prepared her for the sight that met her eyes. The bruise on the left side of her face stretched from her jawline to her temple and was an ugly greenish blue. The bruise on her right temple was almost the size of an egg, the same hideous dark hue, and the skin was split in the center for almost half an inch. A scab had formed while she had been drugged. She had no idea how bad the cut was or what kind of scar it would leave, but she was certain of one thing: she may have marked Hennessy for life, but he had marked her in return.

Just the thought of Hennessy terrified her. She had never met a man who filled her with such fear and revulsion. His cold and casual use of violence sickened her. His behavior toward her left her in no doubt that she was utterly expendable. If she proved to be too much trouble or if she outlived her usefulness, she knew he would dispose of her in a moment. And he wouldn't be too fussy about how he did it. That was part of the reason Janice had kept to her cabin in the bow. The door was unlocked and she could leave at any time but she tried to confine her trips outside to two or three times a day, appearing only briefly to ask for food or to use the head. They had offered a kind of bizarre sociability in the first two days, inviting her to enjoy the freedom of the boat—as long as she behaved. It was as though they were offering her a kind of undeclared deal, an arrangement whereby, if she made things easy for them, if she acknowledged their absolute power over her, they wouldn't hurt her unnecessarily.

Still, she knew, the time would come when they would hurt her—when they would kill her. She was only useful until they had what they wanted. Until they had Lynch. That much she knew. And when they had him, or the deal went bad, she would suddenly become irrelevant. Just another pawn in the game. Perversely, they seemed to expect her to go along with it, to acquiesce in her own death. To make it easy for them. But she couldn't stand to be in the same room with any one of them. Since that first night, when they brought her out of the engine room and offered her a warm meal and showed her the bunk in the bow, she had tried to keep herself as separate from them as possible. Their attitude confused and disgusted her. The forced intimacy appeared to be a kind of game for them, as though she were a kind of novelty that required only the barest consideration. And then what? She had spent most of the time in her bunk, trying to sleep, willing away the long, despairing hours.

The cabin door opened and she twisted to look over her shoulder.

It was Hennessy. Something about the way he looked at her made her stomach turn. He stared at her for a long time, his face impassive. The dressing had come off his left cheek but there was still a large swelling, a dark, purplish discoloration, and, right in the center, a perfect, round puncture wound.

"What do you want?" she asked. She rolled onto her back and braced herself. If it was what she thought it was, she was going to fight.

"I was wondering what a two-thousand-dollar-a-night whore feels like," he said softly.

She waited. Outwardly she seemed calm but inside she was reeling. She couldn't believe any man would find her desirable in her present physical state. Her face was battered and swollen, her hair tangled and filthy. Her clothes were soiled and dirty and she hadn't bathed properly for a week. She also knew that rape had nothing to do with sexual desire. It was about power and violence. Brian Hennessy loved both.

"What do you do, I wonder, that's so special? What makes you different from any other woman?"

When she had first heard him speak at any length, six days ago on the first night on the boat, she had thought he was English. But now she caught something else in his voice, a slight Irish burr to the words. It was as though the time he'd spent on the boat with the two trawlermen had rubbed off on him. As if he'd picked up their accent.

"Do you do tricks?" he tormented her. "Eh? Is that it, Janice? Do you do tricks? What kind of tricks do you do, I wonder? What kind of tricks do you do that are worth two thousand American dollars a night?"

He stepped inside and closed the cabin door behind him. She could hear nothing else but the slap of the waves on the hull and the occasional burst of static-filled radio chatter carrying down from the wheelhouse, through the tiny open porthole over her head. He leaned back against the door with his hands behind him.

"Do you like to suck dicks, Janice? Are you good at it, eh? Had lots of practice?"

He stepped forward and she lashed out at him with her bare foot. She tried to aim her heel at the wound in his cheek but he was ready for her. He swatted her flailing legs aside with his right hand, then moved forward and pinned her to the bunk with his other arm. She arched her back and thrashed with all her might but it was no use. He was too strong. She felt her strength ebbing away quickly. Pulling the handcuffs from his pocket, he grabbed one hand and cuffed it to the bunk rail behind her head, and then the other.

Janice screamed. It was a sound she couldn't believe had come from her. It was the hoarse, agonized bellow of pain of a stricken animal.

Up in the wheelhouse Liam McKee smoked his cigarette and stared impassively at the horizon. Owen's head jolted upright.

"Mind yourself, boy," McKee growled at him. "Bit of man's business goin' on below, that's all."

Janice stopped struggling and blazed a look of pure hatred at Hennessy. Then she hawked and spat full in his face. Hennessy grabbed her sweater by the neck and pulled; it came away like a rotten rag. He used it to wipe her spit off his face and then threw it to the deck. She wasn't wearing a belt. She was dressed in the same clothes she'd hurriedly put on that night at the town house. He tore open the top of her pants and ripped them savagely from her legs. Janice fought valiantly but her strength had gone. She groaned miserably and closed her eyes. And then she did something she hadn't done since she was a little girl.

She cried. She tried to stop herself but she couldn't. Her body was consumed by a wave of helpless sobs and her face flooded with tears.

Hennessy began to undress.

"That's good, Janice," he said softly. "You're making me hard."

It lasted for an hour. He raped her twice. Between the first and the second time he talked to her as though it were all quite normal. As though she were a willing partner. She thought she was going to vomit but she hadn't eaten since the previous day and there was nothing in her stomach to throw up.

Finally he got dressed and prepared to leave. She lay silently in the bunk with her head turned to the bulkhead.

Before he left Hennessy stopped and fumbled in his pants pocket.

"Here," he said. "Here's what I think you're worth."

And he crumpled a two-dollar bill and threw it on her naked body.

BELFAST, NORTHERN IRELAND, APRIL 11

"Good to see you again, sir," Lynch said as he shook hands with Sir Malcolm Porter on the darkened tarmac of Belfast's Aldergrove Airport. "It's been a while."

"Good to see you," Sir Malcolm rejoined. "You're looking a helluva lot fitter than the last time I saw you."

That had been on the deck of the American aircraft carrier, the USS *John F. Kennedy*, off the coast of Libya. Lynch had been on a stretcher, his body bloodied with shrapnel wounds, several ribs broken, both eardrums burst, and suffering blast trauma following his escape from Tripoli. Plucked from the sea by a rescue chopper, he had been in no condition to exchange pleasantries with Sir Malcolm. They had spoken by phone or radio many times since, but this had been the first time they had met in more than two years.

Despite the khaki trench coat over the civvies there was no

mistaking Porter's military bearing. Whip thin, he stood with shoulders back, head erect; his strong, tanned face contrasted sharply with the white-tinged hair. He was the fittest fifty-eight-year-old Lynch had ever seen. A former commanding officer of the SAS, founder and sole controlling officer of Counter Terrorism Command for almost five years, Porter seemed to thrive on stress.

"And who's this brute?" he asked amiably as Bono lumbered toward them through the blustery night, a full kit bag dangling from one hand as lightly as a lady's purse.

"Sir Malcolm . . . Samuel Jefferson Bono, private first class, United States Marine Corps, Retired."

"Glad to meet you Mr., ah . . . Bono." Porter smiled as he shook Bono's paw. "I understand you're rather a useful chap to have around."

"Yeah," Bono grunted. "A useful chap . . ."

Lynch and Bono had both just alighted from a Fleet Air Wing Orion, diverted at Porter's request from its usual run, which took it, three time weekly, between Gibraltar and the Royal Navy shore base, RN Culdrose, in Cornwall. Instead of wasting the four days it would take the *American Endeavor* to reach Northern Ireland, Halloran had diverted the yacht to within two hundred nautical miles of Gibraltar and the two men had choppered in to the Rock. Freshly rested and kitted out after a week aboard the big yacht, Lynch was eager for action. Bono had insisted he come along. His wounds had healed, he said.

"I'm itchy," he argued. "Outside and inside. I need to be doin' somethin'."

"I'm glad you're both fit and raring to go," Sir Malcolm said as he steered them toward a waiting unmarked Range Rover. "Because we have a situation. I thought you might like to come along. I brought all the necessary toys. I'll tell you about it on the way."

Lynch's adrenaline simmered at the thought. In CTC parlance a "situation" meant only one thing: an emergency. And it had to have something to do with the reason they'd come to Northern Ireland.

Porter confirmed it a moment later as he took the wheel of the Range Rover and drove out of the airport to join the M2 motorway and then eastward toward the waterside Belfast suburb of Newtownabbey.

"Got a tip a few days ago about a chap called Danny Locke. Nasty little beggar he is, too. Provo gunman. Responsible for five murders we know of and probably a few more we don't know of . . . yet."

Bono listened silently in the backseat. He liked the way the British called everybody "chap." An IRA hit man was a "chap." That was nice, he thought.

"Tip came in on the RUC hotline. Smells a bit. Seems to me somebody's setting us up as well as Mr. Locke. Perhaps we've just been used to do some of the IRA's dirty work for them. Perhaps someone's settling a score. Either way, because of who he is they passed it on to the army and the army notified SAS as a matter of course. That's how I know. Being aware of your situation, naturally, I thought it might have some bearing.

"Anyway, army intelligence have had him under surveillance for the past few days. Then, this morning, around ten o'clock, Mr. Locke leaves home, drives to Newtownabbey, and holds up the local branch of the Midland Bank. That's all right until he goes to leave and the two silly buggers from army intelligence decide to tackle him there and then, instead of following him home and notifying the SAS. Anyway, Mr. Locke goes completely off his trolley, shoots one in the chest, shoots the other one in the arse, then runs back into the bank and takes the bank staff hostage, all seven of them. That's our situation. SAS was called in around lunchtime. Captain Gamble is there now. He'll be quite pleased to see you, I should imagine."

"How are the two army men?" Lynch asked.

"Oh, they'll both be all right," Porter said airily. "The chest shot wasn't bad. Went through the top right side, punctured the top section of the lung, broke the collarbone, I believe. Bullet went straight through, didn't fragment. Some of the dirty bastards have been using dumdums, you know. The other one was lucky too. You know what they say about army intelligence—bullet missed his brains by inches."

The digital dashboard clock said 11:33 P.M. as the Range Rover hummed along the motorway between amber colonnades of light toward Newtownabbey.

Well, well, well, Bono thought to himself. He was going to
a situation with a few chaps. One chap had already had his ass
shot off but that was okay. Nobody seemed to mind too much
about that. And in all probability, before the night was through,
some other chap would have his ass shot off, too. What a cheery
people the British seemed to be, Bono thought. Lynch was the
only Briton he'd ever really known. They got along because they
had spent all their lives in the military world. They understood
the military code. And they had cemented their friendship under
fire. There was no better way, Bono believed. Combat had a
habit of revealing the true character of any man, real fast.

It took twenty minutes to get to Newtownabbey. Porter
seemed to know Belfast rather well, Lynch thought. Sir Malcolm
had obviously spent some time there with the SAS. Time Lynch
had never heard about but which he'd like to one day. Porter
steered them through a bewildering maze of twisting, narrow
streets of red brick terrace houses and poky little shops. Lynch
had been away long enough to be shocked at how small everything looked, as though all the buildings had been scaled down
by 20 percent. No wonder Americans thought Europe was
"cute."

Eventually they turned a corner into a main street shopping
center and were confronted by a crowd of about two hundred
people at a barricade manned by RUC officers and armed British
soldiers. The crowd didn't seem hostile, Lynch thought. Only
curious. The same morbid public curiosity that attended death
and disaster anywhere in the world was evident here. Porter was
recognized and the corporal on the barricade waved the Range
Rover through. Lynch noticed the shoulder flashes of the Sussex
Regiment. A hundred meters farther down the road a half dozen
vehicles formed a roadblock. There were a couple of armored
Land Rovers, a police Range Rover, a communications truck,
and a couple of unmarked RUC cars. There was a gap of about
fifty yards and then a similar roadblock on the other side. The
bank was just about in the center. There were still a couple
dozen parked cars on both sides of the road, left where they
stood despite the protestations of the owners.

Porter pulled up just before the roadblock. Lynch could see
half a dozen men in plainclothes, a couple of uniformed RUC

men, and another half dozen soldiers in full battle dress. There was no sign of the SAS. Lynch knew they would be in a house nearby, waiting.

"Just a word before we get out," Porter cautioned. "The army's had a negotiator here since midday. Don't know if he's got anywhere yet, but you know what they're like. He'll try to bore Locke into giving himself up. No sign that the hostages have been mistreated, though, and that's good. Even so, Locke's getting a bit twitchy. They sent in some food and drinks around six."

"Any demands?"

"It took him a while. I don't think he was expecting a situation quite like this. He's asked for safe escort to Aldergrove and a plane to take him and the hostages to Algeria. Says he'll release the hostages when he's been granted political asylum."

"Response?"

"Oh, out of the question, of course. He's going nowhere. He's been offered a deal if he frees the hostages unharmed."

"What deal?"

"He faces charges on the holdup only. We keep it a police matter."

"What did he say to that?"

"Oh, usual nonsense, bit of language. Renewed his demands."

"Has he threatened to kill any of the hostages yet?"

"No . . . but the negotiator says he's getting edgy. Could be a junkie. Hasn't asked for any drugs, though. Could just be the jumpy type. Most of them aren't very bright, you know. They're all right at dragging unarmed men out of bed in their pajamas and shooting them at two o'clock in the morning but give them a real situation to deal with and they get a headache."

"Okay." Lynch nodded. "Where's Gamble?"

"Let's go and see him now, shall we?"

Peter Gamble was with five other SAS men in a small terrace house less than twenty paces from where Porter had parked the Range Rover. The house belonged to a young married couple with a new baby who had gratefully accepted the army's offer of temporary accommodations at the Europa Hotel. The six SAS men were already geared up in black utilities, everything but balaclavas and weapons. The last time Lynch had worked with

Gamble they had cleaned out a Shiite militia barracks together in Lebanon's Beqaa Valley.

"Good to see you again, Lieutenant," Gamble greeted Lynch.

That rank again, Lynch noted. Were they trying to tell him something?

Lynch and Bono shook hands with Gamble and exchanged nods with the other men in the room.

"You running this show, Peter?" Lynch asked.

"Afraid so," Gamble acknowledged. "Been on alert since midday. We'll be standing down in . . ." He glanced at his watch. It was close to midnight. "Six minutes. Second unit will come in and we'll grab a little sleep, I suppose."

"Who's the situation control officer?" Lynch asked mildly.

"Technically, that would be Captain Gamble's CO in Northern Ireland, Colonel Fleming," Porter chipped in. "The secretary is informed of every situation where the regiment has to be involved." Porter was referring to the British secretary for Northern Ireland, who would be kept abreast of the situation, as it unfolded, in Whitehall via the SAS at Hereford.

"The secretary must give his approval before the SAS can come in," Porter went on. "Once he's given the okay, the SAS operates in conjunction with the joint military commander for the area at the scene. They are obliged to try all peaceful means to resolve the situation. If they fail or if the situation deteriorates suddenly then the SAS takes over immediately."

Lynch nodded. "Still all a bit reactive, isn't it?"

"Lynch?" There was a mild note of rebuke in Porter's voice.

"You're handing him all the initiative." Lynch shrugged. "You've got everything you need to resolve the situation inside two minutes . . . and you're just sitting around waiting to pick up the pieces when he decides he's had enough."

The men in the room developed a new interest in Lynch.

"There's a bit of politics involved, dear chap," Porter reasoned. "We are a democracy, after all. We can't be too heavy-handed. We have to try all reasonable means. The secretary insists on it."

"Where's the secretary now?" Lynch asked.

Porter had the grace to look uncomfortable.

"At home in bed, I believe," he said.

"Oh, I see." Lynch nodded. "Wake me if it's important . . . that sort of thing?"

There was silence in the room. The rest of the men in Gamble's unit remained impassive but their ears were tuned to Lynch's words.

"So," Lynch went on, "we've got a snot-nosed IRA thug holding seven innocent people across the road at gunpoint and we're all sitting around with our thumbs up our bums while the secretary curls up in his bed with Paddington Bear."

"We could take him now," Gamble said quietly. He stepped into the corner of the room and produced a familiar weapon with an unfamiliar adaptation.

"The Hockler MP5-SD3," he said, using the service abbreviation for Heckler and Koch, the German manufacturers of the SAS's preferred armament.

"The barrel on the top is a laser sight. We've had infrared sensors and directional mikes on the bank since three o'clock this afternoon. We know where he is just about every minute. We could have taken him out at any time."

"How's the negotiator doing?" Lynch asked.

Porter took a deep breath. "Why don't we find out?"

Porter led Lynch and Bono back out into the street. Gamble remained in the house, away from prying eyes, with the rest of his men.

A group of three men in civvies stood with an RUC chief inspector drinking coffee. The shortest of the group, a fit-looking man in a plain blue raincoat, was Colonel Fleming, the SAS commander in Northern Ireland. The tall man at his side was Colonel Webster, the district army commander. Both military men wore civilian clothes so they could not easily be identified as future targets by IRA spies in the distant crowds. The fourth man was a thin, scholarly-looking type whom Porter introduced as Walter Pryne, professor of psychology at Cambridge, on special assignment to the British army in Northern Ireland. The negotiator.

Lynch and Bono were introduced as observers from CTC.

"Anything new?" Porter asked. No one spoke.

"Professor Pryne thinks it's going to be a long night," Fleming said eventually. "Thinks our man might be a little more amenable to suggestion after going without a night's sleep."

"How does he sound?" Lynch asked.

All the men in the group eyed Lynch with undisguised skepticism.

Pryne shrugged. "Erratic. That's to be expected. He was very agitated earlier today just after the situation began. He calmed down a little after I spoke to him. We've sent him some food. He's beginning to come around, I think. There was a flare-up a couple of hours ago when he realized he wasn't going to get everything he wanted. But he's talking. I think we'll do a deal."

"Do a deal?" Lynch echoed. Even though he said it quietly he was unable to filter out all his own distaste. Nothing had changed, he thought. Waffle and blather, drag out the situation as long as possible until the gunman and the hostages are at the end of their rope; then, the moment it all comes apart, send in the SAS and whine like hell afterward because people died.

Lynch turned and walked away. The group went back to their coffee and conversation.

"Where are you going?" Porter asked after him.

Both Porter and Bono heard Lynch mumble something under his breath but couldn't make out the words.

What he said was, "I have to make a phone call."

He walked down the street until he came to a narrow alley between the red brick houses. He entered it and crossed another two streets until he found what he was looking for. The phone directory had been vandalized but directory assistance had the number.

A moment later the phone in the Newtownabbey branch of the Midland Bank rang. The soldiers and men outside listened apprehensively.

"Damn," Professor Pryne swore. "If the bloody media's got hold of this they could ruin everything."

There was no way they could stop anyone ringing directly into the bank. The RUC had plugged in their own intercept and Pryne spoke to Locke from inside the communications van. The RUC and the army PR officers had spent the whole day begging editors, publishers, TV station bosses, and radio network chiefs to respect the negotiation and keep their people from ringing through to get exclusive interviews with the gunman. So far it had worked.

Inside the bank Danny Locke let the phone ring. He was getting a little tired of that weaseling little English prick on the other end who kept telling him to stay calm and they could work something out. His guts had been on fire all day. He was looking down the barrel of a long time in jail or an SAS bullet in the brain. He wouldn't get the plane, he knew. It had been the only thing he could think of. But neither was he going to give up yet. He hadn't actually decided *what* he was going to do. The idea of wasting one of the hostages and throwing the body onto the sidewalk had occurred to him a dozen times, but that sniveling little shit on the phone was probably right. If he did that the deal would be off and he could expect the SAS through the doors and windows any minute.

And so Danny Locke waited and fretted and suffered the agonies of his ulcerated stomach while the hostages lay nearby on the floor against the wall of the bank, trembling in silent terror. There was the branch manager, the accountant, and five tellers. Three men and four women. He'd kept them on the floor all day, forcing them to use a garbage can in the manager's office, with the door open, when they wanted to urinate or defecate. The toilets were in a back room and he couldn't control all the hostages if he started letting them go one at a time. The manager's office had two doors, one that led to the customer area, the other to the service area behind the counter. He'd locked that door and confined them to the small customer area in front of the counter.

There had been no trouble getting them to do what he wanted when he had rushed back into the bank after shooting two men. They had herded fearfully out in front of the counter and lain, whimpering and shaking, on the floor just as he ordered, and they had remained there ever since. Their only respite had been the few sandwiches and soft drinks sent in six hours earlier. The branch manager had tried to reason with him at one point, to let the women go, but Danny had rushed over to him and shoved the muzzle of the Belgian FN 9 mm in his neck and screamed at him, screamed at them all to keep their gobs shut.

The manager's phone kept ringing on the floor near his foot. The line was just long enough for him to bring the telephone out of the office and shut the door to keep the stench of the shit bucket down. He had just finished speaking to the bastard half an hour ago. The negotiator had offered him the promise of full protection. No bashings by the RUC boys when they got their hands on him. A fair trial on the holdup charges only. He had until six in the morning before the offer was withdrawn. It was a reasonable deal under ordinary circumstances, Danny knew, if they were telling the truth. Especially for a man with his record.

The stupid bastards didn't know it yet but they'd struck gold with him. There was no way he was going to the Maze where his old Provo pals would want to know exactly what he thought he'd been up to. He would negotiate again before morning, he knew. He'd offer to grass, to tell them all he knew. He was sick of the Provos, sick of Tom O'Donnell, sick of it all. He wanted out. But he'd need protection, big protection. A new identity. Relocation. Australia, maybe. He liked the sound of Australia. There was no harm in asking. A man could always deal. The hostages could sweat. They could all sweat with him. He had his own skin to worry about.

He picked up the phone.

"Danny Locke?"

It was a different voice. Deeper, harder.

"Who's this?"

"Colonel Fleming of the SAS."

A jolt of fear seared through Danny's guts.

"I'm only going to say this once," the voice continued in a coldly efficient tone. "So listen carefully."

"Where's the other guy . . ." Danny demanded, the bravado failing to mask the tremor in his voice. "Where's the bloke I was talkin' to?"

"He's retired," Lynch said flatly.

"We had a deal . . ." Danny protested, his voice climbing. "We were making a deal . . ."

"No deals," the voice cut in. "You've got one minute."

"What?" Danny stumbled up onto his knees, forgetting momentarily about snipers.

"When I hang up, you've got one minute to come out with your hands in the air."

That was all. But Danny heard the unspoken threat, too. They were getting ready to assault the bank.

"I'll start wasting them . . ." Danny screamed. "I'll start wasting the fockin' hostages . . . I'll do it now."

One of the men on the floor moaned. A woman started crying.

"We don't want the hostages," the voice said.

Danny's mind blurred. It didn't make sense. It wasn't supposed to happen like this. This wasn't how the hard men in the Provos said it would be.

"We want you." The words had a chilling finality. Danny looked wildly around, as though expecting men in black balaclavas to start coming through the walls and ceiling.

"You're bluffin'," Danny yelled into the mouthpiece. "You're bluffin', ye bloody bastard."

"You have one minute." The line went dead.

"Jesus . . ." Danny breathed. If he walked he could still make a deal. If he stayed they would come in and take him. They had given him a choice. Walk and live. Stay and die. And he had less than a minute to make up his mind. His head swam. Part of him refused to believe it. But another part of him did; the part on which his survival depended told him that the SAS did not bluff.

It took Lynch two minutes to walk the short distance back to the roadblock in front of the bank.

Danny Locke was spread-eagled on the ground in the road with his hands clasped around the back of his head and a soldier's foot in the middle of his back. The hostages were starting to come out, led by sympathetic soldiers to the waiting ambulances at the second roadblock. A small group of smiling officers was gathered around Walter Pryne, shaking his hand and congratulating him on a job well done. Gamble and the rest of his SAS team would be packing up to go home.

Lynch looked around for the Range Rover. He saw Porter and Bono coming toward him through the gathering crowd.

Porter was shaking his head and looked slightly paler. "Which school of psychology did you go to, for God's sake?"

* * *

"I want to question Danny Locke."

"There are a few people ahead of you in the queue, dear chap."

Lynch was in Porter's borrowed office at the British army's intelligence headquarters for Northern Ireland at Lisburn, a grimy southern suburb halfway between the city and the Maze. It was ten o'clock the morning after the bank siege and a lot of people were beginning to wonder why Danny Locke had surrendered on the advice of Colonel Fleming, who had never spoken to him.

"They're calling him the latest supergrass," Porter went on. "He's been an IRA man all his life. He knows it and everybody in it better than I know my own family. But he's dealing like a bloody shylock. Shopping around to see who'll give him the best deal, dropping a few gems to keep them all panting and hanging back on the big stuff till he's got the deal he wants. At the rate he's going we'll be buying him a bloody villa in Spain as an expression of gratitude for his service to Her Majesty's government."

"Sir." Lynch kept his voice steady but the anger beneath was unmistakable. "We've been living with our own hostage situation for twelve days."

Sir Malcolm nodded. He was not unsympathetic. He knew Lynch and Janice Street had been lovers since they had met, both on assignment, more than two years earlier.

"If this bastard knows anything about Brian Hennessy," Lynch added, "I want to know. And I want to know fast."

Porter nodded and stood up. "All right," he said. "The home secretary has given my department his approval to cooperate with the Americans if it will help them get to the bottom of this ghastly New York business. I'd say we deserve a piece of Mr. Locke as well. I'll set something up. One condition?"

Lynch waited.

"Nothing too crude, okay?"

Lynch nodded his agreement. By "crude," Sir Malcolm meant Lynch wasn't to intimidate Danny Locke to the point where he might need hospitalization.

It was after eight o'clock that night when Lynch and Porter arrived at the forbidding gates of Castlereagh, the RUC deten-

tion center where all new IRA prisoners are held and interro-
gated. As had become their habit, Bono sat silently in the
backseat, watching and listening. They parked in the main security courtyard and were met by the RUC senior officer and a
guard who had been told to expect them. He escorted them
inside and along a bewildering series of damp green corridors
that stank of jail until they reached Danny Locke's cell in the
isolation wing.

"You've got until ten o'clock," the RUC officer said. "He's
had a long, hard day. Bit of a celebrity now, you see. Surprised
Mrs. Thatcher hasn't been to pay her respects. We'll be down
there at the checkpoint if you need us." He gestured back toward
the security gate at the head of the isolation wing. Then he left
them, and a moment later they heard the electronic lock click
free. The guard leaned forward and opened the second lock and
then he was gone.

They had decided on the drive to Castlereagh that Porter and
Lynch would orchestrate the questioning between them while
Bono hulked threateningly in the background. Lynch wasn't
convinced it was the best approach. Neither was Bono. He
tugged at Lynch's sleeve and the two men stepped back down
the corridor a few paces.

"This guy thinks he's a fuckin' star, right?"

Lynch nodded. "Apparently."

"I don't think he's gonna tell us shit if he doesn't want to.
Two hours is nothin', man. I think I know how to loosen him
up."

"I'm listening."

Porter was a few paces away, listening.

"We'll do good guy, bad guy . . ."

Lynch shook his head and looked across at Porter. Sir Malcolm
smiled indulgently.

"No, listen," Bono persisted in his low grumble. "It'll work
if we do it my way. We do good guy, bad guy. I'll be the good
guy."

Lynch looked up in surprise. "You're the good guy?"

"Yeah."

"I'm the bad guy?"

"Yeah."

Lynch looked at Porter again. Sir Malcolm shrugged. "I got you here; it's up to you how you want to handle it. Just don't mark him."

"Okay," Lynch sighed. Something told him it wouldn't work. Danny Locke had already been corrupted by official promises. He wasn't going to buy the oldest cop interrogation routine in the world. He didn't have to. But Lynch trusted Bono. Enough to give his idea a try.

"Just follow my lead, okay?" Bono said.

"Okay."

Bono stepped forward, opened the door, and the two men followed him into Danny Locke's cell. Danny's special status was reflected by the size of the cell they had given him. It wasn't what anyone might describe as spacious but it wasn't claustrophobic either. There was a bunk bed, a desk with a chair and a reading light, and a wash basin and lavatory. No windows. Danny, wearing prison pants and shirt, was sitting at the desk. He was turned to face the cell door, waiting to see who his visitors were. There were half a dozen paperbacks from the prison service library on the desk, along with a notepad and a ballpoint pen. He said nothing as the three strangers entered his cell. He was feeling better. He'd had two bottles of magnesia since breakfast and the lining of his stomach was coated with a soothing milky balm. He'd slept a little, had a plain cheese sandwich for supper, with a mug of milky tea, and that seemed to have settled all right. He'd been gratified by the reaction to his offer of information in return for special consideration. When he'd told the men from RUC Special Branch and then the British army intelligence blokes what kind of information he had to swap they'd just about wet their pants with excitement. He could help them put the current Provo leadership behind bars within a fortnight if they gave him something in return. He might not escape a prison sentence altogether, he'd been told. Perhaps a couple of years in a soft jail in England and then relocation to another country. Australia wasn't entirely out of the question, they had said, depending on the value of his information. There were just a few last details Danny wanted to settle before he started singing. Such as which prison, what protection, what privileges, that sort of thing.

He looked up at the three newcomers and smirked. The two smaller blokes were military; he knew just by looking at them. The big, bald bastard with all the fading cuts and scrapes was a mystery. He looked like another prisoner.

Bono discreetly closed the cell door behind him, looked into Danny Locke's eyes, smiled in a friendly sort of way, stepped forward, and kicked him hard in the face. Danny's head snapped back and he flew up onto the top of the desk with a cry of pain. A thin strand of blood appeared on the whitewashed wall behind him. Bono caught him by his shirtfront, held him still, and head-butted him, once and then again. Danny's nose caved in, a number of his upper teeth splintered and broke, and a torrent of blood gushed down his shirtfront.

"Good God almighty . . ." Porter gasped.

Lynch stared in disbelief.

But Bono hadn't finished. Danny's eyes were wide with shock and terror. His whole world had taken a sudden turn for the worse again. Bono kept Danny's shirt clenched firmly in his left hand, hoisted him a little higher, then punched him hard in the gut with his right fist and let him drop to the floor.

Porter moved forward to restrain Bono, but the big man pushed him back, a finger to his lips to warn him to be quiet. Porter glared at Lynch in a mixture of anger and helplessness. Lynch looked blankly back. It was already too late to do anything. Danny Locke was marked. They might as well see what Bono did next.

Danny lay crouched on the floor, bleeding and gasping. His gut felt as though a hole had been punched through it. Bono gave him just enough time to catch his breath but not enough to stop hurting. Then the big man reached down and hauled him up again.

"Hi," he said, holding Danny's stunned and bleeding face only inches from his own. "I'm the good guy. That guy over beside the wall? He's the bad guy. If you don't talk to me, I'll let him work on you for a while. Now, are we pals?"

It was fifteen minutes before Danny Locke could find the strength to speak through his split lips and broken teeth but he knew he couldn't take any more pain. He was willing to tell them everything if they would only leave him alone. He told them about the old man in Donegal called Tom O'Donnell who had a dream about a united Ireland that had somehow become warped by madness and bitterness into a crazed and bloody scheme for self-glorification. About a trained killer called Brian Hennessy who had pledged himself to the plan's execution and success. About the intended assassinations of the entire Provo leadership in Northern Ireland. And about the coordinated assaults on Northern Ireland's two biggest cities.

When he had finished there was only the sound of his own pained and muffled breathing as he tried to keep the cold air from searing the exposed nerves in his broken teeth.

"Have you told any of the other gentlemen who were here today about this?" Porter inquired.

"Only that there was somethin' big on. I didn't tell them any names or places. I'm trying to get a deal an' now you've focked it for me."

"Yes," Porter drawled, his voice oddly lacking in sympathy. "But the game isn't over yet, not by a long way."

Porter was already thinking of the urgent action that would be needed if they were to thwart Tom O'Donnell's plan and help the Americans take Hennessy. It meant a covert operation in the Irish Republic before O'Donnell could even get his men and arms in place to launch the assaults on Derry and Belfast. And the last thing he wanted was a political wrangle involving himself, the army, the RUC, and the secretary for Northern Ireland about the best way to proceed and whether or not they could trust the government in Dublin. By the time that had all been sorted out, the attacks would be under way or something would have leaked and O'Donnell and Hennessy would have gone to ground. He studied the wretched, bloodied figure of Danny Locke. Two or three days, that was all they needed.

He reached down and raised the young man's head.

"Go ahead and make your deal with the others," he said. "Pretend we were never here."

Danny dabbed at his face. "Sure," he said.

"Tell me about Hennessy," Lynch asked quietly.

"What do you want to know?" Danny mumbled through split gums and swollen, bloodied lips.

"When did you first meet him. When was the very first time?"

Danny thought back, to a bitter January night more than five years ago, when he had been stopped by a British army patrol in south Armagh, on his way back to Belfast from Dublin with half a dozen detonators inside the door panels of his car. When he saw the maroon berets, his heart almost stopped beating. The paras would take the car apart and him too, just for the hell of it. He knew his name was on all the suspect lists. His fears were confirmed when he stopped and the lieutenant leading the patrol motioned him with his rifle to stand away from the car.

"Hello, Danny," the lieutenant had said. It was a ploy the British army used often. They memorized the names and faces of all known suspects and then greeted them by first name, to remind them that they were known.

"Been doing a bit of shopping in the Irish Free State, have we? Got any duty free?"

The men in his patrol had sniggered. They liked watching Hennessy work.

Without warning, Hennessy opened fire. He put a single burst into both front tires and watched as the car knelt on the road in front of him. Then he walked slowly around the car and put a short burst of automatic fire in the rear two tires.

"Think you got a puncture, Danny," the lieutenant had said, and then led his men back down the lane and through a hedgerow to continue their patrol.

That was the first time Danny had met Brian Hennessy, he said. Though he didn't know the officer's name at the time. All he knew was that he'd got off light. No search, no pushing and shoving, no interrogation. Just a bit of light intimidation. Enough to keep the other soldiers from suspecting their commanding officer was soft on the IRA.

"When did you see him next?" Lynch asked.

"He came to my house a week later," Danny said. "He was in civvies but I recognized him straight away. He came about tea time. Evil bastard he is. Looks and talks like a bit of a toff, y'know? But it's all fake. He's rubbish underneath." His eyes flickered nervously at the three men gathered around him, listening intently.

"Somethin' else, too. I reckon he's psycho. He likes scarin' people. And he likes hurtin' them, too."

Lynch and Porter exchanged glances. Porter was sitting on the end of Danny's bunk. Lynch was standing directly in front of him, hands in pockets, and Bono was leaning against the shut cell door.

Danny Locke went on. "He just stood there outside my front door grinnin' an' not sayin' nothin.' I thought he'd come to knock me over, I swear to God. And he just stood there grinnin', while I shit myself. Then he walks in, cool as you like, shuts the door, takes me by the arm into my own house, and sits me down."

"And?"

"He asks for a meeting with my battalion commander?" Danny spoke the words incredulously, as though he still had difficulty believing it.

"What did you do?"

"I thought he was settin' me up. Either that or he was an eedjit. I told him there was no way they'd trust him. Especially him bein in the paras an' all."

"What did he say?" Lynch asked.

"He said to tell them anyway. An' he said, as proof of good faith, he'd go easy on the house searches an' stuff an' mebbe look the other way a few times when he was patrollin' the border."

"Did you tell McGlaughlin?" Porter inquired.

Danny fidgeted. Michael McGlaughlin had been the Provo commander in Belfast some five years earlier when Hennessy was doing his tour of duty. McGlaughlin had since been replaced and had moved into the Republic to continue his work, but Porter's intelligence was good.

"Aye, I told him," Danny said.

"What did he think about it?"

"What would you think if you was in his shoes?" Danny snorted. "He thought Hennessy was full of shit. Either he was doin' the world's worst job of infiltration or he was bloody mad. Either way he was trouble. McGlaughlin wouldn't have a bar of him. There was talk of takin' him out . . ."

"And why didn't you?"

Danny shrugged. "His unit had been soft on Catholics. They had to admit that. Other blokes would kick your front door down in the middle of the night, heave you into the front garden, and break all your furniture while they looked for weapons. He'd be a bit easier. Your stuff wouldn't get broken. Nobody got pushed around. That was unusual."

"How did he get to meet Tom O'Donnell?" Porter recollected O'Donnell's name but, like every other British security departmental chief with an interest in Northern Ireland, he'd thought the old IRA gunman had been inactive for years following his defeat in a power struggle for control of the Derry brigades in 1981.

Danny looked uncomfortable. "That was my doin'," he said.

"Ah," Lynch murmured. "So we have you to thank for the loss of nearly two hundred lives in the New York attack."

Danny wouldn't meet Lynch's eye. Lynch reminded him a lot of Hennessy. There was the same intimidating physical presence, the same understated menace. The same whiff of danger that suggested this man lived with a smoldering fuse and would be capable of inflicting terrible damage if his temper ignited.

"I had nothin' to do with that," he said shakily. His gut ached and the acid was climbing the walls of his stomach and into his throat.

"Get on with it, man," Porter snapped.

Danny flinched. "There was no way Tom O'Donnell was goin' to let things go," he said. He struggled for a way to minimize his own involvement in O'Donnell's demented scheme. "He'd waited for years to get back at the Provos for what they done to him. I'd done . . . a bit of work with Tom in the early days."

The three men knew what kind of "work" Danny meant.

"We kept in touch, y'know? Old pals. I used to wonder how he was keepin' and I'd drop in an' see him sometimes at Donegal."

"Ah," Lynch breathed, as if it made perfect sense. "On your way home, was it?"

Danny dabbed his mashed nose tenderly with a wet handkerchief dyed a deep maroon from his blood.

"We'd talk about things an' . . . . I must have mentioned Hennessy's name."

"Must have," Porter echoed ingenuously.

"What did O'Donnell do?" Lynch wanted to know.

"Oh, he was interested straight away. The old bugger was up to somethin' then. He wanted to see him, to meet Brian Hennessy. Wanted me to fix it up."

"And, because you were only helping your pal and you couldn't see the harm in it to anybody, you took his message to Hennessy?" Porter completed it for him.

"I didn't know how to," Danny said. "There was no way I could contact him. He came to see me. It was about two months after the first time he come to my house and he wanted to know what the word was. I told him there was nothin' doin.' He wasn't very happy. Started carryin' on a bit. Accused me of lyin'. So I told him about Tom."

"And thus a beautiful new relationship was forged." Porter sighed.

"Eh?"

"Never mind." Porter stood up and looked at his watch. It was a few minutes before ten. "I think we probably have enough, gentlemen?"

Danny couldn't wait for them to leave. The moment they had gone he was going to start screaming for a doctor . . . and a dentist.

"I'm not finished," Lynch said.

Danny shuddered involuntarily.

"Did Tom O'Donnell ever say anything to you about a girl, an American girl? Hennessy took her in New York a couple of weeks ago. Her name's Street. Janice Street."

Danny thought about it for a moment and then they all saw the look of shock that flooded his face as the comprehension dawned.

For the first time, Danny realized O'Donnell had set him up.

"He wanted me to tell you . . ." Danny mumbled in disbelief.

Lynch grabbed him and Danny winced.

"About the girl," Danny said. "I didn't even think of it at the time. I didn't know why he was tellin' me. He told me to do the job. When I asked him where he wanted me to drop the money he said he was goin' up to the farm."

"What farm . . . where?"

"It's up the top end of Donegal county . . . middle of nowhere . . . place called Bloody Foreland. He said he was goin' there to see a nice American lady." Danny looked up, his face a crestfallen mask of betrayal.

"The bastard grassed on me."

But Lynch had already gone, followed by Porter and the big man.

9 The Siege of Bloody Foreland

It was close to midnight when the Ceilidh Princess made first contact with the Nara Maru. They had motored another fifty nautical miles southwest from Rossan Point, toward the coordinates provided by Hennessy, scanning the radar for the pale green blip of the two-hundred-ton Japanese freighter with her cargo of arms. A month earlier, Abu Musa's man in Cairo had given the skipper of the Nara Maru the latitude and longitude of the rendezvous point and the name of the craft they were to meet. But nothing more. When the mate on the bridge realized the small craft approaching them was either on a collision course or was their contact vessel, he roused the skipper from his bunk. There was no radio contact in case they were overheard. When the Ceilidh Princess was within two nautical miles, McKee flashed his craft's identification by semaphore from a searchlight on the bridge. The skipper of the Nara Maru remained at anchor while the battered green-and-white trawler closed and pulled alongside. The skipper went out on deck to wave a greeting to the men on the smaller craft but few words were exchanged. Not only was discussion unnecessary, it was almost impossible. Neither the skipper nor his crew spoke much English and no one on board the Ceilidh Princess spoke Chinese.

The skipper and crew of the Nara Maru were Taiwanese. Their

home port was Kaohsiung, on the southeast coast of Taiwan.
The vessel was owned by the same company that employed them,
a legitimate Japanese shipping line, headquartered in Osaka with
branches throughout the Far East. The *Nara Maru* usually carried
cargo between Japan, South Korea, Taiwan, and the Middle
East. She rarely ventured beyond Tangier, at the mouth of the
Mediterranean. However, the skipper was an enterprising man.
He may only have spoken a few words of English but he understood perfectly the language of commerce. He wasn't averse
to making one or two short voyages on his own behalf each year,
when he was able to bend the shipping schedule. Even more so
when cash payment in advance was involved. The eleven-man
crew shared their skipper's enterprising spirit. This sixteen-day
detour was worth two thousand American dollars, nearly three
months' wages, to each man.

Both skippers were fortunate there was only a light swell
running. Transferring cargo in the open sea was an awkward,
dangerous business, especially when that cargo involved fifty
thousand pounds of high explosive. If the weather had been
against them, they would have had no alternative but to wait,
and McKee would have hated to be on the receiving end of
Hennessy's wrath.

In her bunk in the bow cabin, Janice heard the sudden flurry
of activity, the sound of a bigger ship, men shouting at one
another in what sounded like Chinese. She wondered if she was
losing her mind. She lay cold and miserable under the blankets
they had given her, wearing a man's work shirt and a greasy
sweater provided to replace the clothes Hennessy had destroyed.
He had come down and handcuffed her to the bunk rail again,
a little before midnight, and she had feared the worst. But he
had only grinned at her and left. She wasn't to get a moment's
sleep for the rest of the night as she listened to the thuds, bangs,
and splashes of one cargo being jettisoned while a newer, deadlier
cargo was taken on board.

Thirteen tons of frozen fish went over the side of the *Ceilidh
Princess* while they made room for one heavy case after another
of weapons and ammunition. Some of the cases were metal and
some were made of wood. Some were stamped MADE IN THE

USA, some bore legends in the Cyrillic alphabet of the USSR, and some were stenciled with the Czechoslovakian word *Semtex*. Hennessy watched in silent approval as the weapons and explosives were lowered carefully to the swaying deck of the trawler in an endless stream. There was enough for a small war, he thought. Exactly the kind of war they intended to fight.

The crews of both vessels worked through the night, carefully lowering the lethal cargo from a small deck crane and then manhandling it delicately into the refrigerated hold of the *Ceilidh Princess*. An hour before dawn, they were finished. Both vessels parted as they had arrived, without formality. The skipper of the *Nara Maru* heaved a sigh of relief and went up to the bridge to get his vessel under way. Hennessy, McKee, and Owen spent another hour covering the arms with the slabs of frozen cod they had kept behind just for that purpose. The sun was rising as McKee gunned the engine and turned northeast toward Bloody Foreland. It was only three to four hours' easy running in good weather, but he would steer a wide loop away from the mainland and make sure they took all day. He had no intention of approaching the coast until dark; then there'd be another long night putting the cargo ashore. He advised Hennessy and his deckhand to catch up on some sleep. Owen would take the noon watch while McKee slept.

Hennessy ate a fried egg sandwich and climbed into his bunk, aft of the galley, but could not sleep. His mind wandered back through the incredible events of the past few years. If anyone had asked him, he would have been unable to name the moment when he decided to turn traitor. To turn against the country where his family had found economic refuge, where he had grown up, been educated, and lived most of his adult life. To turn against his queen, that very sovereign to whom he had pledged solemn allegiance when he had joined her army. To turn his hand against her government and work for the destruction of her ministry in Northern Ireland.

All his life he had felt different from those around him. Growing up, going to school, playing football, fighting, chasing girls—even though he had taken part in all the usual things, he had always felt separate from the people around him. He had never had a best mate. He'd always had the ability to stand outside his body and watch himself do things with what felt like a separate consciousness. And he had always had difficulty accepting that the rules governing the everyday lives of everyday people were also intended for him. Rules, regulations, laws . . . they were for people who couldn't think for themselves. Brian Hennessy had always been able to think for himself.

He'd never felt he needed a specific goal. He had always felt he was learning, watching, waiting . . . for something. But he hadn't known what, until the Falklands. The war there had given him the opportunity for real action. And that was when he'd belonged. That was when he'd fitted in. War had made him come alive in a way he'd never felt before. That was when Brian Hennessy discovered that he loved war.

The greatest disappointment for him had been that it was over too quickly. After years of training, months of preparation, weeks of anticipation, the only real action had been at Goose Green. It was his first taste of a major battle, and he had loved every moment. It had been difficult for him to conceal from those around him how much pleasure it gave him. He felt so alive that he hardly even needed sleep. He loved that feeling of invincibility, immortality. That was what had carried him up that craggy hillside that night at Goose Green, through the machine-gun fire, screaming into the faces of the Argentine defenders. He had felt like a god as he ran across the killing ground, immune to fear and fatigue. And then he'd seen their faces, the faces of the enemy, materializing out of the smoky darkness, streaked with dirt and sweat and fear, their weapons down, hands raised high in the air, trying to surrender. And he had fired and fired and fired until his rifle emptied and they all lay dead and bloody on the ground. He hadn't come that far to be cheated of his moment of glory by cowards. His mates had come panting up behind him a few seconds later to finish off the stragglers and take prisoners. He killed eleven men that night. It was only the beginning.

He'd come back from the Falklands a war hero, a man earmarked for advancement. Sandhurst had changed it all. He knew then that he didn't belong. He would never belong. But there was something else, as well. A new and deepening awareness that it wasn't which side you were on that really mattered. The struggle was the thing. The battlefield was where you tested your mettle, the elemental arena where men fought one another the way they were always meant to fight and where only the strongest prevailed. Northern Ireland had decided it for him. *That* was where he belonged, and not with a peacekeeping force. He belonged on the other side, the side that was fighting to win. He could help them win.

He had met Tom O'Donnell in the last months of his tour of duty. It had been a wary, difficult meeting until Hennessy had convinced the old man of his sincerity. Told him how he belonged with his people, fighting their fight. Fighting for a united Ireland. O'Donnell had wanted to believe him, Hennessy knew. The old man saw in Hennessy the strong right arm that would destroy his enemies and give him victory. Hennessy had demonstrated the strength of his commitment by refusing a new promotion and resigning his commission. He had returned to Ireland a free agent and spent that summer helping O'Donnell lay the groundwork for their plan. He had traveled secretly between Belfast and Derry, helping O'Donnell recruit the men, persuading them they could win. It took time, it took argument, it took conviction, and sometimes it took terror. At least two good Provo gunmen disappeared when they refused outright and seemed ready to blow the whistle to the army council. Both disappeared suddenly, presumed murdered by a UDF hit squad acting on a leak from the British army. Eventually, O'Donnell had his men. They trusted O'Donnell, sympathized with him. But they believed Hennessy; they believed he would make it work.

At the end of the year O'Donnell had taken Hennessy into his fullest confidence and mentioned his old PLO friend, Abu Musa. That was when it had all neatly coalesced for Hennessy. He had known then that Musa might prove to be the linchpin of their operation. It was Abu Musa who had the resources to be their treasurer and their quartermaster. A few days later, from a public telephone at the post office in O'Connell Street, Dublin, Hennessy placed a call to an answering machine in a tiny office in Amsterdam, using a telephone number he had stolen from

O'Donnell. Then, in August 1989, without Tom O'Donnell's knowledge, Hennessy had flown from Dublin to Rome, caught a connecting flight to Ankara, and then on to Tehran, where he had been met at the airport by one of Abu Musa's men.

Musa already knew of Hennessy from O'Donnell and he was intrigued by the young man's ambition. Hennessy stayed at Musa's villa for two weeks. He and Musa found they had much in common. They were both men with an independent perspective of the world. Toward the end of the two weeks, Musa confided that he had friends in the Arab world who were not happy with certain people in America. People who had caused his friends considerable pain and inconvenience in recent years. These people were close to the seat of power in the United States, but it was known who they were. It was to be a bargain of mutual convenience. It was sealed the day before Hennessy flew back to Ankara and then on to Heathrow.

O'Donnell was not at all the master strategist he fancied himself to be. He was merely another pawn played between Hennessy and Musa. Hennessy smiled as he recollected how easy it had been to manipulate the pathetic old fool. The puppet had controlled the puppeteer since the day they'd met. It was Hennessy who had suggested, months earlier, that O'Donnell ought to find an isolated farmhouse to bait their trap. It was Hennessy who suggested they sacrifice Danny Locke. It was Hennessy who told O'Donnell to make sure he mentioned the girl in his conversation on the phone with Danny. O'Donnell would serve his purpose. He would provide the Republican facade. But when it was all over, Hennessy would be the power behind the throne. Hennessy was the man who would have made history. Hennessy was the man who would have outwitted, outmaneuvered, and outfought the British in their own backyard, blasting them and their phony laws and their hypocritical system back across the Irish Sea . . . right into Maggie Thatcher's lap. O'Donnell had liked that image above all the others Hennessy had painted for him.

It was all coming together precisely as Hennessy had planned. He lay in the gloom with his hands behind his head, his face a stony mask. He knew they would come for the girl. Lynch, especially. Reckless with hate and anger and distracted by fears for her safety. He was looking forward to meeting Lynch. He had studied the profile Abu Musa had given him. There were similarities between them both. Many similarities. It was ironic that they should finish on opposing sides. But he knew who was the better man, who was the stronger. Lynch was flawed. Hennessy would never allow himself to be weakened or distracted from his purpose by sentiment. He would give Lynch a lesson in professionalism. And, once Lynch was gone, he would be poised to administer the coup de grace . . . the checkmate. In blood. Hennessy turned onto his side and drifted into a deep and untroubled sleep.

A mere ten yards away, in the darkened bow cabin, Janice Street lay in utter torment. Hennessy had forgotten that she had been handcuffed to the bunk rail since the previous night. She stayed there until the morning of the following day, manacled in her prison, fouling herself where she lay, her whole world a squalid pit of humiliation and despair. And hate. Most of all, she felt hate. It was what kept her going.

BELFAST, APRIL 13

"You do understand that it's a trap, don't you?" Porter asked.

"Yes," Lynch answered.

"She could already be dead."

"No."

"Why not?"

"He wants us there. He won't kill her till he's sure he's got us."

Sir Malcolm paused. "I thought the whole thing smelled," he said. "He's been playing us, you in particular, like a bloody fish."

Lynch, Bono, and Sir Malcolm were seated around Porter's desk in his temporary office at Lisburn, drinking coffee. It was a little after eleven in the morning. They'd all slept briefly and badly after breaking up their discussion of Danny Locke's confession at three o'clock that morning. Porter had retired to his comfortable accommodations in the senior officers' quarters while Lynch and Bono had to settle for makeshift beds in a room hurriedly commandeered for them by CTC inside the intelli-

7

gence center. It suited Lynch. Lisburn made an ideal operational
base. When they left here it would be to rescue Janice and to
nail the bastards who had hunted and tormented them for so
long. They had forty-eight hours to formulate a plan and to
launch and execute a covert operation into the Irish Free State.
If it went wrong it had the potential to create a massive crisis
between London and Dublin, to spark an ungodly row between
Downing Street, the army, Whitehall, and CTC, and to present
Britain with a massive international humiliation.

"It's a terrible risk," Sir Malcolm said. "Even if we pull it off
there will still be an awful lot of people who won't be very happy
with us. If we get it wrong . . ." He shook his head. "We'll be
finished. All of us."

"So what's new?" Bono rumbled.

Lynch realized what was new. Sir Malcolm Porter was going
out on a very long and creaky limb for them. If this operation
failed, this time he would go down with them.

"Either way," Porter said. "Within forty-eight hours the army
will have everything Danny Locke told us. I put it all into a
report before I went to bed this morning. They have to know.
If we fail, they have to stop the proposed attacks on Derry and
Belfast city centers."

"Why don't you just tell them?" Lynch asked.

"Because I won't be able to," Porter said. "I'm coming with
you."

Lynch and Bono stared.

"Sir, with all respect—" Lynch began.

Porter cut him off. "I know what you're going to say, but I'm
fitter than most men half my age. That's not the point. The
point is that if my career is going to end in a blaze of ignominy
then I don't want to be sitting in an office when it happens and
have some fat-faced Whitehall warrior telling me what a fool
I've been. I want to be out there, on the ground . . . where I
can bloody well make sure it doesn't go wrong."

Lynch and Bono swapped wry smiles.

"Glad to have you along, sir," Lynch said. Sir Malcolm
thought he detected just a trace of irony.

"I've taken the liberty of calling in Captain Gamble, too,"

Sir Malcolm said. Lynch and Bono waited. Having made up his mind, the old man had obviously decided to run the operation. That was fine with Lynch. As long as the old man didn't get in the way when he went after Hennessy and O'Donnell. Lynch wanted them both. It no longer had anything to do with politics. This time it was personal.

"Peter will be here shortly," Sir Malcolm went on. "We can discuss our plan of attack and work out our equipment needs then. I've ordered satellite maps of Bloody Foreland and the surrounding area. The enlargements are being prepared now. Our greatest worry, of course, is that we're expected. There will be no element of surprise. They'll have it all in their favor. If they decide they've had enough they can start yelling for the Garda and the Irish army and then we're really in the shit. We'd just have to get out the best way we can."

Lynch shook his head.

"I beg your pardon?" Porter said softly.

"You can leave. I stay."

Sir Malcolm took a deep breath. He was about to argue but the look on Lynch's face told him it would be fruitless.

"Once started, there's no stopping. If we don't do the job, we don't come back. Your words, sir. Yours and Jack Halloran's."

Porter smiled. He knew he was trapped, too.

"Speaking of Jack Halloran," he continued, "the *American Endeavor* passed the Scilly Islands at 0800 hours this morning. I've already spoken to Jack. He was intent on coming here, to Belfast. I told him that wasn't a good idea under the circumstances."

"Where is he headed now?" Lynch asked.

"I've asked him to steer a course for a rendezvous point eighty nautical miles northwest of Bloody Foreland. We'll use his yacht as our jump-off point. It's in international waters and it will be ideal for an operation of this nature. We must have some deniability in case even one of us is disabled and taken alive by the Irish authorities. Jack wants to take Hennessy back to the United States to stand trial. You remember what happened the last time the Americans intercepted terrorists after the *Achille Lauro* affair? They forced the terrorists' plane down at a NATO base in Sicily and the bloody Italians insisted on taking over and they let the ringleader go. Abu Nidal, no less."

Lynch remembered.

"Jack doesn't want anything like that happening again. His first choice is to get Hennessy out, in one piece, and onto his yacht. From there he goes direct to the U.S., and he'll grow old in an American prison cell."

"Second choice?" Lynch asked.

"You know what Jack Halloran's fallback position is," Porter answered. "Brian Hennessy is the man who committed one of the worst terrorist outrages of modern times. He destroyed most of a Manhattan skyscraper and killed one hundred seventy-four people. Jack Halloran's people. If Hennessy can't be pulled out in one piece, you are to . . . exercise ultimate discretion."

"Yes," Lynch answered quietly. "I'll see what I can do."

"My proposal," Porter went on, "is that we leave the *American Endeavor* by chopper. We drop you and Peter Gamble on the seaward side. Mr. Bono and I will come in from the landward side. We get in as close as we can and hit them with all we've got. Let them think the bloody army's coming in for them. You and Peter will use our diversionary attack to come in from the seaward side. They'll have it covered, might even have it mined. But both you and Peter can deal with that. We'll give you as much time as we can. When you're in close enough, you and Peter hit them hard. If the two of you working together can't clean out a farmhouse between you then we may as well stay home. If Miss Street is in there the best way to get her out in one piece is to lace the whole place with stun grenades and go through the windows shooting. It's what you and Peter are best at. They may be expecting you but you can clean that place out in seven seconds if you do it right. Nobody is prepared for that."

There was a knock at the door and a moment later Peter Gamble stepped into the room, dressed in civilian jeans, sweater, and brown leather jacket.

"Well," he greeted the three men, "understand we've got a spot of bother needs clearing up, eh?"

Bono cleared his throat. Here he was again, going off with a few of the chaps to clear up a spot of bother.

"Good." Porter smiled. "Let's go and see if those map enlargements are ready, shall we?"

WASHINGTON, D.C., APRIL 13

"I don't like it, sir," Clayton Powell told the President. "If the
source of the attack can be traced back to the Irish Republic,
we can't risk Jack Halloran attempting a hit or snatch operation
on his own. If it goes wrong, think of the international reper-
cussions. American nationals committing kidnap and murder on
Irish territory? The international fallout would be appalling. I
recommend we pull him back in. Besides, we can't be sure it's
Ireland. Our assets abroad still haven't ruled out a Middle East
connection. The whole thing reeks of Arab extremism, sir. If
there is anything to Jack Halloran's theories I think we should
let the agency handle it."

The President nodded. It was close to eight-thirty at night in
Washington and he was seated behind his desk in the Oval
Office with three men facing him from the other side of the
desk. Secretary of State Clayton Powell, FBI Director Wesley
Hatten, and the President's most recent successor to the direc-
torship of the CIA, Henry Stanford. It was Stanford who took
his cue from Powell.

"Our European section can give us an authoritative and updated situation report on Ireland within twenty-four hours," he
said. "I can reinforce our agents there with extra men from
London within two hours of leaving this office. If Jack Halloran
is right, as he may well be, we take it from here. We'll keep
you informed as the situation changes, sir."

The President nodded thoughtfully and looked across at Wesley Hatten.

"All domestic leads have gone dead, literally, thanks to Mr.
Lynch. Victor Flannery was our best prospect and he's been
silenced. John Ritsczik and the team he has on the case have
drawn a blank in New York. Victor Flannery had a lot of
friends. He was a popular guy. He was an active fund-raiser

for Noraid and Mr. Ritsczik had concerns about him, but, as I said, we can't talk to him, and his friends aren't saying much to us either. The NYPD isn't happy and they're making waves about their man getting involved in a bureau snafu. I'm sure there will be more to come on that, sir."

Yes, the President thought to himself, there probably would be.

"We still haven't put a face to the prints from the screwdriver," Hatten went on. "The autopsies on the four bodies found at the farmhouse at Hibbing have proved inconclusive. All that remained of the man in the cellar was a bit of bone and jaw. Not even enough to provide good dental information. Forensic is proceeding with DNA analysis. The man who was burned to death by napalm—"

"Napalm?" the President echoed.

"Yes sir." Hatten felt the coolness in the room intensify. "There was enough to check dental records but there's nothing to show he ever existed in the United States. Could well be a foreign national employed by Arabs to do the hit. The third man was pretty badly cut up by shrapnel from a Claymore mine—"

"Shrapnel . . ." the President repeated. "From a Claymore mine?"

"Yes sir. His clothing has been traced back to a thrift store in the Bronx. All purchased recently for cash and, in all probability, for the purpose of the hit. Again we got good dental records but nothing has shown up on this side of the water. We got good boot prints but they were from recent purchases too. We found no weapons at the scene but plenty of spent 5.56 mm cartridge cases, which came from an Armalite. That is a weapon favored by the IRA. However, we did retrieve the weapon used and spent casings at the house in Greenwich Village. That is a Skorpion submachine gun, a popular weapon with Arab terror groups, especially the PLO. But not the IRA. So," the pink-faced FBI director concluded, "it's still an even bet at this stage. We're following all of this up with Interpol and the British."

"Well, you've been thorough, Wesley," the President complimented him. "You said four bodies . . ."

"Yes sir," Hatten added promptly. "Fourth body was canine. We believe it belonged to the occupant of the house, Mr. Bono."

"A dog?"

"Yes sir."

The four men sat in silence. The three on the open side of the desk felt they'd made their case. Clayton Powell had warned them beforehand not to overstate it. The President looked troubled.

"Gentlemen," he said finally, "as you know, I've been in touch with Mr. Halloran since he departed these shores and he has assured me he will not act without consulting with me first. So far, he has kept his word. He has taken his vessel to Europe to use it as a base from which to conduct his own intelligence operation. He has always proved to be a most loyal and effective servant of this office. I'm inclined to let him proceed a little further. He can only add to our store of information in this investigation. I have warned him, explicitly, if he embarks on any course of events likely to embarrass this office, I will order the United States military to act against him."

"Sir . . ." Clayton Powell attempted to interrupt.

"Clayton, I am aware of your concerns and, despite your known disapproval of Jack Halloran's methods, I am satisfied that you are not acting from personal bias and that your concerns are legitimate. According to our last contact the *American Endeavor* was in the northeastern Atlantic, approaching the British Isles. Henry here can keep us informed of her progress through our satellite tracking network, on a ninety-minute basis, if need be. In the meantime, Clayton, you will prepare a list of our military facilities in the British Isles and a short list of those air and naval units in the region which would be able to act at short notice. In the meantime I'll order Delta Force moved up to sixty-minute readiness. That ought to satisfy all your immediate concerns, gentlemen. We're watching him closely. I'm talking to him regularly. If he breaks his word again . . ." He let the last word linger for their benefit. "If he should be so foolish as to betray the trust of this office and initiate a clandestine operation without my knowledge or approval . . . . I will order the military to intercede within the hour."

It wasn't everything Clayton Powell had hoped for but he was still smiling as he followed his two colleagues out of the Oval Office. One by one he was putting the nails into Jack Halloran's coffin.

BLOODY FORELAND, APRIL 14

"Brian!" In the early morning dark, O'Donnell clasped his arms around Hennessy like a father greeting a son come home from the war. The shingle crunched beneath their feet as both men trudged up the steep incline of the crescent cove to the base of a terrifying cliff. In the watery moonlight it was just possible to see a long line of men toiling up a narrow and treacherous path that zigzagged dizzily down the cliff face. The path had been there longer than anyone could remember, a dangerous, crumbling umbilical from the wild heathland above to the tiny cove below. Through the centuries it had been employed as an avenue for every secret human endeavor, from the smuggling of contraband into the country to the smuggling of fugitives out of the country.

A hundred yards offshore the *Ceilidh Princess* sat at anchor, rocking safely in the lee of a protective, craggy arm, jutting out like a fist from the foreshore. There were two small dinghies, their muffled outboard engines sounding disturbingly loud in the enclosed calm of the cove. Up on the wind-battered clifftop, O'Donnell assured Hennessy, nothing could be heard. The dinghies scurried back and forth between the steep shingle beach and the trawler, ferrying case after case of arms. O'Donnell's men hauled them up the path as best they could and loaded them into two waiting Bedford lorries. From there they had a short, bumpy ride across virgin heath to a stony track that cut across a narrow and deserted coastal road. Eamonn Docherty was at the road with his Garda van and wearing his uniform to make sure no random, late night traveler saw something he shouldn't. From the road it was a half mile to another track through more heathland, slopping down from the roaring clifftops, until it reached a long, narrow, whitewashed farmhouse.

Once there the lorries were unloaded and the arms and ammunition carried into the kitchen and relayed down into the dry cellar. There they were stacked in neat rows around the solid, earthen walls.

O'Donnell noticed the recently healed wound on Hennessy's left cheek, an ugly, sunken circular scar still caked with blood.

"Good God, Brian," O'Donnell asked. "Did you get hurt?"

Hennessy patted the scar on his cheek tenderly. He'd only taken the dressing off in the past week to let the salt air help it heal. He thought of Janice and the way he would finish her when he was ready.

"The American bitch on the boat," he said dismissively. "I'm leaving her there for now. She's our insurance. I don't want her getting hurt by accident at the farm until we're sure we don't need her anymore." He stopped and glanced around. "We'll leave the Semtex and the Stingers on the boat, too. We don't need them yet and they're safer there."

O'Donnell nodded his big, white head in solemn accord. Hennessy was more knowledgeable in these matters. Hennessy was the professional.

"Did you bring all the stuff I asked you to bring?"

"It's all at the farm," O'Donnell said. "Though I've no idea what you'd be wanting with all those car headlights and the two dozen pairs of overalls."

"It'll be fine, Tom." Hennessy squeezed the old man's shoulder. It was the wounded shoulder and O'Donnell winced. Hennessy pretended he hadn't remembered.

"We'd best be getting up top," Hennessy added. "It'll be light in another two hours." He walked back toward the nearest dinghy, plucked out a case stenciled ARMALITE CORPORATION OF AMERICA, hefted it atop his shoulder, and began trudging through the deep shingle toward the footpath. O'Donnell struggled to keep up with him.

"How many men, Tom?" Hennessy asked a half hour later when they reached the top of the cliff and slid the rifles into the waiting Bedford. Hennessy was panting and sweating lightly. He enjoyed the exercise after being cooped up on the boat for two weeks. It took O'Donnell several minutes to regain breath enough to speak. Hennessy waited with ill-disguised impatience.

He hoped the old man would be able to keep up the pace. They had a lot of hard work ahead and they had just started. If O'Donnell didn't have the stamina to lead the Derry assault, Hennessy knew, he would have to put Eamonn Docherty in his place. The old man would squeal but he was rapidly outliving his usefulness.

"Twenty-six, including you, Eamonn, an' me," O'Donnell gasped at last.

"Shit." Hennessy spat into the thick, spongy turf that kept local villagers warmed with peat slabs through the winter. "That's only twenty-three had the balls to keep their word." He was angry. It wasn't as many as he'd hoped for. They would be enough to manage the ambush, when it came, but they were hardly enough to take and hold Derry city center for a fortnight. There were still men in Belfast who had committed themselves but Hennessy couldn't afford to spare any of them for Derry. He would have to go up to Derry himself in a day or two and sort a few of the bastards out.

"Good lads," he called out, clapping the shoulder of a sweating IRA man who passed with another case for the lorry.

"Good to see ye back, Brian," the man answered breathlessly. "Ye've been busy."

"Just the beginning, man," Hennessy answered. He couldn't recollect the man's name. But he knew they'd all be impressed by this consignment. There wouldn't have been a bigger consignment of arms loaded in one day in the recent history of the struggle. Wait till the word got around after tonight and the days that followed. Then there'd be no shortage of volunteers. They'd be flocking to him.

Hennessy stayed up on the cliff until dawn, making sure the last ammunition case had been brought up. He rode carelessly back to the farm in the back of the open lorry with the last cases of land mines. He had a long day ahead of him yet and he had plans for those mines. Mr. Bono had demonstrated how effective they could be. Perhaps not against experts like himself, who had plenty of time to thread a way through the outer defenses. But the men he expected wouldn't have any time at all. He would make sure of that. He jumped easily from the back of the lorry as it swung into the farmyard, every step and movement the gesture of a leader who demanded to be admired. He examined the earth cellar and grunted with satisfaction. No stray bullet would pass through those walls. The only possibility was a ricochet from upstairs, but the floor was a slab of packed limestone rubble except for the wooden trapdoor. The cellar had been hollowed out from above by a man with a pick and shovel a long time past. They could reinforce the trapdoor with a few layers of metal packing-case lids and blankets from the bedrooms.

O'Donnell and Docherty had brought in enough food and drink for a week. There was a keg of Guinness on a wooden trestle outside and the men gratefully took turns filling the tin mugs O'Donnell had provided. Hennessy smiled. Irishmen could live on stout alone if they had to. He'd make sure they didn't overdo it. Besides, they'd be sweating most of it out through the coming day.

No one passed along the blustery coastal road that day. It was too early for the tourist season and the nearest villages were Dunfanaghy, twenty miles to the northeast, and Crolly, another twenty miles to the southeast. The locals had no reason to venture out to Bloody Foreland. If they had, they would have glimpsed a few men digging in the heath near a distant farm. They could have been cutting peat, even though it was the wrong time of year and that would have seemed a mite unusual, but they wouldn't have given it much thought. Residents of the Irish Free State in the areas along the border with Ulster learned to mind their own business. By nightfall Hennessy was finished and he and his men could afford to grab a few hours' sleep.

"What next, Brian?" O'Donnell asked, as they each sipped a mug of tea at the kitchen table.

Hennessy gave him a relaxed smile.

"We wait, Tom," he said easily. Everything was ready. His visitors could come any time now and he would be ready. "That's how a soldier spends most of his life, didn't you know? Just waiting around for the killing to start."

THE *AMERICAN ENDEAVOR*, APRIL 15

"Tomorrow morning at 0300 hours. Agreed?"

The five men standing around the polished rosewood table in Jack Halloran's shipboard conference room all nodded approval. It couldn't be any later. They were all running out of time.

Lynch, Porter, Bono, and Gamble had choppered out from Londonderry aboard a Westland Lynx-3 requisitioned from the army by Porter using his senior intelligence authority and claiming an urgent intelligence mission. By the time the army found out it would all be over—one way or the other. The pilot seemed delighted to have drawn a bit of soft duty for a change. His name was David Hood and he was a startlingly cheerful RAF flight lieutenant on special attachment to the army in Ulster. Much of his tour of duty in Northern Ireland had been spent choppering SAS ambush units in and out of the IRA badlands surrounding Armagh, Newry, and Enniskillen, along Ulster's southern border.

The army had insisted the chopper's TOW missiles and cannon be disarmed before it was released for the supposed intelligence operation, but neither Porter nor Lynch was concerned. They had ruled out a direct chopper assault on the farmhouse because they could easily be shot out of the sky, and Janice would have been executed before they could land. They had chosen the Lynx-3 for other reasons. It is small enough to land on a ship. And it is the only battlefield chopper in the world fitted with blades constructed from a kevlar-titanium compound designed to minimize noise. It isn't silent; no helicopter is. But a man half a mile away would not hear it land or take off.

Gamble had acquired all the equipment they would need, including a laser-sighted Hockler MP5-SD3 for each man. He had not been able to find a black utility suit large enough to fit Bono but he had given the big man a load-carrying vest to wear over his old jungle greens. They had agreed to Porter's plan, with a few minor modifications. They ended the conference at eight with a break for a light supper. Hood, the chopper pilot, wouldn't be told where they were going until they were airborne. He was invited to join them for dinner and told simply that they would be running a snatch operation. He would be required to put the two-man teams ashore at two separate locations and then to wait at a quiet landing zone of his own choice, close enough to come in fast when they had their man. They all noticed that Hood's cheeriness appeared to have been tempered by a certain doubt. However, he had the good grace and the good sense to keep his doubts to himself. He had learned enough about the kind of men who do high-risk, low-profile security assignments to know that he complained afterward, not during the job.

After their meal Lynch, Bono, Gamble, and Hood went to their cabins to get some sleep before jump-off came around in five hours. Halloran and Porter stayed below at the dinner table in the master stateroom, talking. Both men were aware that they had embarked on operations where their own positions were in direct jeopardy.

"Does the President have any knowledge of this at all?"

"Well"—Halloran sighed heavily—"yes and no."

"More no than yes?"

Halloran smiled.

"I told him we were running our intelligence operation from the ship. I told him that it had brought us here."

"But he doesn't know we're going in tonight?"

"He will the moment you all take off in that chopper and I can't see you anymore."

The two old warriors had poured themselves a small glass of port each. Porter raised his glass in salute.

"I did something similar," he said. "Tomorrow morning at nine o'clock, a plain brown envelope marked 'top secret' will be delivered by courier to the office of the commanding officer of all British troops in Northern Ireland." Porter sipped slowly. "By that time we'll know it all, won't we?"

Halloran eyed his opposite number across the table.

"Hot damn," he said, except it wasn't the usual cowboy exclamation Porter heard on television. It was a slow, soft release of tension.

"We're betting it all on this one, aren't we, Malcolm? And there are no guarantees. No guarantees at all. Men will be dead by morning."

Porter finished his drink and got up to go.

"Either we believe in what we're doing or we don't," he said.

"We lead cosseted lives compared to the men who have just left this table. They put their lives on the line for what they believe in. Until now, we've only pointed them in the right direction, then sat back and watched the sparks fly. Now it's our turn. The rest is all politics and horse manure."

Halloran got up to see his old friend to the door. Then he returned to his conference room and considered all the maps and plans scattered across the table. It was a desperate plan, thrown together in a hurry by desperate men.

"Dead by morning . . ." he heard himself say.

It was one o'clock when Lynch woke up, alert, nerves and reflexes silently thrumming. He'd only slept three and a half hours. It was all he needed. He got dressed and went out on deck. Bono was in the adjacent stateroom and he was already dressed and standing at the rail.

"Can't sleep?" Lynch asked.

"Nah," Bono said. "Never could before these things. I like it when we're movin'."

The two men leaned against the rail and watched the pale quarter moon flirt with the wave tops.

"We're going in to nail some kind of bastard this time, ain't we, boss?" Bono grumbled after a while.

"They just seem to keep popping up and we have to keep coming back and knocking 'em down, don't we?" Lynch responded dryly. "I think it's called democracy."

"This guy really a traitor?"

Lynch shrugged. "I suppose it depends where your true loyalties lie. He sees us as the bad guys."

Bono pressed a fleshy forefinger to his right nostril and fired a glistening bullet of mucus into the sea.

"Helluva thing to turn against your own country. Your own people."

Lynch shrugged. "People don't seem to have countries anymore. Only beliefs. Sometimes they're willing to tear their country apart for the sake of their beliefs."

Bono looked at him. "What do you believe in?"

Lynch smiled. "I believe we're the good guys and they're the bad guys."

Bono grinned. "You sure 'bout that?"

"No," Lynch answered. "Sometimes I don't like the things I have to do. But it only makes me hate the bastards more who make it necessary for me to do them."

There was a long pause as both men entertained their own thoughts.

"Well." Bono leaned away from the rail. "Time to get ready for battle." He turned and shambled along the deck toward his cabin.

"Bono?" Lynch called after him.

It sounded strange and self-conscious but Lynch had to ask. "Do you ever worry about what we're doing?"

Bono looked at him.

"No," he said. "I've always been one of the good guys." Then he disappeared into his cabin.

BLOODY FORELAND, APRIL 16

The chopper lifted off the helipad on the afterdeck of the *American Endeavor* at one minute past three in the morning. Halloran watched them go. The chopper had no lights and with her soundproofed rotors she had vanished into the blackness in a twinkling. He turned and walked slowly back down to the conference room and dialed his special number for the White House. It was eleven o'clock the previous evening in Washington. The President of the United States was preparing for a rare early night.

He greeted Halloran warily. "Jack? What do you have?"

"Sir, I have just launched an operation into the Republic of Ireland to snatch the man I believe is responsible for the massacre of my people in New York twenty-seven days ago."

The anger that swept through the President's body was instant and total. He struggled to keep his voice calm.

"You've what?"

"I have received accurate intelligence about his location. I have very good reason to believe he is the man responsible. I have sent my people in to bring him out and to return him to the United States to stand trial. I am doing it with the knowledge and the cooperation of the British government."

It was another lie but Halloran was in so deep now it didn't matter.

"Jack," the President said, his voice lethal. "You recall your people now."

"I'm afraid that would be impossible, sir. If I were to break radio silence now I would endanger the lives of those men and jeopardize the success of the operation."

The President's head flooded with fears and warnings about covert government departments exceeding their powers through an excess of zeal and patriotism. The military and the intelligence services were full of people who still believed that Ollie North was a hero. That was what he had now, the President realized: another Oliver North. The specter of twenty million Irish-American votes dematerialized in his mind's eye. He could already see the beginning of an international embarrassment that would threaten his incumbency.

"Jack," he said, "I gave you fair warning. I have gone much farther for you than I have for any other member of my administration. I'm sorry, Jack, I truly am. But you leave me no alternative."

"Sir . . ." Halloran protested. He was about to ask for six hours. That was all, but it was already too late.

"Clayton, this is the President. You were right. I was wrong. Jack Halloran has gone over the top. I want you here within the hour. I'll have the Defense Department secretary here by then, too. I'm ordering Delta into the air. I want them to drop onto the *American Endeavor* and put all those on board under close arrest. I want the nearest warship to divert to the area and put a crew aboard to escort her back to Chesapeake."

Clayton Powell put down the glass of bourbon on his bedside table.

"Yes sir." He smiled. He contained himself just long enough to put the telephone down and then he pounded the table and let out a loud whoop of Texan jubilation.

"The bastard's done it," Powell yelled to his startled wife on the other side of the bed. "That crazy bastard Halloran has finally shot himself in the foot."

Just as Clayton Powell was hurrying to his waiting limousine in Washington, five thousand kilometers to the northeast, across the Atlantic Ocean, the Westmoreland Lynx was approaching the northwest tip of Donegal at wave height. Two nautical miles before his radar screen told him the coastline began, Hood pulled back gently on the stick and moments later the chopper hurtled over the onrushing, surf-fringed cliffs with only meters to spare. They'd insisted he take them along, he thought; he might as well give them a ride they'd remember.

Hood's passengers sat silently in the small cabin, faces streaked and blackened with camouflage grease. Hood took them well to the south of the promontory named Bloody Foreland and looped around behind the farmhouse now identified by a winking green blip on his map screen. Five minutes later he settled briefly on the heath while Bono and Porter jumped out and melted instantly into the darkness. Hood took the Lynx up again and backtracked. A few minutes later he hovered briefly over the clifftops at Bloody Foreland and dropped his last two passengers off.

Lynch and Gamble got a good look at the two-hundred-foot cliffs and the waves dashing themselves on the black rocks far below before the chopper settled. A moment later they were gone, the chopper was gone; there was nothing to suggest anyone had landed anywhere. Hood banked steeply out to sea and then circled back down the coast to look for a quiet resting spot. As he did he caught a glimpse of something odd, hidden in the folds of the corrugated coastline. Keeping well out to sea to make sure that whoever it was wouldn't know he was out there, he scanned his radar. If it was a boat it was too close to shore to differentiate from the radar profile of the land mass.

He made two more passes and caught it again on the second pass. This time he saw. It was a boat, a white-topped fishing trawler tucked into a small cove for the night. That wasn't unusual, he thought. It might just be a coincidence. But he made a mental note of its location anyway. A few minutes later he saw the lights from the village of Crolly slide past his portside and then, three nautical miles south, he found what he was looking for: a clearing amid a patch of coastal scrub. He brought the chopper down, landed softly on the thick spring grasses, and cut the engine. A moment later the silent darkness enveloped him completely.

Bono and Porter moved in tandem for the first couple of kilometers on the ground and then separated as planned. It was a steady but gentle uphill climb toward the coast and neither man found it tiring. They estimated that they could approach the farmhouse safely to within about three kilometers before they had to adopt extreme caution. After that they both began to move forward in short, quick bursts, lying low for several minutes to watch the ground ahead and listen to the night sounds, then dashing silently forward when they were sure it was safe. They saw nothing but the dense blackness of the heathlands rising to the horizon where a line of almost geometric perfection separated the land from the sky. They heard only the sound of the wind, its constant roaring and buffeting nagging in their ears.

The wind was a godsend, in one respect. It muffled any noise they might make. But it was equally a curse because it chased the scudding clouds across the sky and kept the horizon illuminated by the pale light of the quarter moon and the stars. In other circumstances Porter would have spent the whole night creeping painstakingly across the ground toward his target, making absolutely sure that he wasn't seen. At dawn he would have dug himself into the ground and lain still all day, ignoring the ants and beetles and worms that crawled over him and threatened to drive him mad with their itching. Nibbling only on a couple of protein bars, urinating where he lay. Then, the next night, he would have moved in for the kill. Tonight he didn't have time. They were in a hurry, and they were both decoys.

Hennessy had laid his defenses and set his traps well. Both Bono and Porter detected the outer layer of thin nylon fishing lines that wove a deadly tapestry of alarm and destruction beneath the thick grass. Both were expecting that. They found the first lines a mile before the farmhouse. Too far out, Bono thought. Not enough mines. Too many gaps. He got through first. About a mile and a half away on his right, Porter picked out his own path, a little more slowly, a little more carefully, conserving his strength for the sudden, explosive burst of energy he knew he would need when the action started, soon enough. And it was Bono who got caught first. By the unexpected.

He was worming his way gradually across the ground, submachine gun slung across his back, fingers in front, feeling the ground as delicately as a blind man reading braille. When he felt even the slightest pull of something unusual, he froze, followed it, and if it was a line, he got up onto his haunches, checked the ground on the other side, and then stepped quietly over and started again. When he didn't expect was the voice that came out of the dark a few meters to his right.

"Freeze where ye are, ye bastard, or I'll blow your fockin' head off."

Bono lay absolutely still. Close by, a clump of heathland seemed to detach itself from the ground and move toward him. As it approached, Bono saw that it was a man wearing coveralls with thick clumps of heath grass fastened to his head and back. He was holding an Armalite. The mines and tripwires were Hennessy's outer circle. What they hadn't expected was that Hennessy would put most of his men outside, too. In foxholes, a little trick he'd borrowed from the SAS. Except, unlike the SAS troops, his men had grown up in this country. They were fighting on home ground; they knew the country and all its features and sounds. They could detect the sound and movement of an intruder half a mile away. Hennessy knew the intruders would have to come across country and he knew there would be only a few of them. Four, perhaps six at most. Hennessy's gunmen waited in the dark. They would pick the first one or two off as they approached stealthily across the heath, then fall back to the third line of defense.

"Stand up," the man hissed.

Bono reluctantly got to his feet.

The man snatched the H&K off Bono's shoulder and jabbed him viciously in the back with the Armalite.

"Fockin' move."

Bono began to stumble in the direction the man indicated. It was another hundred yards before he discerned the ghostly white shape of the darkened farmhouse materializing out of the blackness ahead. Minutes later the man leaned forward, opened the door, and shoved Bono inside. It was even darker and it took a moment even for Bono's night-adjusted eyes to see anything. A soft English voice came out of the darkness.

"Ah," it whispered. "The first of our guests." The next moment Bono felt a stabbing pain across the side of his head and he stumbled heavily to his knees.

"Jesus," the voice said. "You're a strong bastard." The second blow plunged Bono into deep unconsciousness.

When he came around he had no idea how much time had passed but he suspected it hadn't been long. Ten or fifteen minutes perhaps. Long enough to show him he was in serious trouble. The first impression he had was that he was looking at the brilliant white death mask of a man. Then the mask spoke.

"How does it feel?" the mask said. It was the same soft voice.

Bono struggled. He couldn't move but he rocked slightly back and forth. His arms and feet were tightly bound to a chair.

"I watched you do this to a friend of mine at your little shack in the States," the voice said. "I heard what you did to him. I heard how he screamed. Now it's your turn."

Bono understood. He was in a darkened room and the man facing him was holding a flashlight between the two of them. Exactly the way Bono had done with the Irishman in Hibbing. The big man took a deep breath and flexed every muscle he had. He grunted with pain as the cords around his wrists and ankles bit deep. They only pulled tighter. He gave up. He glanced quickly around for the knife, but there was none. No table. No pet dog to devour him one piece at a time.

"We've got our own way of doing things here," the voice said, reading Bono's eyes. The man tilted the flashlight to the automatic he held in his right hand. Bono had seen one like it before. It was a Browning Hi-Power. A devastating weapon at close range.

"How many pals did you bring with you?" Hennessy asked.

Bono dropped his head forward on his chest.

Hennessy shone the torch directly into Bono's face, then reached forward with the Browning and tapped it sharply against the huge red lump that covered the right side of Bono's head. The big man gasped with the pain.

Hennessy noticed the almost healed burns and cuts. "You've got a few marks on you." He tutted mockingly. "Did I do that?"

Bono remembered the figure silhouetted in the shattered storm-cellar doors of the farm. The blaze of automatic fire . . . then the satchel full of grenades.

Hennessy was growing impatient.

"Is Lynch out there tonight? Is Jack Halloran waiting somewhere while you guys do his dirty work?" Hennessy paused only a moment. "How many more are out there, Bono? I want to know."

Bono lifted his head and stared back though the dazzle of the flashlight beam with eyes of dark, glittering fury.

"My," Hennessy exclaimed lightly. "We are getting angry." Then the voice changed again. To Bono it almost sounded as though two people were talking to him.

"Have you heard of kneecapping where you come from, Mr. Bono?"

Bono closed his eyes and concentrated on holding his nerve. Any moment, he knew, the firing would start outside. Any moment. It had to. Jesus, where were those bastards? How close did they have to come? What was going wrong out there? And then he knew. He knew how the man in his basement had felt. And, at that instant of realization, Bono knew, too, that his time had come.

"What we do is place the muzzle of the gun directly behind the knee," the voice said. Jesus, Bono thought. That voice. It was like a dripping tap. So even and controlled and insidious, just eating through your defenses to find the deep hidden core of all your greatest fears.

"You'd think it would be quick, wouldn't you?" the voice said. "A single gunshot at close range. And then the shock would take away most of the pain." The voice paused.

"It doesn't, you know. I've seen it done. I know what happens. The bullet enters through the back of the knee, bores a neat hole through the center of the joint, blows away all the cartilage and sinew holding the femur to the tibia, and shatters the kneecap into a fine white powder. It comes right out through the front of the knee . . . like a spurt. A red-and-white spurt that, well . . . it just seems to go everywhere. The pain is quite unbearable, I'm told. And they don't pass out, you know. That's the worst of it. There's no relief. And then, of course, when they've been really bad, there's the second one. And you can see it on their faces, you know. They understand that they'll never walk again. But they want to live. That's the strange part. They still want to live. I don't understand that. Do you? I wouldn't want to live like that. Especially when you do both elbows next."

It was cold in the room but Bono could feel the sweat beading on his forehead.

The face disappeared into the swarming blackness. The flash-light danced around the farmhouse room and Bono saw other faces, other men standing silently, grimly, letting it happen. He glimpsed a heavy blanket pulled across part of a wall and guessed it was a window. Then there was a sharp jab of circular metal behind his left knee. He heard the safety catch of the Browning click off. He braced himself.

"Are you ready Mr. Bono? Are you sure you're ready?"

"Jesus, Brian," a voice said out of the gloom. It was an old man's voice. Once strong, now fearful and alarmed. "Do ye have to. Can't we just—"

"Shut up," the voice behind the chair snapped. "Just shut the fuck up, Tom."

Bono slowly shook his head. He didn't know if he could deal with it a second longer. Somewhere, deep inside him, a scream was forming. A scream of pure, animal terror.

There was a burst of firing from outside. A pause and then a sudden crescendo as several heavier guns joined in.

"Ah," the voice whispered in his ear. "The rest of your friends have arrived." The muzzle of the Browning pulled away from his leg. The flashlight went out and there was the sound of scuffling boots as several men hurried from the darkened room.

Hennessy strode into the kitchen and pulled a blanket away from the window. The countryside was alive with livid slivers of tracers stitching the night sky. Hennessy had positioned his men to protect the circle with a series of overlapping crossfires. He had told them, when the firing started, to fire their weapons at ground level first, then up a fraction, then up a fraction more, then down again. That way the farm was protected for 360 degrees by expanding circular ripples of withering gunfire. Nothing could survive out there. Nothing could come within a mile of that intensity of crossfire and survive.

The first stuttering burst of submachine-gun fire had stopped. The sound of the Armalites died away to a rattle and then ceased. A moment later the first of the men came jogging back to the house, dark lumpy figures emerging out of the dark. Just as he had ordered. He counted them in until all were back inside. They dumped their camouflage at the door and took up predetermined positions at the darkened windows and doors. When they were all inside, Hennessy stepped back to the kitchen table, where a switch was attached to an octopus of electrical wiring running up into a ragged hole cut in the ceiling. He flicked the switch and a great circular ball of light flamed out from the farmhouse over the surrounding heath from a battery of two dozen car headlights he'd rigged around the roof. The wire for each light led to the octopus in the kitchen and a central cable attached to the two truck batteries on the kitchen floor. Nothing moved outside. Nothing could move for two hundred yards without being seen.

"Now, boys," he called to the men inside. "We sit tight until morning and we've got the buggers cold." He looked at his watch. "That's ninety minutes from now. Anything moves out there, anything at all, blast it to pieces."

He looked toward the living room where Bono waited, tied to a kitchen chair.

"Now," Hennessy said, the sadistic silkiness back in his voice. "Where were we . . . ?"

There was the muffled thud of a mine exploding outside. Hennessy turned and looked through the window. A cloud of smoke scurried and vanished in the wind and a small shower of earth and stone rained harmlessly to the ground.

"Did anybody get it?" Hennessy called.

No one in the house had seen a man anywhere near the mine when it exploded.

There was another explosion and Hennessy saw it this time. A vivid spear of red flame leaped violently out of the ground and vanished into the sky like the jet exhaust of a rocket. Again the smoke danced and scattered and pieces of earth spattered harmlessly to the ground. Still they saw no one outside. There was a ripple of uneasiness among the men.

"How can they do that?" one of the gunmen at the second kitchen window asked. "Where are they?"

"They're just playing with us, boys," Hennessy called out to his men. "They've figured out the wires and they're tweaking them from a safe distance, one at a time, letting us know they're still out there."

There was a louder, concentrated blast as three mines went up together. The windows shook and the furniture rattled throughout the farmhouse. Still no one moved outside.

"Bugger this," said a man at the far kitchen window, and he began firing again. It was Eamonn Docherty. He was joined instantly by a louder, deadlier chorus from his pals as the Armalites opened up in unison, all around the house, scorching the open countryside with a firestorm of bullets. Tom O'Donnell had picked up a rifle and was standing beside Docherty, blazing randomly into the night.

"Hold your fire, boys," Hennessy yelled after a moment. "You don't want to waste all your ammo before we get to Derry."

Somebody gave a nervous chuckle and the gunfire faded and died.

One of the headlights wired to the outside gutter disintegrated in a spray of fine glass and a funnel of darkness marched sharply across the heath toward them.

"Jesus," somebody said. "Where are they? How can they still be standin' out there?"

"Calm yourselves, boys. They can't take the house. There's too many of us and we're too well covered."

Another headlight exploded and died. Then another and another. Whoever was firing had a silencer and flash suppressor, Hennessy realized. And he was good. A marksman. A row of lights on one side of the farmhouse popped out in quick succession, like clay pipes at a fairground. The night charged in on them again with frightening speed. The last headlight went out, plunging the heath into total blackness, and the IRA men renewed their fire with a frenzied determination. A man at the kitchen window suddenly reeled back and hit the floor without a sound, half his face shot away. It was Eamonn Docherty. O'Donnell dropped his own rifle with a clatter and knelt down beside Docherty but there was nothing he could do. Tom O'Donnell's loyal and brutish strong-arm man from the old pub days in Dublin was dead before he hit the ground. There was a scream from the other side of the house as somebody else got hit. Hennessy stared wildly around. He caught the briefest flicker of a sinister red light, just a needlepoint of red light on the kitchen wall, and then another man screamed and went down.

"Fucking laser sighting," Hennessy spat. "That's what they're using."

"What's happening, Brian?" O'Donnell looked up from the floor. The note in his voice struck a common chord of alarm among the men. It was turning against them, they felt. Now it was they who were trapped.

"Right," Hennessy said. "It's time we took care of that bastard in there."

He pushed past the old man, strode into the darkened living room, grabbed the back of Bono's chair, and dragged it into the middle of the room. The blanket on the window had been torn down so the men could fire freely, and there was just enough light from outside for Bono to make out Hennessy's shape as it ducked down quickly behind him. Then he felt the Hi-Power jab into the back of his knee.

"Can you hear me, Lynch?" Hennessy roared in a voice that rose above the rifle fire and boomed across the heath. One by one the rifles stopped and everyone paused to listen.

"I killed your pals, Lynch," he taunted. "I killed them one at a time. Burned them like pigs on a spit." His voice seemed to echo eerily through the night, carried on the howling wind that mourned down from the clifftops across the bent and stunted turf.

"I took your woman, Lynch. I took her like a bitch," he screamed. "You want what's left of her? You want what's left of your pal?" His voice rose to a pitch of madness.

"Come and get them, Lynch. Come on and pick up the pieces . . ."

He started to squeeze the trigger of the automatic.

A hail of bullets lashed the outside walls of the farmhouse.

A man staggered back from the curtained window, his chest a cratered mass of blood and bone. Hennessy hesitated.

A grenade glinted evilly in the moonlight as it curled through the shattered window, hit a wall, and skittered hypnotically across the floor. The eyes of every man in the room followed it. It wasn't a stun grenade. It was a live grenade, packed with high explosive.

Bono roared and threw himself backward. The Hi-Power fired and blew a hole the size of a man's head in the opposite wall. Men scrambled desperately for the door, colliding, fighting, tearing at one another in the dark. The first men through the back door went down screaming in a stream of bullets. Porter was out there alone with the Hockler and wasn't taking any chances on being rushed. The men inside balked as they saw their pals die, only to be pushed forward again by the panicking men behind, trying to escape the deadly blast of the grenade.

A window shattered in the back bedroom as a stun grenade went in. A series of deafening bangs and blinding flashes strobed through the farmhouse. Gamble followed the stun grenade, a shadow moving with deadly purpose through the blinding, strobing light. He had ditched the Hockler PSG1 sniper rifle and used the MP5 to take out two men in his first roll. The others, eyes shut and disoriented by the stun grenade, began throwing down their weapons and thrusting their hands into the air, pleading for their lives. The same shouts were taken up throughout the house as men began yelling their capitulation. Porter stopped firing and snapped at the gunmen to line up along the outside rear wall of the farmhouse. A moment later he emerged, flushed and breathing heavily, from the darkness, eyes battle bright in his black-streaked face.

Lynch came through the shattered living room window in a long dive, rolled to his feet, and took the room at a glance. One man on the floor, dead. A man with white hair crouched in a corner, head down, trembling. No Janice, dead or alive. Bono on his back on the floor, still tied to the kitchen chair, his eyes clenched shut, face contorted and bellowing with rage and fear.

"You can shut up now," Lynch said calmly.

Bono still bellowed, unable to hear, trying to shut out the noise of his own dying.

"Shut up, you noisy bugger," Lynch snapped harshly into the big man's ear.

Bono's eyes blinked open. He looked wildly around, saw Lynch, the room, saw his own body, his legs, his arms still intact.

"Funny thing, isn't it?" Lynch remarked as he stooped to pluck the unexploded grenade off the floor and then twirled it lightly in his hand. "As soon as everyone sees something like this, they automatically assume the worst."

Bono stared through stinging, sweat-filled eyes. The pin was still in the grenade. He moaned softly, closed his eyes, and the last ounce of strength evaporated from his body.

The chaps had arrived.

A quick tally showed eight men dead and three wounded. But there was no sign of Hennessy.

Porter called Hood on the chopper. Two minutes later he was airborne. With Bono free, Lynch, Gamble, and Porter herded their captives into a line, then forced them onto their faces in the dirt.

Hood's voice suddenly crackled over the radio in Porter's hand.

"One man," he said. "Running hard. He's heading for the point. There's a fishing boat there."

Lynch snatched the radio from Porter's hand before the CTC chief could answer.

"Pick me up," Lynch snapped. "I want him first."

A moment later the Lynx-3 thrummed quietly into view and hovered a few meters clear of the house. Lynch leaped up onto the skid nearest the pilot's seat, one fist holding on to the helicopter, the other holding the submachine gun. At his nod, the chopper lifted sharply and reared backward into the sky. Seconds later they were streaking through the darkness toward the distant cliff tops, like a black bird of prey hunting down its quarry.

The tears streamed from Lynch's eyes as he squinted into the blasting wind, straining for a glimpse of Hennessy in the rushing darkness, but there was nothing. The ragged fringes of the great cliffs raced toward them and then Lynch saw him, a single dark figure, sprinting toward the edge cliffs and the sanctuary of the trawler in the sheltered cove. Lynch opened fire and watched with satisfaction as a stream of bullets howled down around the fleeing man. Hennessy began to zigzag and Lynch fired another burst. Then they were past him and over the ocean and Hood wrenched the chopper around for another pass.

As they banked, Lynch caught sight of Hennessy silhouetted against the cliff top. There was just enough light to show the thread of a narrow footpath winding down to the beach. Hood flew the chopper in a direct line toward Hennessy and Lynch fired a long burst. Hennessy threw himself onto the ground, waited for the chopper to pass, then leaped to his feet again and began sprinting along the crest of the cliffs. If he took the footpath, he knew, the chopper could hover in front of the cliffs and Lynch could blow him away at his leisure. Hennessy looked like a hunted animal as he ran in a frenzied dash along the cliff. Lynch struggled to work a fresh clip into the Hockler. The heat of revenge burned through him. Hennessy wasn't leaving alive.

Hood banked the Lynx around again. This time, they both saw, they had Hennessy cornered. He was running fast onto a long, crooked finger of land that narrowed sharply until it ended in empty space. The two-hundred-foot cliffs yawned away on three sides, ending in a deadly jumble of fallen rocks and a crashing, merciless surf. There was nowhere for Hennessy to go. He would have to turn and face his pursuers. Lynch tensed and slung the gun to one side. He didn't want to shoot Hennessy at all. He wanted to feel his hands on him.

Hood brought the chopper as low as he dared and they screamed across the turf, no more than waist height from the ground. Lynch watched the gap close between the chopper and the running man with a deadly fascination. He poised himself to jump. It was going to be close. But Hennessy did not stop and turn and face Lynch as a man. He ran till the last fragment of rock disappeared beneath his feet and hurled himself with a triumphant scream into the blackness. Lynch caught just a glimpse of Hennessy's face as he leaped and on it seemed to be a mix of triumph and elation. He had cheated Lynch of his moment of victory. The chopper turned again and hovered for a moment as Lynch's eyes followed the tiny, falling figure, its arms and legs flailing in a dreadful parody of death. And then it was swallowed by the boiling surf.

10 The Long Good-bye

The wind buffeted the hovering helicopter and powerful, invisible hands tried to pluck Lynch from the skid and hurl him to his death below, after Hennessy. Lynch turned and signaled to Hood to take him down to the trawler. Janice would be there, he knew. Hood nodded, gave the thumbs-up, circled around once more, and came down on the trawler from the seaward side. Lynch held the Hockler ready. The chopper slid slowly around the protective arm of land, her muffled rotors drowned in the roar of wind and the enveloping thunder of the surf. No one heard the chopper prowl gently across the wave tops until it was above the boat. Lynch dropped nimbly to the deck and booted open the galley door. Liam McKee and his deckhand looked up from the table in astonishment at the black, paint-daubed figure in the doorway pointing a submachine gun at them both. Both men were playing cards; Owen had a pot of coffee steaming on the gas stove. McKee stared in a mixture of fear and horror, the smoldering stub of a hand-rolled cigarette stuck to his bottom lip.

"Where is she?" Lynch asked. McKee heard murder in the voice.

"In the bow cabin," he answered. "She's fine. Honest, she's all right. We treated her fine."

"Get her."

McKee put down the greasy yellow playing cards and squeezed out from behind the galley table and toward the door to the bow cabin. He opened the door and pushed it open. Even from where Lynch stood at the galley hatch, the smell that gusted out was foul.

"Janice?" Lynch called.

Owen remained in his seat, paralyzed with fear.

For a moment there was nothing and then he heard a faint, unbelieving voice.

"Lynch?"

It was Janice but her voice sounded different. Weak. Beaten.

"Can you walk?" Lynch called.

"Ah, Hennessy cuffed her to the bunk rail before he left," McKee interrupted before Janice could speak. "He told us we wasn't to go near her. We had to leave her there. Honest mister, it's God's own truth."

"Where are the keys?"

"I've got them, I've got them." McKee fumbled in his jacket pocket and produced a small metal key. He knew his life hung in the balance. "I kept it on me so I'd know where it was all the time, y'know."

"Take them off her. Bring her out."

McKee disappeared into the cabin and there was the sound of the manacles clicking loose. He backed out a moment later and had to sit down behind the galley table because there was no more room. A moment later the bedraggled figure of a bare-legged woman wearing a filthy gray fisherman's sweater stepped timidly into the light. If Lynch had not known it was Janice, he wouldn't have recognized her. Her hair was dirty and matted thickly to her skull. Her eyes were dark hollows and one side of her face was still swollen by a disfiguring, yellow-tinged bruise. She looked like a tiny, emaciated, and terrified child. When she was able to look at him it was with the eyes of a woman he had never seen before. They were the eyes of a woman who had died. There was no expression of relief on her face. It was as though she still could not believe he was here and she was free. Her face was set in a frozen mask of pain and humiliation. The handcuffs with the key still in them swung from her right wrist where he could see a deep, raw welt.

"You two," Lynch snapped at the two men waiting silently and fearfully on either side of the cabin. "On deck."

They didn't have to be told twice.

Lynch backed out and they followed him onto the open deck with their hands raised high in the air. They heard the chopper now, thudding dully as it hovered a mere thirty yards away.

McKee took the full force of the kick under the chin. His jaw shattered into fragments and the impact lifted him off both feet, over the gunwales and into the water with a heavy splash where he surfaced and lay facedown, drowning in a mixture of seawater and his own blood. Owen saw his chance and dived over the side. Lynch reflexively aimed the Hockler after him and squeezed the trigger, then decided to let him go and slowly lifted his finger. He was only a dumb kid, Lynch knew.

Lynch turned as Janice stepped timidly out onto the open deck and looked around. She behaved like a woman who hadn't been outside or smelled fresh air in a lifetime. He watched her for a long moment while she stood there, silently, thankfully, breathing in the clean air. Then he let the Hockler drop, walked to her, and pulled her closely to him. There was no answering hug. No reciprocal squeeze as her arms wound around his waist, the way she had on other occasions. This time she just seemed to hang limply against him, her arms dangling weakly by her sides. He kissed her on the forehead and wiped away some of the matted strands of hair.

"It's over," he told her. "It's over." He signaled to Hood in the chopper. "I'm taking you to Jack's boat now . . ."

The kick hit him with devastating power down the right side of his body as Hennessy erupted, streaming, out of the water, and swung over the gunwales with a roar of rage to strike Lynch hard with the heels of both feet. Lynch was thrown against the starboard gunwales with a sickening crash and lay there stunned as Janice staggered backward into a corner. Hennessy looked around for a weapon.

He had known exactly what he was doing when he jumped from the high cliffs around the point. He knew that if he leaped hard enough and far enough he would clear the rocks and hit deep water. To a man who spent nine years in the parachute regiment a fall of two hundred feet held few terrors. He had flailed his arms and legs while he fell in an effort to stay upright, and when he hit the water it was with his feet and knees together and his head tucked hard into his chest. He had gone deep and the current had been strong but he was a fit and powerful man and he had calmly unlaced his boots, kicked them off, and fought his way back to the surface. Then he had swum powerfully and steadily around the point to the trawler.

And now he had Lynch exactly where he wanted him. He saw a white plastic bin full of rusted steel shackles used for securing broken chains. Each shackle was solid steel and weighed six pounds. Hennessy plucked one out of the bin, fitted it over his fist like a massive knuckle-duster, and launched himself with a snarl of triumph at the man slumped groggily in the gunwales opposite. Lynch sensed the blow coming, rather than heard it, and heaved himself out of the way. The shackle smashed through the deck rail and bit deep into the timber where Lynch's head had been a moment before. Hennessy spun around with the shackle still in his fist and padded across the deck on bare feet, pursuing Lynch.

Lynch scrambled awkwardly away on his back and felt his hands touch something hard. A length of chain. He grabbed it and swung it hard across the deck. The chain lashed against Hennessy's shins and smashed down onto his bare feet, crushing and splitting several of his toes. Hennessy shouted with pain and hurled the shackle at Lynch with murderous force. Lynch dodged and the huge steel link blurred past his shoulder to splash harmlessly into the sea. It gave him the time he needed to get back onto his feet and face Hennessy. One on one.

The two men circled each other warily around the deck of the trawler, each one knowing that only one of them would leave that dark, sheltered cove alive.

Hood, in the chopper, had seen Hennessy emerge from the ocean and attack Lynch, but he was powerless to intervene. He guided the Lynx forward until he was directly overhead and switched on his spotlight. The trawler and surrounding water were suddenly bathed in a brilliant pool of light. Hood saw the two men circling each other around the deck and saw a woman huddled helplessly in a corner. Hood swore. He didn't know if the light was helping or not. It might at least distract Hennessy, he thought. The man would have to know he was finished now, whatever happened.

Hennessy leaped, grabbed the trawler boom with both hands, and aimed another deadly, double kick at Lynch's head. Lynch dodged it easily and Hennessy dropped back to the deck, oblivious of the pain in his feet. Quickly scanning the deck for another weapon, he spotted one of McKee's fishing tools lying in a nearby corner. He bent and snatched up McKee's homemade gaff. It was a short-handled gaff used for hooking big fish under the gills and flicking them back over the side if they were worthless. The wooden handle was about half a meter long, well balanced and polished by years of use. At its tip was a large, forged steel hook, about the size of a sickle, and sharpened to a needle point. Hennessy rushed forward and slashed at Lynch with a grunt of malicious satisfaction.

Lynch heard it hiss through the air, inches from his face, and backed across the deck. He felt the heel of his boot touch Janice and she whimpered. Hennessy lunged forward and slashed wildly at Lynch's head and shoulders, trying to hook him somewhere, anywhere. Lynch flung the galley door into Hennessy's face and the hook bit deep into the timber and stuck.

Lynch saw his chance and hooked his left knee around the side of the door, catching Hennessy hard in the ribs. It was just enough to loosen his grip on the gaff. Lynch leaped out and put the toe of his boot into Hennessy's right armpit. It staggered him and Lynch followed it with a second kick that caught him on the breastbone and sent him flying backward into the galley. The galley table splintered underneath him like a child's toy. His flailing arms raked dirty dishes and half-empty cans of food off the benches and brought them smashing down around him. The coffeepot, left by McKee, was steaming violently on the stove. Hennessy stumbled to his feet, grabbed the pot, and hurled the boiling contents up into Lynch's face.

Lynch saw it coming and dodged, but half of the black, boiling liquid splashed across his combat pants, soaking through the thick fabric and scalding both thighs. The sudden, searing pain was intolerable. His instinct told him to dive over the side into the soothing balm of the cold sea water, but he saw Janice, cringing fearfully in the corner, and fought the pain. Hennessy launched himself out of the galley with a bellow and charged at Lynch. Lynch tried to sidestep, but too late; Hennessy hit him and knocked him into a pile of net floats. The heavy black floats, as large and as hard as bowling balls, scattered like marbles across the deck as the two men rolled about, grappling for an opening, the first lethal advantage. They smashed hard against the deck capstan and the impact loosened each man's grip on the other.

Momentarily free, Lynch heaved himself up onto his knees and unleashed two stinging punches into Hennessy's face. They would have staggered an ordinary man, but Hennessy's blood surged with the adrenaline of combat; he shook them off as he would a minor irritation. Instead of reeling from the blows he grabbed Lynch by the lapels of his combat vest and butted him savagely in the face. Lynch leaped back, blood streaming down his chin from badly split lips. Hennessy followed him. The two men squared off in the center of the deck and traded body punch for body punch until Lynch feared his ribs would crack.

Jesus, the thought flashed through Lynch's brain, the bastard is indestructible. He put all the muscle and power he could muster into a vicious, short-armed blow that caught Hennessy just below the heart. Lynch heard the blond man grunt and hit him again in the same place. Before he could hit him a third time Hennessy screamed with a mixture of pain and outrage, lunged forward, grabbed Lynch around the waist, and hoisted him high into the air. Then he brought him crashing back down with his spine against a steel winch mounted on the stern rail. Lynch screamed in pain and for a moment thought his back had been broken. He slumped to the deck at Hennessy's feet and braced himself for the finishing blow.

Between Hennessy's spread legs he could just see a threatening red glow flaring in the galley. One gas ring had been left burning on the stove to heat the coffee. When Hennessy had crashed into the galley, spilling food and broken crockery everywhere, he had knocked over an open bottle of cooking oil. The oil had scattered a shiny, viscous membrane over everything. Some of the oil had splashed across the top of the galley stove and the flames from the gas ring followed it hungrily onto the countertop, where they branched out in a dozen different directions. One tiny sliver of spitting blue flame reached into the mouth of the gurgling bottle of cooking oil and it went up like a Molotov cocktail. The galley was soon ablaze and the fire was spreading fast. Only Hennessy knew there were still fifty thousand pounds of Semtex and two dozen Stinger warheads in the hold.

Hennessy clenched his fists together and brought them crashing down toward the back of his opponent's neck. This would finish it, he knew, and he put all his strength into the blow. It would break Lynch's neck. Lynch struggled to ignore the agony in his tortured body and lashed upward with the points of his fingers into Hennessy's groin. The blow took Hennessy completely by surprise. He howled in pain and staggered backward across the deck, falling absurdly into a sitting position, with his back against the galley door. Lynch struggled painfully to his feet and lumbered clumsily across the deck toward Hennessy. He saw the flames behind Hennessy's shoulder, roaring through the galley, lighting Janice's prison in the bow, flickering up the galley steps, eating through the decking toward the hold. The refrigeration unit had been turned off since the trawler had arrived at Bloody Foreland. The metal casing of the dead refrigerator began to heat up.

Lynch, too, knew that he had to finish it. He could feel his strength draining away through the curtain of pain. The boat was ablaze. He had to kill Hennessy and get Janice off the trawler. He balanced himself for one last kick. A lethal kick to the throat. Hennessy somehow found the strength to move first. His scrabbling fingers clawed up the galley door and found the handle of the gaff still hanging there. He grabbed it and pulled himself to his feet.

Lynch was too late. Hennessy yanked the gaff free and slashed at Lynch's body. Lynch retreated along the starboard rail. Hennessy followed him, exhausted, one hand on the rail to steady himself, the other clenched around the handle of the gaff.

Both men were near the end, their bodies beaten and battered to the breaking point. Lynch bumped against the stern rail, cornered. Hennessy struck. Lynch tried to ward off the blow,

but the gleaming steel point of the hook plunged into the back
of his hand and Hennessy yanked it down against the bulwarks
where it stuck fast, impaling Lynch's right hand against the boat.

Lynch screamed hoarsely with the pain, his whole body spasm-
ing in agony, but he couldn't move. Hennessy gave a low animal
growl of pleasure and looked around. He knew the things McKee
kept on deck. He leaned back toward one of the plastic utility
bins and plucked out a black-handled filleting knife. It was used
for decapitating and cleaning fish. Balancing it lightly in his
hand, Hennessy clenched his fist tight around the handle and
turned back toward the man he'd impaled in the corner of the
boat. He was going to gut Lynch. Open him up from belly to
throat.

Something cold clasped his wrist and tugged him sharply backward. Hennessy looked around in bewilderment. The hand he'd
been using to hold himself upright was now manacled to the
deck rail. Janice backed quickly away from him. She looked like
some kind of wild, feral creature, her filthy black hair framing
a white face set hard with loathing. She lifted her hand and
held something small and silvery in front of her. It was the key
to the handcuffs. Then she smiled and threw it over the side.

Hennessy yanked his arm but the cuffs were locked solid.

"Suffer, you bastard," Janice hissed at him. "You stay here
chained like an animal . . . and you suffer."

Lynch reached down with his free hand and agonizingly
worked the gaff hook free from the side of the boat. Each tug
and jar sent waves of nauseating pain through his body. Finally
it came loose and he pried the deadly hook from his hand. Then
he swung it sharply at Hennessy's free arm and the filleting knife
clattered harmlessly to the deck.

A violent gust of flame belched out of the galley and Lynch
saw smoke sifting through the deck planking beneath their feet.
Janice seemed to notice the fire for the first time. Hood brought
the chopper down low against the stern. Janice had to pull herself
aboard the chopper with only the aid of Hood's free arm; Lynch
was too weakened to help. He was bleeding badly from the brutal
wound in his hand, his back throbbed with pain, and the skin
on both his thighs was still burning. Somehow, with Janice and

Hood helping, he managed to climb aboard the chopper. Hood closed the side hatch and took the Lynx up. He shut off the spotlight and below in the cove they saw Hennessy struggling hopelessly in the lurid light of the flames. Suddenly, a fiery fist punched through the deck with a shower of sparks and burned brightly around him. The flames grew and Hennessy's struggles became more frantic. Then they saw him leaning across the deck, straining.

"Oh my God," Hood exclaimed.

The three of them knew what Hennessy was doing—he was trying to reach the knife. He was going to hack off his hand. More flames burst through the deck and danced around him. They knew it was impossible but they thought they heard a scream.

"Let's get out of here," Lynch grunted. "We don't want to see this."

Janice reached down and cradled his head in her lap. He shifted position to try to see into her face. He couldn't be sure in the dark but he thought he saw her smile. The chopper hummed gracefully over the wave tops toward the waiting *American Endeavor*, eighty nautical miles and only twenty minutes distant. Minutes later the horizon behind them lit up with a flash of brilliant yellow and scarlet light. A moment later the weakening shockwave and the rumble of a massive explosion from the direction of Bloody Foreland reached out and rocked the fleeing chopper.

"Jesus," Hood breathed. He wrestled the chopper back on course and then slowly shook his head. "That man was in a big hurry to get to hell."

WASHINGTON, APRIL 16

"Our closest warship is the USS *Benson*," Defense Secretary Dick Warren was explaining to the President in the Oval Office. The only other man in the room was Clayton Powell, and he was listening attentively. It was almost four o'clock in the morning and they had been at the White House all night, acting as liaison between the President and their respective departments. Now, they were ready to act on his orders.

"The *Benson* is a missile cruiser and she's paying a courtesy visit to the city of Glasgow. That's only six hours' cruising time from the *American Endeavor*'s latest reported position, sir."

Powell took over: "The aircraft with our Delta team on board will be over the *American Endeavor* within one hour. They can drop right on her, secure all personnel, and hold the vessel till the navy gets there."

The President nodded. He was unshaven but had changed into slacks, an open-neck shirt, and a golfing sweater before the secretary of state and the defense secretary had arrived. He was still furious with Halloran but he was worried, too. Even if he did commit Delta and the navy it was still too late. It would be a punitive exercise only. That would please Clayton Powell, he knew, but it wouldn't do anything to get him out of the corner Halloran had backed him into. The phone on his desk buzzed. His White House secretary had been up all night, too.

"It's Mr. Halloran, sir. Do I put him through?"

The President sighed, thinking he might as well hear firsthand how bad it was.

"Yes, Jack," he said a moment later, his voice as tired as he felt.

"Mr. President," Halloran greeted him formally. "I'm glad to report that the operation has been a success. My people were in and out in less than six hours. Our information was correct. The person we sought to apprehend was the person responsible for the attack on my people in New York. He was an active member of a rogue branch of the IRA . . . and he was killed while offering vigorous resistance to my people. All my people have returned safely. The operation was restricted to an isolated area and was completed before dawn. There is nothing to connect us with the incident at all. When the authorities investigate they will find evidence to indicate a feud between IRA factions. Our investigation is closed. We can be well out of the region within a few hours. Do I have your permission to proceed, sir?"

The President snorted in disbelief but a slow smile had started to form on his face.

"Nothing to connect this administration with the operation in Ireland, Jack? Are you absolutely positive about that?"

"Yes, sir. Have I ever let you down, sir?" Halloran couldn't resist scoring at least one point off the President of the United States.

"No, you haven't, Jack," the President conceded. "All right, get the hell away from there. You can come home now."

He hung up and looked at Clayton Powell's crestfallen face.

"Recall Delta Force," the President ordered. "Dick, the boys on board the *Benson* can carry on with their shore leave. Thank you, gentlemen. It's been a long night. I think we should all get some sleep."

"Shit," Powell swore softly.

"You know, Clayton," the President added disapprovingly. "I've been meaning to have a word with you about your language. I'm not entirely convinced it's appropriate for a secretary of state . . ."

BLOODY FORELAND, APRIL 16

Half an hour after Hood had deposited Lynch and Janice safely aboard the *American Endeavor* he was flying back toward the coast of Ireland. Long before he got there he saw a column of thick white smoke rising from the foreshore, lit from the east by the rising sun. As he swept low over Bloody Foreland he saw that there was nothing at all left of the fishing boat, and several huge new sections of the cliff had fallen away, turning the cove into a sinister black pool. The smoke came from the farmhouse, torched by Porter, Gamble, and Bono when they found the weapons cache in the cellar. Hood could still hear the crackle of exploding ammunition from the farm, two miles away, when he settled briefly on the headland to pick up the three men.

They had already sent their captives scurrying away across the heath with a few bursts of submachine-gun fire to speed them on their way. They could take their chances with their own kind. Porter would make sure enough disinformation was sewn

throughout Northern Ireland in the next few weeks to indicate
the IRA had just gone through another of its eternal bloody
purges. As he lifted off from the soil of Ireland for the last time,
Hood saw a lone, white-haired figure in a black overcoat stumbling forlornly across the point, staring wildly around as though
looking for someone or something.

"Poor old bugger's mad," Porter remarked as he saw the old
man flash below.

"You ask me," Bono grumbled, "they're all fuckin' crazy down
there."

Tom O'Donnell heard the chopper hum past and looked up.

"Don't leave me . . ." he called out vainly, his words whipped
away by the wind. "Don't leave me here . . ."

No one in the helicopter had noticed the dark blue Ford
Granada speeding through the dawn light along the road to
Bloody Foreland. A few minutes later it stopped, close to where
Tom O'Donnell stumbled across the heath. Three men climbed
out and walked in a line toward him.

"Oh," the white-haired man said in surprise. "Hello, Ronnie
. . . what are you doin' here?"

Ronnie Carson stared at Tom O'Donnell for a long time
without speaking. The old man stood quite still and stared back,
his watery eyes uncomprehending.

The commander of the Derry brigade had suspected something
big since the murder of Billy McCormack. His suspicions were
confirmed when Kevin Bourke's wife came to him and asked
when her husband would be home. Carson began making his
inquiries, only to find that twenty-three longtime Provo men
had gone missing. They weren't the most loyal members of the
Derry battalions and Carson was able to put it all together quite
neatly after that. He knew a coup was brewing.

"You know what you are, Tom?" he asked in a conversational
voice.

"What, Ronnie, what do ye mean?" O'Donnell asked.

"You're a traitor, Tom," Carson said quietly. "You're a traitor
to the Cause."

"Me?" A baffled smile of denial flickered briefly across
O'Donnell's face. "Not me, Ronnie. I'm a patriot. An Irish
patriot . . ."

"Good-bye, Tom," Carson said abruptly, and turned away.

O'Donnell watched him go and then noticed Carson's two henchmen had produced guns from beneath their coats. Shotguns. Twelve-gauge, sawed-off shotguns.

O'Donnell stared in disbelief. "No, boys . . ." he protested faintly, backing away. "Not me . . . I'm no traitor . . . I'm a patriot . . ."

Both shotguns crashed in unison and Tom O'Donnell was hurled backward into the spongy peat grass, his dying eyes staring up at the brightening sky. The echo of the shotguns faded away and minutes later the birds began to sing again, oblivious to the death and destruction around them. The sun stroked the emerald grasses of the heath with fingers of warm white gold. It was going to be a beautiful spring day in Ireland. As Tom O'Donnell lay on the cliff at Bloody Foreland, somewhere in the deep, dying recesses of his brain, a woman's voice could be heard. "You'll die bloody, Tom," Mavour told him again. "You'll die bloody . . ."

Epilogue

Four days later, Abu Musa was eating breakfast in the courtyard of his villa when the call came soon after morning prayers. Sheikh al-Mahouraq, the mullah in charge of the Iranian foreign ministry, would like to see him that day. When he emerged from the ministry later that afternoon and walked thoughtfully down the steps with the letter folded neatly in the jacket pocket of his double-breasted, Italian-made suit, he looked like a deeply troubled man. It was bad enough that he hadn't heard from either Hennessy or O'Donnell in several days. But he'd just been handed a copy of a letter that came to the ministry from the Cuban chargé d'affaires in Tehran the previous day. The letter explained that President Castro was most disappointed with an arrangement that had been made between him and Abu Musa, an esteemed representative of the people of Iran. It also carried a short and tersely worded account that spoke volumes. It was for lives and equipment lost at the behest of Abu Musa. In crude terms, it was a bill. For eleven million American dollars.

Frowning, Musa climbed into the back of his waiting Mercedes and the driver pulled quickly away into the traffic. Many of his clients were concerned about the amount of their money he had already spent, the mullah had said. Abu Musa nervously fingered his beautifully trimmed beard. Business was not good.

BIARRITZ, FRANCE, MAY 1

A beautiful, dark-haired woman wearing a fetching pale blue dress appeared on the deck of the *American Endeavor* and walked toward a dark-haired man leaning against the rail around the fantail. He had been idling, watching the windsurfers and yachts trace white lines across an inky blue sea against the backdrop of expensive harborside houses shimmering on an unusually hot spring day. When he heard her approaching footsteps he turned and looked at her. It was as though Lynch were seeing her for the first time. The lovely white face with full red lips contrasted by black hair cut in a neat pageboy, the figure, the walk. Most of all the walk. Provocative, confident, just a hint of swagger. The bruise on Janice's face had gone, and with makeup she looked as though she'd spent the last month in a health resort. She'd lost weight and she looked a little drawn, but the shadows beneath her eyes had gone and her dark eyes sparkled with mischief and challenge.

Only if you looked closely into her eyes could you still see the pain. Lynch could see it. It was only during the last five nights that she'd been able to go to sleep without taking pills. It had been two weeks since she was plucked from the deck of the doomed Irish trawler off the shores of Donegal and brought to Halloran's yacht. All the hot baths and soaps and medicines in the world hadn't been able to wash the stain off her mind. It would take a while.

Lynch's arm was healing inside its sling. The bones hadn't been broken but there was nerve and tendon damage and extensive tearing of the muscle, which would take months to heal. The X ray had shown two chipped vertebrae in his spine. The Royal Navy doctor whom Porter had choppered out had told him if the fractures had gone any deeper there would have been nerve damage inside the spine and he may have ended up a paraplegic. The burns on his thighs were the least of it, almost unnoticeable.

He would recover. She might. Their love would not. They had seen little of each other the past two weeks, when Halloran had decided the *American Endeavor* should play the role of hospital ship for a few weeks and cruise calmer waters till they were all strong enough to go on. Janice and Lynch had stayed in different staterooms the whole time. As soon as he could walk he went to see her. They had spent a few hours together on recent afternoons, lounging on the fantail. But the magic had gone. They both knew it. They were in that awkward transition where lovers somehow have to find a way to be friends.

"You look beautiful," he told her. He meant it.

She smiled. "How are you feeling today?" It sounded strange, almost too proper coming from her.

"Better," he said, and shifted the weight from one foot to another in an attempt to ease the ache in the middle of his spine.

"Made your mind up yet?" she asked brightly, putting both hands on the rail beside him.

"About what in particular?" he asked.

"About where you go from here?"

"Well," Lynch sighed. "I can't go back to the States. Halloran says even he can't protect me from the FBI. He's offered to set me up someplace else . . . anywhere."

"Got anywhere in mind?"

"No." He shook his head. "Maybe buy that place in Scotland I thought I wanted once. Porter says I can have my job back any time I want it. Same rank, same pay. No loss of seniority." He looked at her and and smiled his awkward schoolboy smile. Once it had made her melt inside. Now, it only made her feel tender, compassionate toward him. It made him look lost and afraid to ask for help.

"I don't know," he said. "I really don't know."

They heard the chugging of powerful launch motors as the *Junior Endeavor* started her engines down at the pontoon anchored amidships.

"I think that's my signal," she said, and leaned away from the rail.

"You leaving today?"

She shook her head. "Just going into Biarritz to do some shopping. A few simple, normal things first, you know?"

He understood.

"Want some company?"

She looked at him. "No thanks," she said softly. "I want to

be on my own. Besides, I don't think you'd be able to get too far with your back the way it is."

"Yeah." He nodded. "Let me walk you to the gangway, at least."

She waited while he hobbled painfully along the rail until they had reached the top of the gangway leading down to the *American Endeavor*'s launch.

"Bye," she said. She kissed him lightly on the cheek and hurried down the gangway. Halfway down she stopped, turned, and walked slowly back toward him. He waited at the top of the gangway, a puzzled but expectant look in his eyes. This time she kissed him full on the lips.

"You know the trouble with you, Lynch?" she said, the familiar deep red spark firing up again in her eyes.

"What?" he asked.

"You're just a little too damn exciting."

Then she turned and walked away from him. And this time she didn't come back.